A HOLY MAIDEN'S GUIDE TO GETTING KIDNAPPED

A HOLY MAIDEN'S GUIDE TO GETTING KIDNAPPED

SCANDALS OF THE GIFTED
BOOK 1

KATY NYQUIST

Podium

This is a work of fiction. Names, characters, places, and incidents are either products of the author's imagination or used fictitiously. Any resemblance to actual events, locales, or persons, living, dead, or undead, is entirely coincidental.

Cover design by Mario Teodosio

ISBN: 978-1-0394-8246-3

Published in 2025 by Podium Publishing
www.podiumentertainment.com

To my sister, my very first reader

A HOLY MAIDEN'S GUIDE TO GETTING KIDNAPPED

CHAPTER ONE

I have four months, three weeks, and two days left to live. That's still a hundred and forty-five days more than the poor bastard lying on my examination table. Both his legs got crushed under a carriage's wheels. The yellow pus reeks like overripe cheese, too strong to be hidden by the sandalwood scent packets hanging from the clinic rafters. A scraggly beard marks him more a boy than a man. From the crackling wet sound emerging from his mouth with each breath, I give him minutes left to live. Thanks to some quack letting the leeches feed on him, he's as pale as undercooked dough. I need a smoke or a stiff drink. Not both: I learned from bitter experience on my knees in the outhouse that redleaf and alcohol do not mix.

Clearing my throat, I tap the doctor on the shoulder. "Allow me, please. Nothing but the Sun God will save him now."

"Who do you think you are?" The doctor curls back his lip and glares at me. He must be new. Looking around, he says, "This young woman appears hormonal. Will the head doctor remove her from the premises?" He grabs my arm. That's a mistake.

My bodyguard, Alzira, lunges forward and knocks away his hand. Her scimitar snaps to his throat without her even needing to draw it from the scabbard. If she's using magic, then she's angry. "Holy Maiden Ysabel *is* the head doctor," she growls. "Of all the relics, gifts, and magic in the world, Her Holiness is the one and only Holy Healer. Even the elves travel across continents to visit her clinic. Yet you dare call her hormonal? Do you recall the fate of the Dark Lord who presumed to lay hands on her?"

The doctor shudders, probably more in response to the blade touching his skin than from his realization of my identity.

I appreciate it when Alzira brags about my greatness so I don't have to look immodest by saying it myself. Alas, they're both still between me and my patient. With false sweetness, I say, "I'm merely a humble servant of the Sun God. Gentle Alzira, please don't spill blood in my sacred clinic." I push down the sword. "I'm sure the distinguished doctor only meant that all humans have hormones. So yes, I am feeling a tad hormonal today." I lower my voice to a hiss, my smile becoming toothy. "Now get out of my way before you make me angry."

Babbling about how honored he feels by my presence, the doctor leaps aside. I reach toward the patient's feverish forehead. All it will take is one touch from me, and he'll be healed of his mortal wounds, and any hangnails, as a bonus.

The door of my clinic crashes open. The doctor bumps into me as he flees, sending me stumbling backward. Armored men pour in. Unfortunately, they wear the yellow coats and black pants of the Head Cardinal's guard. They sport bandages and bad-tempered expressions. Cardinal Jiang stalks in after them, gemstones rattling on his coat and pantaloons. He takes his silver cane everywhere, despite having no disability that requires it—he just uses it to smack people. I hate him with every fiber of my being.

"Noble Jiang, how kind of the Sun God to send you to my doorstep," I say with an elegant curtsey. I mentally apologize to God for dumping the blame on Him. Despite Alzira's bragging, I can't pull rank on the Head Cardinal. Diplomacy it must be with this creep. "If you'll give me one moment to finish—"

"No." Jiang glowers. "You'll come with me to heal my men this instant, then I'll let you get back to your peasants. I left the worst injured back at my church. Hurry up."

The patient on my table won't live that long. Even a glance in his direction would tell Jiang that. Yet Jiang's guards surround me, scowling as if I'm the one responsible for their numerous injuries.

So, I faint.

It takes skill to fake a faint. I crumble sideways in a swirl of skirts while simpering and throwing up a dramatic hand to protect my head from any serious injury. I land on a pair of forceps. *Ow, my poor buttocks.* If I find out which son of an orc dropped that thing, I'll curse his family until his great-grandmother's ears are burning. Only a small whimper escapes my lips. Reclining with my hand on my brow, I am the picture of feminine elegance.

Now what can the guards do? If the Head Cardinal's thugs dare to manhandle the Holy Maiden, it will be an epic scandal. *Your move, Jiang.*

"Fetch me a bucket of ice water," Jiang says. "The Holy Maiden has swooned and needs to be brought back to her senses." *Damn him.*

"How dare you?" growls Alzira. I crack one eye open. She marches forward and plants her feet in front of me. One hand rests on her scimitar.

Wincing, I mouth, *Don't!*

With her back turned, Alzira can't see me. Jiang can. We lock eyes. He points. "Her Holiness seems quite recovered."

I pretend to be dead.

Jiang makes a sound between a teakettle whistling and an angry bear. "Ysabel, if you don't stand up right this instant, I'll 'accidentally' step on you."

I exclusively enjoy stepping on my lovers, not the other way around. Not that I'd take Jiang if he delivered himself hog-tied and tonguing a ball gag. Though he's handsome, like a fallen angel, the devil's temper lurks in his eyes.

Alzira says, "Touch her, and I'll take off your head." The cabinets on the walls rattle with the force of her fury. She knows it will end her life if she harms Jiang, but she doesn't care with my safety on the line. However, I care quite a lot. I'm seriously rethinking if I should spend my political capital here. It's not as if I've ever met my unfortunate patient before. Maybe he's a terrible person who kicks puppies and kittens. Maybe he secretly longs for death. All I know of him is that his name is Balt, his wife gave birth a few weeks ago, and when I told her the leeches the idiot doctors used on him had been killing her husband, she cried so hard I knew she'd never forgive herself if he died. Not that she or the baby would last long without their provider. In the Holy City, charitable funds end up in the pockets of the likes of Jiang, not the people they ought to help.

Shit, now I'm rethinking my rethinking. A conscience is a most unpleasant affliction.

Alzira stares Jiang down. The tension is thick enough to choke me. Jiang holds all the political power, but Alzira's gift could slaughter everyone in this room. Neither Alzira nor Jiang is the type to relent.

Which means I'm going to have to. I lower my forehead to the ground. "Head Cardinal, I plead for mercy. Of course, I will heal all your men, but first, allow me to save my patient. The entire Holy City will praise your kindness." I strive to strike the right balance between subservient and annoying him into letting me have my way.

The only sound in the room is Alzira grinding her teeth. She cannot bear to look at me bowed down.

Finally, Jiang says, "You have ten seconds. One . . . two . . ."

I spring to my feet, shove aside a guard, and grab poor Balt by his oversized ear. Momentarily, I hesitate.

Each use of my gift costs me a day of my lifespan.

But in return, this man and his family will gain decades. Under that kind of pressure, I can't bring myself to refuse. I steel myself and heal.

Balt's legs snap straight. Flesh regrows. Color returns to his face, and his breathing steadies.

Healing never hurts. It briefly feels like cold flashing through my veins. I can sense the lost time slipping out from under my skin, leaving me lightheaded and empty.

A rush of adrenaline fills me with an urge to run from this place and never let anyone steal what little remains of my life. It would do me no good to try. My healings aren't the only reason that I won't live past four months.

As I release Balt, Jiang finishes counting. "Ten. Time's up."

Disheveled, a flower of blood blossoming on my lacy white sleeve, I glare at Jiang. "It would be my pleasure to tend to the wounds your men obtained in service to the Sun God, Head Cardinal," I say, enunciating each word. "I'll fetch antiseptic and bandages."

"There's no need," Jiang says. "Since you'll be healing every last injury personally." His cold stare scares away the doctor peeking from the doorway.

I'm not supposed to waste my limited lifespan on nonfatal injuries, but this is my punishment for not jumping the moment Jiang called for me. Alzira puts a hand on my shoulder. "I could still kill him," she whispers. We both know Jiang's influence isn't something a bodyguard can shield me from, but I appreciate the thought.

Jiang's men escort me and Alzira to a hill of churches. There's a high steel fence surrounding the bottom of the hill, to keep out the riffraff (aka the people we're supposed to be helping). Beggars used to sleep against the fence, until Jiang added spikes.

As a guard opens the gate, my eyes are dazzled by the summer sun bouncing off all the precious metal. On these slopes, colloquially known as the Afterlife Auction, ten churches compete for believers using gold and glamour. The newest Sun God sects at the bottom of the hill try the hardest. We pass a blinding building with domed caps made of platinum. Another church has four red sandstone towers. A marble square building has a single steeple topped by a golden rooster, their sacred animal. Gold has long been prized by the church for representing the Sun God, or at least that's our excuse for hoarding so much of it.

Next, we pass Cardinal Lector's Maplewood church, shaped like a dragon with a doorway for a mouth. It's gauche, and everyone but him knows it. The bright colors were never destined to survive our local thunderstorms. His junior priests used to add fresh paint to the dragon every week, but they gave up. Now the poor wooden creature looks like it has mange.

At least there is peace to be found among all the posturing. Our pathway up the hill is lined with magnolia trees, which *I* planted, in full bloom. A soft breeze tosses petals in my path, tickling my nose with a lightly fruity scent. Today, the sky overhead is pure blue, with nothing but the sun beating down on us. Before long, my hair becomes soaked with sweat and the heat weighs me down. My feet drag. I'm exhausted, and I don't want to do this.

Halfway up the hill, a giant oak tree holds a church within its massive branches. Thanks to the magic of a long-dead priest, the wooden walls grow straight from the trunk. Inside, a dozen people sing a slow, deep, a cappella choir. The Order of Saint Nora rotates singers constantly because they believe the world will end on the day their choir stops. The tree house has a bittersweet and earthy scent, and—I sniff—do I smell roasted pork?

My head shoots up. The tempting odor comes from a small yet elegant brick cathedral, with religious murals running down the walls. The priests are holding a barbecue outside, roasting a whole pig on a spit. Several of them fan the smells toward the treehouse downhill.

I sigh. The eternal song of the Order of Saint Nora is so beautiful that pilgrims travel from around the world to hear it, but even the most melodious music grates on the ears when it never, ever stops. In revenge, the other churches have started hosting barbecues whenever the wind is directed at the tree house, knowing full well that the priests of Saint Nora are vegetarians. I'll bring it up at the next Council of Cardinals, where I play peacemaker among the sects because no one else will. Frequently I feel like I'm managing children, not cardinals.

The hum of a giant bell tells me that I'm almost at the top. I coax a bit more energy from my tired feet.

Cardinal Jiang's church is the most ridiculous of all, from the dragon statues bristling under the curved roof to that stupidly large black-and-yellow striped dome. It's supposed to be decorated in the colors of a tiger. It looks more like a puffed-up bumblebee. Hundreds of solid gold bells circle the roof. The breeze makes them chime melodiously, and it only worsens my mood. I tap my foot as one of the guards pushes open the elm door decorated with ironwork.

Boot prints and blood drops stain the entryway carpet. Injured men fill every available space, stretchers even placed on top of the golden coffins holding the saints. A handful of guards move around the wounded with water and bandages, but the bulk of Jiang's men are missing.

Have Jiang's corrupt, bullying guards been wiped out? Bad things do happen to bad people! This will be a real blow in our private war over who polices the city. Who would have dared do such a thing? Who has the power to strike such a substantial blow against our great leader? And are they looking for a new best friend?

I gasp, then sway as if I might faint. It's worth it for the infuriated look on Jiang's face. Before he completely snaps, I get to work.

Alzira sticks by my side as I move throughout the room. Every single surface is painted with pictures of saints. The dying men propped against the walls practically blend in with the murals. They're only identifiable by the pungent smell. I step around the colorful pillars and arches to kneel down in front of each stretcher. By the time I'm done, the hem of my dress has been soaked with blood and clings to my legs, damp and fetid, every time I move. Five guards died before my arrival. I heal forty-six total, and I'm counting every last damn day wasted on this lot.

It's not tiring physically, just mentally. This is not how I want to sacrifice my remaining lifespan. These men were injured in the service of my worst enemy. I'd rather push them into hell than put them back on their feet to cause me more trouble. Jiang recruits for loyalty, or more accurately for willingness to do his dirty work. Just yesterday, Jiang pardoned a guard who I'd put in a cell for beating his wife. Hopefully I didn't have to heal that one, but I can't tell—I'm face-blind.

Although prosopagnosia is called face-blindness, I can still see facial features. I just can't see *faces*. This may seem like a fine distinction, but since I can't put the features together into one picture, it's achingly hard to memorize them. Fine details elude me. All someone has to do is scrunch up their face, and they become a completely new person. Jiang's only good traits are that he wears the formal robes of his office and has a very memorable voice that could break glass at twelve paces. I'll never fail to recognize him. But when it comes to his guards who all wear the same uniform, I'm completely lost.

As I rise from my last healing, the patient stands up and joins the rest lining the wall. Several of them touch their bodies as if in disbelief to find no scars under the holes in their clothing. One of them pockets a golden relic box, but I'm too tired to care. Sweat drips down my forehead and my head throbs, but I refuse to show weakness under the eyes of so many enemies.

Marching over, Jiang issues his final orders. "For the foreseeable future, you are not to visit your necro-servant kin in their hideous shanty town. It's a waste of your energy, and it's about to get too dangerous. You are forbidden to leave the city at all."

Head Cardinal Jiang can go fuck himself with a cactus. His slur dates back to when our neighboring nation Conollia was terrorized and enslaved by the Dark Lord Chingis. An enchanted blight struck their lands, and the church proclaimed it a curse on those who had (unwillingly) served a necromancer. Conollia has slowly collapsed into starvation as the blight spreads with each decade, and the trade embargo makes their suffering worse. The centuries-dead necromancer has nothing to do with the refugees outside our city but has proven a convenient excuse for Jiang to deny them charitable aid. *Necro-servant* is a common slur hurled at anyone with darker skin, but in my case I *am* half-Conollian. If I have to heal his band of bullies, then I won't stop helping my countrymen on the paternal side.

Serenely, I say, "I vow to the Sun God that I will only bestow the great power He has granted me in places of safety." And I feel a lot safer visiting the camp than I do here on Jiang's home turf.

Something of my rebellion must glint in my eyes. Jiang frowns. "We must speak alone." He gestures toward a side room and orders Alzira to guard the door while we speak.

"Your Holiness?" Alzira asks.

"Please do," I say between clenched teeth. Anything Jiang tells me, I'll tell Alzira later. But there must be a reason why Jiang didn't send his men to a hospital, and I want to know it.

Once we're alone, Jiang takes the room's only chair. His cane, topped by a white orb, rests on his legs. I stand before him like a penitent. My breath comes out unevenly.

I don't like being here. This is the same room where Jiang once bent my fingers backward to force me to swear an unbreakable life-oath. The one that, in a little more than four months, will kill me.

Jiang appears too young to be a Head Cardinal. He has a neat black beard, a positively royal nose, and a full head of straight, shiny hair he keeps shoulder-length. What really irks me about him is that he doesn't just have the looks—he has a presence that fills a room. I have a professional envy for his aura of domination. Each gesture and word contain a total confidence that sweeps up people in his wake. When he fixes his eyes on me, I hate how it makes me tremble. Here I'd normally say something unpleasant about his mother, but I can't insult whatever unfortunate woman had to squeeze such a bloated head out of her womb.

His next words echo around the small room. "I have unfortunate news. The Holy City may shortly face a siege from Dark Lord Kaine."

This is bad news in the sense a hurricane is slightly wet.

"The Sun God will protect us from such perfidy." The fear in my voice isn't faked this time. I have a painful history with dark lords. "Why would Dark Lord Kaine break our truce?"

"Because the truce is already broken." Jiang drops this confession casually and with no remorse. "I sent my guard to assassinate Kaine during his journey here. They were supposed to wipe out his entire escort so no one would find out. Without their leader, Conollia would have descended back into harmless chaos. It did not go according to plan."

So this is all Jiang's fault to begin with. "Sweet Sun God. You broke the truce of the World Games. I can't remember the name of the last kingdom who broke the Games truce, probably because they were *erased from history*." I swallow my profanity. I've already provoked Jiang enough today. One more open insult and I'll lose another day of my life healing a twisted ankle or persistent cough for one of his cronies.

Jiang shoots me a cold look. "I refuse to let that jumped-up heretic participate in the World Games like a legitimate ruler."

"How astonishing that the Sun God would allow your guard to be defeated," I simper. Actually, I mean that to defeat Kaine, he would need divine intervention. Kaine's gift is even more legendary than mine. People whisper he has the ability to steal the magic of others, which would definitely put him among the strongest in the world. It would give him a very good chance of winning this year's World Games, hence why Jiang tried to kill Kaine before he could participate.

"I had Kaine poisoned with Nightwish. It should have completely incapacitated him." Jiang's hands clench on his armrests. "I sent three hundred Gifted Knights. The man could barely stand, yet he still annihilated them. The survivors only came crawling back because they took Kaine's whore hostage. Then they let a mere girl gut two of them and escape."

If only I could have seen that. I hide my glee behind my best Terrified Female face. It's a half pout with my hand on my cheek.

Jiang continues, "Not a word of this may leave the room." His glare reminds me of how many threats and hostages he has to keep me under his thumb. "Now you understand why you need to stay behind the city walls until this misunderstanding has been sorted out."

"Misunderstanding? This isn't a misunderstanding! You broke the truce and tried to have a foreign ruler assassinated. Kaine will report us to the Conclave of Kings. They'll figuratively declare the dissolution of the Holy City, then step back and let Kaine literally rip us to pieces."

"I've prepared a scapegoat." Jiang flicks his fingers. "I'll transfer the surviving members of my guard to Cardinal Lector's command. That way, he'll be able to tell a Seer that they're his men with technical honesty. He'll be of little loss to the Council of Cardinals. Come now, Ysabel. There's no need to fear. The Conclave of Kings hates dark lords. I have many allies there. They'll be happy to arrest Cardinal Lector as the sole traitor and sweep away this incident with a bit of compensation money."

Jiang acts like as long as Kaine can't prove anything, we're safe. *Fool.*

War is forbidden by the Sun God—and rationality. No sane ruler wants to trigger the end of the world. Magical gifts range from mundane to apocalyptic. Many people go their entire lives without even noticing their knack for finding mushrooms or singing in perfect pitch has a magical element. But when a teenage boy in the local countryside accidentally flooded his family farm, the cardinals and nobles started a bidding war for who would accept him as a trainee knight. In Alzira's home country, their emir has the power to burn down a city in minutes. Legends say their founder could turn a country to ashes, and it's not an entirely implausible boast. The orcs fought a civil war between a gifted king who could cause earthquakes and a would-be queen with the power to completely erase matter. Now there's just ocean where their continent used to be. This convinced every surviving sentient species to forgo war for the World Games. Monarchs can pick their champions and safely watch tidy little battles happen from behind enchanted glass.

The world fears dark lords because when they gather the remnants of a broken country or build an army of bandits, they don't play by our civilized rules. They wreak havoc on nations unused to war. Dark Lord Kaine became the world's worst nightmare: an untamed gifted strong enough to destroy continents. But instead of attempting world domination like the previous dark lords, Kaine voluntarily offered to sign the truce and enter the World Games. It was a smart move, in my humble opinion. The entire world would have banded together to destroy him otherwise. With his strong gift, he's guaranteed to do well in the Games and bring prosperity to his nation. Many monarchs and religious leaders didn't like the prospect of losing to a dark lord. Alas, my own less-than-beloved leader has become the first fool to rush forward and attack. Millions will die for our precious Head Cardinal's arrogance if Kaine decides to invade.

Ugh, I really *need that redleaf.*

Before letting me leave, Jiang holds out his arm. "Your healing services."

I knew this would happen. Teeth clenched, I grab his hand.

Death bubbles under Jiang's skin. Something unnatural has left a layer of rot across his organs. He must be in agony, but he never shows it, the stoic bastard. I'll give Jiang credit for a high pain tolerance. His affliction must be magical in nature, because it keeps coming back no matter how many times I heal it. I've lost track of how much life I've sacrificed for my worst enemy. Once again, I summon my magic and burn away the darkness. I have no choice. Still, I always feel like apologizing to the world whenever I extend Jiang's tenure in it.

When done, I turn and march for the door.

Jiang calls after me, "Keep an eye out for Kaine's whore. A hostage would make everything go more smoothly."

I grunt. *Poor woman. I hope she escapes the city.*

Outside, Alzira asks, "How are you, princess?"

Though I'm as common as stable muck, Alzira likes to call me princess. As the best damn Gifted Knight in the world, she can call me whatever she wants.

"I'm fine. You know I was faking the faint." I wink. One hand creeps to my bruised backside. I can't heal myself, proving the Sun God "blessed" me with the crappiest gift in existence.

She hands me a water flask. I chug it. "Thank you. You're an angel."

Alzira salutes. "It's my privilege to be of service." She has tanned skin a shade lighter than mine, aquiline features, creaseless monolid eyes, and silken black hair shaved to a crew cut under her head scarf. As a shorty, I envy her height and her muscles.

While we walk, I fill Alzira in. She greets my news of incipient war with adequate profanity. The summer air is sweltering, and my dress has too many layers. Wiping sweat off my forehead, I pick up my pace. The city rioted in order to force the church to allow me to heal commoners, so I'd better not keep everyone waiting.

My healing clinic, a flat-roofed brick building, sits a block away from the hill. My forsythia has spread and intruded on the pathway like a weed. Jiang's goons dented my front door, much to my annoyance.

Inside, the central room has floor-to-ceiling shelves stocked with medicinal bottles, mortar and pestles, and surgical equipment. A hamper sits next to the closet, full of used blankets and clothing soiled by all types of bodily fluids. The bone saw hanging on the wall glows red. It's a relic, enchanted to cauterize the wounds it creates. Relics are objects that have been used by a gifted often enough to pick up a bit of their magic. No one knows how to create them deliberately, so they're rare. I traded a healing for this one, and it's saved many lives since then.

Over the cast iron stove, I brew myself a nice cup of tea doused with redleaf so my hands won't shake with fear. Healing has gotten harder lately. All types come through my clinic, from infants with blue faces to elderly nobles begging for a bit more time. One of my former patients invented the first flying shuttle for automatic weaving. Another became a world-renowned poet. I once traveled to the Elven Empire and healed a whole town infected by a plague. The disease could have spread across the continent if left unchecked. These stories are my legacy. All my healings have used up about fifty years of my life. At age twenty-five, I have as much time left to live as a seventy-five-year-old, despite my outward youth. Just one more healing might turn out to be the last day of my natural lifespan. Not that it matters. I made my life-oath, and I'll not live longer than four months when Jiang finally has his way.

Doing my best not to tremble, or worse, have a panic attack, I drain the rest of my cup. My headache eases, replaced by a feeling of floatiness. I walk down the hallway to the patients' rooms.

A husband and a wife lie in adjacent beds, delirious. I tried to sweat the fever out, I tried coriander, and I even tried a bit of unicorn horn. Nothing worked. I have need to stop the disease from spreading. A touch of my hands cools their skin. After waking, they effusively thank the Sun God and leave without looking me in the eye.

I'm the one giving up a day of my life. Would it kill them to thank *me*? Of course, I know why everyone prefers to call my ability a miracle. Without the church telling people I'm a blessing from the Sun God, they might feel half a moment of discomfort when I die.

Maybe I brewed the redleaf wrong. My mind isn't floaty enough. To the only nurse remaining, I call, "Thank you for staying late. You can leave. I'll lock up after the last patient. You're, uh . . ." Uniforms are the bane of my face-blind existence. The white nurse's cap even covers hair, rendering people completely indistinguishable.

"You don't know my name." Her lips twist. "Of course you don't."

"I only asked because I want to add you to the list for overtime pay."

This promise shakes loose her name, but her sneer remains as she leaves.

I hate when someone thinks I'm a snob because I'm incapable of recognizing faces, and I hate myself a little for not being able to do something so innate to everyone else. Dammit, I try twice as hard to remember every single acquaintance's hair, height, body type, and mannerisms. But I'm never going to remember a face. It's a neurological disorder. I once failed to recognize Alzira because a cold changed her voice, and she hasn't left my side in seven years.

In the last remaining room, a preteen girl sits in bed reading. She has twisted legs in a brace and spots on her face. The nurses moved her up my list because of her sleep paralysis, which often turns fatal. My spirits rise. Not because I'm a sadist (though I am—it's just only directed at consenting adult men), but because I enjoy healing children.

The child looks up. "I don't want any more painful treatments." She tucks her withered legs to her chest.

"I won't hurt you, I promise." I take a seat next to her bed. "What are you reading?"

"It's a math book. Boring."

Her tone tells me she doesn't actually think it's boring. "I love math," I say. A slight exaggeration—okay, a blatant lie.

With a little coaxing, I learn her name is Terrial, she's the middle of seven children, and she wants to attend the university even though her merchant parents don't think it worthwhile for girls. When I finally stretch out my hand, she clasps it in hers.

Terrial's muscles regrow before my eyes. The fever heating her hand fades away. My gift can even regenerate limbs. I've never met a patient who I couldn't heal. Even if their heart has stopped, I can haul them back from the dead if I get to them within the first couple minutes. "See? Good as new." Smiling, I help her take off her braces.

"I want to show Mom," she cries. Gripping the walls like she's forgotten how to walk, she stumbles out of the room and into her parents' waiting carriage. Still no "thank you, Ysabel." Oh well. I shouldn't be petty. Her happiness is all the gift I need, even if I'm one day closer to dying.

While sipping another cup of redleaf tea, I talk to God. Of course, I have to hold up both ends of the conversation, but it's my way of drawing strength from the bit of God inside all of us.

"It's not that I mind them thanking You. I just want to be thanked as well. Is that too much to ask?"

I hesitate, stirring my tea. "Good point. But I'm not the one who claimed my power came from You." About one person in a hundred has a gift. It's pure luck. I treat mine like an incurable illness that I have to live with. It's easier if I pretend there's nothing I can do about it, and my death is already a foregone conclusion.

It is, really. If I try to run, the church will hunt me down like the previous Holy Healer, Noretho. Though it's not public knowledge, he tried to escape twice: Once shortly after the church found him, and once after Jiang executed the first and only girl Noretho kissed. Supposedly we lose our healing powers if we have sex, although that's nonsense. Every gift comes with exactly one price, and ours is far heavier. Holy Youth Noretho was publicly known as an invalid who had patients brought to his room because he couldn't leave his bed. Jiang cut his hamstrings. He's threatened to do the same to me if I ever try to run.

A cold laugh forces its way up my throat. "I suppose they don't thank me for healing them because they know I have no choice."

"What are You talking about? Oh, fine, maybe they'd let me get away with not healing the poor, but that would only slow down my death. I could never bring myself to close this clinic. How can I choose to let thousands of people die to save myself? Is that what You call free will?" With just one day of my life, I can save all of someone else's. That's a trade anyone but me would call a good bargain. I've never had the strength to stand up against the will of the entire world.

God goes silent on me. Grimacing, I drain my tea so fast it burns my throat. It brings no calm or brightness to the world. Definitely a weak batch. I've been relying too much on alcohol and redleaf lately. That has to stop. While my liver has no long-run future to worry about, I need to stay alert until the World Games. I've come up with a plan to protect my people after I'm gone. Afterward, I can drown myself in mind-altering substances, and no one will complain as long as I get my healings done.

The backroom door opens. My head shoots up as I quickly compose my expression to be less self-pitying.

"May I escort you back home, princess?" Alzira walks over and sweeps away my empty cup. That's not her job, but she's always given me more than I ask for. *She* would care if I fell to pieces. That makes it both easier and harder to hold myself together.

I manage a smile—more a quirk of my lips, but this one is real. "You don't have to clean up after me."

"It's my pleasure, Your Holiness." Alzira picks a discarded doctor's coat off the floor and opens the wardrobe to put it away.

A bleeding man tumbles out, hitting the floor with a force that rattles the shelves.

I run toward him. He's slight, with black, close-cropped hair, a neat, oiled beard, dark skin, and fine features decorated with several thin white scars.

"He's one of Cardinal Jiang's guards. Be careful." Alzira puts out a hand to stop me. I can't blame her, because she's correctly identified his black-and-yellow uniform—and because his hand clutches a recently used dagger. Alzira disarms him in a flash.

The recumbent man is soaked with sweat and blood from numerous shallow cuts and bruises. His belt has been tied over the worst injury on his stomach. My eyes widen as I notice tatters of a different gray uniform poking out from under his coat. I lean down for a closer look. A black claw around his neck: Dark Lord Kaine's insignia. One of his men in disguise?

As I reach for him, his hand shoots forward to grab my wrist. The man's bruised eyes snap open. They're so strikingly dark brown as to be nearly black.

Alzira bellows, "How dare you assault Her Holiness!"

His grip doesn't hurt. He's only loosely holding my dress sleeve.

I hold up my other hand to restrain Alzira. "I'm fine." To the man, I say, "You're safe here." I'd rather Alzira not have to subdue him, since he looks like he's been through enough already. "I'm Holy Maiden Ysabel. I'll heal your injuries." Then he'll owe me a few answers. "I'm not going to turn you over to Jiang." Whatever else I may decide, I can promise that much.

"Thank you, but I must decline." He clenches his square jaw. "I've heard of you. The price of your healing is a day of your life. I can't accept."

"It's just a day," I say, unable to believe this alien response.

He grins in a proud, roguish manner. "As Dark Lord Kaine of Conollia, I have a principle of never owing anything to anyone. I cannot take your life from you, not even a day."

What. WHAT? My mind goes blank. The reactions of everyone I've ever healed flash across my vision. The people who thank the Sun God but not me. The people who avoid looking at me. The people who pretend they aren't killing me. The people who genuinely don't care. Never once has anyone turned my powers down. I'm their Holy Maiden, and I'm here to heal them. Here to sacrifice for them. Here to die for them.

A single tear trickles down my cheek. I've always longed for someone to tell me that a day of my life matters. That I shouldn't have to die for everyone else's sake. I've never received my simple, selfish wish until now. It fills my heart with an odd mixture of joy and gratitude and something approaching terror. If I ever stop to think about how much I don't want to die, then I don't know what I'll do.

Then the rest of my brain catches up. "Wait, did you say you're Dark Lord Kaine?"

CHAPTER TWO

"No, no. I definitely didn't say Dark Lord Kaine. Never heard of the brave, handsome, undefeatable warrior. I'm, uh . . ." Kaine checks his badge. "A guard for Cardinal Jee-ah . . . ng."

"You just admitted to it, idiot," Alzira says, with the enjoyment of someone who rarely gets to be on the giving end of that insult.

"Whoops." Kaine scratches his head. He does not look particularly concerned. Perhaps he thinks he could take a pair of women in a fight. Even with his injuries, I'm no match for him, but Alzira would be. With her by my side, I'm not helpless, not even before the reigning dark lord.

"We're no friends to Head Cardinal Jiang." I'm in a bind. It's not as if I approved of Jiang's assassination attempt, but I don't want to be blamed for foiling it either. Maybe I can shove him outside and pretend I never saw anything. Since I'm not a complete monster, first I say, "At least let me bandage you up."

"Thank you, but I know how to look after my own injuries." Kaine keeps an arm firmly wrapped over his chest. I knew the newest dark lord was young, but that vulnerable expression emphasizes that he's about the same age as me.

"You can apply the bandages yourself." I turn around. "Alzira, please guard the door."

Eyes on Kaine, she says, "I don't want to leave you alone, princess."

"You'll be in easy earshot, and I need you to keep watch. We can't afford to be discovered with him."

Alzira's face says she doesn't like it, but she also doesn't disobey direct orders from me. She nods and departs, not without one last glower in Kaine's direction.

I turn to our uninvited guest. "Can I ask you some questions?"

Kaine flashes me a grin as innocent as a child's. "A lovely lady wants me to talk about myself? Go ahead." Is this really the greatest dark lord since the majestic and terrible Chingis? Not a random beggar who took a few too many hits to the head?

As Kaine retreats behind a bed screen, I ask, "How did a legend like you end up in such a bad condition? I need to know in order to treat you."

Frustration creeps into Kaine's voice. "Some sort of sleeping drug. I still can't use my gift." This matches Jiang's story. Sleeping drugs can sneak past even magical resistance to poison because they don't harm the body. Nightwish in particular blocks magic. I'm impressed Kaine made it to my clinic, and curious how. Also, I'm surprised he admitted so easily that he currently can't use his prodigious magic. Surely a fool wouldn't have lasted so long as a dark lord.

First, I fetch bandages and pain-easing herbs. I've put great time and effort into studying medicine in order to avoid using my gift as much as possible. Fear of death makes a great motivator.

I find the antidote on the top shelf in the back. Holding the light green vial in my hand, I hesitate. It would be easy to pretend I don't have the antidote. Nightwish is an obscure drug. Should I risk Jiang coming after me for treason? Do I want to give aid to an enemy of my city? Interrogating Kaine would go smoother if he's helpless. I could claim his gratitude just for bandages.

But Kaine didn't harm me even when it would have made sense to hold me hostage. He refused to take a day of my life, which is more than Jiang or anyone else has ever done. Without the antidote, Kaine probably won't be able to escape the city. A true holy healer would give treatment to anyone, even an enemy. I've always thought of myself as a fraud. Even so, I make a split-second decision to be a proper Holy Maiden for the first man who didn't force me into that role.

Fortunately a doctor left behind a spare waistcoat and britches. Kaine insists that I nudge the medical supplies and fresh clothing over with my foot while he stays behind the screen. Such maidenly modesty for a dark lord.

Thanks to the church's prying eyes, this is the closest I've gotten to a naked man in months. My healing gift is considered proof I've been divinely chosen for a lifetime of no sex. Since the Sun God has yet to descend from Heaven to consummate our marriage, I consider myself a free woman. The cardinals wouldn't see it the same way. They think I'll lose my oh-so-useful holy power if a man penetrates me. Imagine the stunned looks on their wrinkly old faces if they knew I have a taste for penetrating men.

"Did you come here to save the woman Jiang took hostage?" I ask.

"Who?"

"You don't have to tell me if you don't want to."

"I already freed her. While I held them off, she ran away. When I felt on the verge of collapsing, I beat up a bee-uniform and stole his coat so I could follow them in here. A healing clinic seemed like a good place to hide since I could steal some bandages once all of you left."

I nod to myself. "But you passed out inside the wardrobe before you could leave."

From behind the screen, he chuckles. "It's good you found me first. If Jiang's men had discovered me, then I might have cracked your lovely tiled floor with their skulls."

I shift my feet uneasily. He's bragging to me. A part of me feels flattered. But the same men who play nice in an attempt to get me into bed have been known to turn on me for not living up to their image of purity. I would like to believe that the first man to care about stealing my life is different. But Kaine is a dark lord. I trusted a dark lord once before, and that didn't end well.

Striving for a neutral tone, I say, "I can ask my spies to investigate whether your companion got out of the city if you give me a description."

"Please don't. Uh, I used a gift to send her far away."

Funny, he just said he can't use his magic. He's a poor liar. Not to mention, wouldn't this unknown woman have been better off sticking close to Kaine for protection? His story smells fishier than the wharf during the fish market. "Then I won't bother."

"Thank you for helping me." There's a rustling as he ties the bandages. "I know you're taking a risk. I'll protect you."

Does he have no fear that I might yet turn him over to Jiang, or is he only pretending to trust me? He promises to protect me, a woman from an enemy nation, with such easy sincerity. Either he's a smooth talker or an idiot. Perhaps I'm too harsh. He has the right to his pride, given his track record of defeating armies single-handedly. But he's currently weakened, and a gift as powerful as his must bear a heavy cost, like mine.

As he steps out from behind the screen, his straight frame and swift stride show no trace of his serious injury. He moves in a lethally graceful swagger, as if everyone else had better get out of his way.

"That was fast. How are you doing?"

"I have several regenerative abilities. When not damped down by poison, I could take a brick wall to the face without damage. Thanks to your antidote, my strength is gradually coming back."

Is he warning me not to attack him? Or am I massively overthinking it because I've spent too much time in politics? Trying to outthink this man is giving me a headache, maybe because he's not even playing the same game as me. "You look better already." The shallow cuts visible on his arms have turned into red lines. I'm glad I didn't waste a day of my life on that.

Kaine's voice takes on a formal note. "I vow to repay my debt to you."

I incline my head. "Thank you." Since he values debts so greatly, I expect a generous favor. "I can help you get out of Arahasnor." It's worth the risk of crossing Jiang, if in exchange Kaine will agree not to take revenge on us for breaking the World Games truce. Plus his impressive pecs are a national treasure of Conollia.

"Then I'll owe you twice. Whatever you desire of mine is yours." Sincerity glistens in Kaine's big eyes. "I'll spare you and anyone you care about when I sack this city."

Pardon me? There will be no sacking of my city. My hands clench. Perhaps I should drug him and turn him in after all . . . or I could use Kaine's interest in me. It wouldn't be the first time my cleavage talked a man out of murder. "Since you owe me, I hoped that you could forget about this little misunderstanding. We've already established Jiang could barely scratch a big, strong man such as yourself. I'll sneak you out of the city, you won't report this to the Conclave of Kings, and we can go back to competing fair and square in the World Games." I flash him my best winning smile, then stretch my arms in a casual way that pushes out my breasts.

Kaine's eyes snap down for a moment. But he doesn't smile. "I was nearly murdered under the flag of truce. It was neither little nor a misunderstanding."

I become painfully aware that I'm not facing a courtier who likes to flirt—this man is a dark lord. A shiver skitters like a centipede down my spine. After my nasty betrayal at the hands of Dark Lord Yarthor, trust doesn't come easy to me. But Kaine doesn't seem capable of pretending to be nice. He acts like it would be beneath him to pretend anything.

Kaine seems to appreciate bluntness, so I switch tactics. "Unfortunately, you have no proof you were poisoned. If you attack my city, then you'll be the one blamed for breaking the truce, not Cardinal Jiang. It will mean war."

"I know." His tone is level. "I've tried the legal way. I agreed to abide by your so-called civilized rules. In exchange, I've had repeated assassins sent after me. It turns out no one follows their own rules. And not a single monarch wants to face me in the World Games. So now they'll face me on the battlefield instead."

I open my mouth to argue. But he's making a very good point.

World peace is enforced because every monarch has sworn a magical oath that will stop their hearts if they wage war. The problem arises when someone who's not a noble, and thus has taken no life-oaths, raises an army. Every nation in the world unites to destroy these "dark lords." As someone who fakes being a saint, I know being called a dark lord doesn't make someone evil. The Conclave of Kings brands the title equally on both cruel warlords and rebels revolting against a tyrant. Kaine won't be treated fairly by them, and we both know it.

Our raised voices draw Alzira from her position at the entrance. She taps the wall once with her sword, meaning she's watching for my signal, a nose scratch, to surprise-attack Kaine. Hopefully it won't come to that.

I give Kaine my best Holy Maiden smile. "I know you're angry. Anyone would be after Jiang's treachery. But the Holy City's civilians don't deserve to be pillaged, raped, and murdered."

"The penalty for rape in my army is death."

Unlike talking to a politician, he's so straightforward. "I—I think I like you."

"Thanks. I like you, too." He winks at me, flashing his dimples. Slight men with muscles and pretty faces are my type. He definitely has the cheeky confidence I enjoy flirting with. Ugh, where is my mind going? He's a dark lord about to invade my city! Now is not the moment to contemplate how nice it would be to push him down on the clinic bed and put his mouth to another use.

I stand up straighter. "What about your own people? If you attack my city, then sure, you'll get your revenge." Unless Alzira kills him first, but we won't talk about that option quite yet. "But if you enter the World Games as you planned, then Conollia will be reinstated as a country. A victory would bring you much-needed food aid, gold to rebuild your infrastructure, the removal of the trade embargo, and a mandate to return your kidnapped citizens. You're the first person to unite the starving, desperate people of Conollia under one banner. Don't waste that because of Jiang. He's not worth it."

Since kings can no longer determine who has the biggest dick through warfare, teams of each nation's five best Gifted Knights fight in a yearly tournament. The World Games are no mere entertainment: monarchs wager land, resources, and even national policy as a proxy for war. The last-place country has been known to disappear after everyone takes a bite out of it. It's a lawful form of pillage.

Conollia hasn't qualified for over two centuries. The Conclave of Kings only agreed to allow Kaine to compete because he'd somehow united his fractured people across the blighted land, making his illegal army much larger than any dark lord ever raised before. Kaine was also smart enough to refuse to disarm until after the Games, leading to our current precarious political standoff with an army lurking at the borders of my city-state.

Kaine frowns. "I just want to kill one person who tried to kill me first. You can tell the Conclave that I'll still join the Games afterward."

"Here's the thing." I exhale. "Jiang has a different cardinal set up to take the fall. The Conclave of Kings doesn't like you, and Jiang has the political connections to make them pretend to believe him. If you attack him, the Conclave will ban you from the World Games."

"So what you're saying is that to get to him, I'll need to go through the whole city."

"No! There will be no sacking of *my* city! Do you know how long I spent getting the roads in good repair and improving sanitation? People used to toss their garbage down the well, then wonder why they got sick. Our river was so full of dirt that you could walk across it before I cleaned it up. Now we have boats bringing in trade. What do you think corpses will do to our water quality? Also, I added landscaping to all the public areas, and dead bodies hanging from the trees would not match my aesthetic. I've got a new shipment of granite for the walls coming in next week, and if you knock them down before then, I will have wasted *thirty thousand aracoins*. Everyone told me I shouldn't put flower gardens around the moats because they'd be trampled in event of an attack, but I said this city hasn't been hit by raiders in decades, and you will not make a liar out of me."

"You're begging me to spare your begonias?" Kaine's anger fades into bafflement. "Most people are more upset about the gold and jewels. Or, you know, the lives of their families."

Not everyone has great parents. Crossing my arms, I mutter, "Have you seen my flowers? They're just going into bloom!"

My distress draws my bodyguard over from her hiding place. Kaine doesn't look surprised to see her step into view. I think he knew she was there all along. Alzira puts an arm around me and glares at Kaine.

Her fury makes Kaine take a step back. He clears his throat. "I didn't realize this city belongs to you, my beautiful savior, not that ass of a cardinal who tried to murder me in my sleep."

"The city isn't mine. I just do all the hard work of maintaining it," I mumble, restraining an embarrassing sniffle.

Keeping one hand on her sword, Alzira pats me on the shoulder. "The old men on the Council of Cardinals don't lift a finger to help her. Then they cut her budget to fund orgies."

"They're not even good orgies," I add. The cardinals are obsessed with the notion that all group sex should involve one man and a large number of women, and they don't even make a token effort to ensure their prostitutes enjoy themselves. I want to be extremely clear that I appreciate orgies, but theirs are an insult to the word.

"Terrible." Kaine shakes his head. "You should overthrow them, behead them, and claim the city as your own. Then use their skulls as drinking gourds."

A snort escapes my lips. I wish. When all us leaders have been magically bound not to use military force against one another, we're left only with political intrigue.

Luckily, that makes me good at persuasion. I summon my most forceful tone. "Revenge isn't worth it. Don't throw away your one chance to remove your dark lord status and make Conollia a real country again."

Kaine's eyes narrow, and I sense that I've miscalculated. He says, "Conollia is no longer considered a 'real country' because your high and mighty Conclave of Kings deemed it so. We suffer because we're trapped in a land where nothing grows."

I bite my lip. "That is true."

"Do you know what the main export of Conollia was before I took charge? Slaves." The word cracks the air like a whip, making me flinch. "We bought food to survive by selling our own people. When I was only a child, my brother and I were sold. I don't know where he is or if he's even alive."

My stomach sinks. He's right to be angry. Much as I would never want war back, the Games can also be oppressive. Conollia has been in a state of perpetual civil conflict for two centuries while the other nations raid them for slaves. Those Arahasnor calls dark lords, Conollians call saviors. "I really do care. I'm half-Conollian myself. My father was a refugee, and I've been doing everything in my power to help the refugee camp outside our walls."

"While I slept at your refugee camp, someone poisoned me for your Head Cardinal."

"Oooo. See, I did not know who did that. If I'd known, I wouldn't have brought the camp up. I hate my father anyway." I'm babbling.

"I get it. I've never seen my dad's face, so he's nothing to me either." Kaine nods his acknowledgment. "I never thought you were involved. But I don't consider myself responsible for looking out for former Conollians who left my country behind. They're not loyal to me, so they're not my problem. The one who poisoned me will need to die."

His hostility makes me wince, but it doesn't surprise me. A lot of Conollian refugees hate dark lords because Yarthor, the previous holder of the title, betrayed more people than just me. They're mostly ordinary folks who want to avoid war. They want what's best for their families, and they oppose Conollia's current military aggression, perhaps partly as a show to help them better fit in while living in Arahasnor.

"I was born here, so I don't think of myself as a citizen of your country, but I truly do want to help the Conollian people." I take a deep breath and marshal my arguments. "Trust me; if there's anything I know as well as healing, it's politics. The other monarchs don't want you in the Games because they fear your strength. Jiang tried to sabotage you so they can go back to the old system where whenever a dark lord rose up, the armies of the world ganged up and one-sidedly slaughtered you. For the first time, a dark lord can beat them by their own rules, so they don't want to let you play."

Kaine strokes his chin. "What you're saying is that if I attack, my enemies get what they want. I'd be playing into their trap."

"Exactly." I clap my hands.

"You sound like Durrian, my second-in-command. He insists I have to get into the World Games no matter what shit I have to swallow." Kaine grins. "He'd like you. You two should meet so you can be boring together. Fine, I agree." His mercurial change of mind catches me as off guard as his shift in mood. "Jiang still dies, though. I'll kill him before I leave the city."

My smile falters. "That sounds . . . obvious. How about instead we gather evidence of his crimes and expose him? I'll help. I *hate* him."

"That sounds . . . slow." Kaine ponders. "Can't I at least maim him?"

I have trouble figuring out when this man is serious. "Err, how about this? If we can't manage to convict him legally, I'll let you maim him until he wishes for death." I say it like I'm doing Kaine a huge favor.

"Deal." He sticks out his hand and we shake. I feel a brief tug to heal his injuries, like an instinctive urge to catch a falling glass or straighten a crooked painting. But I make a conscious decision not to heal him, as he requested.

Kaine says, "My friends will already be bringing my army to claim bloody vengeance. I'll need to move quickly to intercept them."

"I can smuggle you out of the Holy City."

"My debts to you keep piling up." He makes a face. "I promise I will pay you back."

"I know you're good for it, Your Darkness." I flip a hand. "But there's no need. Consider it a gift from a friend. I have a hunch your friendship is valuable."

He throws back his head and laughs. "I *really* like you. Maybe I won't introduce you to Durrian after all."

"Afraid of a little competition?" I arch an eyebrow. "I have a thing for intelligent men, and you're making him sound smart." My tone is jesting. It's been a while since I've had such a fun flirtation.

"I once lost a game of chess to a five-year-old, but I've never lost a real battle." His eyes dance with merriment and challenge.

Alzira steps forward. "Anyone who seeks Her Holiness's hand must defeat me in single combat."

Kaine looks Alzira up and down. "I've heard of you, Alzira of the Holy City. Humanity's Strongest Monster. The Holy Maiden's bodyguard. I wouldn't insult Ysabel by fighting over her like an object, but I'd love a shot at you. It's so rare I get an opponent worth my time."

Alzira and I exchange glances. "He passes," I say.

"Only halfway," she disagrees. "He's not trying to fight me for you, but he still thinks he can take me."

"Kaine *is* a dark lord. It's justified."

"You think he could beat me?" Alzira very slightly pouts.

I wave my hands. "No, no! You're the strongest!" In truth, I wouldn't place bets on that fight, but that's not something to tell my angel. I'd better head this off at the pass. Gifts like Alzira's and Kaine's are the reason we have one less sapient species and a global truce. A fight between these two could leave the continent a smoking crater, to say nothing of my begonias. "I'm just pointing out it's not male arrogance for him to think he's on your level. He *is*."

"Nobody is on my level," Alzira mumbles, but she no longer sounds quite as upset.

"Are we going to fight or not?" Kaine's fingers flex and he rolls on the balls of his feet.

Alzira draws herself up to her full, majestic height. "I'm ready anytime. Do you have your weapon?"

"My hammer is back at my camp."

"Then I won't use mine." She begins to unstrap her scimitar.

Are these two swords-for-brains seriously intending to go at it here? In my healing clinic, full of fragile, expensive medicinal bottles? With Kaine a wanted man? I jump between them. "Don't you dare. We need to get Kaine out of here before anyone tracks him down."

"I lost my pursuers . . . around the time I got lost myself." Kaine shrugs.

"They'll be looking everywhere for you. You'll need a disguise and to get back beyond the walls as soon as the gates open for the drovers at dawn. You can stay at my place overnight." I fetch the aprons the healers throw over their clothes to avoid bloodstains. I cut one into a scarf while Alzira turns a mop into a wig. Luckily, terrible wigs are in fashion.

Kaine offers no objections to following me to my home, where I could easily capture him after he goes to sleep. By the Moon Lady, I have increasing respect for the lieutenants who must have worked hard to keep his overpowered ass alive.

The mop over his head fails to impress me. To Alzira, I say, "I don't want to risk running into an observant guard. We'll need to hide him in the rag cart. Can you pull it?"

"I could pull the cart," Kaine volunteers.

We turn on him with identical expressions. Slowly, I say, "You'll be hiding in the cart."

"Ah, right." With no further protest, Kaine curls up on a small oak cart and allows us to pile used bandages on top of him. We leave his disguise on as a backup plan.

Before we're done, there's a knock on the door. "Coming," I call. To Alzira, I hiss, "Get Kaine into the storage room and don't let him out from under the rags." She obeys with due haste.

The pounding on the door starts to sound like a threat to break it down. I run to unlock it.

Cardinal Jiang stands in the doorway. I'd know *his* face anywhere, because I see it in my nightmares—just kidding, his white cardinal's robes have a red tassel denoting him as our glorious leader. I ought to be horrified, but I'm too stunned. A dozen guards crowd behind him. Aha, there's my horror.

It would be no exaggeration to say my heart stops. My chest contracts. I can't breathe. Shakes run down my arms and legs. All the telltale signs of a panic attack. I need to think of a plan, but my mind is stuck on a repeated chant of "Run." Standing still couldn't be any harder if I'd been set on fire.

If he insists on searching my clinic, the law is on my side, but a lot of swords are on his. Alzira could beat them all, but her life-oath prevents her from attacking another sect's guards. Their life-oaths in turn will kill them if they harm her, but I can't play chicken with Jiang when he places no value on his people's lives.

As it often does during a panic attack, my mouth moves on its own. "Sun God watch over you, Head Cardinal." I curtsy. My body is going through the motions—I just can't think. I have to hold it together. If Jiang sees I'm panicking, then he'll know I'm hiding something. If I throw a fit, he may claim it's demonic possession and lock me up in a dark dungeon, and oh sweet Sun God I am not helping myself calm down. I take deep breaths and tap two fingers against my cheek, a calming exercise. It makes me feel something approaching human.

"Cut the crap. I have your spy." Jiang steps back, revealing a guard holding a sword at the throat of a young man. He's about my age, short, and wearing Jiang's uniform smeared with dirt. His mouth is compressed into a thin line of defiance.

So Cardinal Jiang isn't here about Kaine? All my fear escapes my body in one huge sigh. "I've never seen that man before in my life." Though I've been trying to plant a spy in Jiang's guard for years, I've been unsuccessful.

"You're a natural at playing dumb, Ysabel." Jiang shakes his head. "All those times you passed by him and never a flicker showed on your face. You could have had a great career as an actress or a whore."

Jiang sounds really, really certain I know this man. With my face-blindness, it's tough for me to be equally sure he's wrong. I have to be careful here. What if he's testing me? If Jiang finds out about my face-blindness, he'll have another weakness to hold over me. I take a closer look.

Faces are like a foreign language to me, where I can memorize a few words but don't understand the grammar well enough to translate a whole sentence. They generally have two eyes, a nose, a mouth, and two ears, but any minor distinguishing features are lost on me. Trying to remember a face is *exactly* as hard for me as memorizing someone's whole wardrobe, so I rely on both methods of recognition. I'm not blind. I don't mistake a halfling for a human, or a man for a woman, but put two women of similar age in the same clothing next to each other, and even if I've known them for years, I just plain can't tell who is who. It makes my life so damn difficult.

The supposed spy is even shorter than Kaine. He's handsome, with brown skin, hazel eyes, and curly light brown hair. His button nose has a rash of freckles. As I peer at him, he turns away from me, making my job harder. I say, "If you want me to save you from Jiang, then tell me why I should." His shoulders stiffen. How odd. Someone in his position ought to be begging me for help.

The supposed spy doesn't match anyone from my painfully memorized list of people's distinguishing features. I straighten. "He's not one of mine. Have fun executing your own loyal guard." Heartless, yes, but I have a dark lord hidden in my storage room. I need Jiang out of here.

Jiang sneers. "Nice try. You're too soft to let me kill your half-breed brother."

My vision blurs and my breath falters, pushing me back toward the edge of panic. I grab the man's cheek and force him to show me the side of his face he was hiding. There's a white scar below his ear.

This is my older brother, Calum.

CHAPTER THREE

My brother got his scar the day our father sold me into slavery. I was ten years old, and he was twelve. When I climbed an old willow tree to hide, Calum coaxed me down by promising to help me run away. As soon as my feet touched the ground, Dad and five armored men ambushed me with manacles. Dad laughed and promised a strawberry tart to Calum for finding me. I kicked Calum, the closest target. When he fell, he cut open his cheek on a rock.

So no, we're not close.

After I spent two years being owned by crime lords, Cardinal Jiang brought me into the church as a Holy Maiden. My father sent me letters asking for money, and I burned them.

When I turned fifteen, Calum sought me out. Thin and shaking with hunger, he begged for aid. My mother's newest baby had sickened and died. He apologized over and over again. I almost fell for it, until the scar of his betrayal glinted on his cheek.

My mind went white with fury. I revealed the real reason why I have such an exact time frame to live. In four months, three weeks, and two days, I'll fully come into my power as a Holy Healer. On that day, Jiang will rip out my heart in a ritual designed to give himself immortality.

Skirting the edge of breaking my life-oath to stay silent gave me a mild heart attack. The last words I spoke to him before passing out were: "Fine, I'll give you a monthly stipend for the sake of our little siblings. On one condition: You never show your face in front of me again."

He never had.

So what in the unholy fornication of the Sun God and the Moon Devil is Calum doing in Jiang's guard? If he intends espionage, it has nothing to do with me. I haven't seen his treacherous, backstabbing face in a decade. Did I call him handsome? He gets uglier the longer I look at him.

Misinterpreting the shock on my face, Jiang says, "Of course I guessed. Without his disguise, you two look very much alike. Don't pretend. You'd never let me kill your only brother."

Calum speaks in a voice tight with fear. "Her last living relative." Our eyes lock, and I know we share at least one common goal here: If Jiang doesn't know about the rest of my siblings, both of us would like to keep it that way.

Why is Calum only speaking up now? I know the answer; I just don't want to accept it. Calum knows I can't recognize faces. He didn't want me to identify him by his voice. He was trying to keep Jiang from using him to threaten me.

Jiang says, "He'd finally acquired the right blackmail material to free you from our bargain. It took him five years, and he finished four months before you'll be sacrificed. But I intercepted and destroyed his letter to you. It's over. I've won."

Reluctant though I am to admit it, because hating my family keeps my cold heart warm late at night, Calum must have infiltrated Jiang's sect guard in a misguided attempt to save me. Because I told him my death would be his fault. *Shit.* I do not know how to deal with this.

If I have a second panic attack in a row, I'm going to collapse. *Breathe, you pathetic lump!* I tap my cheek rapidly. "What do you want for his life?" My words come out harsh, without a trace of the wheedling tone I use on men. I may not like my brother, but apparently I still love him.

Jiang smiles, and I've never hated him more. "You can't figure it out? I suppose half-breeds aren't very intelligent." His tone makes it clear being half-Conollian is worse than full in his eyes.

I've been politically scheming with the best of them since I turned fourteen. Yet I have to swallow the insult. In fact, I understand clearly what Jiang wants—to end my rebellions against him. I beg, "Please let me stay on the council so I can keep the refugees from being driven away. If they're forced back to the blighted lands, they'll starve."

Almost certainly, Jiang has only allowed the Conollian refugees to stick around this long to create hostages. Life-oaths aren't good at stopping someone from committing suicide, since the penalty for breaking them is, well, death. Whenever I get uppity, Jiang brings up how easy it would be for him to write a sermon denouncing the refugees as lay-about heretics.

Cardinal Jiang says, "I'll leave the migrant rats alone—if you obey all my orders and stop trying to escape your sacrificial duty."

Relief makes my knees go weak. That's easy enough. I never planned on surviving. I can still protect everyone.

Calum jerks down on the arm of the guard holding him, shouting, "His murders are—"

The guard slams a sword hilt into Calum's midsection. Another man grabs my brother by the throat, cutting off his words.

"Stop!" I scream.

"Stop once he's unconscious," Jiang orders. Calum goes limp, and the guard releases his throat.

I let out a whimper of relief, then step forward, hand outstretched.

"If she moves one hair closer, kill him," Jiang says.

I freeze. "I only wanted to heal him."

"I'm not taking any chances." Jiang sneers. "He'll be under guard in a secret location. There will be a crossbow on him at all times. If you in any way defy me, your brother dies. If I die, your brother dies. I can always go back to using the necro-servant migrants as hostages. He's expendable. From now on, no more lip or cheek. You come when I call, you do as I say, you heal who I wish, and you die at my command. Do you understand?"

Wordlessly, I nod.

As Jiang and his guards leave, my fingers twitch with longing to snatch Calum away from them. I slump against the doorframe.

Oh, Calum. I can't believe he did something like this, but it's been so long since our childhood, I don't know him at all. I've always told myself that he doesn't care about me, only the money I send every month. But if that were true, he wouldn't have spent five years trying to save my life.

My big brother was always my hero. He grew up too fast, looking after his younger siblings because our parents didn't. A thousand memories flash across my mind. Calum stealing apples from the neighboring farm to feed us. Calum shoving the girl who'd called me a half-breed into the river. Calum spitting out blood after our father had punched him, then getting to his feet to stand in front of us younger siblings again. Of course he'd stand up to an even bigger bully named Jiang for my sake.

I remember the day so long ago when Calum found my hiding place. He had bags under his eyes and a bruise on his left cheek. Was he threatened into giving me away? When I try hard to think back, I recall seeing sincere surprise on his face when the slavers grabbed me. Maybe he didn't know. Or maybe I'm remembering wrong after so long.

If he dies before we speak again, I'll never know the truth or be able to sort out my complicated feelings. The thought of my brother dying brings stinging tears to the corners of my eyes. The intensity of my own feelings surprises me. I thought I'd cut ties with him, but apparently that was another lie I told myself.

Arahasnor has never been one of those countries where the laws apply to important people. Jiang has clipped any political influence I might use to rescue my brother. Calum tried to tell me something important, but I have no idea what. He's going to die once my use to Jiang is up, and I'm not going to be able to save him.

I put my head in my hands and try very hard not to cry.

Alzira steps out of the storage room. "Princess? What did Cardinal Jiang want?" Upon seeing my wan face, she charges forward. "What's wrong?"

Lucky thing I sent Alzira away. She knows nothing about my role as a human sacrifice. If she did, she'd try to stop it and die breaking her life-oath. "He just upset me. You know what he's like." My brother, I'll tell her about later so I can get one of her hugs. I can't cry yet, because we're not alone.

Kaine pokes his mop-covered head out the door. "Are you sure I shouldn't kill him?"

"Don't," I growl, and Kaine recoils. He doesn't know why this is no longer a joke to me, and I can't tell him.

I have only one thing that Cardinal Jiang would be willing to trade for my brother: the life of Dark Lord Kaine. Conversely, I have no way to win against Jiang. But Kaine might be able to.

I have to go all in or all out. Betray Kaine. Or throw my full political weight behind the dark lord and destroy Jiang until he gives me my brother in exchange for his miserable life. No denying which of these would be more satisfying . . . but also more dangerous. For Calum: I'm dead either way.

The idea of selling out Kaine makes my stomach turn. He seems like a decent person despite his quickness to violence. Distant Conollia means little to me compared to the Conollian refugees I grew up with. Still, it would be an evil deed to sell out an entire country of innocent people just to save my brother.

But can I trust Kaine to value my brother over his vengeance? He doesn't act very discreet. Calum dies if Jiang gets the slightest word of our alliance.

I don't have to decide yet. If I give Kaine up now, Jiang would just murder him and keep my brother anyway. I'd need to arrange a Seer to create a life-oath. I have time to get to know Kaine better, to decide if he's worth trusting.

"Let's go." I sigh.

Kaine wiggles back under the rags on the cart. Alzira grabs the handle and squeezes the cart out the door.

It's still light outside. The scalpel-shaped bruise on my buttocks gives me little tinges of pain with each step. We pass high-end shops selling perfume, jewelry, and fancy clothing, with big glass displays and banners announcing outlandish wares. Carriages bustle by, the occupants wearing awful giant wigs. Gradually, the shops become smaller, now with homes above them. Barefoot workers in caps or bonnets pass us on the dirt path. A stray dog paws at trash left on the street for the rakers. In the distance, smoke rises off the textile factories built just a few years ago. As the Age of Science has driven urban migration and doubled the Holy City's population, more and more beggars sleep on the sides of the street. There have been three riots as the poor scrabble over scarce resources, and Jiang blames the refugees while pocketing most of the church's charitable donations.

A cane blocks my path. I can tell from his square cap that this is Cardinal Farruco, not a beggar. He turns his expensive official robes into rags because he thinks it makes him look holy. His oniony stench knocks me back a step.

As I pass around him, his eyes fix on the V-shaped collar of my lacy white dress. "Whore."

Alzira whirls around. "Do not speak that way to Her Holiness."

Dammit, Alzira, just keep walking! We're smuggling a dark lord in the cart you dropped . . .

Farruco sneers. "That thing on your head is disgusting," he says, pointing his cane at her headscarf. Yes, he criticized me for not covering up enough and her for covering up too much in the space of a minute. Farruco is the only cardinal on the council who's never broken his vow of chastity. But he's no better because he never shuts up about how much he wants to sleep with women, in the form of long rants about how we're all seducing him.

As Farruco lunges forward, his spittle strikes my face. "Your sole purpose is to heal in the name of the Sun God, yet you deal in politics. I should cover your sinful face and beat you."

If you're going to use a blindfold, at least take advantage of the increased reactiveness from sensory deprivation with a dab of hot wax or ice. Amateur. If Farruco knew I have far more experience dominating than him, he'd do me a favor and have a heart attack.

Unlike Farruco, I'm not into dominance because I hate the opposite gender. For me, it's about trust and honesty. When a man allows himself to be entirely vulnerable, this allows me to return the same level of trust to him. I'm able to see him at his absolute limit and push myself to my limit. It forms a connection between us. In that moment, we're both completely stripped of our masks and illusions. That's a state I rarely get to be in. Of course, it's also a whole lot of fun. Adrenaline, letting loose, and primal joy. The taboo is part of the pleasure. Not going to lie, I love thinking about how shocked the cardinals would be if they could see their Holy Maiden in full dominatrix mode. Of course I'd never actually let Farruco anywhere near my bed, but the fantasy keeps me from completely snapping after he spat on me.

Wiping my cheek, I say, "I'm dreadfully sorry to have offended you, Cardinal Farruco. As the Sun God wills, I have the highest respect for my elders." *The Sun God says you're a creepy fanatic and you should talk to someone about your hatred for women. Not Him, though. He's heard enough on the subject.*

Farruco brings his cane down toward my head.

Alzira catches it before it can touch me. Her other arm draws back for a punch. I grab her bicep, hissing, "Let it go." To my horror, Kaine's hand emerges from the rags. I step forward to block him from sight. It's true what they say: better a thousand enemies than incompetent allies. "Cardinal Farruco, please accept my humble apologies."

Farruco opens his mouth, looks at Alzira, and shuts it. The cardinal slouches away, muttering insults under his breath. "Painted eyes and suntanned skin. Slut."

Perhaps Farruco has lived so long because the Sun God is avoiding the creep. The conversation where He'll have to explain to Farruco that he doesn't actually speak for Him is going to be so awkward.

"Has he ever hit you before?" Alzira demands.

"Of course not." Excluding that one time I deliberately stepped into the path of his cane. After I showed off the bruise for sympathy, the council voted to send a thousand tents to the refugee camp.

Kaine whispers, "Are you hurt?" His sincere concern takes the edge off my anger.

I sigh. "I'm fine. I appreciate the thought, but please stay hidden. If anyone found out I'm sheltering a dark lord, I'd get in far worse trouble than anything Farruco could do to me."

"He was imagining breaking your bones with his cane." Glinting among the dirty rags, Kaine's eyes burn very cold.

My heart rate accelerates. "Your magic has returned?" That would make it obscenely hard to (theoretically) capture him for Jiang.

"Only partly."

Summoning all my acting ability to look disappointed rather than relieved, I say, "Let me know as soon as you're fully recovered."

Hands flexing, Alzira hisses, "Your Holiness, please allow me to teach that vile fiend Farruco a lesson."

I'm unwilling to openly discuss committing a crime on a public street, in front of Kaine. "The Sun God in His never-ending mercy forbids us from unnecessary violence."

Alzira grabs the cart and pulls it along. "So I should put on a mask first, then beat him?"

My dear Alzira, I'm the only sect leader who hires women for guards. A disguise isn't going to hide who sent you. "The Sun God is all-knowing and all-seeing."

Her brow wrinkles with concentration. "I think . . . what you're saying . . . is that I should cover his face instead of mine, then beat him."

Exactly. "Of course not. The Sun God would never permit any such thing." I wink.

Voice muffled under the rags, Kaine calls, "I'd be happy to help."

Alzira glances over her shoulder. "Find me the smelliest bag in that pile. I need to do violence to an elderly nose."

I love Alzira.

Just a block away from my house, I freeze. Two carriages, both surrounded by guards, are on a path to bowl us over. A white flag emblazoned with a violet narcissus flies over the first carriage: the symbol of the queen. I have a bad feeling about this. Arahasnor nobility only lower themselves to visit the poor part of town when they want healing. They're here for me.

"Ysabel?" In a blur of motion, a tall woman jumps out of the coach. Lean and angular, pale skin clashing with dark brown hair, she wears a red dress tailored with buttons to resemble a man's coat and a slit for easy movement. Her crimson top hat has a cluster of silk flowers and a tall feather on the side. The clothes make it easy to recognize her where faces usually fail me: Countess Donya, renowned women's rights activist. I'm delighted to see her. I hold Donya in much higher esteem than the queen.

Her thin lips purse. "How dare you have no women's bathrooms set up for the World Games? Sellout."

My love for Donya is not mutual. We lead two very different women's rights factions. Hers stages protest marches, chains themselves to lampposts, and publishes angry pamphlets. Mine goes around afterward to say to powerful men, "Oh dear, those loudmouthed troublemakers, such a disgrace, and I'm sure the situation would calm down if you signed this teensy-weensy bill on women's property and that one on divorce law." In other words, Donya plays the radical and I play the suck-up, and together we've negotiated significant improvements in women's legal rights in Arahasnor. Except only one of us knows about the arrangement.

My fake smile turns real as I see an opportunity to obtain the bathrooms we both want. "It's my sincere desire to help you, but I am sworn to poverty."

"I'll provide the gold." Donya crosses her arms. "There, now you don't have any excuses." Her organization is generously funded, with patrons including the elven empress.

"I commend your generosity to the Sun God. I'll put your proposal into action without troubling the cardinals. It's just like the time we worked together to open that school for refugee children."

Donya puts her hands on her hips. "When you hijacked a fundraiser I'd been planning for months to hawk your own cause?"

"How dare you point it out when Her Holiness rewrites the truth," Alzira growls.

If even Alzira doesn't believe me, I must have lost track of my lies. It's been known to happen when you're juggling as many balls as I am.

Donya steps in front of me. "While I have you cornered, why aren't your Dragon Maidens participating in the Games? Your team is far better than you deserve. You could win."

My smile falters. This is a sore subject. I plan to negotiate land for the refugees by agreeing to keep my team of fighters—especially the deadly Alzira—out of the matches. No one knows that because of the secret price of Alzira's gift, she can't fight effectively in the Games anyway. "Everything happens according to the Sun God's will."

"Must you mention the Sun God every sentence? You're so silly!" Donya throws up her hands.

I can never get upset at Donya's insults. They're harmless. When a cute kitten bares her claws at me, I take out a ball of yarn and play with her. "My faith in the Sun God is as strong as a snowstorm."

"It also melts when exposed to sunlight," Donya retorts.

I'm glad she got the comeback I fed her. Donya is absolutely brilliant, but a terrible public speaker. I've been secretly training her during our debates. "Spoken like Queen Bianna's errand girl."

Donya glares. "Do you have a problem? Her Majesty is the kindest person I know."

So I thought too, when I first came to court. Donya will also learn Bianna's true face the hard way. I pause, debating if I can put off whatever the queen wants from me. In principle, I'm subservient to the church, not the monarchy. In practice, the monarchy has always acted like they rule us, and they have more guards.

Arahasnor is the name of the Holy City and also the name of Arahasnor the country, which is exactly as confusing as it sounds. The city-state is ruled by the church and entitled to our own World Games teams for each sect. Surrounding us is Arahasnor the country, ruled by the king. We've long had messy power struggles with the royal family—they tax our imports and exports absurdly, and we swallow up bits of their territory as the city grows. It's like the gang war over control of our first horse-pulled railroad station, except on a geopolitical scale.

I paste on my fake smile. "Our kindhearted queen will surely understand I'm exhausted from carrying out my duty to the Sun God and succoring the sick. I'll speak to her tomorrow."

Sympathy flashes across Donya's face. "She ordered you to come immediately. The king needs you for a medical emergency."

I wince. Under our agreement with the government, I have no right to refuse healing to the king and queen. "Of course I will obey our divinely consecrated leader. Just give me a few minutes."

Kaine sneezes.

The guards run forward. Blue light shoots from one's hand to strike the cart. "Please, he's just a beggar!"

The guard freezes, a sheepish look on his face. "I used a sleeping power. I feared he might be another kidnapper after you, Your Holiness."

Kaine isn't moving. My calm mask cracks. "Please let me drop him off at my home for treatment. He's very sick."

"We can't." The guard captain with a plume in his helmet steps forward. "Their Majesties ordered us to bring you at once."

I turn to make another appeal to Donya, but she's already vanished into her carriage. When I turn back, the guards are lifting Kaine's limp body into the second carriage.

My eye twitches. They may not recognize him yet, but if we're driving right into the heart of the palace, then someone could. "The Sun God would appreciate your understanding—"

The guard captain ushers me into the carriage. "We can't delay another second, Your Holiness. It's lucky we found you."

Lucky? I've been called to attendance before the King of Arahasnor with Dark Lord Kaine in tow, disguised with a mop for a wig. *Lucky* is not the word I would use. The word should be *fucked.*

The royal carriages are magical relics. No one can eavesdrop on the conversations inside. Stuffed into the second carriage with Alzira and Kaine, I ought to be scheming my next move. Yet all I can do is stutter. I don't even have the excuse of a panic attack. I'm so far past fear I'm circling back around to angry.

"Should I beat Countess Donya, too? It's no trouble," Alzira says.

What? I like Donya. "The Sun God promotes mercy and forgiveness."

"So I should put a bag over her head before beating her?"

No, I don't want you to beat her at all. Huh, I don't think we have a code for that. I slip out of my Holy Maiden voice. "Donya means well, unlike Cardinal Farruco. Besides, she's right about me being a fraud."

Alzira mutters something about a sharp tongue needing a whetstone. I've been a terrible influence.

I'll order some servants at the palace to take Kaine to the kitchens for a meal. Maybe he'll stay out of sight long enough for me to avoid execution. I reach for Kaine's dirty face, planning to heal him awake.

Again, his lightning-fast grip seizes my hand. "I told you. I won't shorten your lifespan," he growls.

"You're not sleeping?" I ask dumbly.

"I dodged the spell." Kaine sits up. "I was pretending because you said not to start fights."

Oh. He trusted me and listened to me. Pleasure wars with my guilt, since I still haven't decided if I will betray him. If everything goes wrong because I told Kaine not to fight back, then it will be my fault. "Sorry, now you're stuck going to the royal palace with us."

"I've gotten a little more magic back." Yanking the mop off his head, Kaine waves a hand over his face. His hair turns red, his skin pales, and his nose elongates. Several moles obscure his features. His face ages twenty years.

"You can shape-shift?" I blurt out.

"Magical modification kills living beings." Kaine's tone is wistful. "It's merely an illusion."

"What are your limits?"

"I can only make small changes, I can't hold it for longer than an hour, and it won't stand up to touch." Kaine shakes his head with discouragement. "I don't *feel* any different."

"That's good enough to hide you until I return. Just . . . don't talk. Not one word. Pretend you're mute."

Kaine frowns. "I wouldn't give you away."

Alzira says, "You introduced yourself to us as *Kaine*."

"It's a common name. I could have been any Kaine."

I raise an eyebrow. "You said *Dark Lord Kaine*."

He winces. "It's easy to blurt out your real name."

"For you, which is why *you're* not talking." I draw myself up to my full, tiny height and glare him down.

He sighs and nods. "Are you in trouble with the local Useless Rich Nobility?"

"The king wants a healing." His Majesty probably has a tummy ache from overeating sweets. It wouldn't be the first so-called emergency.

Kaine tilts his head. "You look like it's been a long day. Thank you for risking yourself to help me."

Guilt chokes me. I want to confess everything. My brother's life stops me. I have to save Calum before I die. Though it would be nice to save Conollia, that's a lower priority.

But I really, really don't want to betray this man.

King Uctor's castle is the second largest building in the Holy City, after the council's headquarters. Both buildings keep adding new wings in a juvenile competition. The royal castle is made of brilliantly red sandstone. The airy towers and huge glass windows favor beauty over functionality. The carriage lets us off at the moss-covered steps framed by sculpted bushes. It takes four guards to hold the bronze doors open.

The hallway ceiling depicts ancient kings and queens sailing, battling, and in one case making a rude gesture. Tall blue-and-white furnaces alternate with swords encased in glass. Since it's currently summer, the furnaces are turned off. The swords are frost relics, made by a long-dead gifted with an ice power. Each one stands as tall as me. The thick blue blades have ridges resembling waves. Every time the rune in the hilt flashes white, sparks dance down the blade and cold air puffs out. The previous king used to tell foreigners they could become the destined monarch of Arahasnor if they drew the sword from the case, just to see if they were stupid enough to actually try it. We keep the ice statues in the ballroom.

The king's steward, Owlert, rushes forward. "You must make haste at once." He waves his hand at the air around my back. Alzira has trained men to never, ever touch me.

"Wait. I brought an ill beggar with me. Please take him to—"

"To the commoner's balcony, of course." Owlert's nose wrinkles at the odor of stale blood wafting off Kaine.

"I'd rather get him a meal in the kitchen." No one listens. Several guards peel off to escort Kaine away. He glances over his shoulder. I mouth, "It's fine." Anything is better than Kaine starting a fight. If he can just shut up for a few minutes, we can all get out of here with our heads intact. If. “Alzira, watch over him. You'll still be able to see me from the commoner's balcony.”

“As you command, Your Holiness.” Alzira sprints after Kaine.

At a barred silver door leading to the throne room, Steward Owlert bellows, “Presenting Holy Maiden Ysabel to His Majesty, the Fifth of His Name, Uctor the Magnificent.”

Guards in blue-plumed helmets with rapiers line the carpet leading up to the throne: the King's Guard, drawn from younger sons of nobles. Behind them stand a row of men in heavy armor carrying pikes: the real guards. It used to just be the King's Guard, until someone assassinated the monarch a hundred years ago and the royal family realized nobles are far less willing to take an arrow for them than commoners.

The room is designed to impress and intimidate. White-gray pillars supporting busts of the king's ancestors alternate with chandeliers. Paintings from artists around the world hang on the walls. The great Riyardo himself did the mural of martyred saints on the ceiling. Everything from the candlesticks to the stained-glass windows are antiques. Even the graffiti on the pillars comes from princes and princesses of centuries ago. The huge silk carpet is emblazoned with the royal emblem, a purple sword and sickle. The chairs upon which nobles sit to await their audience are miniature thrones with golden sun backs. Commoners can petition the king from the alcoves above, since only nobles are allowed to set foot in this room. I'm as common as the dirt on my family's farm, but as long as no one challenges my right to be here, I'm not going to say anything. Above, guards escort Alzira and Kaine to the front of the balcony.

The king's throne is made of solid gold. Two employees are dedicated to polishing out the dents every day. A red curtain hangs around the back of the throne. Above that, a giant golden hoop suspends a glowing ball. The sun relic casts light over the throne and its inhabitant, the fifty-fifth monarch of Arahasnor.

King Uctor is a corpulent fellow with golden curls and a tiny blond beard and mustache. His round head and pudgy nose have the innocence of a baby. He reminds me of a bad portrait done by a painter, too heavy with red on the face, but that's actually how he looks. The bejeweled robes splayed around him make him seem even bigger. A diamond the size of an egg hangs around his neck. More gemstones drip off the many rings on his fingers. The crown on his head is big enough to give someone brain damage, which would explain a lot. Let's just say there's a reason Jiang, a suspicious priest of unknown origins, runs around unchecked in this country.

Despite me being emergency summoned here, the king looks perfectly healthy to me.

I launch into my usual speech. "Great King Uctor, I'm pleased the Sun God has brought me here. Blessed light radiates off you . . ." I can go on like this forever, and he always eats it up.

When I pause for a breath, Uctor waves at me. "Ysabel, you're as beautiful as always. Such a pity the Sun God strikes dead any man who touches you."

Normally I resent that myth, but in this case, God is welcome to bring the entire heavenly choir to keep the king from laying a finger on me. "I flew to your side the very moment the Sun God delivered your message to me. You look terribly ill, Your Majesty."

"What? No, it's not me. It's Theodesius Carston Wormington Wattlewaggler the Fourth." The king gestures at the elderly poodle lying on a cushion in his lap. Ribbons adorn his fur, pompoms decorate his legs, and a tiny crown sits on his head. "Her Majesty told me not to let him eat chocolate, but I only left the bowl of candies alone for a few seconds."

He wants me to heal his *dog*? After he irresponsibly poisoned his pet? My virtuous smile freezes in place. "The great gift the Sun God has bestowed upon me must be reserved for the direst of circumstances."

"Can't you heal animals?" King Uctor's mouth puckers up. "I can't bear to see my Theodesius suffering. I insist you try." Sweat and sickly perfume wafts off him.

The criminal gang that owned me as a child forced me to heal their racehorses. No one since then has had the nerve to ask. Too bad I can't afford to upset this pompous ass. My anger collapses under the weight of bitterly familiar resignation. "It's my honor to be of service." I accept the cushion holding the sleeping poodle.

Every time I do this, it could be the last. Usually I summon my will by reminding myself that at least I would be dying to save someone else's life. This time, the angels would be dragging me kicking and screaming to the afterlife. I've been given a graphic lesson on how little my sacrifice means to those who use it.

My life is worth less than a dog's.

"What's taking so long?" Uctor leans forward on his throne. "Performance anxiety?"

The crowd laughs. He's the king—they'd laugh if he made a fart joke. The many eyes bore into me. I want redleaf. I *need* redleaf. Without noticing, I've bitten my lip so hard it's bleeding. I place my hand on the cream fur.

A man jumps down from the balcony and lands with a force that shakes every lamp in the room. Kaine. His disguise is gone, revealing the angry face of a dark lord. Tiny red and black sparks dance over his body. The air around him crackles with such force that static dances off the carpet. His eyes are glowing. He snatches the cushion away, waking up Theodesius, who leaps down and hides behind my legs. "Don't! You're dying!" His body trembles with suppressed rage as his eyes plead with me.

"Who—what—it's only a day of her life," Uctor says with a familiar whine preceding a temper tantrum in his voice. "Guards!"

"Go stuff a cock in your mouth, you inbred fuckwit," Kaine says, then punches the King of Arahasnor across the jaw.

CHAPTER FOUR

He punched the king in the mouth. He punched the king in the mouth! The king! Mouth! His Majesty went flying! Noooo, don't turn around and grin at me. Don't give me a thumbs-up. I have nothing to do with this. I'm not an accomplice to an assault on royalty. I've never seen this man before in my life.

I'm almost relieved when the closest King's Guard swings his sword, distracting Kaine from incriminating me. The blade breaks against his arm, then Kaine tosses the sputtering boy across the room.

The crowd goes silent, except for King Uctor the Fifth wailing like a baby. Blood trickles down his lip. The real guards, the Gifted Knights in armor, start forward. One summons a cage of ice. Heat roars off Kaine's body, melting the ice into a puddle. Then he backflips over the wall of men and lands behind them, touching the ice-user's neck. An odd, hungry look crosses Kaine's face. A spark dances from the knight's body to Kaine's hand as he absorbs the power. Kaine freezes the guards' legs to the ground. It leaves a small bit of frost on his face.

"I—I can't use my ice," a Gifted Knight whispers in shock, staring down at his feet frozen using his own stolen gift. "His Majesty! Someone save His Majesty!"

Kaine can steal anyone else's gift permanently with a touch. He can wield an infinite number of magics. Only one man has ever possessed this awesome power, and it may very well make him the strongest person alive. (Though I would never tell Alzira I thought that.) It also makes him very obviously identifiable.

"It's *Dark Lord Kaine*!"

The same cry emerges from many throats. The nobles stampede for the exit. The King's Guard flees too. The Gifted Knights, to give them credit, try—even though they'll lose their livelihoods if the dark lord steals their powers. With them frozen, Kaine easily takes from one after another, before they have time to do more than make the air rotten and the candle flames flicker. Their armor warps into cuffs on their wrists, their eyes close with slumber, and they're all lifted up and propped against the wall.

Steward Owlert throws open the doors, and a veritable army pours in. Kaine strides forward. The fleeing crowd means nothing to him; his power lifts them aside without harming them. The guards also mean nothing to him. Arrows bounce off his skin. Swords shatter. Magic dissipates. They look like gnats trying to attack a giant. Kaine is simply too strong.

After he's swept everyone from the room and sealed the door with ice, Kaine turns toward me. He has the nerve, the colossal nerve, to smile. Moon Devil take him, there isn't a scratch on him. What a magnificent ability, one that allowed him to conquer an entire country single-handedly. After all the warlords he sliced through like butter, rumor has it he obtained thousands of powers.

I'm in no mood to be smiled at. "You promised me you wouldn't do that. You *promised.* All you had to do was sit still and not act like a barbarian for a few minutes."

"He deserved it for how he was treating you."

"So now it's my fault?" My body shakes with rage. It's all the same song and dance, whether it's "you're a weak and feeble woman so I'll ignore what you say to protect you" or "you were too pretty, so I raped you." The mysterious power of women's beauty to free men of all responsibility for doing whatever they already wanted to do.

"That's not what I meant." Kaine's puppyish eyes plead with me. "Look, sometimes I have trouble controlling my temper."

"Is that *my* problem? Are you going to claim I owe you for what I never wanted?"

"No, you don't. I made my own decision." He takes a deep breath. "I can't bear to watch them slowly kill you."

At least he took full responsibility. Deflating, I sag against the pillar. "You've put me in danger, my plan in danger, and your entire country's future in danger."

"I know." His face is serious. "I removed my disguise first so no one would connect me with you."

"That's something, at least. It's lucky you didn't kill anyone." I pause. "Did you?"

"Relax, the truce is safe." Kaine wrinkles his nose.

I bite my lower lip in thought. The noise outside makes it hard to plan. Splinters of ice fall across the ballroom floor as the army chips their way in. "It's going to be much harder, but I can still sneak you out of the Holy City."

Kaine flips a hand. "I've already caused you too much trouble. There's no need. Nothing in this city can stop me from leaving now my magic has fully recovered, even if I have to knock down the walls."

"Whoa, whoa, remember what I said about not destroying my walls?" I glare. "It's not too late for us to save your treaty with the Conclave of Kings, as long as you don't kill anyone. Sneak away and meet me at—" I almost said *my house*, but I can't trust him not to lead an army to my doorstep. "Find me at the oldest church at the top of the hill. Giant and painted yellow, you can't miss it." If Kaine does bring an army at his heels, I'll have plenty of time to escape while he destroys the buildings of people I don't like on his way up.

"Agreed." Kaine shivers.

"Are you worried? I can try to think up a different plan . . ."

"Don't worry about me. I'm cold because I used an ice power." Kaine rubs his arms. "That's the usual price for that type of ability. I can handle it."

The price of his gift is to suffer all the effects of the magic he stole? I'm surprised that he revealed a state secret so easily. On second thought, he probably has an additional price. Many weak gifts come with merely a little exhaustion, but the strong ones always have a high cost.

A larger block of ice hits the tiles with a crack. An armored glove sticks through the hole. "I'll see you soon," Kaine says with a cocky grin, turning toward the enemy.

As the first knight breaks into the room, I duck behind a pillar. The clash and flash of magic resumes. All Kaine does is walk toward the door at a steady pace. He doesn't even need to fight. Magic and weapons bounce off him. Ineffectually, the guards chase after him down the hallway.

Alzira slides down a pillar to land beside me. "I could take him."

I raise an eyebrow at her. "He could steal your power."

"It wouldn't do him any good if I'd already leveled us and this entire city." In response to my raised eyebrow, Alzira crosses her arms. "I never said I'd actually do it. Just that, theoretically, I could." She's very proud of her unofficial title as Humanity's Strongest.

"I can't believe he punched the king." I roll my eyes. "Goddamn male pride."

Alzira shrugs. "I would have ripped His Majesty's bloated head off his shoulders if my life-oath didn't prevent me."

"I'm *glad* you didn't do that." It's tempting to imagine a world where life-oaths don't exist, and I could use Alzira to destroy all my enemies. But they're necessary when every major power bloc has someone with a gift capable of incredible damage. A world war could easily end in global extinction.

Theodesius the poodle nuzzles my ankle. He seems to have recovered on his own. All of this fuss was for nothing. The perfect shit ending to a shit day. I sigh. "Please get me out of here."

"As you command, princess." Alzira scoops me up in her arms. Not the most efficient way to move, but she loves doing it. A little magic later, she's busted a hole in the wall for our escape.

We're halfway out of the palace before I realize the option to betray Kaine in that moment never even occurred to me.

At the palace gate, I run into Steward Owlert issuing orders from a safe distance. I take the chance to practice my innocent act: *I have no idea what happened. I fainted when the horrible man attacked from the ceiling. That was the Dark Lord Kaine? May the Sun God punish him. The hole in the wall was totally him too. I'm not paying for that.* Not my finest line of nonsense. Anyone with the tiniest respect for my intelligence would have seen through it. Happily, I rarely have that problem.

The sounds of Kaine's destruction echo behind us. "Let's take a carriage for hire to Cardinal Santos's church," I tell Alzira. I picked our meeting place partly because Santos is one of my rare semi-allies on the council. "We'd better disguise ourselves first." I have zero desire to be implicated in Kaine's current chaos if anyone sees us together.

We swing by the clinic. First, I put on a gray wig that none of our balding patients ever want because they all prefer younger hair. We take turns applying a paste to each other's faces to make it look like we have boils.

Looking at myself in the mirror, I ask, "Did we overdo it?" With red lumps all over my skin, I look like I should be under quarantine. A lump on one of my eyelids makes it flop down.

"Probably," Alzira admits, her face equally obscured. "But if we wash some of them off, we might be too late to catch Kaine."

Who knows what trouble that walking disaster will get into? I wince. "Let's hurry."

We head to the top of the Afterlife Auction hill. Santos's sect of the Sun God is the oldest one, and thus the only church with the confidence to be squat and painted a brilliant yellow instead of using actual gold.

Despite having an exterior beaten down by age, the inside of Santos's church blinds my eyes. The gold-encrusted shrines host icons and relics of saints, three of whom are buried here. Ugh, including that dreadful Saint Vernon, who had a dozen wives and was caught in a brothel after faking his own martyrdom. The palace was centuries old, but this place has stood for millennia. Despite very careful upkeep, the silver candleholders are tarnished, and the pews have worn grooves from many parishioners' usage. The king and queen have personal thrones for their visits. Not many people climb all the way up here except for sermons. Today, two trash rakers still wearing their uniforms have come to donate coins in the box and pray. Their indistinct murmurs echo in this large, silent space. Alzira and I slip into the pews. My feet are killing me from the long walk up the hill.

As we wait for Kaine to arrive, my eyes wander along the frescoes on the nearest pillar. They tell holy stories for those who can't read. The top shows the birth of Holy Maiden Ava, founder of the Church and Bride of the Sun God. Then her visions, her healings, and her rebellion against the orc overlords. The final paintings show Ava dying to heal a nonbeliever king who'd pretended his cold was pneumonia to test her. The happy ending: the Sun God resurrects Ava with a new gift to revitalize the war-ravaged cropland. The king and all his people convert out of gratitude.

My breath catches, as if there's a pocket of air stuck in my lungs. I jerk my eyes back to my hands. Holy Ava is the reason Healers hold a special place in the church of the Sun God, but I've always hated the moral of her story: that we're supposed to heal anyone without question, and if the Sun God wanted us to live, He'd bring us back to life

Himself. My personal interpretation: maybe the Sun God removed Ava's gift because people wouldn't stop abusing it. And if the Sun God married Ava, He probably doesn't want *me*. I'm not nearly as curvaceous.

As the setting sun creeps through the stained-glass windows, I become anxious and hungry. I nudge Alzira. "We'd better let the Dragon Maidens know we're safe. I gave Cardinal Santos a book linked to ours at home."

After the invention of the printing press, people with book-related gifts began to appear. Bookmakers can create paired books, such that words written in one book will appear in the other. The strongest can even send images. The nobility, the wealthy, and the church compete to hire them. Knowledge is a matter of life or death on the political stage. Gradually, the books have spread until the middle-class can afford to visit a church and borrow a page to send a letter to a distant relative.

The priest at the door shows us where the enchanted books are kept. Alzira writes a note of vague reassurance, then the paper burns away. The lucky Bookmakers have a cheap price for their magic, unlike what healing takes away from me and my unfortunate predecessors.

When I hear distant shouting, I have a bad feeling that Kaine has gotten himself into trouble again. Although I'm less worried about him and more worried about anyone who gets in his way. I put on a pleading face. "Alzira?"

Her brows draw up sternly. "I cannot leave you unprotected, princess."

"It's probably Kaine."

"Kaine can take care of himself. People try to kidnap you once a week."

A gross exaggeration. It's more like once a month. "I'm in disguise. I swear I won't set foot out of this church, in the name of the Sun God. I'll be safe."

Her look says she's not buying my bullshit. "This is a public church."

"Protected by a relic that strikes down anyone who uses violence in this holy place." I use my last resort. "This is an order, Alzira."

"As you command," she says. Ugh, now she's making that face. The one she knows makes me feel guilty.

I turn on the charm. "You're the only one I can count on. I'm placing my trust in you."

"Understood!" She salutes. "I'll drag Kaine back by the neck." She marches away.

The church has emptied. Even the priest at the door went home for dinner, confident in the relics to protect all the treasures here. My stomach rumbles as the door creaks open.

I duck down in the pews. Alzira has made me paranoid. I peek over the edge. The woman walking to the shrine wears the red coat of Donya's women's rights posse. That thick, brown hair and angry, aggressive stride, it has to be . . . "Countess Donya?"

She turns around. "Excuse me? Do I know you?" Her eyes are red and puffy.

My political rival would never want me to catch her crying. I have no good explanation for my disguise either. In the first trick I can think of, I pull out the Conollian accent of my childhood, extending my vowels and speaking like one of my nostrils is closed. "I'm a huge admirer of yours, my lady. I deeply appreciate what you've done for women in this country."

Her smile chases away the shadows in her eyes. "Thank you. Call me Donya, please. What's your name?"

My mind goes blank. I blurt out my sister's name. "Bora."

Completely taken in by my clever disguise, Donya sits down next to me. She doesn't flinch away from my apparent skin disease. "Nice to meet you."

"If you don't mind me saying so, you look upset. Would you like to unburden yourself? Sometimes talking to a stranger can ease your troubles." Yes, I'm curious. Yes, I'm fishing for useful information. It's not my proudest moment.

"That does sound nice." Donya lets out a deep breath. "There's this older woman, who I admire for her accomplishments."

In other words, the queen. I murmur encouragingly.

"We don't agree on everything, but I've always believed her to be a good person." Donya flinches. "Until now."

I knew Queen Bianna would show her true colors to Donya someday. Sincerely, I say, "I'm sorry. What happened?"

"Her husband, he . . . threatened a maid. Said she'd lose her job if she didn't . . . uh. Then he grabbed her, and she kicked him where, uh . . ."

"In the weak spot a kind and loving God created for the sake of women in need of a quick escape?"

"Yes." Donya manages a weak laugh. Her eyes well up again.

Uctor has always been a pervert, making inappropriate comments and lingering openly with his eyes. It seems he's finally crossed the line (or finally been caught). Normally I have ways of dealing with such men, but he's the king. *Dammit.* I'll have to drug his tea to make him impotent. I wish I could use fatal poison instead but that would violate my life-oaths.

Donya continues, "I thought she would help me. I thought she was the only one with the power to help me."

"She let you down."

"The first words out of her mouth were to call the maid vile names."

"Fucker." I'm so angry I forget my accent. Another person I might pity since it's hard to believe terrible things about loved ones, but Bianna doesn't love anyone as much as her wigs.

"The maid went missing today." Donya looks at her shaking hands. "I came here to pray for guidance. Last time we talked, the girl was raging about reporting this to Head Cardinal Jiang. I tried to tell her Jiang is as corrupt as they come. What if she went to him anyway?"

This is bad. The queen would never let Cardinal Jiang obtain a valuable piece of blackmail material on the royal family. It's too easy for commoners to disappear . . . like Calum. "Perhaps you should keep your head down, seeing how one person involved has vanished already."

"Too late." Donya rubs her forehead. "I know a scribe in Jiang's household who attends my rallies. This afternoon, she glimpsed someone short being dragged into Jiang's carriage."

Hold it. Based on the timing, I'm pretty damn sure that was actually my shrimp of a brother. My voice shakes as I ask, "Did Cardinal Jiang leave with him? I mean her."

Proving my hunch right, Donya says, "Yes, and he came back hours later, carriage wheels muddy and without his prisoner. My comrade fears the worst." Donya grips her arms. "I shouldn't be telling you this."

Dear, overly honest Donya really shouldn't, but I'm glad she did. This conversation has already paid off for me. I have no idea if Jiang has Donya's maid, but now I know Jiang took my brother somewhere outside the city. "I promise to keep this to myself. I only sought to ease your mind."

Donya fidgets. "I have to do something."

"Did you consider going to the Holy Maiden for help?" *Crap, that sounds suspicious.* I hasten to add, "I'm a huge admirer of both of you."

"She's not who you think she is." Donya's pug nose wrinkles. "Ysabel is a power-hungry fraud."

Sure, but I also have great hair. Look at these lovely natural curls. "She fought for laws criminalizing domestic violence and allowing common women to own property."

Donya's lip twists. "She's only interested in advancing her own ambitions. The first time I met her, I was giving a speech about how my deceased father supported my education and taught me to swordfight. Afterward, she told me he must have wanted a boy, and if my mother lived long enough to give him a son, he never would have even glanced at me." Her voice shakes on the last word.

Moon Devil fuck me, because I deserve it. I don't remember telling Donya that, but I know exactly why I would have if I'd been high or hungover. Because Donya's father loved her, and mine sold me into slavery.

I clear my throat. "Ysabel . . . has her virtues, but she's also a shameless liar."

Donya half laughs.

Encouraged, I say, "Remember the time she told the king that babies are created by true love, and half the city was laughing about it?"

"I hate it when she does that." Donya clenches a fist. "She's encouraging the men who think us all stupid. Dressing up pretty and talking in a breathy voice and so proud of her project covering the city in flowers. It's all the more maddening because she's capable of so much more."

"I—*she* accomplishes more by acting weak."

"She causes more harm than good. She embodies the idea that a woman's only worth is her virginity. It disgusts me that she fakes being chosen by the Sun God."

Guilty as charged there. It makes me unbearably sad that people who hate the corruption of the church like I do also hate me for being part of it. "Your concerns are valid, but maybe she can create change from the inside."

Donya raises an eyebrow. "She plans to decrease corruption by lying?"

With no defense there, I go on the offense. "Don't you see the problem in you criticizing Ysabel for liking frills and flowers? Look at you." I wave a hand over her dress imitating trousers. "You preach that women can be as good as men . . . as long as they dress, talk, and speak exactly like men."

"I like my clothes!"

"Maybe Ysabel likes dresses. Does that make her worth less?"

"I didn't mean it like that," Donya says slowly. "But I can see why you'd take it that way. It's easier for me to gain respect by boasting and swaggering like a man . . . and that's not very fair, is it?" She smiles at me. "Thank you. You've given me a lot to think about."

"You've given me a lot to think about too. There probably isn't one right answer to questions like these. All of us women are trying together to find our answers in a world just starting to change for us."

"Tell that to Ysabel." Donya makes a face. "She keeps sending her henchwoman to intimidate me."

Goddammit, Alzira. "Somehow I think you won't have that problem again." My dear overprotective Alzira has the makings of a fanatic. It's lucky she fell into the hands of someone responsible like me. I'll have a talk with her later.

"I feel a lot better now." Donya rises to her feet. "My faith in the sisterhood of women has been restored. Thank you."

"It was my pleasure." I feel the same way. There's a bit of warmth in my icy heart.

"I still hate that fake witch Ysabel."

"I still like both of you."

We exchange grins. Donya leaves me alone with my thoughts.

I hate the "holy" part of my fake image even more than the "maiden." I truly believe in God, a kind and loving God who cares about everyone, not just those who can afford a cardinal's blessing. Sometimes I fear I'm a disappointment to Him. My faith helped me through the darkest times of my life, when I was the property of a crime lord. After I was beaten over and over again, I felt something touch deep inside me and comfort me. I knew my own tale might not end happily. But through God, I could believe in the ultimate triumph of goodness in the world.

To me, my faith is a private thing. Talking about God in public feels like standing naked before a crowd of strangers. That makes me a shitty excuse for a Holy Maiden. Preaching is in the job description. Some people are called to that and find strength in sharing their faith. I'm not one of them.

I don't want to be a Holy Maiden.

But I never had a choice. At age twelve, Jiang told me I was the Bride of the Sun God, and no man could touch me. I had my reasons to avoid men at the time. As a twenty-five-year-old, it's no longer what I want. Clandestine meetings are no longer enough for me. I want to get married. I want a life shared. I want children. I've started to feel the dim ache of desire when I see babies or imagine being pregnant. My dreams are haunted with images of the happy life I want, barely out of reach.

Aloud, into the silent church, I say, "God, I want a divorce. It's not You, it's me. I hope we can stay friends. I'd miss our little chats."

The weight of the world lifts off my shoulders. I have a feeling of peace, of contentment, of approval. I don't know, maybe I imagined the last one. I'd hate to be someone like Cardinal Farruco, who only hears God tell him what he wants to hear. All I know is that if I've ever felt God inside me, I felt it then. It was a very warm, kind feeling.

I'm not sure what to do with this revelation, given my death is mere months away. But somehow, I know something is about to change for the better.

Someone taps me on the shoulder.

CHAPTER FIVE

I jump in the air. Screaming happens. A completely understandable reaction to a strange man sneaking up behind me. I don't recognize Kaine until I see the clothes I lent him. He uses a purple carpet tassel to wipe mud off his boot.

Gesturing at my fake boils and wig, I ask, "How could you possibly recognize me?"

Kaine tilts his head sideways. "I don't know. I just thought there was a kind of Ysabel-like feel to you. And hey! It is you!"

What keen instincts. I click my tongue. "If you don't stop damaging that carpet, you might set off a relic alarm."

"Sorry." Kaine picks up the carpet and wrings out the mud into a gem-encrusted cup attached to the end of the pew.

"Stop!" I hiss. "That's a Holy Chalice!"

He cleans the cup out with his sleeve. "A what?"

"You're supposed to dip your fingers in it in order to purify yourself."

"There's nothing in there."

"I know. The Council of Cardinals blesses all the cups."

"People pay your priests to fill up these cups with nothing?"

"Enough to fund our annual Sun's Day party."

"So it's a Useless Rich Person Spittoon." Kaine laughs at my glare. "I'll be more careful. Durrian is always getting upset when I break fancy stuff. Whoops!" The cup snaps off. He tries to push it back into the indentation.

I've never met this Durrian, but I have a lot of sympathy for him. "Were you followed?"

"I wasn't." Kaine's face turns serious. "I turned invisible and snuck up the hill."

I frown. "If the commotion outside wasn't you, then—"

Alzira thrusts the double doors open, disheveled and panting. Sweat has caused the paste to partly fall off her face, making her look even more frightful. "A mob was trying to lynch two Conollian pilgrims, a husband and a wife. I rescued them and got them on a carriage out of town." Her eyes light up as she spots Kaine. She runs over, grabs him by the arm, and yanks him in front of me. "And I found Kaine for you, princess!"

"That you did. You're the best." I stand on my tiptoes to pat her on the head.

Alzira says, "I ordered another carriage to wait outside for us. The driver ran off, though." She fingers her scimitar in a way that means I'm going to have to track down someone and make apologies.

Before leaving the church, I help Alzira mop the paste off her face, and she does the same for me. Otherwise everyone back home won't recognize us.

At the bottom of the hill, there's an overturned signpost and a bit of blood on the ground. I frown. Corrupt priests used to rile up mobs to murder supposed heretics, then seize the victims' property. The heresy laws were overturned in a prior World Games. Disgustingly, it still happens. How strange for a priest to stir up trouble for poor pilgrims instead of wealthy political rivals. Maybe it's tensions over the refugee camp.

Kaine helps me into the waiting carriage while Alzira takes over as coachman. The purple sunset casts shadows over the velvet cushions. I turn to Kaine. "How long do we have to get you out of the city?"

"If Durrian orders a hard march?" Kaine shrugs. "My army could arrive as soon as tomorrow."

Exhaling, I close my eyes. If I had a choice, I wouldn't sneak anyone out of the city so soon after an attack on King Uctor. My tone hardens. "We'll leave early tomorrow morning."

"I wish I could stay longer." Kaine's eyes drift to a place below my chin, jerking away fast enough that I know he didn't do it on purpose. He stutters, "This is a beautiful city. Back home, we don't have such pretty decorations." He points at the flowers lining the road.

Aw, he noticed my petunias. Be still, my heart. "I borrowed the idea from elven cities. Many of the people who come here from the countryside looking for work appreciate a touch of green."

"I've always wanted to visit the Elven Empire. I'm due for my pilgrimage to the Great Tree, but it's hard to obtain entry to foreign countries when you're a dark lord."

"You're a Dharist?" It surprises me that a Conollian human worships the predominantly elven religion, which believes in nature spirits and reincarnation.

"My older brother, who raised me, is a half-elf. Different father." Kaine's face scrunches up in pain. As I recall, his brother was abducted by slavers. I feel for him. I understand how binding family ties can be, even after years apart.

"I'm sorry about your brother. The Elven Empire sponsors an organization devoted to reuniting freed slaves with their families, and I sponsor the branch in my city. When you return for the Games, I'll help you . . ." My voice trails off. This is, of course, assuming that I haven't betrayed Kaine to Cardinal Jiang by then. I just can't seem to make that plan stick. I swallow. "I have an older brother too." I don't know why I'm telling Kaine this. "We had a fight in the past, but when I needed help, he got into trouble trying to save me. Now I blame myself." Am I asking for Kaine's forgiveness? What a coward I am.

Kaine's eyes fill with warmth. He reaches out a hand, stopping just short of touching me. Heat radiates off his long fingers. Those dangerous hands are capable of stealing my life or my gift. Yet that's not the only reason I'm scared to touch him. My heart pounds. He says, "I know how you feel about family. My brother, Alesh, shielded me from the dangers of the brothel where we were born. When I was six, I followed a 'nice' customer into his room. He ripped off my clothes, then punted me into a wall in disappointment. He, uh, had expected different bits under my pants. It was a lucky save."

I shudder. "Kaine, I'm so sorry."

"Alesh got us out of there quickly. I'd never seen him so mad. He had a deal that he would take any customers as long as they left me alone. He tried to keep it secret, but looking back as an adult, there were signs. Alesh disguised his ears at his new docks job because slaves with elven blood are valuable rarities. The slavers finally caught him when I turned fifteen."

So young. Ineffectually, I repeat, "I'm sorry."

"I kept making mistakes after that. First, I went after the wrong gang trying to rescue him. I got myself captured too. My magic manifested shortly after. Then I stupidly slaughtered my way through every slaver in the city, when I really ought to have left someone alive so I could interrogate them for information. And I should have retrieved the client list from the brothel before burning it down. It made hunting down every single former customer so much harder."

"Uhhh . . . let me once again try to persuade you that murder and burning shit down should not be your default solution to all your problems."

"The brothel dealt in raping children."

I try really hard to dig up any moral qualms and fail. "Welp, some buildings need to be razed to the ground."

"That's how I got started on this whole dark lord business." Kaine leans back against the cushions and sighs. "All I wanted was to hunt down the war band that took Alesh. I stormed a few of their cities single-handedly, then the next thing I knew, I was in charge. Everyone expected me to feed and shelter and rule them. I found a bunch of people to handle the tough bits for me, which somehow turned us into a faction. Eventually all the warlords banded together to come after me. When I defeated them, I ended up with even more territory. It's been exhausting."

"You're doing a good thing for Conollia. If you succeed under their flag at the World Games, you could win completely new lives for your people. It will be difficult, but I envy you the chance to rebuild a country from the bottom up. I have to work around the people in power. The cardinals put me in charge of the budget because no one else wanted to do it, so I've tripled the amount spent on church cleaning so I could also clean up the streets and local river. Nature is part of the Sun God's kingdom, after all. I created a fund for people with injuries rendering them unable to work. If I had access to the entire national budget, I'd create a minimum income for everyone in the country. I think that would be a fascinating experiment for you to try."

Kaine shrugs. "Whatever I win in the Games will be my loot. Why should I share it?"

I should have expected that reaction, but I'm still somehow disappointed. I suspect he'll respond better to practical rather than moral arguments. "Because the people in your country need help to get back on their feet before they can start producing wealth for your nation. You'll make more in the long run off taxes from a prosperous country. Speaking of which, you're going to need infrastructure to restart trade. Build some roads and name them after yourself, and you'll win popularity with your subjects. That means fewer assassins and revolts. We both grew up poor. You've seen with your own eyes that most crime isn't caused by evil, it's caused by poverty. If people have food and shelter and good lives, then not so many kids like us will end up sold."

As I warm to my subject, a small smile forms on Kaine's face. "I need people with experience running a country. Would you prepare a couple different plans for how you'd rebuild Conollia depending on where we place in the Games? If your advice proves useful, I'll give you a favorable trade deal."

"I'd be delighted." I grin. Finally, a chance to get paid for my work! And maybe even appreciation and credit! Wait, I don't want credit for helping Conollia because that will get me in trouble with the Council of Cardinals. Dammit, I'll have to content myself with the warm fuzzy glow of helping others. "Spread the gold around and hire some bards to sing about it, and you could change your title from Dark Lord Kaine to King Kaine the Kind."

Kaine looks at me with opaque eyes. "My brother was a kind person, and he was turned in to the slave catchers by one of the street children he slipped food to. You're a kind person, and you're dying for it. I admire kind people, but I don't want to be one."

I don't know what to say to that. I'm not kind at all. Otherwise I never would have considered for one moment turning Kaine over to Jiang. Our conversation has reminded me how many other people's lives rely on Kaine. I . . . I can't do this. He's not just another dark lord; he's someone who wants to save his brother, like me. I can't betray this man. Not when I know full well he'd never betray me.

I open my mouth, but nothing comes out. Kaine watches me patiently. I'm sure he'll understand if I tell him the truth. I can trust him, right? Except that's what I thought about Dark Lord Yarthor. All my doubts come rushing back. Speaking a single word feels like swallowing a nail. "My brother . . ." My tongue catches. I've known Kaine for less than a day. Can I truly trust my instincts? Can I risk not only my own life, but also Calum's? "I'm worried about my own brother. He used to spy on Jiang, but he ran away, and now Jiang wants him dead." If there's a competition for cowardice, I've won the championship. Everything feels like too much. I burst into tears.

Kaine's hand hovers, not quite touching my back. "Can I give you a hug? Only if you want to."

I give a little nod and lean into Kaine's arms. He's nice and warm. The rattling of the carriage jerks us. Kaine pulls me onto the bench alongside him and strokes my hair as I inhale deep gulps of air. Slowly, my sobs subside.

He murmurs, "I think I met your brother, when I was fighting Jiang's Gifted Knights."

What? Then why is he not suspicious of me? I look up and ask the only question I dare to. "Calum has a gift?"

"He's got a better disguise ability than mine. I wanted to steal it." Kaine rubs the back of his neck. "With his real face, you two could be twins."

I have trouble recognizing my own portraits, so this is news to me. "He fought you?"

"More like he ran away from me." Kaine chuckles. "Once I caught him, he begged me to spare his life. He said he only joined Jiang for his little sister's sake, and that he'd been trying to desert in the confusion so he could send her information that would save her life. So I let him go."

"Thank you." I poke his chest. "Not a kind person, my ass."

"I save it for people I care about." His eyes lock with mine, and there's a bit too much meaning in them. I swallow.

The carriage lurches to a stop. I dry my eyes. "Give me a moment. I don't want Alzira to see I've been crying, or she'll"—*leap into the carriage and try to behead you*—"worry."

Offering me his arm, Kaine escorts me up the cobblestone path leading to my humble home. I snagged a former inn cheap after my new domestic crime unit arrested the owner for murdering his wife. Who says good deeds don't pay? My building is surrounded by a massive stone wall, with spikes on top to prevent climbers. Compared to the other elegant inns in the area, my home resembles a stumpy armored tortoise squatting among swans. No matter how much it pains me, I must favor defense over beauty.

After I unlock the front gate, we walk along the path lined with flowering trees and lanterns. The door is a stone archway with a wooden roof squatting over it and two towers on either side. Protruding windows resemble eyes.

One of my Dragon Maidens always stands guard. Today Nakimé and Ua'la'sur are arguing, a familiar sound.

"It's half an hour before my turn on watch. You woke me early on purpose," Ua'la'sur growls.

Nakimé sniffs. "Last time it took me an hour to get you out of bed."

"That's because you were breathing in my face, you low-class criminal. The depths-dwelling stench knocked me unconscious."

"Has royal inbreeding made you too lazy to get out of bed? Too bad you no longer live off the sweat and blood of peasants."

Ua'la'sur tuts her tongue. "As if a thief like you ever paid any taxes."

I push the door open. "Ladies, break it up. We have company." Nakimé has her hand on her whip. Shadows dance around Ua'la'sur's body, obscuring her face. They're just playing around. Probably. They haven't killed each other yet.

Nakimé's up-turned, freckled nose twitches. "My, who's the man bold enough to lock arms with our beloved leader?" The former thief is red-haired, fair, and slender as a boy. Nearly every inch of her visible skin is covered in plant tattoos, a garden of roses, belladonna, oleander, pitcher plants, lily of the valley, and corpse flowers. She winks at me, blue-gray eyes sparkling with mischief.

"He's a cutie, too," Ua'la'sur purrs. Why do they only get along when they're ganging up on me?

Ua'la'sur's shadows retreat to reveal a heart-shaped face. She's a beauty, from her high arched brows to the single mole over her lip. Most dwarves tend toward stockiness, but she has a lithe grace like a snake. Thick black hair escapes in all directions from her waist-length braid. Ua'la'sur is an exile. The previous dwarven ambassador made it quite clear she would never be welcomed back, once he recovered from fainting at the sight of her.

Alzira fixes them both with a death glare. "You two 'guards' didn't even notice us coming in. Disgraceful."

While the troublemaking duo cower under my bodyguard's lecture, I escape down the hallway. Things will get much more peaceful around here once those two decide if they want to murder each other or make out. The way Ua'la'sur looks at Nakimé would get her burned at the stake by two sects. Another upholds romance between women as the purest manifestation of love without lust, which goes to show how much Santos's sect knows about women. The Holy City is ruled jointly by ten very different Sun God sects gathered from different parts of the world, each represented by a cardinal. Due to lack of agreement, we have no laws interfering with romantic relationships, only degrees of social acceptance varying drastically from person to person. The dwarves have no prohibitions, so that's not what's stopping Ua'la'sur. I've a harder time reading Nakimé's feelings, but if she feels the same way, I'm rooting them on.

Climbing the stairs, I ask, "Kaine, how do you feel about sharing a room?" It would be ideal to put him with one of my Gifted Knights for protection.

"No. I need my own room." His tone shifts abruptly to harshness. Lines harden on his face.

I raise my eyebrows. Here's the dark lord arrogance I've come *not* to expect from him. Unfortunately, I don't have any guest rooms worthy of someone of his stature. Every gem-encrusted candlestick and golden-framed painting in this hallway is fake. Since I wasn't born noble, I keep up the appearance of affluence before visitors. "Our only open room is the size of a closet and dustier than the queen's wigs."

"A closet would be great," Kaine says, sounding relieved. I recall his odd modesty at the clinic. I wonder why he doesn't like disrobing around other people, since he seems like he'd be proud rather than ashamed of any scars. Does he have an embarrassing tattoo? I bet it's an embarrassing tattoo.

As I open the door to Kaine's new room, my stomach rumbles. "Are you hungry?"

"Starving," he admits with a lopsided grin.

I've missed one meal, but he's probably missed several. "I'll find us dinner."

Not wanting to wake the cook, I head to the kitchen myself. The house is eerily silent except for the ticking of a grandfather clock. I scrounge up pheasant, crab bisque, and steamed vegetables. We keep our leftovers in a silver icebox, an elven relic with the shield of a frost-user melted into the side. While the food heats over a fire relic, I run to the basement to fetch my most expensive bottle of wine. The bedroom might be subpar and the meal leftovers, but this wine is fit for a king. I've been saving it for an important guest who I actually like.

When I arrive, Kaine opens his bedroom door. "Thank you. This looks delicious." He takes the tray from me.

His smile is enough to make a lady blush. "I have an extra surprise." I whip out the wine from where I stashed it in my cleavage, the only available location with my hands full—totally not me putting on a show. "This is an Alexandrina Astara Ashia Aquamarine." I hand him the bottle. "From year '21, no less."

He turns it over in his hands, peering at the picture of halflings trampling grapes. I don't think he can read the label. He blinks. "It's a fancy beer?"

"It's wine." I eye the bottle, longing to snatch it back now I realize how unappreciated it's going to be. "Would you mind if I joined you?" By the Sun God, at least one of us is going to properly enjoy that Aquamarine.

"I'd be delighted." Kaine waves me in. We squeeze in side by side on the lumpy mattress. Only a small gas lamp lights the cracked walls.

The poor dark lord tears into his meal like a starving lion. I open the bottle, pour a glass, and take my first, very small taste. It's the perfect mix of acid and sweet. A sigh escapes my lips.

"That good?" Kaine asks, a bit of broccoli sticking to his facial hair.

Reflexively, I wipe it off. "It's everything I dreamed of. Take small sips and roll it around in your mouth."

Obediently, he pours himself a dollop. Smacking his lips, he swallows. His eyes widen. "Oh, that's unusual. It tastes rich."

"Right?" I beam, glad to see that high quality is recognizable by everyone.

While we both eat, I end up telling him all about the underground auction where I purchased the bottle by outwitting two crime lords and a foreign queen.

"Didn't anyone try to kill you for it as you were leaving?" Kaine asks, wide-eyed.

"They wouldn't be so gauche." I wave a hand. "Queen Nevik of Rashiba sent men later, but that's what I have Alzira for."

Kaine flexes a bicep. "If you let me follow at your heels next auction, I could slay assassins for you."

"Oh my, talk pretty to me some more." I bat my eyes.

I'm tempted to place my hand on top of Kaine's, but I don't. I'd never let our flirtation cross the line when Kaine already has a lover. Or does he? Jiang called his escaped hostage "Kaine's whore" but I have no idea if that was a verbatim description of the lady's profession or a general measure of his contempt for women. Not going to lie—I really want Kaine to be available. I venture a lure. "I'm sure a handsome dark lord already has plenty of attention waiting for him back in his dreaded moving fortress."

"I'd much rather be here with this beautiful woman," Kaine says, his gaze intent on mine.

I can't tell if he's being dense or evasive. He was reluctant to talk about the unknown woman from the beginning. I could press him further, but I'm too nervous. We really shouldn't. I depend on my Holy Maiden reputation for political power, so I have to be careful. I still haven't been completely honest with him. Besides, I'm dying, and everyone knows it. What if he's just being kind to me? What if he's a natural flirt with those big dark brown eyes? I tell myself the odds of Kaine being into my specific inclinations in bed have to be low. A girl can dream, though. And I'll be dreaming of spanking that round ass tonight.

I step back from the metaphorical cliff. "I should go to bed."

"Thank you again, Ysabel." Kaine meets my eyes. "Perhaps I can host you next time when I return for the World Games."

"A chance to visit the infamous fortress on wheels?" I press a hand to my heart. "I'd love to."

That night, I toss and turn in my bed, unable to sleep. Guilt and indecision and fear for my brother have done a number on my nerves. I shouldn't have flirted with Kaine when I haven't yet told him everything, even if I already realized I won't be able to turn him over to Jiang. I'm being foolish. I need Kaine's help to save Calum, so I need to tell him everything.

There's a reason I can't bring myself to completely trust Kaine, despite his kindness and his trust in me. That reason is named Dark Lord Yarthor.

The Conollians have banded together under dark lords over a dozen times despite their long string of defeats. Watching children starve makes parents desperate. When I was a child, it was a merchant named Yarthor who professed to be different from the warlords of the past. Instead of trying to expand his territory, his warband mostly stole food and left civilians unharmed. As his followers gained a reputation as chivalrous thieves, his numbers swelled. The Conclave of Kings declared him a dark lord. The Conollians called him a hero.

After I was forbidden to join a mercy mission of nuns carrying medicinal supplies to Conollia, I stowed away in a wagon. Fourteen years old and full of youthful idealism, I chose to spend my life saving my people over the church's gilded cage.

A few days later, Dark Lord Yarthor was carried into our camp with an arrow in his gut. I dragged him back from death. When Arahasnor's guards came chasing after him, I stood before his tent with my arms outstretched and told them that to touch a Holy Maiden was to die. In one of those little moments upon which the course of history changes, the superstitious men believed me.

The day I lost to heal that fucker Yarthor is the number one day of my life I want back—and I've healed Jiang.

My gift wasn't fully grown, so I could only take Yarthor from mortally wounded to probably-going-to-pull-through. For two days, I tended to his injuries and brought him food and water. He called me an angel. I was flattered when he discussed literature with me as if I was an adult. He compared us to the love ballad of Dark Lord Chingis and Holy Maiden Sarra. That should have been my first warning sign.

His soldiers whisked him away shortly before Jiang's men arrived to take me back. Then the letters and gifts started, delivered by bribed servants. He sent me jewelry and dresses and even a pony. I received airy poetry praising my beauty. Then the poetry became cruder. I knew this wasn't how a grown man talked to a child. But Yarthor was my hero. Surely he'd understand if I told him I was uncomfortable.

He sent me back an effusive apology. All was well, for one letter. Then he told me some things I didn't want to know about his masturbation habits. Once my return letter arrived late, and he sent me a profanity-filled rant. I'd had it. I asked him not to send me any more letters. He sent me a long rebuttal.

I showed the letters to my elderly nanny. She said this man was dangerous and made me promise to never write to him again. Her good advice might have worked—except this particular pedophile had an army.

After I threw out his next five letters, Dark Lord Yarthor made a daring foray into Arahasnor to knock on the gates of the Holy City itself. Cardinal Jiang was away on a diplomatic meeting. The rest of the cowards had me stuffed in a wedding dress and dumped outside the city walls before anyone had time to tell them our forces outnumbered Yarthor's five to one. They told me as long as I was a pure virgin, it was impossible for a man to rape me. My nanny gave me a knife shaped like a pin to stick in my hair.

What hurt the most was that I'd truly thought Yarthor was my friend. I saved the fucker's life. When he hugged me, as if he hadn't just abducted me, it made my skin crawl. The only time he struck me was when I begged him to let me go. Then he was all gentle apologies and promises . . . assuming I didn't act up again.

Yarthor took me to a hastily erected shack where he'd laid out a candlelit dinner and a bed covered in rose petals. I played along with his delusions out of fear. Halfway through a meal that tasted like dirt, he stood up to recite poetry to my breasts, and my mind snapped. I knocked us both into the wall, put my knife to his throat, and demanded he let me go.

A guard flung open the door, knocking Yarthor into my knife and messily slitting his throat. There was blood everywhere. Of course that's when my body decided to have its first panic attack.

Here is where the dark comedy becomes an outright farce: my attack saved my life. The soldiers thought I was possessed and fled in terror.

I walked right out of that camp. No one tried to stop me. Most people did not know I was supposed to be a prisoner. Yarthor's followers weren't bad people. They'd believed in his illusion like I had. All they'd wanted was to survive.

When I returned home, I was treated as a runaway, not a victim. I was hauled before the Council of Cardinals with blood still staining the sleeves of my dress. I'd supported Yarthor's cause in the past, so they refused to believe anything I said. Half the cardinals wanted to strip me of my title and pack me away to a nunnery. Until Cardinal Jiang explained to the council that when I became a full-grown Holy Healer, I could be sacrificed in exchange for eternal life. Dangling immortality before a pack of old men (at least some of whom weren't eager to test how God felt about the stains on their religious vows) was like throwing fresh meat in a kennel of starving dogs. Jiang became their master.

They discussed the Conollian refugees pouring across the border after Dark Lord Yarthor's army had collapsed into chaos. Chin in hand, Jiang pointed out it would be easiest to kill them while they were still disorganized.

He proposed genocide. The church would announce the Conollians were infected with plague. The lie would serve as a justification.

I'll never forget the cold look in his eyes as he said: "People will commit any atrocity if they first convince themselves they're the victims, and the people they're hurting are evil."

They discussed food laced with poison. Soap infected with disease. Guards to round up and kill the rest. My siblings were in the refugee camp. I pulled my still-bloody dagger from my belt, then swore I'd slit my own throat across their golden table unless the refugees were accepted into my sect, giving them the legal right to live in Arahasnor.

Okay, I'd actually lost the dagger back in the blighted lands. And I pissed myself a little. It had been a rough day.

But they couldn't risk me suiciding later and stealing their one chance at immortality, so they took my deal. I swore a life-oath to keep their secret and die at their command. I saved my people and doomed myself. As my one act of rebellion, I've tampered with the records of my healings so no one realizes how close to death I am. It would be hilarious if I die before Cardinal Jiang has the chance to rip out my heart in his ritual. Sometimes I pray for it.

Although I've had ample time to regret my choice over the years, I still don't see any other way. My guilt forced my decision. Yarthor might have been a disgusting pedophile, but at that point in time, he was Conollia's only hope. Late at night, I used to wonder if I should have given in to him. From a strictly utilitarian standpoint, didn't the suffering of all Conollians outweigh one little girl getting raped? How many refugee women would suffer assault in my place? If Yarthor had been alive, he might have saved everyone. I killed him, so it was up to me to protect my people instead. I bargained with Jiang to save everyone because I'd caused this. I'd left my people leaderless and scattered their army right before Jiang's attack. I had to take responsibility.

And I've spent the last decade fulfilling my responsibility. I've schemed so hard, trying to do right by both the Conollians and the Arahasnorians. Only once did I act selfishly and put myself first: when I told Calum the truth. It had been a test to see if he would betray me again. As I'd screamed curses at him, I'd secretly wanted him to tell me that I should run away. I thought maybe he'd take my hand and offer to escape together to make up for the time in the past when he failed to keep his promise. The child inside me had hoped for my big brother to come to my rescue. He'd only stared dumbly, and I'd hated him for it.

Fuck. Fuckity fuck fuck fuck. With my stupid test, I drove Calum to throw his life away. I'd only wanted him to say he would save me so I could nobly decline. Instead the crazy bastard decided that he, an ordinary farm boy, would take on the head cardinal. It was hopeless from the beginning. I've been amply punished for refusing to die in silence like a good girl.

I'm still not certain if Calum betrayed me to our father or if our father tricked him. But frankly, it wouldn't have made much difference in the long run since I couldn't have hidden up a tree forever. Years later, it was our cowardly old dad who sent a teenage Calum to ask me for money. Our younger siblings were starving. Calum had no choice.

Why did it take me so long to see? I never should have blamed Calum for what our father did. He was only twelve. When I was ten, twelve had seemed a great age of wisdom, but now I see he was a child too. I lost years that we might have enjoyed together because I closed myself off.

Now I'm making the same mistake again with Kaine. He doesn't deserve to be held responsible for Yarthor's actions. They're different people. All this time, I've been afraid if I join Kaine's side, no one will ever believe I didn't run off with Yarthor willingly. If he betrays me, everyone will think I deserve it. But why should I care what those people think? At least, I don't *want* to care.

I make a conscious decision to take a leap of faith. Even if I can't fully erase my doubts and fears, I won't be held back by trauma any longer. Tomorrow, I will tell Kaine everything.

With my decision made, I'm finally able to slip off into a pleasant sleep. I dream of pitch-black eyes and a mouth suited to begging.

Alas, before I can get to the good parts, I wake up to the oh-so-dulcet sound of Cardinal Jiang's voice, coming from a book in my closet. "Ysabel, I have an order for you. Stop Dark Lord Kaine's army from invading the city."

CHAPTER SIX

"Five more minutes," I beg, kissing my pillow.

Cardinal Jiang growls, "The dark lord's army is currently approaching the city."

"Urmph. Isa he tha one spinning my bed in circlesh?" My head throbs. I shouldn't have finished off the whole bottle of wine.

Even though he can't hear me with the book closed, Jiang makes that special angry sound of his resembling the love child of a hunting horn and a bear. "If you don't have my book open in five minutes, I'll order my guards to murder the first Conollian beggar they find."

I roll out of bed in a heartbeat, the movement turning my stomach. The sunlight through the curtains hurts my eyes. Dizzy, I fling open my closet door. Two books fall off the shelf, one hitting me in the stomach and one on my bare foot. Oofing, I grope for the book linked to Jiang. On the third try, my sausage fingers get it open.

The first page reveals a moving picture of Cardinal Jiang, dressed in full robes and sitting behind his desk. "Why did you call me?" I gasp out. "There's no way I can stop Dark Lord Kaine's army." Surely he can't know Kaine is in my house. He's not omniscient, whatever the nightmares of my childhood might say. Remembering my brother's status as a hostage, I add, "Please, Head Cardinal. I'm sorry."

Jiang rubs his forehead. "You stupid girl, I need you to send your pet to deal with the army we have on our doorstep."

Oh, right. Humanity's Strongest Monster Alzira—that's his aim. I try to think, which is never easy right after I've woken up. If I stall for time, I can sneak Kaine out of the city to get his damn army off my lawn before Alzira has to kill anyone.

I lock eyes with Jiang's tiny image. "I want proof that my brother is alive and well."

"If he wasn't, I'd deliver his mangled, tortured corpse to your door in a box," Jiang says, ever the ray of sunshine.

Though I'm already planning to stop the invasion, giving in too easily would set a bad precedent. I clench my teeth. "First, swear a life-oath to release Calum after you've sacrificed me. Second, let me see him."

Jiang's eyes narrow. "Very well."

As the Head Cardinal reaches out to touch his book and link me to another place, my page becomes filled by his blurry finger. Then the image swirls into a dingy brick wall. A man with a familiar cheek scar sits on a stone bench with no mattress. Manacles fasten his legs. The only light comes from outside the barred door, casting shadows over Calum's torn uniform. His head hangs down, hair obscuring the bruise on his cheek and fingerprints on his neck. From the lack of windows, I think he's underground. Alas, that's a mostly useless piece of information.

Whoever holds the book clears their throat. The page presses close to the cell bars. Calum spots me and leaps to his feet. The manacles stop him from getting very far. "Calum, how have they been treating you?"

He looks happy and unhappy to see me at the same time. "I'm fine," he says unconvincingly. He has no outward sign of new injuries, but his voice is worryingly hoarse. "Ysabel, don't listen to—"

I raise a finger. "Stop. If you try to talk me out of saving you, Jiang might cut off our conversation. I've got plenty of reasons to ditch your dumb ass already, yet here I am."

That came out meaner than I intended. To my surprise, Calum laughs. It goes on a little too long before he buries his face in his hands. Through his fingers, he says, "Ysabel, I'm so sorry I gave away your hiding place to Dad all those years ago. It wasn't on purpose. He followed me. No matter my excuses, I promised to protect you but I helped them grab you instead. I've been ashamed to face you, especially after taking the money from you knowing you earned it pouring out your lifespan. Brother or not, you don't owe me anything."

Ugh, now I have to apologize too. "I'm sorry I believed Dad." In retrospect, our father never said that Calum willingly betrayed me, just promised him a reward for being a useful tool. "I'm even sorrier

I dragged you into this whole mess. You shouldn't blame yourself for what happened when you were just a kid."

Calum tries to cross his arms, but the chains don't quite reach. "You were just a kid too when you saved our people by selling your own life to the council."

I shrug. "Yeah, well, sometimes I regret doing that." This time both of us laugh a little too long.

In a more serious voice, Calum says, "You didn't drag me into anything. Even if you'd never told me, I still would have come to the city to save you as soon as I understood the price of your gift. Because you're my sister."

My stomach squirms. I'm bad at soppy stuff. He knows it, because he winks and adds, "Besides, it was entertaining watching your fake Holy Maiden act."

This jerk! He hasn't changed a bit since he used to tease me as a kid. I want to chew him out for observing me for years without revealing his identity to me. But I refuse to expose my face-blindness to Jiang. Faux-cheerfully, I say, "I can't believe you successfully infiltrated Jiang's guard. But look where you ended up." *Hint, hint. Give me a clue so I can find you.*

Calum bites his lip. He speaks slowly, as if measuring each word. "I figured out how to play Jiang. I faked an ultra-macho personality, and he ate it up. He's like the kid who reads all day but longs to be a sword master."

"Really? I do the exact same thing with the Council of Cardinals! They're the type who visit prostitutes and idealize virgins." I grin at Calum, instantly recognizing what he is doing. He twisted the word *play* slightly to resemble the Conollian word for *heretic*. These days, most Conollians speak Standard like everyone else, with a few native words mixed in. Our dad had pretentions of being a scholar, so he taught us all Old Conollian. We used it as a code in our childhood.

He also turned the word *sword* into *death*—wait, that's not a location. I think he's passing along his blackmail material from his intercepted letter. Even now, he's still trying to save me. Why is he being stubbornly self-sacrificing when we both know cowardice runs in the family?

The book starts to close. Maybe we shouldn't have been insulting the cardinals. I shout, "Jiang promised me twenty questions!" A brazen lie, but Jiang must not be paying close attention on his end, because his guard leaves the book open.

"How did Jiang catch you?" I'm both stalling for time and genuinely curious. According to Kaine's story, Calum should have gotten away cleanly in the confusion of their battle.

Calum sighs and looks down. "I was close. So close, dammit. A palace maid came to Jiang for help after the king tried to rape her. Jiang encouraged her to give a public speech. Afterward, he planned to kill her and frame the royal family to maximize the scandal."

Donya's missing maid! The world is full of coincidences. "That sounds like Jiang," I mutter.

"I was nearly out the door, but I just—I couldn't leave her there. I got her out of the mansion, but Jiang caught me. You know the rest." Calum pauses. He's dropped the Conollian words for map, ritual, four, and months. So this is connected to my impending human sacrifice.

Calum's fingers spasm. "Ysabel, if you die because I stopped to save a stranger, I'm sorry."

"I wouldn't blame you. I'd blame her."

Calum nods. "Well, she *was* dumb enough to trust the Head Cardinal."

"How mean." I arch an eyebrow.

"I never said I liked her, just that I couldn't bring myself to let her die."

"I never said I disagreed." Frozen hell, I completely understand how he feels. I'm always stuck doing good person things while secretly not wanting to.

Calum locks eyes with me. "No matter what happens to me, it's not your fault. Because I'm not just doing this for you anymore. Even if I die, I won't have any regrets."

I listen very carefully. Our unwanted listeners will probably think this is a nobly sacrificial speech, but my brother and I are alike enough that I know better. He's telling me whatever he uncovered is bigger than my death.

Calum continues, "I'm standing up against darkness—"

The book on his end snaps shut, plunging my picture into literal darkness. The last word Calum spoke, *darrvessen*, is the Old Conollian word for *necromancer*. Is that why Jiang cut him off, or is it just a coincidence?

Several pages of the book burn away as an aftereffect of the magic. I've gnawed my lip bloody by the time Jiang reappears on a fresh page. "You've wasted enough time." He doesn't seem angry. Surely he wouldn't speak Old Conollian or recognize an obscure word like *necromancer.*

Maybe Jiang's patience ran out. We took long enough that he's summoned a Seer, recognizable by the eye emblazoned across her robe. She wears earplugs, an old trick for when Seers bind secret life-oaths.

I cross my arms. "Calum sounded thirsty. Bring him a jug of water."

"He won't have one morsel of food or drink until you stop Dark Lord Kaine's army." Jiang's cruelty pierces me like a lance.

Like always, I'm too easily scared by him. Substituting loudness for firmness, I demand, "You'll get nothing from me until you swear not to hurt or starve him."

Jiang touches the Seer's bare hand. "I swear that I will not physically harm Ysabel's brother Calum unless she disobeys one of my orders, acts against me, or attempts to rescue him. After her death, I will release him and never again seek to harm him directly or indirectly." Light dances between his hand and the Seer's, a true life-oath. His gaze rakes me. "Is that all?"

Without me even asking, he closed all the loopholes. This level of cooperativeness makes me wonder what will be the catch. "Don't I need to swear, too?"

Brusquely, Jiang waves the Seer out of his office. "No, you might give yourself a heart attack trying to find a loophole. I have a better idea. If you fail me, I'll torture your brother until even Dark Lord Chingis himself couldn't resurrect the corpse."

That's a hell of a great incentive. My fists clench. "Please, just give me a few days, and I promise that Kaine's army will leave—"

"You have until the end of today." Jiang closes his book, ending our connection.

Strange that he swore so easily. Life-oaths are nothing to play around with. Even accidentally breaking one can kill you.

While I remember, I scribble down Calum's code words: *heretic, deaths, map, ritual, four, months,* and *necromancer.* Is Cardinal Jiang the heretic? Technically yes, since none of the current cardinals obey their own rules. But then what do deaths have to do with anything? I remember Alzira stopping two people from being murdered as heretics yesterday. Calum used *map* as a verb, so I'm guessing he wants me to create a map of all the religiously motivated deaths in the Holy City. If it turns out that Jiang has a connection to the crimes, that wouldn't surprise me one bit. But what's the point? Why did Calum even bother? Whatever Jiang is planning, I can't stop him. I'm going to be sacrificed in four months. I only hope to save my brother before I die.

I set my quill pen back on its stand. My eyes fall on the bundle of letters from my younger siblings: Bora and Benoni. We also had one stillborn and one who didn't survive infancy. I try to write to them as often as I can around my busy schedule, and they've always been faithful about sending me letters every week. I pick up the newest letters, skimming them again. Benoni likes his new teacher and classmates. Ah, now I remember why I took advantage of Donya to fund a new refugee school—my brother was being bullied in his last one. Bora asked me to visit Mom, who's having a rough time after discovering Dad's extramarital affairs. I've been putting off answering that letter. Mom stood back and let Dad sell me into slavery. She didn't divorce him then, yet she's considering it now that he hurt *her*. There's no forgiveness for either of my parents in me.

But for Calum? Calum, who used to be my number one accomplice when we stuck a toad into the neighbor's bed and baked tarts to surprise Mom. Calum, who gets my dark sense of humor, who refused to accept my fated death. Calum is still my weakness. His betrayal all those years ago gave me permanent trust issues because I loved him so much. It's an amazing weight off my shoulders to finally believe, wholeheartedly, that he never abandoned me.

He came to save me, and I'm going to save him in return.

My breath hitches. Crying, I slump down in my chair and muffle the sound with my hands. Part of me wants someone to hear, wants to be comforted, but I also don't want anyone to see me like this. I cry harder.

A hiss comes from the huge glass tank on the other side of my room. I've woken up Evilrina, my pet snake. Her tail slaps the glass.

I run over to soothe the agitated serpent. Flicking her tongue, she rises from her dish of water. As I pet her, I let her wrap around my shoulders and nuzzle my ear. It calms both of us down. Maybe she's only trying to absorb my body warmth, but I like to think she's comforting me.

Evilrina is a gorgeous royal python almost as long as I am tall, her scales dark brown with lovely black and golden dorsal blotches. She's not venomous. Instead, she's timid and adorably affectionate. She flees if anyone but me tries to pet her head. Her tank has an enchanted heating pad, a gas lamp for basking, and fake branches with colorful leaves I crocheted myself. I'm one of those pet owners who spoils my baby rotten.

According to my clock, my Dragon Maidens should be awake. I need to warn everyone about the approaching army. Also, I fear for the refugee camp outside the city walls. I down a glass of water to clear my head, then get dressed.

I grab Alzira and send her with messages to the others. We have preparations to make. A letter from the royal palace waits for me. I don't want to be alone right now, so I read it over breakfast in the kitchen. Chatting with my cook refreshes my spirits. By the time I've finished eating, I've solidified my plan. I summon the relevant parties to our meeting room.

Feiyan raises her hand to greet me as I enter. Known as the Axe from her days as a mercenary, Feiyan is so tall her head brushes my chandelier as she sits down. Her bulk ripples equally with fat and muscle. Rumor has it she might trace her bloodline to the extinct orcs, though she told me she doesn't know anything about her parents. She wears her graying black hair in a spiral braided bun. Her dark eyes are kind, softening the tiny scars dotting her face.

Alzira sits across from us. Feiyan is my captain and Alzira is my vice-captain because Feiyan has the brains and Alzira has the brawn. Typically the most powerful member of a Games Team becomes captain, but Alzira is ill-suited to leadership and would be the first to admit it, so she happily lets Feiyan do the job.

Suzette strides in, escorting Kaine. The curly-haired platinum-blonde woman in her bejeweled blue dress exudes a dizzying scent of flowers. My official quartermaster and unofficial spymaster can roll out of bed every morning looking perfect, which ought to be magic. Even though I know she must have gotten up early when I sent her my orders.

I rap on the table. "We're here to discuss smuggling Dark Lord Kaine out of the city. Everyone, this is His Darkness."

No one looks surprised at this news. I keep nothing from my Dragon Maidens, my most trusted people. Of course, none of the regular staff can know.

"Pleased to meet you." Kaine smiles roguishly. The light glints off his pearly teeth.

Suzette props her chin in her hand. "You're shorter than I thought a dark lord would be."

"Short men are always trying to conquer the world because of our inferiority complexes," Kaine says, deadpan. He's a couple inches shorter than Alzira, though I still only come up to his shoulder. My dad used to tell me I'd have a growth spurt someday, which turned out to be one of his many vile lies.

I clear my throat. "Arahasnor is sending a peace mission to find out why Kaine's army wants to burn us to the ground. King Uctor doesn't know about the poisoning. Cardinal Jiang is pretending not to know. The fastest way to get Kaine back to his people, and to stop a war, is to sneak him out with the envoys."

Suzette pulls out an envelope. "I've prepared a false identity for him as one of your guards."

"Thank you." I grin at her.

Suzette turns to Kaine. "I need to list an ability for you, one useful enough to guarantee the king's diplomatic corps will want you along. What have you got?"

"I can detect danger and bad intentions. I can generally tell if someone means me harm in the short or long term, too," Kaine says. "It's an active ability, not a passive one, so I have to be consciously using it." She writes all of that down.

I choke, suddenly realizing why Kaine trusted me when we first met. He would have been warned in advance if I'd tried to betray him. He'd probably exaggerated his inability to use magic. I'd been right the first time when I wondered if a dark lord would truly be so trusting. In the future, I'd remember not to underestimate him. He didn't detect those times when I fantasized about spanking him, did he?

"Will we be fast enough?" Kaine asks.

"The envoys leave within a few hours. The royal family has a teleportation relic that can take you straight to your army."

"Sounds like a good plan." Kaine inclines his head at me.

"I'm coming with you to the castle, because the king has summoned me and Alzira." I rub my forehead. "There's a good chance he plans to have me order Alzira to kill Kaine. Who, farcically, will be part of the royal diplomatic party."

"I saw a comedic play with this plot," Kaine says.

"I need to at least appear to obey the king and Cardinal Jiang's orders." I clear my throat. "Alzira, if you have to fight, then please hold back both Uctor's and Kaine's people to prevent war from breaking out—but no killing!"

Alzira never looks happy about leaving my side (or not killing people), but she nods.

Suzette asks, "Do we expect Alzira to see combat?"

Everyone in the room is thinking about the worrying price of Alzira's gift, but no one else figured out a way to casually ask without tipping off Kaine. "She may need to hold back the army briefly, but hopefully no more. I'm sending the rest of the Dragon Maidens outside to guard the camp."

Suzette nods, satisfied. I have a backup plan if Alzira needs to use more power, but no one will like it, so I'm keeping it a secret.

I continue, "Kaine, please cast a different disguise on yourself. And if you publicly reveal you're a dark lord again, I'll be sneaking you out of the city by beating your pretty face until it's unrecognizable."

Kaine glows. "You think I'm pretty?"

Suzette interrupts, "Her Holiness needs to get ready for court. Feiyan, please arrange formal clothes for Kaine."

As we leave, Feiyan whispers, "We could body-modify Kaine for a better disguise."

"A bit permanent, don't you think?" I murmur back. "I'm not sure Bei Ren would appreciate us letting a dark lord know her secret either. His disguise should be enough."

For a royal audience, I change into a formal gown with flowing sleeves and a laced bodice. Pure white is traditional (the obsession the old men who run the church have with my sex life is skin-crawling), but I add a dash of color in the pink pleats and laces. I wear the ruby necklace the king gifted me for my birthday, although the stone has been replaced with a fake. I built two homeless shelters with that oversized rock.

Suzette knocks on my door. Even after her promotion from maid to spymaster, I rely on her as the only one who can properly do my hair.

As Suzette winds my curly brown hair into two braids, I explain my brother's situation and his cryptic message. "Could you order your agents to make a map of every heretic death in the city?"

"Of course." Under Suzette's skilled hands, my braids form a looped bun. "One of your brother's words was ritual, yes? Do you think Jiang could be causing murders at strategic locations as part of a necromantic ritual?"

I jolt, stabbing my ear with a hairpin. "Ow! That would make a lot of sense. If it involves a huge number of deaths, it must be a powerful one." I sit still as Suzette finishes my hair. If her suspicions are right, this might have something to do with my own death, since Calum mentioned four months. I don't tell her that part.

"I'll compile a list of deadly rituals and search the city for necromancers. I've heard a rumor there's a necromancer among the Faan Games delegation."

I raise an eyebrow. "The World Games are in about four months. That could explain Calum's message."

She squeezes my shoulder. "We'll save your brother."

The concern in her voice makes me choke up. "What would I do without you?" If Alzira is my right hand, then Suzette is my left. My workload has decreased by more than half since she floated down from heaven into my life.

"Probably starve to death when you forget meals." Suzette's voice lowers. "Let me know if there's anything else I can do to make you feel better. You don't have to go through this alone."

I squeeze her hand in reply. "I promised to create a governance plan for Kaine. Could you pull up the figures on how cleaning the river decreased illness across the city? I need evidence to back up my ideas. Also, can you collect together all the dirt we have on Cardinal Jiang? I told Kaine we'd punish him legally. The Conclave will probably only hand out a slap on the wrist for the assassination attempt. That won't satisfy Kaine."

"Good idea." Suzette's mouth hardens. "If we use Kaine's political power, then we could finally get justice for the Head Cardinal's crimes."

"Exactly." I've never been in a position to openly defy Jiang, but now I can use Kaine to do it for me.

"It will be my pleasure, as soon as we finish getting you ready for court." She grabs the powder jar.

A lot of work goes into my Holy Maiden look. My political influence extends from my perceived virtue, and there are a lot of idiots who equate beauty with goodness. I've been blessed with a shapely nose, ears, and mouth, but my acne has regrettably persisted into my mid-twenties. It's so damn expensive to get brown face powder in a city where most of the locals are pasty.

Sometimes I wonder if it would be easier and politically beneficial to make my skin lighter or my eyes darker so I don't look multiracial. Instead, I draw attention to my lovely hazel eyes with a dash of eye shadow. Let them cast slurs my way—it will only look like envy.

The effect of my dress on Kaine is most satisfying. He perks up like a terrier, taking effort to tear his eyes away. His new disguise is a fair-skinned, pointy-jawed blond man with deep-set blue eyes. Feiyan dressed him up in a red doublet that accentuates his muscles.

I smile. Hopefully my fabulous dress will ease the blow of what I'm about to admit. My nerve falters, but I brace myself when I remember how I wronged Calum by mistrusting him for years. "Kaine, we need to talk."

"Already? What have I done?"

"You've done nothing wrong. *I've* been keeping a secret. This afternoon, when Cardinal Jiang came to my clinic, he brought my brother with him." Everything pours out in a rush: Jiang's threats and Calum's unknown location. As I start to explain why Calum infiltrated Jiang's guard, my chest begins to ache. I cut off. A decade ago, bending my life-oath to tell Calum about my impending human sacrifice nearly killed me. I can't afford to be bedridden for weeks right now. The pain makes me double over.

"Hey. Look at me." Kaine holds out his hand. Shaking, I accept it, clinging to him like a raft in a shipwreck. "I owe you an apology."

I jolt. "*You* owe *me* an apology?"

"Yes. I was still planning to kill Jiang. I figured he'd give me another excuse later to claim self-defense." Kaine scratches the back of his neck. "I would never do that now, of course, not until we've beaten your brother's location out of him."

That surprises a croaking laugh out of me. I really, really like him. "Idiot. I'm the one who's sorry. Don't you realize I was thinking about turning you over to Jiang in exchange for Calum?"

Kaine nods. "That's what I figured. My ability to detect danger started going off after Jiang visited you, so I knew he'd threatened you. But I decided to wait for you to tell me what was wrong."

He knew . . . he knew all along . . . and he kept on trusting me. Or perhaps he was testing me, turning his back on me in order to see if I'd put a knife in it. I can't figure out if he's smarter or dumber than I thought. I laugh again.

His tone sobers. "I'm going to save your brother. I promise." There's a weight behind those words, from a man who does not make promises lightly.

My leap of faith has left me confident and invigorated. "I believe you." And I really do believe him. "We should leave—"

"Wait!" Sigma Songheart calls, rushing out the front door. It's always easy for me to recognize the only halfling in the Holy City. Very few halflings leave their distant homeland. My last Dragon Maiden is plain, muscular, and freckled, with a pale complexion and brown hair cropped short. Unlike dwarves, halflings' ears point slightly upward. The other way to tell the two short species apart: Halflings grow hair on the tops of their feet. A few tufts creep out from Sigma's slippers.

She waves her hands. "The royal family has refused to allow any refugees into the city, supposedly to preserve our supplies if this mess turns into a siege."

"Well, fuck," I say, a reasonable enough reaction.

Sigma's face has lost all color. "Guards are herding the refugees toward the Conollian army to use them as shields."

I dropped my "fuck" too soon, and now have nothing to say. "I won't let that happen. We're going to stop this war. I promise."

The relief in her eyes only makes me feel worse. Unlike Kaine, I'm a filthy liar.

CHAPTER SEVEN

The palace gates are packed with nobles' carriages. News has gotten around, and everyone is helpfully panicking. I direct my driver around the back to the queen's private entrance.

Beaming at the gate guard, I say, "The Sun God whispered in my ear that it had been too long since I'd attended one of Her Majesty's salons."

He looks confused by my nonsense but lets us in. Every noble banging on the main gate is an idiot. Anyone worth playing political games with knows Queen Bianna is the power behind the throne.

As the guard flings the gold and glass doors of the salon open, I brace myself for the most dangerous part of this den of starving dogs: figuring out who's who.

The queen is easy. In a blue hooped dress and a tall white wig, she sweeps forward to clasp my hands and kiss the air around my cheeks. "Ysabel, I'm so glad you were able to join us." Her wigs keep changing, but she has a distinctive soprano voice. Her Majesty cuts a ram-rod straight figure, her face subtly made-up and perfumed with a rose scent. She wears a perpetually kind smile. I've used fake smiles often enough to recognize them.

I gesture behind me. "In hope of being useful to the Sun God's chosen monarchs, I've brought Humanity's Strongest Monster Alzira and a young guard who can detect danger."

Bianna's eyes light up. "My dear, true friends are the ones who stand by you in times of need. I won't forget this favor."

Fool me twice, shame on me. "In return, the Sun God would require of Your Majesty a favor," I say, forcing my lips to remain in a smile.

"I'm sure 'the Sun God' would." Queen Bianna raises an eyebrow.

"If you would open the Holy City's gates to the frightened refugees outside, it would show mercy befitting your distinguished lineage."

"Your charity cases are Conollians just like the dark lord himself. He wouldn't endanger them by attacking us," Bianna says. "Or, since it seems Dark Lord Kaine was visiting the refugee camp when something upset him, he might satisfy his anger on them."

"Which one is it?" Alzira mutters.

The queen overhears. "Why, whichever Dark Lord Kaine chooses."

Except Kaine isn't leading this army. Who knows how angry his second-in-command might be about his poisoning? No matter who's in charge, it will be hard for them to avoid hurting a bunch of stampeding civilians being driven into them.

I came prepared to compromise. "Think of how it would look to the dignitaries soon to arrive for the World Games if they heard of you using innocent people as shields."

"Innocent? They're necro-servants."

"With *Alzira's aid*, I'm sure this could be settled fast enough that no lives need to be lost." Maintaining my smile at this perfumed monster threatens to split open my face.

Queen Bianna taps her chin. "I'll pull back my troops . . . for now. Please enjoy the party until the delegation is ready to depart." After exchanging a few pleasantries, we part ways.

"The diplomatic party should leave at once," Alzira growls. "These fools would party while the city burns."

"Bianna is evil, not stupid," I whisper. "The royal family's teleportation relic has a limited range, and we're waiting for the army to get close enough."

Kaine's brow furrows in contemplation. "She's got a vaguely malicious vibe but no immediate plans to off you."

I look up. "Huh?"

"According to my danger detection."

I'd forgotten we weren't lying about that. I perk up. "Can you tell me who present hates me, and who's planning to do something about it?"

"I, too, want this valuable information," Alzira mutters, fingering her sword hilt.

"It would be my pleasure to start repaying my debt to you." Kaine beams. "Can I kill them and bring you their heads?"

"No!" I glare at both him and Alzira. "Suzette and I will handle any threats *subtly* and without getting caught breaking the law."

"I'm good at not getting caught," Alzira says.

"I'm not," Kaine admits.

My eyes sweep across the blur of people, hoping to recognize someone by their outfit, but nobles always have new clothes. They're also dreadfully touchy about their precious long names. One wrong guess could be political suicide. My quick scan categorizes everyone by body type, hair color, skin tone, and age, which narrows it down. Then I try to guess by other contextual clues—wedding rings, family crests, who's arm in arm with whom. For example, whoever is kissing someone must be their spouse—except for that one awkward time.

The domed room is decorated to dazzle and show off wealth, from the chubby angels holding potted plants to the huge mirrors. Flames from the candles hiss and crackle, casting light that bounces off the amber-paneled walls and the blue-green mosaics on the floor. Shelves protruding from the walls hold statuettes. Nobles are packed tight between the tables of light refreshments. They fill the room with a steady level of garbled chatter, sweat mingling with the stench of a dozen perfumes. Quite a few nobles like to smoke, casting a faint haze that tickles the back of my throat. A cherub holds a vase pouring out a chocolate fountain. The crystal punch bowl has two rams locking horns painted on the front. Each cup is shaped like a pink lotus flower. The far-right table displays a rainbow of glass bubbles floating in a tube of water, used to tell temperature. Science is in-fashion, and the queen likes displaying the newest creations of the inventors she patronizes. Queen Bianna would be smarter to pay attention to how the Age of Science has led to a rising middle class. But if she and Jiang prefer to act out the passé church-state power struggle, I'll be happy to form alliances with the new-money merchants.

"Ysabel! It's been a long time." A man wearing a generic outfit, with dark brown curls—a popular hairstyle, unfortunately—approaches me. I force my lips upward as I narrow down a list of noblemen roughly his age.

"I want to introduce you to my fiancée, Areline." He gestures at a blonde woman with golden spectacles and a soft face. I don't know the name, but taking my cue from the man, I adopt a friendly attitude as I introduce myself.

Kissing my cheek, she whispers, "I hope we can become good friends. We have a lot in common." *Who the hell does she think she is? Is she hitting on me?* I know all the major players among the nobility. "Areline" isn't on the list.

The man casts anxious eyes at me. "We'll have to catch up later. I swear this isn't an excuse, but we were just leaving. Dinner with my parents." *Aha!* That saucy tilt of his hip and the way he brings his thumb up to his lip when nervous. This is Rachpard, my former lover.

We've barely spoken over the last two years. First, we were avoiding each other while the wound was still fresh. Then he returned to his ancestral estate. I'm glad he's extended a peace flag. I don't have enough true friends to afford to lose one.

My smile genuine this time, I shoo Rachpard toward the door. "Go where the Sun God calls you. Send a card to my humble home." More quietly, I add, "It would be good to catch up."

"It would be." His smile is relieved. "I'll be here until after the World Games."

"Rachpard, we should leave or we'll be late," Areline calls. *"Now."*

He jerks to attention. There's a familiar glaze of desire in his eyes. *Well, well. So this is what Areline and I have in common.* I'm pleased Rachpard found a woman to his tastes. His shame over his desires drove us away from each other. He wanted to be forced more, but he wasn't willing to tell me how. I refused to guess. My games are supposed to be mutually fun, not a weapon for his self-loathing. Since then, he seems to have come to terms with himself. I'm relieved. He was so repressed, I feared he'd make himself miserable marrying some unfortunate girl who'd been taught her body was evil and her duty was to lie on her back and move as little as possible.

"All the happiness in the world to you, Rachpard," I mutter under my breath, making a mental note to have Suzette do an investigation into Areline's background. I have to make sure she's good enough. Once I've had a man suspended from a rack and completely at my mercy, I'll forever be a bit protective of him.

When I turn around, Kaine's picking up pigs in a blanket with his fingers. I hand him a fork.

"Thanks," he says, switching without batting an eye. "Are you actually friendly with that one, or faking it again?"

"We're friends," I say.

"There's someone in this room planning harm to him."

My spine snaps straight. "Who?"

Licking grease off his fingers, Kaine points at a tall pale man with tight blond curls. I've got his name from how he waves his hands as he talks energetically. Viscount Derall, a notorious blackmailer. Rachpard should have said something to me if that one is giving him trouble. The dear is probably too proud. My eyes narrow. "Alzira?"

She materializes at my elbow. "Your Holiness?"

"The Sun God has called me to another room . . . and summoned Viscount Derall to join me."

Her grin is wicked. "As you command, princess."

The queen's salon has a dozen parlors with claw-foot couches for political deals and the occasional seduction. I pick a lovely pink room with lacy curtains and a carpet close enough to the color of blood. A sour smell exudes from the corner where someone drank a bit too much and got sick. Since the carpet will already need to be replaced, it shouldn't matter too much what additional mess I create.

Alzira knows the drill: a dagger subtly placed at the viscount's back while her arm guides him, as if helping a drunken friend. As soon as I close and lock the door, Alzira throws Derall to the floor by his belt. On his hands and knees, he looks up at me and gulps.

"Viscount Derall." I kick him in the face. "I told you what would happen if you ever messed with my people."

Blood trickling from his lip, he says, "I haven't breathed a word about you."

"You've been feeding Jiang information about my movements for years." My words elicit a whimper. I kneel down beside him and grab his hair to force him to look me in the eye. "It's okay. I don't expect you to be more scared of me than the Head Cardinal. What I do expect is your fear of me to outweigh whatever coins Rachpard's broke family can scrape together. Don't pretend you didn't know he was off-limits. You're the one who ratted our romance out to Jiang. I had to sit through an entire council meeting of his backhanded comments."

"You two haven't even spoken in years!" Derall protests.

"Irrelevant. When you touch one of my friends, you disrespect me. Isn't that right, Alzira?"

"Please allow me to kill him for you, Your Holiness." Alzira holds Derall steady as he tries to bolt.

I pretend to consider. "I don't think we need to go that far. Worm, what dirt do you have on Rachpard?"

Derall growls into the carpet. "He likes to take it up the ass like a woman, by women, even, of all the depravities—"

"Is that all?" I roll my eyes. Imagine if this lout ever finds out about the really kinky stuff. Hardly worth my time, but Rachpard would be upset if it became public gossip—enough to do something stupid like paying off this weasel. "Who told you such tales?"

After he surrenders the name of a voyeuristic maid, I unlock the door to allow Derall to scramble away, telling him, "There won't be a third warning."

When I emerge, Kaine stands by the door, eavesdropping so shamelessly that nobles are giving him dirty looks. It's considered tasteless to get caught.

I take his arm. "I've more nobles to investigate, if you're willing."

"If? This is fun." He laughs. "Kind of like a battlefield but with catering." He scandalizes a butler by snatching an entire tray of pastries out of the man's hands.

Although I should scold him, I can't bring myself to spoil his fun. I like watching him eat. He grins with each bite, then does a little happy jiggle as he finishes a pastry. It's cute.

As I escort Kaine around the room to meet people, I'm in my element. This is what I love doing. Once we're done, I find a free parlor and write down Kaine's who's-out-to-get-who encyclopedia while I remember it. Every parlor looks about the same with the same couch, armchair, and bookshelf. I picked this room because it's the queen's favorite, so this particular bookshelf always has an empty notebook that she uses to write notes for herself. It brings a smile to my face to think how annoyed she'll be when she discovers it stolen. The too-bright room has a pearl wool white carpet and pure white walls—not the cream color people usually paint walls, but actual white. The queen loves that color and resents me for wearing it to every occasion. I wish I could tell her that she can have white, because I'm sick of it. This room is already starting to give me a headache. Even the furniture and the cushions are devoid of color. A portrait of Her Majesty glares down at me as I write. Alzira waits outside the door, but Kaine follows me in.

There's something endearingly doggish about how he sits down across from me and patiently waits for me to finish before speaking.

"Aren't you afraid of being blackmailed by the scrawny fellow yourself? It wouldn't be hard for him to guess that what your ex was into, you're probably into."

And what does Kaine think about my hobbies? There's no disapproval on his face—a good sign. "The first rule of being a holy virgin: every man claims he's bedded you." I lean back in my armchair with a smug grin. "Never deny the accusations. Ignore them, because everyone knows they're fake. The rumors about me tying up men and having my wicked way with them are so positively laughable amongst all the false rumors that no one will ever take them seriously. Even if someone like Derall gathers evidence, it doesn't matter. The church says I can only heal if I'm a virgin, and the church speaks with the infallible voice of God."

"Your church hates to admit it's wrong," Kaine says. "Aren't half of your sects still claiming the sun rotates around the earth?"

I nod. "Six out of ten. In this country, where the cardinals control the schools and libraries, facts die stillborn. As long as my pure image is useful to Jiang, I could fuck a horse on the main street and still be called a Holy 'Maiden.' Though I suspect Cardinal Jiang might have believed the stories back when he had a maid executed for kissing my predecessor, Holy Youth Noretho. Now he's stuck, because it would be rather awkward for him to admit the poor teenage girl wasn't a temptress sent by the Dark Moon Lady herself."

"You sound bitter."

"I tried before to convince people I wasn't a virgin. It didn't work." I look away. "These days . . . the image is useful. Though it is detrimental to my personal life. Men have certain expectations when bedding a Holy Maiden. I'm supposed to say, 'Whoa, I never dreamed it would be so big, I'm sooo scared, whimper, whimper.' Not: 'Nice! Want to see my collection of strap-ons?'"

Kaine strokes his chin. "I feel you. Expectations come with the dark lord business too. Women who approach me want a rough, conquering beast to manhandle them."

What an interesting thing to say. Especially how he says it, looking down and then glancing over at me to see my reaction. I wet my lips and deliberately keep my tone casual. "And that's not what you want?"

"Not my taste." This time he flashes me a sly grin. "Although I have nothing but respect and admiration for people in the business of dominating. Nothing is more powerful or beautiful than a woman who knows how to take control."

A prickling runs down my arms. That smile went straight to somewhere lower. I've got to be certain before I let this go any further. It's exceptionally risky for a lady of my social position to flirt with the wrong man. "Do you like your women in control?"

"Sometimes it can be a relief to let someone else be in charge for once." His voice is soft, but his gaze remains steady.

He actually . . . he wants . . . my inner wolf roars at the moon. I want to pounce on him and rip off his clothes. Those unfulfilled fantasies of his? I can make them all a reality. My eyes jerk around the room, finding curtains to use for bindings and blindfolds. The smell of my own power is tangible. If I order him, I bet he'd get on his knees.

Luckily, I'm not crazy, so I don't make a spectacular fool of myself by mistaking my fantasies for reality. That sort of thing takes careful negotiation, and Kaine will be leaving the city in less than an hour. Good thing, since my libido is trying to override my brain. The two of us would be a political disaster. Besides, I like intellectual men who enjoy discussing literature with me, blush when I tease them, and make me want to protect them, not oblivious barbarians who use books for campfire kindling. That's why the depth of my attraction to Kaine catches me off guard.

I fill my tone with supportiveness for the secret he bravely shared. Just like I'm taking a risk when I approach men, I know he's risking his own reputation exposing such scandalous interests to me. "That's hard. Other men have complained to me about the same expectations."

"I like to cook, but after a few too many people told me it was feminine, I got . . . nervous."

"They were just jealous. Women love a man who can cook." I draw out each word flirtatiously.

"Then I'll have to make something for you. I cook for all my friends these days. It took me a while to figure out that being a man didn't mean I had to spend every waking moment worrying about if my decisions and preferences were manly enough. Once I learned to stop caring what anyone else thought, my life became much happier."

I wish I had that luxury. Being a dark lord sounds fun. In all honesty, I hate my Holy Maiden image and the box it shoves women into. "I'm glad for you." I dare reach out and touch his hand.

He turns his hand to hold mine and squeezes. There's a sparkle in his eyes. I lean in closer for a better look. Belatedly, I realize that might seem like I'm leaning in for a kiss. But why stop when he's not pulling away?

Alzira knocks on the door. "Queen Bianna has called the diplomatic delegation to gather in the hallway."

We yank our hands apart.

"I guess I have to go." Kaine sighs.

I pat him on the shoulder. "I'm counting on you to stop this war. There's a lot at stake here. The fate of your country, the people in my city, and the refugees outside who will be stomped in the chaos." I look into his eyes and lower my voice. "Alzira can be a little, uh, violent, so I'm relying on you to keep the situation from escalating. You're much more experienced with battle."

Kaine's shoulders snap back. "You can count on me."

"Look out for yourself, too. You'll be in danger if anyone finds out your identity." I touch his forearm.

"So will you, for helping me."

"Don't punch out any kings, then." I wink.

He laughs. Then he leans closer. From the certain look in his eye, I know he's about to kiss me. I *want* him to kiss me. I close my eyes—then open them. "Wait, Kaine, don't you have a woman waiting for you? The one you invaded the Holy City, while heavily injured, to rescue?" I have the right to know under these circumstances.

He's so close that his breath tickles my face. "Ysabel, I don't have anyone waiting for me."

"Oh. Then who was she?"

"Ah, about that." Kaine hesitates. He scratches his neck. When an entire army tried to kill him, he didn't look this nervous. He gnaws on his lip. "I promise, I have a good explanation. Just . . . give me a little time to work up my nerve to tell you. I'll return soon to the Holy City for the Games. Then—" His hand stops inches from my hair. "I promise I'll tell you everything."

The excitement returns to my heart. I believe him. Whatever secret he has can't be worse than the time I considered betraying him. I wish I hadn't stopped that kiss. My voice is a little higher than I like as I say, "I'm looking forward to seeing you again." Locking eyes with him, I bring the back of his hand up to my mouth to kiss it. He yields and lets me move his arm despite his superior strength. I love the way he looks at me like I'm the most beautiful woman in the world. The slight tremble in his hand. The intimacy exceeds a kiss on the lips.

"We'll meet again. I promise." Kaine speaks with certainty, and it inspires complete faith in me. This man valued one day of my life so much he wouldn't let me heal him even when he was wounded and trapped in a city that wanted him dead. He'll keep his word to me no matter the cost.

Very reluctantly, I release his hand. He lets go with similar unwillingness.

We catch up with Queen Bianna's group in the hallway. She glares at me for making her wait thirty whole seconds. Her gaze intensifies when she notices her notebook peeking out of my purse.

I tug Alzira down and whisper in her ear, "Slip away from the delegation as soon as you can. I'm counting on you to prevent this situation from turning violent. Kaine, he's hot-tempered. But I know you'll obey my orders perfectly."

"Of course, Your Holiness." She thrusts out her chest. I laugh internally. Both of them are too easy.

"I want a promise from you in return, princess." Alzira's eyes drill into me. "Since I can't guard you, you'll head straight home."

Dammit, Alzira understands me just as well as I understand her. "I could go to the king and pretend I had a holy vision—"

Alzira crosses her arms. "Remember how well that turned out last time?"

The first time I met Alzira, it involved me trying to bluff a gang of bandits. They didn't buy my "God will strike you dead if you touch me" story, so I would have died if not for her. Then she followed me around for a week until I accepted her as my bodyguard. Best defeat I ever suffered.

I didn't trust Alzira at first because I didn't understand why she would offer her service to me, a Holy Maiden with more restrictions and obligations than power. She had better offers from more prestigious members of the church. With her gift, she could have formed her own power base. But I came to understand that like many of my past lovers, Alzira wanted to hand over power to someone else, except in a platonic way. She sought a cause worthy of her great gift. For reasons I will never fully understand, she saw that in me. I can remain standing tall if the whole world turns on me, just as long as I never disappoint *her*.

Although technically Alzira can't make me do anything, in practice she has a really scary glare. I hang my head. "I'll wait for you at home."

Her eyes soften. "Thank you, princess. I'll be able to fight with confidence knowing you'll be safe. I vow to bring you victory."

Really, I almost feel bad about lying.

As the diplomatic party leaves, I cast one last longing look at Kaine's backside. Noticing, he winks at me before striding down the hallway with the confidence of a beast who knows he's stronger than anyone else in the whole damn city. Oh, how I long to have all that power beneath me. It would be one last treat before my date with death. Around Kaine, I want to pretend my hourglass isn't almost up.

I head to the throne room. Time to do what I do best and bluff like crazy.

CHAPTER EIGHT

I lay a hand across my brow as if I'm about to swoon. "The Sun God has granted me a vision."

No one is listening. The throne room has been thrown into disarray as the assembled nobles talk over each other, clustering around the giant mahogany mirror before the throne. It's a relic allowing the viewer to see across distances.

I elbow my way forward, digging my high heels into a few stubborn feet to reach the thrones where Queen Bianna just joined King Uctor. This gives me a clear view of the glass showing the Holy City's guards lined up at the top of the wall. The rumble of many rattling weapons can be heard through the mirror. About half the troops belong to the royal house. The rest fly banners of the ten religious sects. Our numbers look painfully small in comparison to Conollia. By global treaty, we're only allowed to maintain a small force for self-defense. Cannons bristle through the wall slits . . . and a couple canvas-covered gaps. I would have had those walls repaired by next week, Dark Lady be damned, but of course the only existing army in a world that bans war just *had* to show up before I finished. As the mirror view drops to ground level, my heart clenches. Refugees pour around the walls, trying to flee the oncoming army.

The Conollian refugees belong to the Pacifist Order of Saint Nora. I give their faith credit for the lack of panic. I'd expected a few elderly and children to have been stampeded to death by now, but they're moving slowly and nonviolently. They're unwilling to abandon their animals, leading to a mooing, crowing mess. I fear the people below think that they're going to be let into the city. They're in for a shock.

My hands clench. In the distance come the first antlike figures of Kaine's army. They look like tiny specks in the mirror. It makes my head spin to realize there are tens of thousands of soldiers marching in orderly rows. The legendary black castle on wheels looms high above the ranks. Bells jangle on the black harnesses of the cavalry. The siege weapons stand out in the front, the metal gleaming under the sun. Due to the World Games, the Holy City hasn't had to deal with more than mere raiders in centuries. If Kaine's forces do attack, we don't stand a chance.

"The Sun God has granted me a vision!" I shout again. Cramped by the crowd, I squirm forward. "If Your Gracious Majesty will refrain from attacking—"

"Later, Ysabel." King Uctor finally glances at me. "This is important."

"But the Sun God—"

"The Holy Maiden seems hysterical." Uctor looks around. "Someone fetch smelling salts for her."

Humiliated, I clamp my mouth shut. I have no real power here. The cardinals might occasionally let me get my way when it comes to hospitals and hyacinths, but ultimately they pay the guards' wages. I do the work of running the city they own. All my influence comes from wheedling old men, and I'm left with nothing when they choose not to listen. Anger brings me to the point of tears, but I have to hold it back, or they'll have another excuse to dismiss me. I bite my cheek.

Queen Bianna hisses, "They're not slowing. The assassination attempt failed."

I knew her "peace envoy" was up to no good. Kaine stopped them, I assume. Or hope. Same difference.

With a flick of Uctor's fingers, the mirror zooms in on the royal guards below. They've formed a line to stop the refugees' flight. Lowering their pikes, they advance, trying to drive the civilians at the approaching army. I can't see the shocked looks on the faces of the people below.

But I hear the screams.

I barely even feel betrayed. From the beginning, I knew Queen Bianna was probably lying. Fortunately, I made a backup plan.

My Dragon Maidens push their way to the front to stand between the guards and the refugees. I bring my hands together to disguise their shaking. My Dragon Maidens have some of the strongest gifts in the city. Because the other sects don't accept women as fighters, I took my pick of the best. But only I know that Alzira is at a disadvantage because of the price of her gift. If she proves necessary, I will have to intervene.

Feiyan makes their armor so heavy they fall to the ground. Sigma's water magic creates a moat. Nakimé grows a wall of trees between the refugees and the royal guards while Ua'la'sur's illusions send them running away.

Of course, all gifts have consequences. Sigma must be frantically guzzling from her water bottle right now. Nakimé's trees will be impossible to remove and suck up all nutrients in the area, posing a real risk to my flowers. Ua'la'sur's power only works during daytime, and only when the sun is out. Feiyan has probably fallen over unconscious. But no one tries to take advantage to kill her.

The guards and my Dragon Maidens have to avoid harming each other because of their life-oaths. No signatory to the Conclave of Kings can use fatal force against another member. This sword of Damocles prevents wars and enforces the outcome of the World Games. The refugees have no nation, so no life-oaths protect them. But our life-oaths don't stop us from doing our damnedest to protect a group they're trying to use as a human shield. I shoot a look of pure hatred in the direction of Uctor and Bianna.

The dark lord's army moves forward. *Come on, Kaine, come on . . .* I'm not certain if he'll be fast enough. Uctor shifts the mirror's image again to focus on Alzira. He must be wondering what she's doing and why she hasn't fought yet. His principles against women fighting have faded fast in the face of danger to his royal person. Unfortunately, he's about to get his wish, because Alzira can stall no longer.

Alzira faces down the dark lord's entire army. She raises her hands in the universal signal to stop. "Sinners, halt in the name of Her Holiness! This is your last warning!"

Now everyone in the room notices me. My cheeks burn. Alzira should be declaring herself in the name of the Holy City, not me, but try telling her that. She's loyal to the only member of the church she personally considers worthy, and she doesn't care who knows it.

Alzira snaps her fingers. Bits of metal dust spring up around her to form a shield. She points at the army, still a good mile away.

Every single soldier stops.

Of all the numerous metal-users, Alzira is the strongest. She's the first person in history to be able to manipulate even the iron in blood, though she can't hold thousands of people in place for very long. Of course, she could have already strangled them dead if I let her.

Suddenly I have a lot of space on either side of me. It's a good feeling. Unlike my other forms of power, Alzira can't be taken away from me.

"Excellent job, Ysabel," King Uctor says with false boisterousness. I incline my head at the murdering rapist very slightly.

The battlefield is uneasily silent for what feels like eternity but only lasts a few seconds. Then one soldier steps forward, and another.

Not good. For Alzira's power to have run out so fast, it means the conditions of her gift haven't been properly activated.

As her price, Alzira can only use her power to defend the lives of people she cares about. She can't use her power in self-defense. If a gang of regular ruffians cornered Alzira alone, they'd be able to kill her without her being able to access even a tiny bit of her prodigious magic. No one knows that Alzira follows me around as my bodyguard as much for her own protection as mine. As long as we're together, anyone threatening her will also be threatening me.

Alzira's strength is proportionate to the danger to her loved ones and how much she wants to protect them. She's been able to use her ability to defend the other Dragon Maidens, but her friends are avoiding directly confronting the enemy forces, so they must not be giving her enough magic.

Only one thing can give Alzira the power she needs to stop an entire army: a direct threat to my life.

I know what I must do. I edge toward the door.

Queen Bianna looks over the crowd. "Where is the Holy Maiden? She must order her bodyguard to fight!"

Bianna believes that Alzira let the soldiers escape her control deliberately. I can't explain otherwise without revealing our secret. I give up on subtlety and dash for the door, as fast as I can shove through the crowd.

"Stop her!" Bianna shouts. Her eyes narrow. "Anyone who threatens the Holy Maiden would control her bodyguard. I wonder if any soul in this room might be brave enough to save our city."

Moon Devil take me. I should have listened to Alzira and stayed out of the throne room. Ironically, I'm in danger, but it won't help Alzira if she doesn't know about it. Nor can I let myself be used to force her to kill.

I still have a chance. Bianna can't order her guards to take me hostage or her life-oaths will kill her. However, many an assassination has been instigated by a noble wandering into an assassins' guild and casually commenting about how much they hate so-and-so, and whoops, did a purse of gold fall out of a sleeve? The Conclave of Kings has never been able to gather enough votes to close the assassination loophole. The people who raise the issue keep ending up mysteriously dead.

The circle around me gets wider. A man in an olive doublet steps forward. There's doubt in his eyes as he fingers his sword's hilt. "Your Holiness, if you'd just—"

I toss back my hair. "Lay one finger on the Sun God's Blessed Bride, and He will strike you dead. Recall the fate of Dark Lord Yarthor."

Though he reaches for me, the man sweats. He's trying to skirt the edges of breaking his life-oath by taking me unharmed. The perspiration could be nervousness or, better yet, a punitive heart attack. Life-oaths can be tricky. It's hard to gauge exactly how close you can come to breaking one. I've experienced the initial chest pains before.

In the mirror, the line of soldiers halts once more. One of my Dragon Maidens must have self-injured to give Alzira power. But Alzira can't hold on forever without me.

My would-be attacker falls over, clutching his chest. No one else dares grab me. I do not wait to see if he's dead. I run for the door.

Outside, I scream at the first carriage driver that the Sun God demands he take me to the walls. My fake visions are more effective on people who haven't grown weary of them and have less authority than me. He immediately complies. The guards at the wall let me pass for the same reason.

By the time I climb to the top of the city wall, I've attracted a curious crowd of guards trailing after me like a line of ducklings. Hiking up my dress, I peer over the top of the wall. The army looks far bigger and more real in person. Alzira still has them frozen for now. I can barely make her out among the tiny figures below. Vertigo makes my head pound. That's a long way down. If only I can attract Alzira's attention, then she'll know that I'm close enough to be in danger, and she'll be able to fight. (She'll also be furious at me, but that's a problem for future Ysabel.) Finally, I make out the gold thread on her headscarf gleaming in the sun. She's standing near the wall, almost directly below me. I instructed my Dragon Maidens to stay as far from Kaine's army as possible, so as not to risk a stray arrow.

A roar attracts my gaze. The royal army pours out of the East Gate. *Dark Lady, send us to hell.* After I left, Bianna must have given up on peace. It makes a hideous sense from her perspective, and it's completely and utterly screwed my plans. My throat clenches. War is about to start, and the refugees will be crushed in between like grapes pulped into blood wine.

As Alzira turns toward the second army, Kaine's soldiers begin to move again. She can't hold two armies at once.

There is only one way for me to unlock Alzira's full power.

I whisper a prayer under my breath, then climb on top of the battlement. The crowd behind me murmurs, but no one dares touch me. Or perhaps they trust that I know what I'm doing. I hope I know what I'm doing. I tell myself that this is nothing special. I sacrifice my life every single day. But this feels a whole lot worse.

"Alzira!" I scream. Her head jerks up. Over the distance, our eyes lock. Her mouth is moving. I can't hear from this distance, but I know she is ordering me to stop.

I planned a fancy speech during the carriage ride, but it deserts me. "ALZIRA, PROTECT ME!" Before my survival instinct has time to reassert itself, I fling myself over the wall.

I plummet headfirst. The wind rips my elaborate hairstyle to pieces. Air pricks my skin like needles. I have mere seconds to regret all my life choices.

A gentle force grabs me and pushes me upright, using the metal on and inside of my body. I can't move, or I would be sobbing in relief. I float down and land in a bridal carry in Alzira's muscular arms.

Her face contorts with rage. I flinch, for a second imagining that it is directed at me. Alzira growls, "How dare you sinners force Her Holiness to risk her life?" Looking down at me, her face transforms into a saint gazing at an idol. She sets me gently on my feet. Stepping in front of me, she raises her scimitar over her head. Her rage-filled gaze sweeps across both armies. "In the name of Holy Ysabel, face the wrath of Heaven!" The blade glows the color of moonlight as it absorbs and increases her power. A spark blazes from the tip.

This close to the battlefield, the sound of thousands of footsteps nearly overpowers me. The smell of unwashed humans reaches me even from a distance. I feel faint and dizzy. My ears ring. The sound of my own heartbeat echoes the loudest. Alzira's voice is lost in the rumble of the charging armies.

The wrath of Heaven comes at Alzira's call.

The first meteor strikes the ground before the East Gate, roaring into the earth in a spray of dirt and sparks. The air screams like a living creature being tortured. The earth shakes from the impact of a rock the size of a horse, and men fall all around us. The wind carries the smell of burning and a whiff of something bitter and metallic.

The rubble from the impact flies so far that a pebble nearly strikes my feet, before Alzira floats it away. "My apologies for allowing a speck of dirt to approach you, Your Holiness." Her blade gleams, making her whole body seem to glow.

As the dust settles, both armies go silent. Their awe cuts through the battlefield chaos like a blade. The soldiers would have heard legends of Humanity's Strongest Monster, but that's not the same as coming face to face with the power to shatter the sky. Even I feel a small shiver of fear. The entire world seems to pause for one moment.

I take advantage of this brief quiet. "Alzira, use your power to collapse the East Gate and separate the armies." That's our best chance of stopping this. "For the love of the Sun God, bring the next rock down slower. You're not trying to trigger a volcanic eruption."

"Your Holiness's will be done!" Alzira shouts, then raises her sword higher.

The next rock rips loose part of the wall, making me wince. It will cost many coins to repair that. I put my hands over my ears. Everyone around me is screaming, even though Alzira hasn't let a single meteor touch a person. She continues holding the troops in place to stop anyone from running into the range of fire in a panic—or trying to kill us. Fire rains down from the sky, the impacts drowning out the shocked cries. The East Gate is completely destroyed, and the guards are trapped within the city.

Alzira's control over metal is so strong she can drag down asteroids. Most countries have at least one gifted capable of leveling a city, but Alzira could cause global extinction. With half a dozen more such people spread around the world, no nation dares start a war for fear of mutually assured destruction. If a dark lord with an extinction-level power ever starts shit, the entire world sends their strongest Gifted Knights to kill him quickly before he can sink a continent. In this manner, so far, we've survived our own stupidity.

I've daydreamed about using Alzira to conquer the world, except she'd destroy it first. Once, when it rained during a picnic, Alzira casually commented that the sun is full of metal so she might be able to nudge it out of the clouds. I told her quite firmly to never, ever do that. The sun is exactly where the Sun God wants it to be and not an inch closer.

The Conollian army turns around and marches in an orderly retreat. I glance at Alzira. She shakes her head. "I'm not controlling them. They're leaving on their own."

Kaine must have finally regained control. I sag to my knees. Taking deep breaths, I resist the urge to cry. The adrenaline has finally caught up to me.

Alzira leans down and extends her hand. I accept, afraid to meet her eyes. She'll be furious with me.

Instead, Alzira says, "I regret that my weakness caused you to be in danger, Your Holiness."

"Huh?" I look up. "It's not your fault."

"This happened because of the price of my gift." Her mouth becomes a flat line.

Prices tend to be related to the nature of the magic, but there's also some evidence they are affected by the user's personality. It's probably not a coincidence that Alzira is a protector by nature, but her price requires people close to her to be in danger.

I slap Alzira on the back. "You stopped a war and potentially saved the world. You are not allowed to be ashamed of yourself. I forbid it. That's an order."

Very slightly, Alzira smiles and shakes her head. "As you command, Your Holiness."

I look around for the other Dragon Maidens. They're already at work calming the crowd of agitated refugees. Sigma has a bandage on her arm.

"Come on." I nudge Alzira. "I need you to help me get everyone safely home."

Nothing brings back Alzira's spirits faster than being needed. "Silence for Her Holiness!" she bellows, marching forward.

Needless to say, after Alzira's display, she gets silence. I quickly give orders to the Dragon Maidens. We turn to the work of rebuilding the camp.

The refugees live in heavily patched tents. On better days, the dirt path would be lined with street vendors hawking crafts and textiles, often singing along with the buskers. Today, every home and shop alike has thrown open their tents to offer food and shelter to those who were displaced by the army. The Order of Saint Nora may be scorned by some for cowardice, but they're also known for generosity and compassion. I nudge a chicken out of the way with my foot. While the other Dragon Maidens are busy helping put up tents, Alzira trails after me.

My footsteps tread a path I've traveled many times before toward the shop of Urew the Praying Mantis, Conollian smuggler turned leader of the camp.

I'm within eyesight of the blighted lands, where the ground is dried-up and barren. A distant tornado dots the lifeless landscape. The blight kills all plant life and small animals. Corpses of diseased fish then poison every body of water. Worse, it's still spreading.

In 335 A.G. (After Games), the blight struck Conollia. In the two centuries since, close to half the Conollian population has died. Many fled to other lands, where they were often met with violence due to grudges left over from Dark Lord Chingis's brutal invasion. Every year, our royal couple threatens to kick them out if they don't pay an exorbitant tax. Charitable donations raise most of it. The elves have donated a lot and taken in some refugees. The lands across the west sea have some unsettled farmland for those who brave the journey. But many people still live on scraps of semihabitable land outside our city walls.

I absolutely have to secure the refugees a portion of fertile land in the next Games wagering before I kick the bucket. If only Alzira could participate in the World Games, everything would be easy. But Alzira's price makes her gift uniquely ill-suited to the Games, where matches are not fought to the death. Fortunately, no one knows this. I plan to bribe/threaten the king and queen with an agreement to keep Alzira from the World Games as long as they give me concessions to protect the refugees. When Donya wondered why I didn't let Alzira fight, I could not answer her. Unfortunately, this is the best I can do. It's not fair. But the World Games are still better than war.

Urew's shop is a rare one built out of wood and stone. It squats like a loaf of bread with the red tiles on top gleaming under the sun. "Alzira, guard the door."

She salutes. "Yes, Your Holiness."

Inside, the shop is crammed floor to ceiling with pet supplies and exotic animals, from snow foxes howling to parrots chattering. The back wall has tanks of colorful fish stacked on top of each other and separated by who eats who. Bird cages hang overhead, bathed in sun from the skylight. I stop to peer at the tank of reptiles heated by a relic pad. My personal favorite is the copperhead snake curled up around a hunk of tree trunk. Urew has always collected more than he can fit in his shop. The boxes full of fabrics and incense are stacked high, contents spilling out the top. The smell of so many animals close together makes my nose wrinkle. A tapestry of Saint Nora's winged snake hangs on the wall, but I know that's for show. The refugees are divided into two categories: genuine pacifists and those who took vows to Saint Nora because it was the only way a Conollian would be allowed to camp outside the Holy City. Urew is the latter.

Urew has one eye, a harelip, and skin the texture of a dried apple. He hands me a cup of tea as I perch on the part of the couch not chewed on or covered in bird shit. I clench my jaw. "Give me the worst news first."

"Our tank of rainwater cracked in the confusion."

Pretty bad. I take off my ruby necklace and earrings. "These are fake, so please try and sell them to someone who deserves to be tricked." After a group of elders quietly walked into the blighted lands to save food for the rest of the camp, I stopped caring about the legality of Urew's methods.

"It will tide us over." Urew tucks away the jewelry.

Draining my tea, I rise. "Tell me the rest as we walk to the injured."

Urew looks away. "You can't have that much time left, Yzzy."

I shrug. "I'd be lying if I said I'm ever happy to heal, but I'd rather spend my life for our people than King Uctor's stomachaches." Urew has a harder time than most accepting my death as the Sun God's will because he's my uncle. And more of a father to me than my actual father, which is sad given his contributions to my upbringing were showing up every Sun Day with tales of his travels and mailing birthday presents. He also beat up his own brother for selling me as a child. I appreciated that.

I start walking toward the medical tent. He runs to catch up, his face twisted. "Have you heard anything odd lately from Cardinal Jiang?"

I stop and stare. Guilt reddens his face. Uncle Urew has been feeding me information on Jiang for years, but he always refused to reveal his source. "It was you. You gave Calum the fake identification papers to sneak into Jiang's guard! And you must have altered the records to conceal the rest of our family if he got caught."

"How'd you know?" Urew pales as he realizes. "Calum missed our last meeting."

"Jiang took him hostage."

Urew closes his eyes and whispers a prayer.

"Why in the frozen hell did you let him do something so stupid?"

"He wanted to help you. So did I." Urew runs a hand down his face.

"Great job. Now Jiang can kill him along with me." I storm past my uncle.

As I reach the tent with a blue star symbolizing medicine, Uncle Urew grabs my arm. "Yzzy . . ."

Seeing his sadness, I relent. "I'm going to save Calum. I have a plan."

"I meant . . . you don't have to heal anyone. We've got . . . bandages."

He can't even say they have medicine. The camp is too poor. I open the flap and point to the line of bleeding patients. The closest is a girl no older than five, and some cock-rotting bastard cut off her arm. She pants as blood seeps through the tourniquet. A missing arm might be survivable, but not when we lack herbs to soothe infection. I shake off his hand. "She's going to die if I don't save her."

Urew opens his mouth, then closes it. I feel a tiny bit of malicious satisfaction. No one has ever been able to tell me that my life is worth more than the many people I heal.

No one except Kaine. But he isn't here, and I'm left to listen to the sobbing and moaning of the people lying in the healing tent.

Hanging his head, Urew leaves just as Alzira catches up to us. I order, "Help move rubble off the well."

She frowns. "I must stay by your side, Your Holiness."

"I'll be within shouting distance. The refugees already lost their tank of rainwater. They need this. Please?" I give her my most adorable pleading eyes. She can never resist the eyes.

Alzira sighs. "Promise you'll shout if anyone so much as says a rude word to you, Your Holiness."

"I promise. Thank you." I grin triumphantly.

As I turn to the tent, my smile fades away. I steel myself before entering.

The girl with a bloody stump for an arm rocks back and forth. Her parents hover on either side of her, trying to soothe her sobs. They look up at me, and their eyes go wide with hope.

I save ten lives and tell myself to be proud.

As I approach a middle-aged man in a wheelchair, he shakes his head. "I'm here making painkillers, not as a patient." He points at the mortar and pestle on the table.

"Are you certain?" I ask.

He flashes me a grin with one tooth missing. "I've been in this chair all my life. It's an old friend."

"Thank you," I say quietly.

"I'm not doing anything you should thank me for, Your Holiness. I meant what I said about being happy as I am." He turns back to his work.

I disguise myself before I leave the healing tent, using a wig and face paste for fake boils again. Head Cardinal Jiang ordered me not to heal any of the refugees. I doubt that he'll come out here and check—everyone in the Holy City has bigger concerns—but I can't risk it. A guard in Jiang's pocket might spot me sneaking back into the city.

As the sun moves down across the sky, I head toward the well and Alzira. It's hot, and I haven't eaten lunch. Several turns later, I'm hopelessly lost. I've got no sense of direction. Just as I lack the ability to map faces, I also can't read literal maps. The elf who told me about prosopagnosia said I was born with damage to that part of my brain. I could shout for my bodyguard, but I'd rather not resort to that. If Alzira finds out that I wandered off without her, I'll be lucky if she lets me go to the bathroom alone for a week.

Sitting down by the road, I try to catch my breath. The sun causes my fake boils to start melting off my face. I catch one and stick it back on. A passerby in a familiar red hat stops in front of me. "Bora! Did you come to give aid to the refugees too?" Donya is pulling an empty cart that must have been previously full of medical supplies and food. It turns out at least one person in Arahasnor had the courage to come out to the camp. My disguise wasn't a waste of time after all.

I'm not proud of it, but in Donya's smiling face, I see an opportunity. All I know to find my brother is that he's underground. She has a spy in Jiang's household. I fill my voice with tears. I'm so good, my eyes even well up. "My lady, I just don't know what to do."

Donya takes the bait. "Please, let me comfort you as you did for me." She sits down beside me.

"My sister works as a cook for Cardinal Jiang. She overheard something dreadful. He plans to kill a woman and frame King Uctor."

A pained noise escapes Donya's lips. "Do you think it could be the maid who went missing?"

Nope, because my brother already got her out of the city. "I'm sure of it." I rapidly compose my lie. "He said it would be plausible because His Majesty had assaulted the girl."

"Oh no. Oh no." Donya rocks back and forth.

"He also said something about an underground prison. Do you have any idea where that might be?"

Donya bites her lip. "I can ask my scribe friend, but I'm not sure how much she'd be willing to risk."

I cough. "Suppose you greased her palms with a hefty amount of aracoins for that sick mother you mentioned?"

"I've got to try." Donya clenches her fist. "Please tell your sister to keep silent and safe."

"No, we want to help." I raise my chin nobly. "We'll pass along anything we learn to you." Actually, I expect the information will flow in the other direction. "I'm a nurse at Holy Maiden Ysabel's clinic. I'll investigate what she knows." That will give me the excuse to tell Donya anything I know that might be useful to her. At least then I won't be only taking advantage of her.

Donya shakes her head. "I can't risk your lives."

I toss back my fake hair. "I insist. I'm going to investigate this with or without you."

Donya gives me a look reserved for mental patients. "Please, at least work with me. I swear I'll keep you safe." She mutters, " . . . And mostly out of this."

She's worrying about me even though I'm lying to her. This is wrong. I only wanted a little information. I never meant to drag Donya into conflict with a killer like Jiang. But I'm going to do it anyway, to save Calum's life. I feel even guiltier because I know that Jiang's prisoner isn't the maid, who already escaped. It's my brother. I've recruited Donya to save someone who means nothing to her. It won't be the worst thing I've done while playing politics, but still . . .

At the least, I'll make sure Donya gets out of this okay. "If you ever feel you're in danger, go to Holy Ysabel for help. Word among the servants is that the Holy Maiden will help any woman being harassed by a powerful man." That's not a lie; I spread the rumor myself.

Donya raises a majestic eyebrow. "Ysabel? Really? She's a liar."

"I'm serious. She cares about helping people. If she lies, it's for a good reason." I hesitate, then decide I must convince Donya. "How much do you know about Ysabel's life before the church acquired her? She used to be owned by a criminal gang. When she was twelve, one of them tried to rape her. She could only stop him by claiming that if she wasn't a virgin, her healing powers wouldn't work."

"I never heard that story." Donya looks flabbergasted.

"In the church's version, an angel descended down from Heaven and smote the vile criminal for daring to touch the Bride of God's skin. Strip away the bullshit, and you can see what really happened: a terrified little girl lying to save herself." I lower my head to conceal how I'm shaking like a sailboat in a hurricane. Angels, my ass. I was all alone in that muck-smelling barn.

"And after all that, the cardinals still sold her out to Dark Lord Yarthor," Donya whispers.

The cursed name Yarthor brings back my memories even more powerfully. The scent of his jasmine perfume lingers in my mind so vividly that even years later, I have panic attacks around jasmine. I can almost feel the sweaty touch of his hands crawling down my arms. My nails dig into my palms.

Donya continues, "Poor Ysabel, used by such awful people. No wonder she grew up to be a merciless, backstabbing snake incapable of love."

Whoa, that's going a bit too far. Besides, snakes are kind and lovable creatures that make great pets. I cough. "Uh, be that as it may, will you go to her for help?"

"I can't trust Ysabel. Nor can I forgive her. Tell a story about a girl saved by God from rape and the message is that all the other raped girls just weren't good enough."

Unfortunately, I've heard people claim exactly that to my face. "Other people created her fake miracle while she was a mere child."

Donya's rigid posture holds no mercy. "Now that she's an adult, she could tell the truth."

She makes it sound so easy. In the face of Donya's stubbornness, I give up. "Here's where you can reach me with any information." I name a business fronted by one of Suzette's spies.

"If you insist on helping me—" Donya extends her hand. "Then we're accomplices. I'll obtain a pair of linked books so we can remain in contact."

Perfect. Calum, I'm coming for you.

I shake her hand. "One last thing. Can I ask you for directions?"

With Donya's help, I make it back to the well before Alzira notices I've gone missing. Today is looking up.

Just as I finish my evening sandwich, Suzette knocks on my bedroom door. "May I come in?"

"Please do. I have great news for you." I beam at her as she steps inside. "I have a new source on Calum's location."

"What source?"

I hesitate. I'd rather not say anything about Donya. I already feel bad enough about tricking her. If I share my story with more people, it will feel like we're all laughing behind her back. I do want to be Donya's friend, and I'm a bad enough friend as it is. "Uh, let me wait and see if it pans out first."

Suzette purses her lips, then changes the subject. "I made the map your brother told you to create."

"You work fast." I smile at her.

She tries to smile in return, but her face is strained. "It wasn't as hard to find murders as I expected. There have been too many of them. You need to look at this."

Spurred on by those ominous words, I quickly sweep my plate off the desk. Suzette unrolls a map of the Holy City with red dots all over it, each representing a murder of a supposed heretic or atheist.

"There have been this many deaths?" I shake my head. I'd read of one in the newspaper, maybe two, but there must be at least a hundred dots here. Disgusting. Belief in the Sun God isn't something that can or should be forced. I figure people who don't have any faith don't need it the way I do. "Is this over the last couple decades?"

"It's over the last two years," Suzette says, twisting her hands.

Surprise silences me. This all happened after the repeal of the heresy laws. Are there enough crazed fanatics like Farruco who will risk jail time to kill?

How could this have been going on all this time without me noticing? Although it's an inadequate justification, someone must have been bribing guards to keep these reports from me. I'm seething. Ua'la'sur and Nakimé are atheists, and Jiang tried to use it against me before. I fear for every victim who doesn't have someone as powerful as me to protect them. "I want to see people in jail for this."

"Feiyan is already on it. We never have any trouble taking suspects into custody. The real difficulty has been convicting the priests who always claim their calls to violence were 'misinterpreted.'"

"Typical." I groan. Time for some underhanded justice. "You get me names, and I'll see about enforcing our long-ignored celibacy laws. Since these pure-hearted souls hate heresy so much, we'll have *traditional* punishments."

"Good idea, Ysabel. It's just . . ." Suzette waves the map. "I need you to tell me if I'm crazy. These dots, do they have a shape?"

I look hard. "A house with a door and a window?"

Suzette turns the map sideways. "No, look at it this way."

The top line of dots forms a semicircle and the square in the middle looks sort of like a jaw. "A skull?" More like two-thirds of a skull.

Suzette exhales in a gust. "That's exactly what I was seeing. It gets stranger. See these dots? They don't fit the pattern." She stabs three dots above the shape. "I investigated those incidents in particular. Two victims lived in houses located here and here." She points at spots that would fill in the skull pattern. "They fled from a murderous mob at their doorstep and died elsewhere."

"That's probably not a coincidence," I acknowledge. Calum risked his life for this information. Even as Jiang dragged him away, he kept trying to tell me. He wouldn't have gone so far just to point out our resident corrupt church officials have gotten worse than usual. A chill skitters down my spine like a centipede. "Assign permanent guards to points where we predict future murders. Make it look like we're responding to a request from someone plausible—the Science Guild, perhaps—as long as Jiang can't trace it back to me." I hand Suzette back the map.

"Are you sure, Your Holiness?" The formal address, rare when we're alone, shouts her lack of confidence. We both know this will be ridiculously expensive. "What if it's all a coincidence, and we're both seeing shapes in clouds?"

"I'm sure. I'll eat nothing but bread for a month if need be." Or maybe I can seize the property of priests involved in the murders to pay for the protection.

"Why is Cardinal Jiang doing this?" Suzette swallows. "Surely he's after something more than a demented art project."

"Who knows what goes on in his cesspit of a brain?" My life-oath strangles the truth. If only I'd realized sooner that a ritual to give the entire Council of Cardinals immortality probably needs more blood than just mine. Close to a hundred are dead already. Now I have four months to stop the remaining murders.

CHAPTER NINE

On the day I have four months, two weeks, and one day to live, here I sit, wasting a precious hour meeting with the Council of Cardinals.

Today there's only four out of ten idiots to talk sense into. Fortunately for me, the cardinals come from religious sects with very different dress styles. Rakir's turban decorated with golden suns gives him away. Santos has a distinctive pointy hat. He'll vote with me on anything I can spin as charity. He's the nicest of this lot and probably the only sincere believer, cardinal being more a political position than a religious one these days. I'm probably a jerk for finding him dreadfully boring.

The elderly man in a generic robe as white as his skin? He's bald but that barely helps. I've committed to memory the names of five follicle-challenged cardinals, but I haven't a clue which of them is sitting across from me. It's driving me crazy.

The last cardinal, Orwin, always wears extravagant rings and necklaces. My closest ally on the council, he has the morals of an alley cat, but he's smart enough to have invented the printing press and bribed his way up from a church orphan to the council.

My eyelids droop as Cardinal Rakir finishes his insipid joke. " . . . That should fit in there nicely, as the cardinal said to the maid." Around the table, all four cardinals laugh.

"What did you think of my story, Holy Ysabel?" Mockery fills Rakir's voice.

I widen my eyes. "It was dreadfully entertaining, but I fear it went over my head. The Sun God has not blessed me with a wit equal to you gentlemen."

Rakir laughs even harder. I keep a vapid smile on my face.

Cardinal Santos scowls. "Not in front of Holy Maiden Ysabel!"

"Oh, I don't understand a word." I cast pleading eyes at Santos. Because he idealizes the virgin I pretend to be, he's about to get me thrown out.

When I first dug up a dusty document proving that as a Holy Healer, I was entitled to join the council, the cardinals discovered the presence of a woman made it awkward for them to brag about their conquests during worktime. So I pretended to be too virginal to understand sexual innuendo if it mugged me in a dark alley. Now they make a game of who can get the dirtiest implication past me. I'm still being excluded from the wheeling-and-dealing in their drinking sessions, but at least they no longer "forget" to tell me when to show up at the Cardinals' Chamber to cast my vote.

It's a gorgeous room, paid for by our citizens' mandatory twenty percent to "charitable" tithes. Dozens of angels spread across the ceiling etched in silver and gold. A gas lamp burns in a chandelier shaped like a star. Documents spill across the round table made of pure gold. This ill-thought-out luxury has to be replaced once a month because frequent fist-pounding leaves the soft metal dented. The hand-woven silk carpets don't last much longer on account of the drinking parties I'm not invited to, even though I could drink them all under the table. We have no windows for security reasons, making it too hot in here. Statues of nude men crowd the alcoves, fig leaves covering where the last Head Cardinal went around hacking all their penises off. Nice chest muscles, though. Glancing sideways, I memorize those marble asses so I'll have something to spank in my dreams tonight.

Rakir wastes seven more minutes of my too-short life telling jokes with the punchline "women are sluts." I fantasize about beating him. (Not recreationally.)

Cardinal Orwin finally pulls our meeting back to business. "How is construction going for the stadium for the 549th World Games?"

Leaning back in his chair, Rakir stretches his arms. "I can't speak for the king, but the church's portion is complete and under-budget."

In a voice as bright as the sun, I say, "Then I'm sure you have the aracoins to purchase a new rainwater tank for the refugees. Such wonderful news!"

Rakir slams his hands down on the table. Ouch, that sounded like another dent. "Why should we help the necro-servants when their leader threatens our fair city?"

I learned long ago that there's little point in trying to explain to the cardinals that not all Conollians are the same. In fact, the old Conollian empire was made of a conglomerate of very different nations. Even so, I give it one more try. "The refugees greeted Dark Lord Kaine's visit by throwing eggs at him. One of them even helped poor misguided Lector poison the dark lord." As expected, Jiang wriggled out of the assassination by scapegoating Cardinal Lector, who retired to his wine cellar. "Their pacifist principles reject all warlords. We should support the enemy of our enemy."

I don't agree with the general dislike for Kaine among the refugees, but I'll certainly use it to make my point. Assuming it's possible to reason with a group of men who would drink piss if they mistook it for beer. The cardinals come from royal houses around the world . . . usually booted over to the church because of their incompetence.

My eyes well up. "Though my body is that of a fragile female, my heart longs to bring fresh water to the bedraggled faithful of the Sun God." I hold up one finger at Orwin, promising him one of my votes next time.

Orwin nods. "I call for a vote." With Santos and Orwin voting on my side, we win three to two.

"The Sun God will shine on your benevolence." I dab my eyes, gracious in victory.

I'm glad I won, though this will bring more accusations from the royal court that I favor the country of Conollia due to my father's heritage. I don't actually have a deep personal attachment to a country I've never been to. Conollia and the refugees in my sect are two different groups. Still, I feel sorry for the Conollians and think we've been riding a tiger by bullying a country bigger than us. What if one of these days a dark lord rises up and the Conclave of Kings doesn't come running to save us in time? The Conclave is not known for efficiency. They once spent a year deciding that the title of dark lord should be gender-neutral to avoid confusion with the Sun God's adversary the Dark Lady. Meanwhile the female dark lord in question conquered two countries.

I want the best for both Arahasnor and Conollia. Our neighboring nation would be better as our closest ally than an enemy. Their prosperity would bring new trade to us. If Kaine can become a legitimate monarch for Conollia, then he could both save his people and lay the perpetual threat of war to rest.

Over the last week, Kaine's army has been camped a few miles outside our city while he negotiates compensation for Jiang's assassination attempt. I'm hopeful. There's little I've ever been able to do against the Head Cardinal, bound as I am by life-oaths and hostages, but Kaine can become my front man. My heart races with anticipation . . . and maybe an even deeper feeling. If only I'd kissed him before he left. I'd gotten so close I'd felt the heat off his lips. My cheeks start to flush. Ugh, I need to keep my head in the game.

The rest of the meeting proceeds tediously, but at least I steal a budget increase for my sanitation project by convincing the cardinals that women have special, expensive plumbing needs for mysterious reasons they need not know.

Before I can slip out of the room, Orwin hands me a stack of papers. "Here are dates when the dignitaries arrive. Thank you for handling these arrangements, Ysabel."

I bare my teeth into something resembling a smile. "I'm pleased to be of service."

At least he went through the motions of gratitude. The others don't. "Requests for food stall permits. You're much better at handling such matters than me," Rakir says, a half-assed compliment in place of a thank-you. I know he'll take credit for whatever I do later. He'd take credit for giving birth to himself. My mouth hurting from the effort of maintaining my smile, I accept work from every last man.

Since the cardinals consider matters like law enforcement, clean water, and trash disposal beneath them, they shaft everything off on me. Little do they realize how much power they've handed over. I've hired the first-ever women as bureaucrats and let a boatload of heretics out of prison. No one noticed. Amazing what can be accomplished from the bottom up.

I stagger out of the room, balancing the weight of my new work. Alzira waits for me outside the door. I sigh as she takes half the papers from me. "Thank you."

We have to run in order to make my lunch date with Rachpard and Areline. We meet at a new foreign restaurant I've wanted to try for a while. The stir-fry is delicious and the company is excellent. Rachpard insists on paying while drolly mentioning a spying maid who suddenly decided to move to another continent. He invites me to a folk football game in a few weeks. He knows it's my favorite sport. I like to pretend the ball is Jiang's severed head.

Back in my office, I check for a note from Donya. She sent "Bora" two book relics, one so I can talk to her and one connected to our scribe inside Jiang's household. Her colleague accepted a hefty bribe to spy for us.

Captain Feiyan knocks on my door. Sitting across from me, she unfurls the skull-patterned map. "I have an update."

The entire right side of the skull has been filled in. "There have been *more* deaths?"

"No, I've added unsolved murders from the last ten years." Feiyan frowns. "It could be a coincidence how many of them fit the pattern."

She doesn't sound convinced. Neither am I. "This just got even creepier." According to Suzette's research, the skull symbol is used in necromantic rituals of the most violent type. One that requires so many deaths would be unheard of . . . and very powerful.

Feiyan leans forward. "About the patrols you assigned? Cardinal Jiang claims to need extra security for the World Games, so he had them moved to the stadium."

My knuckles go white around the edge of the table. "If I protest, he'll know I'm onto him." And he'll take it out on Calum. I don't think he'd kill my brother, not for the first warning. But I'm not willing to chance it. I grind my teeth, sparking pain in my jaw. I've been doing that too often lately. "Can we move new guards in secret?"

She shakes her head before I finish. "Cardinal Jiang has too many spies."

"What if we hire some people off the streets?" My voice sounds unsure. I don't want to decide between my brother's life and the lives of innocent people.

"Untrained thugs? The Head Cardinal would notice them the first time they tried to stop a murder." Feiyan hesitates, running a finger down the map. "It doesn't have to be your responsibility to save everyone at the expense of yourself. If there's anyone who has the right to question what this city has ever done for them, it's you."

I blink in surprise. If I could sum Feiyan up in a word, it would be reliable. She's been with me since the beginning, when I first took the refugee population into my sect. In the early days, she did all the work because I had no idea how to feed and govern a civilian populace. She accepted pay far below what she'd commanded when she'd led a mercenary troop because she'd wanted to join the World Games. Yet she stayed without recrimination even as that dream stalled. It's not like her to tell me to pick the personal over the responsible.

"Thanks," I say in a small voice. A trap has closed in around me. But I'm a scam artist—I don't play by the rules. I straighten my spine. "Screw that. If we can't provide the guards, I'll find a patsy to do it for me."

Feiyan looks a bit more cheerful. "Do you have someone in mind?"

"Not yet." I bare my teeth. "But I'm about to attend dinner with the wealthiest, most powerful people in the world. If I can't find a sucker there, I don't deserve to be a fake Holy Maiden."

I devote an hour to getting ready for the pre-Games banquet with global ambassadors. My silvery white dress has ruffles crisscrossed with wine-red embroidery. The sleeves and gloves are made of scarlet satin. Fragments of rubies (fake, of course) form the shape of a rose on the bodice. The red diamond and fire opals in the necklace are real, to be sold after the party. King Uctor has been handing out presents to young women lately like a man made insecure by his sudden impotence.

Suzette braids my chestnut hair with silver beads, then wraps it into a bun with a star-sapphire pin. Two artful curls hang on either side.

"It's perfect," she says, clapping her hands. We've been planning my outfit for weeks. I adore frilly dresses.

"Thank you." I kiss her cheek.

"Here's all the 'unofficial news' I have on the foreign ambassadors."

I accept the papers. "Kaine isn't attending?"

Suzette sighs. "Even after you spent so much time getting dressed, no."

"I have no idea what you're implying."

Her eyebrow asks me who I'm fooling. "It's a pity. He's signing an agreement with Arahasnor tonight. He could be in the city by tomorrow, so try not to end up hungover."

Her teasing has a slight edge, or maybe it's just me. Instead of responding, I flip through the pages. The section on the elven ambassador has been circled twice. "Rumor has it that Ambassador Berylseed is a mind reader?"

Suzette twists her hands. "It worried me given, well, your image."

"Not a problem. I met Ambassador Berylseed when he attended the Games six years ago. I trust him completely. Besides, he wouldn't be surprised by anything in my head."

Saying I "know" the elven ambassador is a euphemism. He was my first lover.

When we met at a boring court session, my mind wandered to what it would be like to undress him. Afterward, he approached me, saying, "I couldn't help noticing your interest in me, and I think we have some hobbies in common."

Once I got over my embarrassment, it turned out to be the luckiest chance meeting of my life. He taught me everything I know about the art of domination and submission. Being an elf, he had centuries to explore his submissive side. He'd been unimaginably patient with me, always making sure I was comfortable every step of the way.

At the tender age of nineteen, I was confused and frightened by my desires. Suspecting it stemmed from the men who'd hurt me in the past, I thought it made me a monster too. He taught me that there are men who want what I want to give them, and that dominance isn't supposed to be about violence.

My first lover taught me all about consent and boundaries and safe words, all while showing me an amazing time. (His tongue. The best I've ever had.) I used to think not being able to remember faces made me self-centered or stupid, until he taught me the word "prosopagnosia" and what it meant.

I loved him, though I wasn't ever in love with him. It was more like love for a mentor or a teacher. He kept a clear understanding of the age gap between us and never would have let me fall in love. I owe him more than I can ever repay. Because I met him, I regained my ability to trust and love men. Because of him, I might yet fall in love in the future. Maybe I've started to fall for a certain someone, if only I can live long enough.

I'd like to tell him how much my younger self gained from him. With a smile on my face, I head to my carriage.

Alzira, waiting at the door, looks lovely and dangerous. Her skirt is made of steel. The vines etched into the metal plates sprout knife pouches instead of flowers. The bodice is closer to a knight's armor than a dress. Tassels hang from her spiked gauntlets. A sheer silver shawl over her back partly covers her sheathed sword. In place of a headscarf, she wears a helmet with beautiful wings on either side. Kohl and glitter sharpen her dark, upturned eyes. She looks ready to kill everyone in the palace, which is the point.

"Princess," she says, helping me into the carriage. "It might be for the best Kaine isn't coming. I'd have to murder him for staring at you. Oh well, there will be plenty of other men to offend your honor."

Even Alzira is teasing me about my love life. My dignity is dead.

At the palace gates, we end up behind a long line of guests getting their invitations checked. Dignitaries from around the world are dressed in their native garments: colorful saris, woven brocades with turbans, tang suit jackets, kimonos, gem-encrusted dashiki shirts, and bark cloth dresses. I keep my eyes peeled for the sequined tunics favored by elven men.

Even the distant dwarves made it on time this year, thanks to our new horse-pulled railroad. The dwarven diplomats wear full armor, men and women alike. Feathers, jeweled horns, horsetails, crests, and even a giant golden dragon decorate their helmets.

The Halfling Confederacy sent a cluster of wealthy citizens. I incline my head at Sigma, who's representing her father, their current president. She waves back. Her puffy skirt is made of silk purple flower petals, and she carries a staff with a sapphire on top. She'll be stuck at a distant table since the halflings have never been good enough fighters to place well in the Games. The Halfling Confederacy eventually started loaning out their strongest members to other teams in exchange for political concessions. That's how I ended up with Sigma. I hate to say it, but I don't even need to compete to win more than they could alone. Just threatening people with Alzira has done the trick.

The Elven Empire spans two continents, and their delegation is too large for me to pick out their ambassador. They range across all the usual human skin shades in addition to green for the forest elves and blue for the sea elves.

The old saying goes: Elves for honor, dwarves for loyalty, halflings for kindness, and humans for adaptability. All of these virtues have their flip sides: Elves can be rigid, dwarves keep themselves isolated, halflings have been called cowards, and humans destroy their own civilizations as fast as they build new ones. Of course, individuals don't necessarily match the stereotypes. Who's to say how much is innate versus cultural?

A lovely woman steps out of her carriage wearing a flowing pink dress. Lace roses decorate the bodice and grow all the way to her slippers. Her belt resembles a thorny vine. Her companions wear both dresses and the dress-doublet hybrids that scandalized the court last year. There's a dagger strapped to her side, too sharp to be ceremonial.

Her eyes fall on me. She frowns. "If it isn't the sanctimonious hypocrite."

As soon as I hear her voice, I recognize Donya. "The Sun God smiles upon us all, even the self-righteous loudmouths." I wave. "Love the dress." Would it be arrogant to think the feminine dress she wears this year has something to do with my conversation with her as Bora?

She crosses her arms. "Insult me all you want. I'm secure enough not to care what anyone thinks, and I like it."

I meant the compliment. Donya's one of the handful of people I've never been able to charm. Everything I say rubs her the wrong way.

"I have a bone to pick with you." Donya steps so close our noses nearly touch. "Stop sending your deranged guard dog to spy on me."

Insulting Alzira is about where my patience stops. "I pray that the Sun God will illuminate your misunderstanding. May His radiance shine on this banquet." Fake smile on my lips, I blow past her.

She mutters something under her breath. It sounds like "poppycock" and "goshdarn it." *My dear Donya, I'm disappointed in your language—you need to learn better swears.*

"I'm sorry for getting caught, princess. She's astonishingly observant for someone who fails to grasp your magnificence," Alzira says. "I swear I wasn't rude in the slightest this time. I tried to explain that you'd sent me to protect her."

"Don't feel bad. I'm glad she's being careful, given her potential danger from both Queen Bianna and Cardinal Jiang."

Alzira stands silent for a moment. Then she says, "It's not your fault people don't appreciate you. I've been watching everything you do. *I* admire you."

My cheeks flush. "Alzira, I don't know what I'd do without you. Marry me already." Joking aside, Alzira is basically my platonic life partner. (In the secret places of my heart, if she had the faintest interest in sex, I could have found my straight preferences flexible for her.)

The usual banquet hall couldn't fit this party, so the royal ballroom was transformed using rows of tables covered by yellow cloth. Guards stand in the archways. Dozens of carpets cover the tiled floor, making a beautiful patchwork quilt. Chandeliers caged by glass beads circle the round room. The golden walls are decorated with paintings of famous religious or historical scenes. My table is located next to a floor-to-wall depiction of Dark Lord Chingis's slaying of the previous Elven Emperor. Jiang ordered a battleship set on fire just so the watching artist could paint a realistic picture. I told him not to waste so many aracoins to memorialize the Conclave's greatest defeat, but did he listen to me? Noooooooo.

The king and queen's thrones were dragged in for the occasion and placed before a dinner table on a raised platform. Exactly four people are privileged enough to share this table: me, Cardinal Jiang, the elven ambassador, and the dwarven ambassador. Despite submitting three requests, the Archpatriarch isn't allowed to sit with us. Or, as Jiang calls him, the head of the heretic faction. Both religions of the Sun God call themselves the True Church and the other side the heretics. The Archpatriarch lost against Jiang's team in the last Games, which is why he ended up at the kiddie table.

I sit at the Games host's table because centuries ago a Holy Maiden was considered even more powerful than any cardinal. If only that was still true. A sweet scent drifts off the spectacular display of flowers in the center of the walnut table: yellow roses for friendship, mayflowers for hospitality, rocket flowers for the rivalry of the Games, and clover for good luck. My seat is cushioned in red velvet with rubies on the armrests in the wrong places to be comfortable. As Alzira pulls out my chair, the dwarven ambassador leans over to whisper something. Ambassador Mo'la'ni is a plump, middle-aged woman with thick dark hair, her ceremonial blue armor covered in gemstones.

Alzira draws back. "I'm not interested." Her voice is too loud to be diplomatic. Mo'la'ni casts me a sheepish look leaving no doubt she tried to poach my bodyguard.

Since she's not allowed to stay, Alzira heads to her designated table. The elven ambassador arrives at a polite run. Sharp disappointment pierces my heart. Even someone with face-blindness can tell a young man from an older one, and he's younger than me. His hair color is wrong. He's not my former lover.

This Ambassador Berylseed must be a relative with the same last name. Judging from the slight curve of his ears and his tall height, he's a half-elf. It's rare for the exceptionally talented Suzette to give me the wrong information, but presumably he can't be a mind reader since that gift exclusively appears among elves.

He looks a few years younger than me, an oddly inexperienced pick as ambassador for a long-lived species. *Curious.* He has reddish-blond hair, reaching almost to his waist in elven fashion. A silver circlet sits on his brow. His skin shines like moonlight and his blue eyes are dark as the ocean. Despite the fineness of his features, there's a strength to his jaw. Arm muscles are firm without bulging, very nice. He slides into his chair across from me as gracefully as a parting wave. A sea-blue sequined tunic clings to his trim frame. He's ravishing as the sun reflecting off a glass full of water. In other words, the single most handsome man I've ever laid eyes on. One-hundred-percent my type. At least no matter how boring this dinner gets, I'll have something to look at.

Huh, did he check out his own reflection in the wineglass? Arrogant prat. On second thought, I'll pass. Wait, now he's stopped. For some reason, his gorgeous smile has an element of sheepishness.

Jiang leans sideways and whispers something to King Uctor. Our dear king ruins the cardinal's attempt at subtlety by looking at Ambassador Berylseed, then braying like a donkey. Jiang's glare at the young half-elf holds an even deeper hatred than when he found out about my mixed blood.

Servants bring out the first course, bread drizzled with honey. The meal starts off with pleasantries. "What a lovely cane," Queen Bianna says, gesturing at Jiang's oversized moonstone cradled between three silver claws.

"Thank you," he says, resplendent in his diamond-crusted robe and a peacock's feather sticking out of his hat. "Your hair looks marvelous. My compliments to your maid." Let the fun begin. He knows her hair is thinning.

"What a lovely dress, Holy Ysabel," King Uctor says, leering. *Oh, saints, this again.* "It's a crime against mankind that you are sworn to the Sun God."

So God is the one who ensured that I've had nothing but my toy collection for the last two years? Please direct me to the Sun God so I can file an official complaint.

Ambassador Berylseed chokes on his food. Eyes watering, he gropes for a napkin.

"Ysabel at least is dressed properly," Jiang says, casting a cold look at the dwarven ambassador's armor. Mo'la'ni's lip curls back.

Oh, don't you even start, and don't drag me into it. I'd look equally fabulous in armor. Aloud, I say, "The Sun God has blessed everyone at this table with marvelous clothes."

Ambassador Mo'la'ni scowls. "Not being a worshipper of your sexist religion, I couldn't care less."

Our beloved king can always be counted on to make matters worse. "It's not as though dwarven women have much to hide behind a breastplate." Then he laughs like a jackass. *No, he's more like an infertile mule—that would explain why there have been no royal bastards despite how much he's fucked around.*

Did Ambassador Berylseed just snort wine out his nose? Is he okay? Maybe too pretty to be able to feed himself?

Next come the plates overflowing with a delicious array of venison, wild boar, salmon, and pike. Most elves don't eat meat, so the cook prepared a lentil dish for Ambassador Berylseed. He eats nimbly, with long, slender fingers. *I could waive my minimum intelligence standards for someone so pretty. Huh, he has a nice blush, too.*

Time to put my plan into action. Barely keeping a straight face, I turn to King Uctor. "Your Majesty's royal guards are doing a fabulous job protecting this city." I don't look at Jiang as I speak. I'm going to maneuver one of the ambassadors into asking about security. It will be risky for me to bring up the topic of heretic hunting around Jiang, but this is my last shot at preventing the murders. My hand shakes on my butter knife.

Ambassador Berylseed chimes in before the king can respond. "My people have heard rumors of so-called heretics being lynched in your city. This deeply concerns us. You have a duty to provide protection for your foreign guests."

Huh? I was hoping someone would take my bait but that was more specific than I was expecting.

Ambassador Mo'la'ni says, "Heretic hunting was globally banned after the elven victory in several World Games."

Sticking in the knife, Ambassador Berylseed adds, "Yet the Arahasnorian guards assigned to prevent the rising deaths in this city were removed from their posts." *Damn, how amazing is the elven spy network given I only found out this morning?* It's convenient for me, though.

King Uctor clears his throat. "I'll assign my own guards as replacements. The state can be counted on, if not the church." *Thank you, my patsy!*

Jiang's lips go white, but he doesn't speak. He cares about the reputation of the church. Which means he must have some reason to allow these murders anyway.

Ambassador Berylseed smiles across the table at me. He caught my cue so perfectly, I can only conclude he deliberately helped me. No doubt he has a common interest with me to protect people of his own faith.

Though everyone is speaking Standard, the artificially created universal language, the large room fills with a blend of different accents. At the table behind us, the Archpatriarch, an elven Dharist priest, and a dwarven shaman debate Holy Maiden Ava's miracle. The elf says any decent necromancer could have brought her back from the dead, and the dwarf lists several documented cases of people losing or changing their gifts.

Red-faced and speech-slurringly drunk, Cardinal Farruco snarls, "Silence, all of you stone-shitters and leaf-lickers!"

I wince. Those are slurs for dwarves and elves.

"Calm your tongue, good sir," the Archpatriarch says. "You're embarrassing our faith. I know our churches have their differences, but aren't you from the Dresde royal family? Most of your relatives have converted to our church."

"My family is full of sinners destined for Hell." Farruco sounds gleeful at the prospect. I've noticed a certain type of religious people love God because there's some part of them incapable of loving their fellow beings. I wouldn't even call it faith, more like justification to inflict their malice. *Moon Devil take Farruco because no other woman will.*

A giggle escapes Ambassador Berylseed's lips. He clenches his teeth to suppress it. Another laugh emerges. "Sorry," he gasps.

The main course arrives: swans and peacocks on jeweled dishes, with stuffed replicas of the beautiful birds as centerpieces. I scan Ambassador Mo'la'ni for points of conversation. Her emerald necklace is shaped like a heart—the actual fleshy organ with two chambers, which dwarves, a literal lot, use as a sign of love. "What a beautiful piece of jewelry."

Her face lights up. "It's a present from my husband."

Jackpot. I've found my lever to repair the damage caused by the bigotry of my dear countrymen. I draw her into bragging about her children and laugh at her stories about mining safety regulation snafus. Finally, I turn our now-friendly conversation to the dwarves' coal mines. The Holy City is desperate to power our new factories since the Rashiban trade embargo.

Then King Uctor just has to butt in. "The coal? Good job, Ysabel, we've been needing that badly since I somehow offended the queen of Rashiba again. Touchy lady, no sense of humor."

Glee crosses Mo'la'ni's face. *Bugger it.* She's going to charge me half again the price we almost agreed on. *I'd like to beat His Majesty's face in. It's my duty to our ruler's spiritual well-being, since his best shot into Heaven is if the Lord of Light can't recognize him.*

Ambassador Berylseed starts rocking back and forth. It almost looks like he's in pain, except he's grinning. Even oblivious Uctor has noticed his current victim isn't paying much attention to their conversation.

I switch negotiations to obtaining some of the brand-new dwarven electrical capacitors. No one has yet figured out exactly how to use a device that stores electricity, but I'm certain this will be a big thing, and I want to get in early. Mo'la'ni plays coy with me for a bit before admitting her superiors won't let her sell any without first exploring the military applications. This surprises me. Military technology lags behind domestic in our peaceful world. When Mo'la'ni tells me that she can sell after the World Games, I realize that her nation is waiting to see if the treaty with Dark Lord Kaine holds.

Jiang interrupts us, offering to introduce Ambassador Mo'la'ni to a great buyer of coal, Cardinal Farruco. What nonsense is he babbling? My blood runs cold with realization. He'll let Farruco the fanatic insult the dwarven ambassador so badly it will ruin my trade deal. Why? Just to spite me?

Excuse me, someone fetch me some stationary, I need to write a note to God:

Dear Sir, Madam, or Other:

I see you have created humanity in error. Please correct this oversight as soon as possible.

Hugs and kisses,

Ysabel, your ex-wife

Ambassador Berylseed stands up. "Excuse me, I have to—" He turns without another word and flees, his shoulders shaking with laughter. Who snuck redleaf into his meal?

"What an odd fellow," King Uctor says. "Are all elves such a jovial lot?"

"He's a mind reader," Cardinal Jiang says. "That's why the discount-rate dryads sent someone so young, and a mongrel. Show more caution around him, Your Majesty."

Crap. The entire dinner flashes before my eyes. Ambassador Berylseed aided my plan to get more guards and laughed whenever I mentally insulted someone. My knuckles whiten as I clench my fork. Mindreading is a gift almost as uncommon as mine. Gifts don't run in families, so the odds against the Berylseeds producing two mind readers must be astronomical. My excuses for my carelessness come too late. I should have trusted Suzette—her intel has never let me down before. Sun God Above, he overheard me fantasizing about his body! I sink down in my seat, cursing out the last ten generations of my family.

With delicious chocolate cake sitting uneasily in my stomach, I seek out Alzira for damage control.

The other elves have already been spreading around gossip obtained by their ambassador's mindreading gift. He dished about the royal couple's relationship (terrible) and Jiang's speciesism (predictable). I shift from foot to foot as I ask, "How bad are the rumors about me?"

She blinks. "There are none, Your Holiness. He said the Holy Maiden's thoughts were too pure and godly to be understood."

Why, what a smart man who doesn't want to be dragged into a dark alley and beaten within an inch of his life! I smile. "Excellent. Never mind about finding that bag for me, Alzira. We won't be needing it after all."

After dinner, the crowd floods into the second ballroom for dancing. I approach the cardinals, aiming to keep Cardinal Farruco far away from Ambassador Mo'la'ni. The council members introduce me to a dizzying number of relatives I'll never be able to remember. (Parents and siblings only; no one admits to the bastard children.) I nod and smile so hard my face might fall off. It's pretty awkward. I've never before been forced to meet the families of the people who I keep cursing. Cardinal Santos's mother tells me how wonderful it is to see human women on a World Games team with such sincerity that I wither with guilt over cursing her to suck eggs in hell the last time her son annoyed me. Then she goes on to talk about how far women's rights have progressed in Arahasnor, which irritates me a little because it wasn't as easy as she's making it sound. Like a graceful swan, my legs are kicking like hell under the water's surface.

From behind, Cardinal Jiang grabs my arm. "Ysabel, the king needs to see us."

"Does it have to be right now?" I'm too angry with him to spout about the Sun God.

"It's about our compensation for Dark Lord Kaine. He's set a new condition that could make or break the deal. His Majesty insists on telling us in private." Jiang looks worried. This I have to see. I follow him to the throne room.

A guard stops Alzira at the door. "No bodyguards allowed."

"It's never been an issue before," she says, flexing her gloved hands.

The guards pale. Even so, the leader insists, "We made no exceptions for even the highest nobles in the land. You have to leave."

"Wait for me at the carriage," I say, laying a hand on her arm. I'm not worried. Kaine is on my side, so whatever this condition might be, it can only be good news for me. I have no need of a bodyguard in this room, where everyone's life-oaths prevent us from harming each other.

The throne room holds the most important people in Arahasnor, from the cardinals to high-ranking nobles like Donya. Numbering no more than two dozen, they sit around a wooden table dragged over for the occasion. There aren't any guards. I've never seen the King's Guard leave his side. What did Kaine demand that can only be spoken in front of so few, the right to punch Jiang in the face? That would be just like him.

Jiang and I take the last two seats. I'll sit back and watch the show, because whatever has people so upset, it's not my problem. Given how much time I spend on other people's problems, that's a welcome change of pace.

"Now that we're all present . . ." King Uctor stops. He stutters. He can't look up from the table.

Queen Bianna smoothly interjects, "Dark Lord Kaine has magnanimously forgiven our blood price—a rather heavy debt we don't have enough gold to pay." Her gaze sweeps the room. The tension in the air spikes. "On one condition."

People around me stir and shift in their seats. Everyone knows that we do not have the ability to refuse. Not a single person makes a sound as they wait for the hammer to fall.

"The dark lord wants the Holy Maiden Ysabel," Queen Bianna says. "All we have to do is deliver her to him, for him to do whatever he wishes, and we're free of all responsibility." She eyes me. "What is it about you that attracts all the dark lords, Ysabel?"

The world blurs. My heart gallops under my chest like a horse gone mad. Kaine has betrayed me. I'm his ransom. Just like last time with Dark Lord Yarthor, I'm to be bartered like a thing, given over to a man to do whatever he wishes. I have to . . . to do . . . but I can't move. I can't breathe. I can't speak. I can't think. I'm having a panic attack.

CHAPTER TEN

I have to speak up, but I can't. My lips feel numb. The world spins, the pillars of the throne room merging together. My head sags. I might throw up. I can't throw up, not in this room full of vultures. It feels like I'm dying. No! I have to RUN, to get out NOW, yet my legs are no longer under my control. My heart beats so fast it might tear itself out of my chest and flee without me.

This can't be happening, Yarthor wouldn't have betrayed me, he's my hero. No, not Yarthor, I meant KAINE. Kaine is not the same as Yarthor. He wouldn't have done the exact same thing. Except he did. I gape at the queen, my lips half-parted like a dumb fish on a hook, praying for her to tell me that this is all a malicious joke. Or I could be dreaming. The searing contempt in her gaze feels very real.

My fate hangs in the balance. I have to do something besides gape like an idiot. Except I *am* an idiot. For a second time, I trusted a dark lord who pretended to care about me. For a second time, he turned out to be only after my body. How could I have made such a colossal blunder? I still want to believe this is a misunderstanding or trick, and I hate myself even more for that weakness. I gave Yarthor so many second chances and the benefit of the doubt. I promised myself I wouldn't do that again.

With the same thing happening twice, am I the common denominator? Yarthor accused me of leading him on. I flirted with Kaine. Did I make him believe I'd welcome this? No, it doesn't add up. No rational person would think I'd be fine with being humiliated before the court, having my position taken away, and being sold as a war prize. An invitation for sex isn't a license to rape. Even (especially) someone into bondage knows that.

Now I've been targeted by two dark lords, no one will ever believe it's not my fault. Just like Queen Bianna said, I'll become the holy maiden known for affairs with dark lords. Kaine could do just about anything to me, and not a single person here will blame him. I can tell from their cold eyes. I'll no longer be able to convince anyone that I didn't want Yarthor, either, not now that I've done it again. Believe it or not, in that moment, I'm almost even more hurt over the inevitable return of the love ballads about me and Yarthor than I feel about what the bards will write to celebrate my latest wannabe rapist.

Distantly, I hear King Uctor speak. "You'll be fine, of course. You are virtuous, so the Sun God will protect you." His tone hangs suspended between disbelief and a desire to believe. "After Bianna reminded me of your divine shield against the touch of a man, I felt quite relieved we wouldn't lose your healing powers."

No one is going to help me.

Part of me knows I have to pull myself together, but the rest of me can't. My mind has gone completely blank. I shake all over. Jelly spreads up my legs to my arms. I sag. When my chair rocks backward, I can't catch myself.

Donya leaps around the table and grabs me before I hit the floor. The table wobbles. She gives it a good kick to knock it over, sending papers flying and providing us with a brief moment of cover.

Cradling my head in her arms, she whispers, "You can do this. You can get out of this. You have to stay strong a little longer. Stand up and spout a bunch of holy nonsense like you always do." Her hands stroke my back, offering what little comfort she can.

It won't work. My own lies got me into this mess. They think the Sun God saved me once, so of course He'll do it again. The Arahasnor court has always pretended that I'm one of them, up until I'm not. It would hurt their pride to hand over one of their own noblewomen, who they think of as their property, to be violated by a barbarian—but at the end of the day, I'm half-Conollian. A tool. Disposable.

I gathered so much power and yet it's not enough. I'm still a pawn. Still worth nothing except how they can use me. And once again, the royals and priests will hand me over to be raped by a dark lord.

A spark of rage pierces my fear. If I'm going down, then I won't do so while spouting the fiction that the Sun God protects virgins from rape. That lie insults the god I believe in.

I stand up.

My eyes lock with King Uctor's. "Bullshit."

He gapes. The room falls silent. No one present but Jiang has ever heard their Holy Maiden curse. I snap, "Virginity has never protected anyone from rape or any other bad thing. Show some common fucking decency."

I've never expected the Sun God to protect me, and I've certainly never expected Him to protect me more than other people, as if I'm better than them. That's not the God I worship. The God I worship lives inside of me, and there's nothing any man could do to me that would take that away.

"Stop," Donya whispers, but I can't stop. *Don't tell me to stop, Donya. My conversation with you gave me the courage to tell the truth. Because of your help just now, I found my strength, and I'll need it.*

Most of the room won't look at me. From my healings, I'm familiar with the evasive eye contact of shame. King Uctor hyperventilates. He likes his rapes kept in the darkness. I have a few minutes before someone shuts me up. Better make the most of them.

I raise my chin. "Dark Lord Yarthor wasn't struck down by divine wrath. I slit his throat with my own two hands." That stirs murmurs from the crowd. I talk over them. "Let me spell it out to you cowards: you're selling me out to be raped by a dark lord in exchange for money. You can lie to yourselves, but not to God."

For a moment that feels like an eternity, silence holds the room still. Then Head Cardinal Jiang says, "Ysabel, people might believe you seduced one dark lord by accident but two looks like a pattern. You should examine your own behavior. But I'm afraid I can't let our Holy Maiden leave the church's service at this point in time. She still has preparations to arrange for the World Games."

Jiang actually means that he still plans to sacrifice me in four months. I never thought I'd be counting on my worst enemy to save my life, but right now, he's the only person who has a (purely selfish) reason not to sell me out.

Queen Bianna's smile could cause flowers to wither and die. "Dark Lord Kaine swore not to kill Her Holiness. He'll be required to release her long enough to attend the World Games. Appearances must be maintained."

"In that case, I will withdraw my objection." Jiang shrugs. He knows he can use my brother as a hostage to force me to show up at his sacrificial altar as long as I'm still alive. He's also fully aware my healing power has never had the slightest connection to virginity. As far as he's concerned, he's found a new way to use me.

My head sags, feeling like an elephant is resting a foot on it. As always, my panic attack has left me exhausted. If I sit down, my legs might refuse to stand again. I can't even speak while these people decide my fate as though I'm not present.

"I feel faint," King Uctor moans in a high, petulant voice. "Where is my doctor? I need the royal doctor at once." He sways, then collapses face-first onto the table.

Nobles rush forward to catch the fallen king and coo over him. Several people elbow each other in an attempt to be the one to carry His Majesty from the room. Everyone carefully does not look at me as they make excuses to leave. Perhaps my speech did bother them, even if I only pricked their cowardice instead of their consciences.

I could try to run. I could shout for Alzira, who probably didn't go far no matter what the guards told her. But if Alzira rebels against royalty, then her life-oaths will stop her heart. If I somehow flee the city, then Jiang will kill my brother. I'm trapped.

In the confusion, Donya fights her way over and grabs my elbow. "I'll help you escape." Her face is pale but composed.

She must be out of her mind. She could lose everything trying to save me: her noble title, her political goals, her very life. We're not even friends. She hates me!

I shake her off. "There's nothing you can do."

She puts her hands on her hips. "I wouldn't be myself if I didn't try."

"Then give me your knife."

Hands shaking, she unstraps the dagger from her belt. I have nowhere to hang it, so I stick the sheathed weapon through my bun. A fitting symmetry to my last kidnapping. "This is all I needed to deal with the last dark lord."

Tears drip down Donya's cheeks. Why is she the one crying, not me? How irritating.

I swallow. "I can take care of myself. But . . . thank you."

A hand grabs me from behind. I whirl around, glimpsing the guard's uniform before I topple over sideways. It must be the guard with a sleeping gift. Bianna apparently does not trust me not to run.

Before my eyes slip shut, I see hands reach for me. Donya, a fool to the end, tries to push them away. Then my world goes black.

* * *

I wake to the bumping of a moving carriage. Sitting up, I touch my throbbing forehead. My hands and legs are not bound. The carriage door is tied shut, and guards on horseback can be seen through the window. There's no way out. A pocket of air forms under my chest. I tap my chin. When I remember, my hand snaps up to my hair. I still have Donya's knife. The touch of cold steel lets me breathe, albeit raggedly. It's possible the guards overlooked it, but more likely the queen hopes I'll stab Dark Lord Kaine.

What happened to Alzira? Without me, she's magicless. Yet she's not the type to go down without a fight. What if they apprehended and injured her? My breath hitches. Animal panic claws under my skin.

Taking rapid breaths, I try to think. I want to believe this is a misunderstanding. Except Jiang and the royal family would have no reason to lie; they don't want to lose my healing power. Perhaps Dark Lord Kaine thinks he's doing me a favor by getting me away from the people who use me, not realizing certain idiots will pack me off to a nunnery if they think I've been penetrated by a penis. Maybe he didn't mean it the way it sounded. Dark Lord Yarthor also said that he was doing me a favor by returning me to my homeland, *and I just needed to repay him by holding still and being a good girl—*

Nausea overwhelms me. I put my head between my legs until I feel less likely to throw up.

I can't believe Dark Lord Kaine would hurt me. It has nothing to do with him being, by his own admission, submissive. I've met men who enjoy being humiliated, so they harass women for the pleasure of their insults. Or the men who think only submissives have the right to boundaries and limits. I don't date them. No, I thought I was safe with Kaine because I thought he was a good guy.

Except I haven't actually known him for very long. Only two days. Any monster can pretend to be a good person for two days. *Dark Lord Yarthor pretended for months.*

With that thought, I bend over again, hands covering my mouth, trying not to cry or vomit. I don't have it in me to keep faith or make excuses any longer. I'm tired of being betrayed. I just want to go home.

This can't be happening. I trusted Dark Lord K—no, *Kaine*. When we first met, he was honest to the point of idiocy, a little shy, and completely lacking in malice even when he discussed sacking my city. Minutes ago,

I would have sworn to a Seer he'd never force anyone under any circumstances. Stupid me. I thought Yarthor was a good man and look how that turned out. Kaine could be even worse because I've started to fall for him. It's as if I invited him into my house, and he set it on fire.

It would serve Kaine right if I did stab him with Donya's knife. It's probably the one way I can come out of this with people believing my "virtue" is intact. Still a Holy Maiden. I have to do it.

Emotion strong enough to cause physical pain stabs into my heart and my eyes sting. I can almost feel Yarthor's blood on my hands. Then and there, I know I can never bear to push a knife into Kaine. I can't kill him.

The image of the blunt, straightforward man who laughed like he loved the world flashes across my mind. I can't harm Kaine even if he would harm me. It shames me, but my heart can't change so quickly. Fine, then. I'll make Kaine understand that he'll have nothing of me that he doesn't take by force, I *won't* kill him, and then I doubt I'll ever trust another man again.

In pitch-darkness, the carriage passes through the city gates. Kaine's army is camped out in tents beyond the moat. Guards with torches escort me to the wooden fortress looming before the mountains: Dark Lord Kaine's famous castle on wheels. It sits on a raised platform with movable stairs in front. Half a dozen spiky towers stretch up into the night and vanish into the clouds as if they rise for eternity, and gargoyles perch on the eaves. A few lights shine from the windows, casting shadows on their leering stone faces. Dark shapes of catapults can be made out at the base. The central tower has metal bat wings spread on top. Torches gleam on either side of the gate like fangs decorating an open mouth.

My teeth chatter with the force of my shaking body. I need redleaf. I reach for the packet in my purse, but of course I don't have my purse. How stupid. Now is not the time anyway, not when I need to stay alert.

As Kaine's soldiers surround the carriage, I press an ear to the window but fail to overhear. I only catch the thundering footsteps as the Arahasnor guards flee. Even the coachman runs after them. One of Kaine's soldiers climbs up to take the reins, then we start moving again. Quickly, I pile up my hair around the dagger, trying to hide it more. Fortunately the sheath looks ornamental enough to pass as a decoration.

At the entrance, a soldier opens the door. "His Darkness asked to see you at once, my lady." He smiles so sincerely that either he's a brilliant actor or he does not understand what his lord purchased me for. "My name is Nix. Will you please remember that I greeted you first? It's an honor to meet you."

My smile in return is all teeth. "Please escort me to Kaine." All this false civility is giving me flashbacks to Yarthor.

They don't search me. That's a relief. Frankly, my dagger isn't very well hidden, but no one comments. Sometimes it pays to be underestimated. As the soldiers guide me to a parlor, my heart hammers as if it's being strangled by a life-oath. With a click, Nix closes the door behind me. Of course this is the type of room Kaine would like. Cushioned chairs designed to be comfortable rather than pretty. A bookshelf full of knickknacks instead of paper. Thick, comfy carpeting and an iron ring of candles overhead. Aggressive animal heads snarl at me from the wall. A short table is strewn with snacks and a bottle of wine. My heart breaks again to remember the way Kaine enjoyed the 521 Alexandrina Astara Ashia Aquamarine when I showed him what the good stuff tasted like. A pounding behind my eyes blurs the room and makes it hard to think. The knife in my bun feels twice as heavy.

"Ysabel!" Kaine jumps up from the sofa. He wears a long blue tunic, simple except for the white fur on the cuffs, no armor at all. "You look absolutely stunning. Bloodred is definitely your color." He moves fast, too fast, and suddenly he's right in front of me with one of his hands resting against the wall. The arm traps me like a metal bar. His body looms over me, making me keenly aware of his height and muscles. "I love the dagger hairstyle." He reaches up to touch a lock of my hair.

Before he can touch me, I panic. Hauling back my fist, I punch him in the nose.

CHAPTER ELEVEN

I do not manage to send Kaine flying the way he did to King Uctor. Instead, he grunts as my fist bounces off his nose. My knuckles sting. I've done no damage, not so much as a drop of blood. Fear sweeps away my adrenaline. From the ache in my wrist, I've quite possibly hurt myself more than him. Heart racing, I draw back my fist again, trying to recall my self-defense lessons. If I strike him in the jaw, maybe I can stun him long enough to put distance between us.

His expression stops me, the look of a faithful hound whose beloved master just kicked him. His eyes scrunch up like he might cry. My fist relaxes, and I step back. My spine digs into the wall. The silence in the room balances on the edge of a knife. Clearing my throat, I say, "Please let me go. This is wrong, and I'm scared."

"I think you've misunderstood. Sit down, and we can talk over the refreshments. I prepared your favorite wine."

His delusion of friendliness, so similar to Yarthor's, enrages me. "How dare you. How dare you pretend everything is fine when you just *kidnapped* me?" I yank my dagger from my bun, a stick shielding me from a giant. "Don't touch me." The blade before my eyes divides my sight of Kaine into two pieces. The sharp silver tip wavers as a drop of my sweat rolls down the beaded hilt.

"Ysabel, I'm not kidnapping you." He sounds like he believes it.

The dagger stops shaking. In my relief, I can almost think again. He doesn't have immediate plans to attack me, but he still hurt me. "Can I leave this place without anyone stopping me, Kaine?"

"I promise you can leave, but please talk to me first. I—"

"No ifs or buts! Can. I. Leave?"

When Kaine takes a step forward, I flinch. Instead, he reaches past me to open the door. "Of course you can leave, Ysabel." His voice quavers as he looks at the floor. His sadness angers me. How dare he act like a victim when he just destroyed my life? The reality of this situation doesn't change regardless of his intentions. The royal court and the Council of Cardinals both abandoned me. My reputation will be in tatters when I return from the dark lord's castle, no matter what I tell people.

I should probably find out what he intended, but I'm too angry to even look at his face. If I'm going to salvage anything from this nightmare, then I need to make certain he won't run around claiming I had sex with him. But I'd rather punch him again than beg for his help. I still have a nagging fear that the open door might be a trap.

Wobbling, I take a step forward. My sweaty hand slips, and the dagger falls out—directly toward my foot.

A gust of wind picks up Donya's dagger and carries it over to Kaine. "You lost this." He offers the dagger to me hilt-first.

Kaine didn't touch me. Even when he had an ironclad excuse—stopping me from impaling my own foot—he used one of his gifts instead, because he knows I don't want him to touch me. This isn't a trap. In the end, he is still the kind of man I believed him to be.

Maybe I always knew that, under my panic. I just couldn't trust myself. This feels less like changing my mind and more like reality reasserting itself after a nightmare.

I sit down on the floor. Too relieved to cry and too overwrought not to cry, I sniffle. Kaine hovers over me, mouth opening and closing. He keeps holding out the dagger.

Eventually, I take the dagger before his arm falls off. I stagger over to the armchair and collapse into it, setting my knife down on the table. "If this isn't a kidnapping, then we *should* talk."

Kaine sits across from me. "Why would you think I was kidnapping you?"

"I didn't want to believe it." My voice rises defensively. Perhaps my panic clouded my thoughts, but he'd given me good reason to distrust him. Even if Kaine's a presumptuous ass instead of a deliberate kidnapper, rape is the one thing he never should have used against me, even as a fake threat. "You demanded my body as 'compensation' from the Arahasnor court."

"No, Ysabel, I never said anything like that." He waves his hands. "But I needed them to free you, and I had to make it seem like it wasn't your choice. They would think I wanted your healing powers."

Wearily, I say, "Kaine, you clueless fuck. The entire court of Arahasnor thinks you're raping me right now."

His face falls further. "Y-you really thought that? I thought . . . we . . ."

"Forget what I thought. If other people think I had sex with you, willingly or not, it means I'm not a Holy Maiden any longer. You ruined my life."

"Ysabel, I wanted to *save* your life. I needed to pretend you didn't have a choice so your brother wouldn't be in danger."

I massage my temples. He doesn't get it. Of course if he made me part of the ransom then everyone would think he wanted a war bride. If he took a life-oath not to kill me, then under the unspoken rules, that implies he planned to commit nonfatal offenses against me. The dagger looks tempting. I don't have to stab him, I could bash his face with the hilt. *Calm down, Ysabel, he wasn't trying to keep you powerless and dependent on him—he's just a moron.* "Why, Kaine? Why would you pull this stunt?"

"To save your life." His face is drawn but composed. "My spies have been investigating Jiang. I know what he's planning to do to you."

"You know about—?" My throat clenches as my life-oath sends a jolt of pain through my chest. I can't say it, but he can.

"Stop, you don't have to talk. I know that he's planning to kill you in a ritual to give himself immortality." Kaine raises his hands as if to soothe a wild animal. "I wasn't sure how long you had before the ritual. I had to get you out right away. I gave up all the other compensation for this. And it was a lot of money." His voice holds a note between pleading and indignation. "The original treaty offered to feed my army for nearly a year, enough gold to fill this room, and a generous trade agreement."

"Then you should have taken the deal," I growl. "If you don't want the food, I have refugees who could use it."

"I won't let you die." Iron lurks behind his words.

"Why do you care so much?"

Kaine pauses. "I owe you a debt." Two dots of color appear on his cheeks.

That's so clearly not the real reason, I feel a little flattered. Logically I know my life has much less value compared to a deal that would have helped so many more people, but I've been sacrificing myself for so long that it feels good to be put first for once. My heart gives a treacherous flutter. I remind myself why I'm angry. "It doesn't matter, this wasn't your decision to make. Why didn't you ask me for permission before doing this?"

"You haven't made any effort to escape. The thought crossed my mind that maybe you couldn't. Or maybe you didn't plan to save yourself." Kaine's piercing gaze captures mine. His voice lowers. "You don't have to say anything if it hurts. Just nod."

I hesitate. "Maybe there are other ways I could have worked around my oaths but—"

"See!" His voice rises in triumph. "I assumed you couldn't just walk out of there. But even if you could, you'd make excuses as to why it wasn't worth it."

He doesn't understand. Even if I'd known he was offering me a way out, I still couldn't have accepted. There are too many lives besides mine at risk. Even if I'm not sacrificed, how many days have my healings left me with? Not enough for my life to be worth saving.

"Good intentions don't make what you did right. Even if you wanted to save me, you didn't give me a choice. You humiliated me before the royal court." That's not the real reason. "You *scared* me." Death is inevitable for me. But being sold is my worst nightmare.

"You had to know I'd never mean anything like that."

"Did I?" My anger rises up again. "Kaine, we've known each other for mere days. You had no right to expect me to trust you."

"I—I see that now." Deep thought tramps lines across his face, resulting in a look of dismay. "I'm sorry. I owe you another debt." His head slumps down, sadness drooping every muscle of his admittedly scrumptious body. His hands twist and untwist.

I've kicked a puppy. Again. Because Kaine trusts people so easily, no wonder he assumed I would trust him. But my life has taught me not to trust.

I clear my throat. "Look—" I bite my lip, do I really want to talk about this? I decide to try and be vulnerable one more time. "I don't know if you've ever heard the story of what happened between me and the late Dark Lord Yarthor. The real story, not the nonsense the bards peddle."

Kaine nods. "We tell the real story in Conollia. I know that you risked your own life to save Yarthor. I never believed that you called down divine wrath to kill him—frankly, I don't believe in miracles at all. It was a pack of lies to make Conollia look bad. And of course Yarthor couldn't have tried to marry you; you were only fourteen."

My bitter laugh interrupts his spiel. "I was fourteen years old when the royal court handed me over to a pedophile to be r—ra—" A solitary tear trickles down my cheek.

Realization and horror fills his eyes. "Ysabel, I'm sorry."

"I killed Yarthor myself. It was an accident." I pour out the grim details as quickly as I can before I lose my nerve. "I'm not sorry I did it, but I've always known I got lucky. I've had nightmares for years about not being so lucky next time." Something between a gasp and a sob emerges from my lips. "When I was called to the throne room and told they were going to hand me over to another dark lord, it brought back memories."

The look on Kaine's face reminds me of a man once brought into my clinic with his intestines reaching his ankles. "I'm so sorry."

"I was in a bad state of mind, or I would have given you more benefit of the doubt."

"This isn't your fault."

We're both quiet for a moment, the only sounds an occasional sobbing hiccup from me as my body continues to calm.

Kaine clears his throat. "Seriously, this is entirely my fault."

I nod, because it's refreshing not to be blamed for once.

"You should hate me. Go on, I deserve it. Hate me. Only please don't hate me. Because actually, I like you quite a lot. How about instead I'll let you hit me as much as you want until you're satisfied?"

I manage a wobbly laugh. When tears sting my eyes, I irately brush them away. "You're a masochist. You'd enjoy it."

He winks at me. "But wouldn't you enjoy me enjoying it?"

I flush scarlet as I imagine bending him over my knee right here and now . . . No, wait. I still haven't forgiven him for the kidnapping.

"If you punch me in the face, I promise I won't get off on it." He points at his nose. "Go ahead and hit me with your full strength, not like that love tap earlier."

I sigh. "I'm not going to hit you. I'm sorry for doing it the first time." What does he mean, love tap? That *was* my full strength! It's not my fault I was born small and my job involves paperwork instead of swords.

"It's okay. I can take a punch when I deserve a punch."

"I understand your intentions. But your plan crashed in without any thought of how it would affect me." I hunch over. "And now the whole world will see me as your spoils. How can I trust you when you have so much power over me? One wrong word from you, and my reputation would be in tatters at a time when I need every last bit of influence to save my brother."

I don't know why I'm telling him this. Since Kaine has left me in a position where I need him, normally I would tell him whatever he wants to hear. I would be a fool not to accept any help he can offer me right now. I ought to let him believe that he can save me so that he'll work with me, even if I don't believe it myself. But I want to be honest with Kaine. It's the only way we can repair this.

Kaine regards me carefully. He seems to reach a decision. "I have a secret. I wanted to tell you before. It would let you hold power over me, like I have over you. If you used this information against me, then you could possibly cause part of my army to revolt and my country to fracture."

I swallow. "Do you want me to swear a life-oath never to tell first?"

He thinks about it for a second.

"No, this leverage belongs to you to do what you will. It's not the equivalent of your brother's life hanging in the balance, but it's the closest I can come to making us even." Kaine sticks a hand down his pants and pulls out a rolled-up sock, setting it on the table.

"That looks like a sock," I say, like an idiot.

Kaine makes a sound between a snort and a whimper. "It is a sock," he says in a faint voice. He pulls up his shirt to reveal a breast binder, keeping his eyes averted. His hands shake. "Don't look at me like I'm crazy, but I'm not a woman."

"I know you're not a woman," I murmur. Perhaps I'm biased by my crush, but his bullheadedness and masculine energy makes it hard for me to see him as anything but a man. "You're a trans man, right?" That's the word the elves use. None of the words in the Holy City are particularly polite.

"That's all? You believe me? Without question?" Kaine shakes his head.

"I know someone else like you," I explain.

Kaine gazes at me with near-worshipful eyes. "You—I can't believe you believe me. You're amazing."

His praise discomforts me. I'm not a saint of tolerance. I already got all my awkward and pushy questions out of the way with Suzette. When I first caught what I believed to be a disguised man among my maids, I had Suzette thrown in the dungeon as a spy. Stupid, because anyone sending an actual spy would have picked someone whose gift has combat application. (Suzette creates flower scents.) Back then I felt hurt and betrayed, so I said quite a few cruel things I'm never going to be able to apologize enough for. I only let Suzette out of jail because I concluded she was nuts. It took me months to even approach understanding.

I'm nearly shaking from shock, not at the reveal but at the complete and total trust and vulnerability Kaine just showed me. In the wrong hands, this information is a blackmail jackpot. The geopolitical stakes far outweigh whatever debt Kaine feels he owes to me. He wasn't kidding about the (unfair and unjustified) threat this information could pose to his position. There are still too many humans in the world who think all leaders should be born with a penis. My heart feels like it might explode. I'd hoped he would reassure me, but I never dared dream he'd instead give me such a tangible demonstration of his sincerity. "I promise I won't tell anyone. I wouldn't talk under torture."

"You're not angry I didn't tell you before?"

"It wasn't my right to know."

He tugs at his collar. "It could be. I mean, I was planning to tell you. Because, well, I thought, ah, I'd started to get the impression, that maybe you wanted to get to know me better?"

My throat is suddenly drier than the blighted lands. I caress his hand and lock eyes with him. "Yes. I'd like that." I lean forward. His lips part slightly, looking very kissable. Then I remember the reason I didn't kiss him last time. "What about the woman Jiang thought was your lover—?" I stop. Several puzzle pieces fall into place. "Jiang captured *you*."

He nods. "The surviving assassins found me lying drugged in the dark lord's bed and jumped to the conclusion I must be fucking myself." His crude hand gesture conveys the impossibility of such an act. "Once I woke up, I bit off a nose and stabbed my way out of there."

A giggle escapes my lips. Then a guffaw. I double over laughing. Jiang's guard captured the real Kaine and didn't notice because they couldn't in their wildest dreams imagine a dark lord without a dick! This is hilarious. It serves their sexist asses right. Wiping tears from my eyes, I say, "I can't even be mad at you now I've laughed my head off. It's kind of annoying."

"If you're not angry at me any longer, then will you stay?"

I gulp. I believe in him now, with all my heart. But I can't. "I could do more good back in the city. I could help out your cause, too."

"You'll drain more of your life doing healings."

"My brother is a hostage."

Kaine's forehead wrinkles. "We can use the time I bought to find and free your brother."

"Then Jiang will switch to threatening the refugees instead." I refuse to allow myself false hope.

"Then we'll beat his ass in the Games and take over the council."

"It's not so easy! My nice, safe plan was to strike a deal with the cardinals to grant the refugees land by agreeing to stay out of the World Games." I'm having trouble controlling my breathing, a warning sign of another panic attack. "Even if I overthrow Jiang, my healings will kill me eventually."

"That's part of why I wanted you here." Kaine runs his fingers through his hair. "What people have been doing to you is wrong. No one in my kingdom will ever force you to heal again."

"It's too late." The adrenaline has long ago drained out of me. It's late at night, and I'm too tired for this conversation. "I'm going to die soon, Kaine. I've run out of days to spend. Each healing could be my last." I should have told him sooner, before he had time to do something stupid like get attached to me. "I was never getting out of this alive. All I want is to save my brother before I die. You should send me back, then get something actually useful as reparations. I'm sorry."

His mouth sets mulishly. "What would your brother think about you giving up? Take it from someone who's lost a sibling: He'll blame himself for your death." His eyes blaze. He wasn't angry when I hit him, but he's angry now—for my sake. His words strike their mark. I feel sick.

"Then what do you want me to do?" I all but shriek.

"Fight to survive until the very end." He cautiously approaches my armchair, watching for any sign I want him to back away. I don't. He halts in front of me. "I'll look for a way to save you. I have more gifts than even I remember. At the very least, I want you to live every day left to the fullest."

I want to feel hope, but I'm hollowed out inside and accustomed to giving up. "I can't get out of my life-oath to Jiang."

"We'll figure something out. I promise." He drops to his knees in front of me, looking up imploringly. The candlelight dances off his dark hair and the obsidian depths of his eyes. "I'm a dark lord. I have power and influence and an army. Because of the debt I owe you, I offer myself to your service. You took control of your city on sheer nerve and competency. Now that you have my resources, what can't you accomplish? My plan failed because I don't have your political savvy or cunning. If we work together, we can do *anything*."

Is it hot in here or is that just blood rushing to my face? I will admit it—I have a huge weakness for flattery. I blame the lack of appreciation from certain council members in my day-to-day life. Kaine's a natural charmer. Plus, guys kneeling at my feet is a big kink of mine. My throat dries. I cannot speak. I want him to make me believe that maybe . . . just maybe . . . I can escape my death sentence.

"Ysabel." Kaine reaches for my face as reverently as a pilgrim. His hand hovers, not quite touching my skin. "Please. Please forgive me. Please trust me. Please allow me to help you. Don't go back to your death. Give me a chance. Please."

As my willpower fails, I lean against his hand. His palm feels big and warm. He watches me as if his everything depends on my answer. I wet my lips. "There might be a way for me to stay here while still keeping my political power. We could tell everyone the truth." *What a shocking idea coming from me.* "Or at least, a limited version of the truth. I'll ally with you officially. You can give me the power to act as your agent. You'll clarify that you did not purchase me from Arahasnor, and you're disgusted at their awful assumptions. If we pull this off correctly, then I could humiliate the king and queen." That thought gives me almost as many butterflies as the sight of Kaine on his knees.

He brings my hand up to his lips and kisses it. "I couldn't possibly have a more skilled political schemer representing my nation. You won't regret this, I promise."

I feel lightheaded. Did I just abandon years of scheming for a man? There's a reason why I dread lovers finding out just how weak I get for men on their knees. Yet in the face of Kaine's sweetness and sincerity, I can't regret my agreement. Honestly, I want to stay. Worst case scenario, it'll be nice to spend what little remains of my life with him. The icy block around my heart collapses, bringing a wave of relief, exhaustion, joy, and even burgeoning love. Thank the Sun God, my faith in Kaine wasn't misplaced after all. I can trust him. Tentatively, I smile. He smiles back.

"Can I assume you don't want me to take him hostage long enough to leave this place and then kill him?" Alzira drops down from the ceiling, the metal on her dress completely silent. "I only want to be certain, Your Holiness, since you do lie all the time."

My heart nearly leaps out of my chest. I shriek and drop Kaine's hand. "How did you . . . ?" There's no point in asking, I already know that Alzira is amazing. "Nope, we're not killing Kaine. It was a misunderstanding. Um, you didn't kill anyone on your way in, did you?" It will get awkward if Alzira just murdered her way through Kaine's army.

Kaine gapes at Alzira. "How long have you been there?"

"Fortunately for you, I came in to find you on your knees, so I refrained from chopping off your head." Alzira sniffs. "Honor forbids me from attacking a man who has already surrendered to Her Holiness's magnificence. Though if she were to wink at me, then I would murder you and bury the body too deep for anyone to find."

I laugh frantically. "No winking here! If I do wink, that means I have something stuck in my eye." Every last bit of metal around the room is shaking. That means she doesn't entirely believe we're out of danger. I put my arms around Alzira. Her body shakes, too.

It was a lucky save that Alzira came in just after the part about me becoming a human sacrifice. If she'd overheard, this room would be in tatters. I've always hoped to avoid that conversation by dying first.

Rubbing Alzira's back, I murmur, "I'm fine, I promise."

"I'm never letting you send me away again," she mutters. It sounds like a threat.

"It was my mistake. I'm sorry." I pull back and look her in the eye. "Did you kill anyone? I need to know, no matter how well you hid the body."

Alzira holds her head high. "I avoided causing fatalities by tunneling into the castle."

Kaine stares. "No one saw you?"

"The tunnel goes all the way back to the Holy City. You'll want to guard that until your people can fill it in, since it's now a prime invasion route. Your security is rather lax. Who's your bodyguard?"

"I've never needed one," Kaine says.

Alzira harrumphs. "You may want to rethink that policy. A good bodyguard is invaluable and would have prevented me from snapping your neck from behind."

"People have tried sneak attacks before. I can turn my skin to granite."

"I can explode your heart inside your chest. Think about it."

"I am," Kaine says, looking queasy. I suppress a chuckle. It's best if men understand early on that Alzira will always be part of my life, including standing guard outside the sex dungeon (which is exactly as awkward as it sounds but has saved my life before). Besides, Alzira still looks like she wants to break Kaine's face. Better to allow her to let off steam in harmless ways.

A knock sounds against the door. A deep voice calls, "Kaine, I apologize for disturbing you, but there's a hole in the hallway floor."

"Durrian!" Kaine's face lights up. "Please come in. I want to introduce you."

The door opens, revealing a dark-skinned giant with a hint of a paunch and calm eyes. He wears armor made of black lacquered leather and a robe-like heavy fur coat. He's middle-aged, with gray streaking his receding hairline and the muscles of a warrior. His beard is neatly trimmed, as if to ask the looker to ignore the weather-beaten skin, oversized ears, and spiral tattoo peeking out of his collar, and not think him a barbarian. He extends a hand with scars where his fingers have been repeatedly broken. "Holy Ysabel. It's a pleasure to meet you after hearing so much about you. I'm General Durrian."

"It's a pleasure." I mean it for once. I have a lot of respect for the man who's been doing all the hard work of running the country Kaine conquered. I place my hand in his, and he shakes it very gently as big men often do.

Kaine looks between us with the hopeful eyes of someone who badly wants us to like each other. "This is Alzira, Ysabel's bodyguard."

"Since she was not part of the arrival party, I take it she left the hole in the castle." Durrian conveys a great deal by raising a single eyebrow.

Kaine fidgets. "It was my fault. I let Ysabel's people worry about her. I'll explain later."

"First, I need to contact the rest of my friends," I say. If news has started to spread around the city, then Alzira won't be the only one worried about me. "They'll be joining us here."

Durrian turns a professional smile on me. "I'll make arrangements. May I have a word with my lord?"

"Of course." I nod, and they step outside.

Once we're alone in the parlor, Alzira murmurs, "Are you sure about this, Your Holiness? You must know what staying here will do to your reputation."

I strive to think of a good reason to give Alzira that isn't *His adorable kneeling temporarily blinded me and I made the decision with what's below my waist*. "Uh, Kaine and I are going to think of a plan to handle the court. I need Jiang to believe Kaine is holding me prisoner so he has less cause to threaten my brother." A great reason. I'm proud I thought of it.

"Of course, Your Holiness." Alzira's eyes sparkle. "I'm glad we're finally moving against Jiang."

I look away so she can't see the truth in my eyes. She'll be devastated when Jiang murders me . . . except I'm not planning to die anymore. Maybe. The thought of survival is new to me.

Durrian returns, bringing a Bookmaker to contact the Dragon Maidens. I put my game face back on. We have a lot to plan.

My Dragon Maidens arrive and wait for me in the entrance hall. I give an impromptu speech to my small staff, telling them that they can return to the city with full pay if they desire. Almost no one leaves.

Kaine has prepared guest rooms for all my people. I retire to my new bedroom. It smells like it's been recently aired out. The wallpaper is colored pale blue with a trim of painted plants on the bottom. Royal blue curtains have crystal tassels in front. The bed has a simple but elegant ebony frame. Half a dozen pillows are piled high on the green comforter. Once again, he's infested the room with dead animals: a deer head over the desk, a stuffed duck on the dresser, an entire bear with its claws looming over the end table, and a wolf rug. Antlers hang over the headboard. An unrecognizable type of horn decorates the door. Alone, I pace with nervous energy.

From outside, Kaine calls, "May I speak to you?"

"Come in." I fill my voice with enthusiasm to soothe the apprehension in his tone. Now that I'm not angry with him, I want to repair things between us.

He holds up a wine bottle. "I found another Aquamarine something, since the last one was so delicious."

It's only a Year 536, but it's the thought that counts. "Let's share the bottle. Do you have any redleaf?"

His nose wrinkles. "Some people in my hometown did nothing but take that stuff all day until they starved."

"It relaxes my nerves. Besides, I—" Better not to mention my likely demise to Kaine again. I only binge when the despair gets really bad and I have the spare time to pass out for a few days. Hmm, when I admit that to myself, it doesn't sound so good. "Maybe I'll stick to one glass."

Okay, I have two. It's not enough to get me drunk, and I've had a rough day. I savor my last sip. An Alexandrina Astara Ashia Aquamarine is good no matter what year. "Thank you again, Kaine. This was very thoughtful. Consider yourself forgiven."

He winces, rubbing his neck. "You shouldn't forgive me so easily. I really screwed up. I'm bad about scaring people accidentally."

"Manners aren't your strong suit," I say dryly.

"It's partly because everyone but my brother treated me as a girl growing up. When I first dressed as a man, the social rules changed. I made missteps worthy of the Dark Lord Chingis." He shudders. "I'm saying this as a reason, not an excuse."

"Like what?"

"When I went out for a walk, the woman in front of me sped up her pace. So I chased after her to tell her I wasn't following her. That did not go well." He looks away. "I'm a hugger. Durrian had to take me aside and tell me that I shouldn't hug the serving girls because I was scaring them." He casts me a pleading look. "Now I'm very careful to always ask before touching."

It's easy to picture Kaine tripping over himself like an effusive puppy. Luckily, he had someone to set him straight. "I noticed you're good about asking first."

"Thanks. Could you teach me how to not scare women? I never again want to hurt anyone like I did to you."

Taken aback, I say, "I don't know if I ever thought about . . ." He's giving me the begging-for-a-treat eyes. "I can try."

From his sitting position, he puts his hands on his knees like a dog sitting on its haunches. "I will pay close attention."

"First, remember that to any given woman, you're a potential threat." I gesture at his thick arms. "If someone seems scared, are you talking loudly? Getting too close? Getting angry? If you don't know, try apologizing and asking what's wrong."

I help him play pretend for half a dozen hypothetical scenarios. Once my imagination runs out, I sit down again. "I'm proud of you for trying so hard. You're a good man." It feels a little like stepping off a cliff to say that out loud. My trust before was fake and forced, so it collapsed easily. This time, I've decided to trust Kaine to the bitter end.

"Thank you." His face relaxes. "You're the only one I can talk to about this. Speaking of which, you said you had a friend like me. Could you introduce us?"

"I don't feel comfortable revealing her identity to you without getting her permission first. But I'm certain she'll want to talk to you once I explain your circumstances."

"Great! How do *you* feel about it? Could you still like me?"

Ah, he's pinned me down with the big question. I'm not sure if I can sleep with a female body no matter who's inside. Yet undeniably, I'm still attracted to Kaine. I just don't know what to do with that feeling. What if it doesn't survive our first encounter in bed? I don't want to hurt him like that. I sneak a glance at his impressive muscles. On the odd occasions I "notice" the female statues around the council building, it's because the pre-A.G. era sculptors liked their women well built. I can work with this.

"I definitely like you. But I've been through too many mental somersaults tonight to make any decisions. There are political risks in a relationship that will affect me but not you. You know, because of sexism. As for your body . . . I'd be willing to try. It's just I'm afraid I'll hurt you if I discover I can't after all."

"I'm not easily hurt. I'm willing to take the chance." He leans forward. "I visited several modifiers, until Durrian made me stop because I got sick. My beard is real and my chest is pretty small."

The blanket term "modifiers" covers all gifted who can transform objects. The very lucky can turn iron into gold. Most can only warp the shape of the same material. But they all have one thing in common: Modifiers kill any living thing they work on. He must have an iron constitution. That or he was desperate. I say, "There's a better way." Then I hesitate, wanting to tell him about my acquaintance's gift but afraid it will come out like I'm only willing to be with him if he has a full-body transformation. It has to be his choice, not mine. "Talk to Suzette. She'll be able to give you a much better idea of your options."

He stares at me. It takes me a moment to realize I gave Suzette away. "Fuck. Can I beg you to pretend you didn't hear that?"

"Of course," Kaine says, amused. He raises a finger. "I just want to point out it's really easy to accidentally blurt out a name."

Is he reverse-teasing me about his dark lord slip when we first met? The smug bastard! The biggest shit-eating grin spreads across his face. I'm not going to laugh. I refuse to. A tiny snort escapes my lips, and he smirks in triumph. Surrendering, I laugh until I'm rocking back and forth like a loon.

Upon hearing a knock, I open the door to let in soldiers carrying my trunks. The last two bring Evilrina's tank. Being moved around has my poor baby upset and hissing. "It's okay. She's harmless," I tell them, but they turn and more or less run away. What big babies. I pet Evilrina until she's soothed.

"What a lovely snake," Kaine says.

The cheesy grin of a proud pet owner spreads across my face. "Thank you."

"It would make a great pair of boots."

"You stay away from my Evilrina." I point my knife at him, not entirely in jest.

He raises his hands. "Sorry. I'm more used to thinking of snakes as food than pets." When I yawn, he adds, "I'll let you get to sleep."

"If you want, you can hug me." I hold out my arms. He looks surprised. "I was serious about forgiving you. It's okay."

Kaine wraps me in his arms. I relax into his support. I'm tempted to kiss him, but I'm not quite ready, so I peck him on the cheek. We're already moving fast. But I've only got four months to live, I don't have time for a slow courtship.

With my exhaustion, it should be easy to fall asleep. Instead, I toss and turn on an unfamiliar bed. I blame all the creepy stuffed animal eyes staring at me. As I'm wont to do when having trouble sleeping, I start talking to God.

My lips barely moving, I ask, "Am I making a terrible mistake considering breaking my oath? I'm afraid of what Jiang might do."

"I know You only help people who help themselves. I'm just saying, I had a plan, and in that plan, everyone except me was going to be safe."

"Does it count as suicide if I let Jiang sacrifice me? It does? Well, I always took issue with suicide being a sin in the first place. I wouldn't be hurting anyone except myself."

"You can stop listing the people I'd be hurting. I get it."

"So what if I talked big about wanting a husband and kids? That doesn't mean I can actually have those things. I can? Do You mean it?"

"Fine, I promise I'll try to live. Heh. It feels good to say that out loud. I never wanted to die."

"Thanks. It's scary but I know You're there for me. What do You think about Kaine? Do the Dark Lord and the Holy Maiden have a shot in this crazy world?"

"You don't need to sound quite so enthusiastic on the subject. Why are You so eager to pawn off Your cute ex-wife on a strange man?"

"You're wrong. My type is shy, intelligent guys who I can easily manhandle. Not barbarian hulks with meat for brains."

"I don't know what You're talking about. Love him? Pshaw. I'm not going to continue discussing this with You. I need to get my beauty sleep for a busy day tomorrow."

I awake to sunlight slipping in through a crack in the curtains. Clanging of metal pots comes from the army outside. Something scratches against my door, a weak knock. "Who's there?" I call.

"I didn't want to wake you," Kaine's voice replies. "Do you have a moment?"

"I just got up. Don't come in!" I pull my covers up to my chin.

"I'll return later. I should have told you last night, it just slipped my mind in all the excitement. There was another pressing reason I had to get you out of the city quickly."

This doesn't sound good. "Tell me now."

"I'm dreadfully sorry. I need to invade after all. Do you have a least favorite city wall I can knock down?"

Goddammit, Kaine! See what I have to put up with, God?

CHAPTER TWELVE

I can't believe this meathead is trying to sack my city again. He has the memory of a guppy. "I told you not to touch a single block of granite on those walls." I shoot out of bed. "Don't you dare go anywhere!" After throwing a coat over my nightgown, I drag Kaine into my room and toss him into an armchair. He lets me manhandle him, which is admittedly arousing. Except now really isn't the time for that.

Crossing my arms, I pace in front of him. "How have my poor innocent city walls offended you this time?"

He has the nerve to look cheerful. At this hour, no less. Ugh, he's one of those dreadful morning people. Bouncing in his seat, he says, "I found my brother! Well, I almost found him. I will find him very shortly."

"That's great news, Kaine. I'm happy for you." I plant my hands on my hips. "What does this have to do with my lovely city *not* being lit on fire?"

"One of my abilities can detect if people are blood-related to me. I acquired it hoping to use it to track my brother, but unfortunately it only works by touching someone, so it proved useless. Until now. I combined it with two other mostly worthless abilities that let me filter the air I breathe and draw air to me from a distance. A day ago, I picked up on a trace of Alesh's breath. Unfortunately, I don't know anything specific. But I think he's inside the Holy City."

"I'm still not understanding. Why aren't you putting up wanted posters instead of conquering Arahasnor?"

Kaine crosses his arms. His lip sets at a stubborn angle. "That's too slow. Once I take over the city, I'll be able to line everyone up so I can look at their faces."

He's an idiot. I want to cry. My hands shake from the effort of keeping my voice calm. "Are you even sure your brother is in the Holy City? I don't pretend to be an expert, but air can travel a long way."

"I'm sure enough to invade." He has the nerve to say it with a grin. As if I don't know how little it takes to put him in invasion mode. "Are you saying I should secure the surrounding countryside too?"

"No! I'm saying that you're jeopardizing your country's one chance at legitimacy and the World Games."

"I don't care." He shrugs. "I raised an army and took over Conollia to find my brother. That's all I ever wanted, not this mysterious political garbage."

"You signed a treaty."

"Durrian put my signature on it, as he always does, since I can't write. I agreed not to touch theirs if they didn't go after mine, but they have my brother. Besides, real promises are made face-to-face."

Rubbing my forehead, I attempt to reason with rocks-for-brains on a level he can understand. "A battle is a terrible time to try to find someone. Chaos and fire everywhere. What if your brother accidentally gets killed during your siege? My spy network can find him without the risk." It would be my pleasure to help. I truly feel for Kaine and his brother. I know what it's like to be separated from family. Besides, I want to shake the hand of the genius who kept chicken brains alive through childhood and even beat something resembling morals into the rock between his ears.

"That's a wonderful idea, Ysabel. Thank you," Kaine says.

I smile back, thinking the problem solved.

"But once I start murdering everyone who's ever harmed Alesh, I think it will start a war anyway."

Rocks can't be reasoned with! Hyperventilating, I demand, "Wait, Kaine, what about my petunias? You liked my petunias!"

"They're lovely, but not quite enough to forestall the vengeance that drove me to become a dark lord. Sorry."

"Have you considered Alesh's feelings? Maybe he wouldn't want you to harm the city where he lives. Maybe he likes my petunias more than *you* do."

"I told you, your flowers are great."

"Oh, really? What color were they?"

"Err . . ." Kaine stares at his feet.

"You don't even remember!"

"I do remember. Uh . . . pink?" He's not meeting my eyes. *Fucking men.*

There's a kind of innocence to Kaine, except pure isn't the same as good. He has the type of purity that starts holy wars. Exterminate evil, wash everything clean, and leave no survivors. I have to stop him. "What about the Conollian refugees? They'll be used as hostages again."

"They don't like me, and one even poisoned me for Jiang, so I don't care."

"A lot of the refugees trusted Dark Lord Yarthor and were burned because of it. Please, give them another chance. I'll speak to them on your behalf."

Kaine lifts his hand limply, palm up in an *Eh?* gesture. "I'll try to protect them, and any other slaves in the city."

"Slavery is outlawed in Arahasnor. You don't know if Alesh remains a slave."

"What, like that stops it from happening?" Kaine raises an eyebrow.

He has me there. The Holy City has an underground human trafficking network I've had little luck uprooting. Too many of the customers are nobles and churchmen. "My point is that you *don't know*. Please give me a chance to pursue legal options before you start turning skulls into drinking mugs."

"I'll think about it." Kaine looks sideways, about as convincing as if he promised to run away from his dark lordship to join the opera.

Time to think like a sword-brain. He believes in debts and fair trade. I steeple my fingers. "You still owe me for the kidnapping."

Kaine's head shoots up. Now I have his full attention. "Do you want me to promise the security of your city in exchange?" He doesn't look happy about it.

"I want you to promise that from now on, you'll listen to me before you rush off and cause chaos. Not just in this situation, but every situation."

"That's the least I owe you, when you could simply demand I do it your way," Kaine admits.

"This is a partnership, not a dictatorship. I won't always be right. But in this case, I believe my plan is better. If you bring an army to find your brother, then you won't be able to hide from the world that you have a brother. You'll have to give your soldiers a description if you don't want them to accidentally kill him, and from there it will leak to your enemies. Alesh could be taken hostage."

"Hmm, true." Kaine gnaws on his lip.

"Remember, you don't even know if anyone in my city has harmed your brother. At least investigate before you break the treaty. Alesh might not want you to uproot Conollia's future for his sake. Remember what happened when you came riding to my rescue without asking me first?"

Kaine flinches. I press my advantage. "We can do this without dragging your followers, the people counting on you, into a war. I promise to find your brother. Then you can ask him what he wants." I dearly hope Alesh is a gentle soul with the forgiveness of an angel, because Kaine is right to be afraid. Any disreputable brothel would pay a fortune to get their hands on one of the legendarily beautiful elves.

Kaine regards me for a long moment. "I'll give you a week. That's about how long I reckon it would take me to conquer the city and find him on my own."

"Only a week?"

"I'm making a big concession." Kaine's eyes burn like dark coals. "I've been looking for Alesh for twelve years. I won't be denied now, not when I'm so close."

"Deal." I hold out my hand, and we shake.

Kaine grins, the white scar on his lip curving upward. "You know, for such a heavy debt, you could have gotten much more out of me than a temporary ceasefire for one measly city."

I sniff. "I was going to let you off with my punch last night before you threatened to sack my city like an uncivilized brute."

"I could have conquered a new one for you if your current one got burned down."

"I'm attached to the one I've got. Go, I need to get dressed." I chase him out of the room.

Now, in addition to taking on Jiang and the Council of Cardinals, I have a week to find Kaine's brother before he goes barbarian on my city. The work of a Holy Maiden is never done. Is this why I feel like God is calling me toward Kaine? So I can do something about him before he attacks the Holy City? *Unfair! Sexist! The Lord of Light is selling out my body! I demand a new mission! Are You listening to me? Sun God, come out of hiding, I swear I'm not angry, I just want to talk!*

* * *

Luckily, Kaine waits in the hallway and escorts me to breakfast, because his castle is a giant maze. The corridors all look the same, with granite brick walls and exposed wooden rafters in the ceiling. He hasn't even bothered to lay down carpet. I suppose he has bigger concerns and no money to spare. My fingers twitch with the urge to decorate. I completely understand the need for ballista around every corner, but they'd look much nicer hidden under a tablecloth. The occasional windows are thin and tiny. As someone from a country with no military, it takes me a moment to realize that these are arrow slits, not windows. I wonder if I could add flower boxes on either side. Sure, the edges are stained with soot from previous attacks, but danger has never stopped me from putting flowers everywhere.

Oak doors lead to a huge, noisy mess hall. This room has the first splash of color: The rafters are painted green and the walls silver. The green spiral carpet is sadly stained from food fallen off a dozen long cedar tables. The copper chandelier overhead is shaped like an octopus, with the candles pointing downward and sideways. Since I don't see any dripping wax, I'm reasonably certain it's a relic. I must admit it looks menacing and dark lord–ish. Kaine and I join the line of soldiers waiting for the buffet. His presence must be normal, judging from their lack of surprise. It's me they stare at. A soldier smiles and waves. He mouths his name—Nix. The soldier from yesterday. When I wave back, his friends cheer and slap him on the back. It calms my racing pulse. I'm popular in Conollia because I'm half-Conollian and because of the aid I've given to the refugees, but every so often I run across someone who refuses to believe the truth about Yarthor . . . or who doesn't care. Hopefully the latter would be unlikely among Kaine's people.

Ua'la'sur and Nakimé sit at a table, speaking with Durrian and an unfamiliar woman. She has bronze skin, an oval face, a stubby neck, and a thin ponytail running from her mostly shaved head. She wears the dark lord's gray uniform with a black claw emblazoned on the back.

Kaine sets down a plate piled high with biscuits and sausages and teetering precariously. "Ysabel, you've met Durrian. This is Ho Tan, my third-in-command. She's mute."

"No, I'm not. Fuck you, Kaine," Ho Tan says, then goes back to wolfing down a massive steak.

Kaine tells Durrian, "We're not attacking the Holy City after all. You can lower the alert."

"Oh, thank the nature spirits," Durrian mutters. "How did you talk sense into him, Ysabel?"

"Feminine wiles." I wink.

Nakimé leans across the table. "I've scheduled a practice spar with Ho Tan this afternoon. It will be nice to have some real competition."

"I'd like a one-on-one match with Alzira," Kaine says. "Where is she?"

"Behind you," Alzira replies.

Kaine whirls around, hand groping for a weapon. "How long have you been there?"

Alzira stares unblinkingly like a snake at a mouse. "I'm not ready to leave you alone with my princess yet. You hurt her. Still, she does seem attached to you, so I'll protect you too as long as you're accompanying her."

"Um, thanks," Kaine says, the heaving of his shoulders calming.

Alzira arches an eyebrow. "I await your challenge for the title of Humanity's Strongest Monster anytime."

To my relief, Durrian says, "Neither of you are dueling until the World Games. You might kill each other or destroy a few continents in your enthusiasm."

"Agreed." I fix Alzira with a commanding glare.

"I'm out today too," Ua'la'sur says. "Sorry—I need to attend court with Ysabel to apologize to the dwarven ambassador's assistant."

"I'm very proud of you," I tell her.

"For what?" Ho Tan asks.

Once Ua'la'sur would have avoided the topic of her past, but now she answers, "I had the royal guards throw him into a fish pond. There were a few piranhas."

Ho Tan recoils. "You're *Queen* Ua'la'sur? The exiled monarch of the dwarves? The Queen of Nightmares?"

"Don't believe everything you hear about me," Ua'la'sur says. "My brief reign was disastrous but bloodless. I inherited the throne at thirteen and didn't know what I was doing."

Nakimé snorts. "Putting a spoiled preteen on a throne is a foolish mode of government." Nakimé is a dedicated proponent of democracy. She's been eagerly watching the dwarves experiment with a parliament and a prime minister.

Ua'la'sur continues, "Ysabel helped me realize that in order to put my past behind me, I have to make amends."

Nakimé's eyes become distant with memory. "Reminds me of how Ysabel and I went around returning a few things I regretted stealing. She even got beaten up alongside me." Her gaze hardens. "That's why I'd be *furious* if anything were to happen to her."

"Me too," Ua'la'sur purrs. "You'd never see either of us coming." They nod at each other, then fix Kaine with identical vicious looks as he chews obliviously.

Oh, sweet Sun God, this is my friends' "if you ever hurt her" speech. I want to die.

Ho Tan slams her hands down on the table. "I'll have you know that before Kaine brought order to my hometown, people were eating their own dead. He's kind, sincere, and doesn't have a setting in between 'stranger' and 'someone I'd die for.' If a stuck-up noble lady ever took advantage of him, I'd ensure she regrets it."

"How dare you?" Nakimé hisses. "You know nothing about her."

Wishing people would stop talking about me like I'm not here, I squirm in my seat. "This is getting awkward," I whisper to Kaine. "Want to make our escape?"

"Sure," he says, tossing the last of his breakfast down his throat, then licking his plate for good measure.

I track down Suzette, who's settling the maids into their new rooms. That lady deserves a vacation. Suzette has two boyfriends and a girlfriend (all of whom know about each other), and she hasn't seen any of them in weeks. Once the World Games are over, I'm giving her a bonus.

After I explain about Kaine, her eyes widen. "I'd love to talk to Kaine. Even before that interesting revelation, I needed to give him this." She holds up a thick stack of papers bound by a leather cord. "Here's all the dirt I've collected on Cardinal Jiang over the last decade. I have enough to topple his position as head of the council and perhaps even see him excommunicated." Her eyes could burn a hole in the papers. "We've never been able to use it because you can't openly defy him. But now we can use Kaine to take Jiang down."

I chuckle. "That's the plan. Make sure General Durrian gets a copy, too."

"Someday I'd like a copy in every newspaper around the city," Suzette mutters as she follows me. I know how she feels. For the first time, we have hope of making that happen.

I introduce Suzette to Kaine, then leave them alone to talk.

In my new office, I file away documents while planning my story for the royal court. Or maybe I'm just stalling. I might as well get it over with.

I catch Kaine as he's leaving Suzette's office. Since Suzette isn't glaring at me, Kaine didn't give me away. A successful lie; I'm almost proud. I wave him into my office. We'd better have this conversation in private—if a dark lord doesn't have spies among his staff, then I'm a virgin. "How did it go?" I ask as soon as the door is closed.

"Suzette, well, it went great. She told me about how her friend Bei Ren gave her a completely new body." He's vibrating with joy and disbelief of what might be too good to be true. "I've never heard of a form of modification for humans."

"No one had ever heard of your ability before you came along. Suzette said it was instantaneous and painless."

He bites his lip. "It's a lot to take in."

"Is it something you want to do?" I ask, then hastily add, "You can take as long as you need to decide."

"No! I want it." He vibrates with eagerness, bouncing on his toes. "Suzette already promised to locate Bei Ren for me. She'll set her spies to finding Alesh, too."

"Did you give her a description?"

"Yes, and she made you a copy." He hands me a paper. "I'm sorry, I couldn't answer most of her questions. I haven't seen him since I was fifteen, and I can only draw stick figures."

"I'll find him, I promise." I skim it. Unfortunately, if Alesh is currently held in illegal slavery, then his captors will have him hidden away. If he's escaped, then he'll be lying low. This task won't be easy either way. "What's your brother like?"

"Alesh is kind to everyone. He always made sure I ate first when we didn't have enough food, and he couldn't say no to anyone who asked him for help. Like you."

I snort. "You have an idealized image of me."

"You might have a few more prickles than Alesh, but you're just as bad at looking out for yourself." He shakes his head. "Alesh is a dedicated Dharist. He danced for the spirits every night and wouldn't eat meat. I'm lapsed in that area, but I count myself lucky to have been raised in the faith. Elves have a concept of a soul being reincarnated into a body of a different gender, so Alesh accepted me immediately when I told him I was a boy."

"Lucky indeed," I murmur. Suzette once showed me the scar on her shoulder left from her experience coming out to her father.

Kaine casts me a sidelong glance. "Can I say thank you? It's great to be around someone who doesn't doubt me."

"Again, you should thank Suzette for that." I wince. "I was not understanding at all with her."

"Now she describes you as her biggest supporter. She says you're the one who convinced the rest of the Dragon Maidens to accept her."

Twisting my fingers around each jewel on my bracelet, I sigh. "I couldn't understand why anyone would want to be a woman. In my life, it's meant nothing but working twice as hard to get half the respect. So when Suzette described herself as a woman trapped in the body of a man, my reaction was, 'Want to trade places? If I woke up in the body of a man, I'd throw a parade.'"

Kaine nods. "It's easier not to be a second-class citizen. I'd know. Still, wanting male power is different from wanting to be a man."

"The thing is, I really did want to be a man when I was younger. I had some issues with hating my own body. My dysmorphia faded as I came to like myself more. At first, I thought everyone should 'grow out of it' because I did. I finally understood when I asked Suzette why she'd go to so much trouble to deceive us, and she said, 'It's when I'm a woman that I'm not deceiving anyone.' That I could get. It wasn't Suzette choosing to give up all the advantages of manhood, just that she had never had the option of being a man."

"You had a completely different experience with dysmorphia? Whoa, that is interesting." Kaine leans forward. "One of the most surprising things about talking to Suzette was how different we were. I told my brother I was a boy from almost the moment I could talk, and her realization didn't hit until puberty. I've hated my body to the point of harming myself trying to modify it, and she says she honestly wanted to be able to live like a woman more than having the body of one."

"Have you made up your mind, then?"

"I want a full transformation. Suzette said I shouldn't feel less like a man if I didn't, but I'm certain. I've been certain for years."

"Then I'll take you as soon as I can find Bei Ren. She's in hiding to avoid being relentlessly used by nobility." I rise. "I wish I could talk more, but I've procrastinated long enough."

"Where are you going?"

"To primp for my visit to the royal court. I have to explain to everyone that you're not a horrible dark lord who carries off maidens after all." I arch an eyebrow at him.

"One more thing first." Kaine takes a deep breath. "I want to give you a regeneration ability. It might at least partly restore your lifespan."

My legs go out from under me, and I sit back down. "You can do that?" I ask dumbly.

"I can transfer the abilities I steal to other people. I have several different regeneration abilities. They can heal even serious injuries and protect against nonmagical disease and poison. Unfortunately, magical poisons work on me—that's how Jiang knocked me out with Nightwish. Since your price is magical in nature, I have no idea if it will help you. I'm hoping that even if your price steals your life, the damage left behind is nonmagical." Kaine's nostrils flare. "If this doesn't work, I'll find another power. I won't give up."

"I, uh, I guess it's worth a try." Odd that I can't muster any more enthusiasm. Why do I have a cold pit in my stomach? Have I given up so thoroughly that hope frightens me? I stuff away that thought down the dark hole where I put everything I drink away and paste a big Holy Maiden smile on my face. "My thanks to you and the Sun God."

He tilts his head sideways. "We could do it later."

Of course he recognized my fakeness. I made him worry about me. We have to do this now. There will be people waiting for me at my clinic to be healed . . . and each one could be the last. "No, no, I'm just . . . nervous."

"Completely understandable." His tense face relaxes. "Let's step into your room. Sometimes people pass out during the process. It's not painful, just tiring. Not everyone can receive every ability, or I'd create my own army of unstoppable Gifted Knights." He sighs at the lost opportunity.

We rise and head out the door. "Next time you have a spare regeneration power, would you consider giving it to Alzira? She gets injured like she thinks it's heroic."

"Is it okay to say that when she's following us?" Kaine looks over his shoulder.

"You've started to notice," Alzira says. "Your observational abilities might become halfway decent with training."

"When she's in bodyguard mode, she expects you to pretend she isn't there." I wink. "Don't let her or any of my Dragon Maidens give you a hard time. They think they're being funny."

His dimples flash at me. "They care about you. I'm glad you have people like that. And my friends like you already too."

"Uh, yes." I think Kaine's people care about him very much and would try to like anyone for his sake.

Once we arrive at my room, I sit down on my bed. "How will you tell if it works?"

"I have another ability that lets me detect natural lifespans."

A Gifted Knight with a similar ability told Jiang how long he'd have to wait for my gift to fully develop before he could sacrifice me. "Can you tell how much longer I have left right now?" My heart clenches. Most of me doesn't want to know. The leader in me has to. My tongue sticks to the roof of my mouth. In the past, I've tried to avoid thinking about my death-by-healing by instead counting down to my death-by-sacrifice.

His gaze is sad. "Five years, two months, and eight days. I'm going to save you." So he's known this since the moment we first met. I don't know how to feel about that.

Those five years will burn by in less than one if I keep healing every day. At least I'll last until after the World Games in four months. "What do I have to do?"

Kaine kneels down in front of me. I try not to drool at how cute he looks doing that.

He offers me his hand. "If you start to feel sick, let me know and I'll stop. That means your gift and the new one are incompatible."

I reach for his hand, then stop. "Wait. I know you bear the prices of your stolen gifts every time you use them, but do you have an additional price for taking powers or giving them away?" The more powerful the gift, the higher the price. What if I'm hurting Kaine in exchange for an attempt to save me that doesn't even seem likely to work? Belatedly, I remember it's dreadfully rude to ask the price of other people's gifts. Especially for someone as powerful as Kaine, it means revealing a weakness. "I'm sorry. You don't need to answer that."

"I don't pay any price to give away powers." Kaine sounds casual. "My price is that whenever I try to steal someone's gift, I must overcome their will in order to claim their power as my own. If their willpower is stronger than mine, they can steal my gift instead."

Wait, WHAT? Did he really just tell me such an insanely important state secret? I gasp. "Kaine, you can't tell anyone else!"

"I know. If people know about my price, they're more likely to fight back. I can grab most gifts easily because no one even tries to resist. Only Durrian knows the price of my gift, and he instructed me to never tell." Kaine tosses off a cocky wink. "But I know I can trust you."

My heart flutters. Damn, that man has no right to be so charming. "Shouldn't you be more careful about stealing gifts? You already have plenty. But if you try to take the gift of the wrong person, you might lose everything. Why not just stop?"

"I can't do something so cowardly." Kaine scowls. "My gift wants to be used. It's the power of a conqueror. I've won every single battle of wills because I'm the person most suited to possess it. If I were to betray my gift by never using it, then it would abandon me."

"You make it sound like it has a will of its own."

"It does. It calls itself Plunder. Sometimes it whispers to me, telling me who has the best magic to steal. It's always hungry."

I open my mouth to explain that gifts aren't intelligent, then close my mouth. Kaine knows how his own power works better than me. Perhaps that's even part of his price, to carry a gift that craves to be used. "Have you ever come close to losing?" I ask.

"No one has ever been able to overcome my will, because I'm fighting for my brother's sake, so I'll never give up." Kaine smiles with total confidence. "But a handful of people have been strong-willed enough to prevent me from stealing their gift, including your older brother."

I blink. "Calum? Really?"

"I told you before about how I tried to steal his power. I wanted a new disguise ability because I thought it would make me more comfortable in my body. But I didn't tell you that I failed. I was careless—I never expected the head cardinal's flunky to be so strong-willed. He might have even stolen my gift if he'd known it was possible. I barely let go of him in time." Kaine locks eyes with me. "Calum could match my willpower because he was also fighting to save someone he loved, just like me. That's how I knew he was telling the truth when he said he had a sister to rescue, so I let him go free."

I shake my head. "I'm surprised you didn't kill him to eliminate the threat of him ever taking your gift. Though I'm glad you didn't, of course." *Very, very glad.*

"I wouldn't be such a sore loser." Kaine wrinkles his nose in distaste. "I respect other people who also want to protect their families."

Knowing how hard Calum fought for me, I feel ashamed of wanting to give up on myself. "I'll take the regeneration power. It's what Calum would want me to do." I press my palm to his, resisting the urge to squirm.

Heat pulses from Kaine's palm and trickles up my arm. It tingles, not painfully but a little ticklish. When the ghostly feathers reach my brain, I gasp. The sensation is everywhere, maddening. I scratch my scalp, unable to reach an itch inside my skull. I fall backward.

My head thumps against the mattress. The crick in my neck is gone. So's the ache in my wrist from too much paperwork.

"Ysabel?" Kaine bends over me, face concerned.

"I'm fine." I sit up. "No, I'm great." It feels like a massage and a long nap rolled into one. "Regeneration must be a good match for healing."

"It took perfectly. Almost no power lost in the transfer." Kaine looks me up and down, eyes focused on something I can't see. "The brightness is already eating into the dark part of your lifespan." He glances away. "By tomorrow I'll have a better idea if it's enough."

Enough to save me? Not likely. The longer I have, the more people will demand.

A little voice whispers, *You could stop healing.*

My breath catches and sweat trickles down the back of my neck. Animal panic lurks just below the surface. I tap my cheek.

Kaine places a hand on my shoulder, his gaze understanding.

I swallow. "I-I'm grateful. I really am."

"Hope can be scary."

"It's not as if I have a choice about healing." I speak more to myself than him.

"Of course you do. No one can compel you as long as you're in my castle. You can make me into the bad guy. Tell everyone that I'm forcing you to stop healing people, or even that I'm holding you prisoner. I don't care what strangers think about me."

I look at my hands. "I'm not going to shaft the responsibility off on you. But thanks."

"You've done enough. You could live your life for yourself now. Be happy. Think about it." Kaine's husky voice tempts like the Moon Devil's whispers.

I have no intention of even considering it. It would be too selfish. Still, that little whisper follows me long after he's left.

Stop healing . . .

Have a chance to live.

CHAPTER THIRTEEN

My battle armor is a bluish-silver silk dress flowing to the floor. A sheer lace shawl covers the pearl-encrusted sleeves and bodice. Ua'la'sur meets me in the hallway, wearing a shimmering black dress and high heels. "Isn't Alzira coming with us?" she asks.

"I don't dare take her along today. People will call me slurs, then she'll explode their hearts inside their chests. It would be a political disaster, to say nothing of trying to get the bloodstains out of my silk dress."

"I hate to break it to you, but she's following us." Ua'la'sur jerks her head at a bend in the hallway which appears empty.

"I know. And she knows that I know. But as long as I'm pretending not to know that she knows that I know, she won't kill anyone." I chuckle. "Though she might beat them up in a dark alley with a bag over their heads later."

"Whatever works for the two of you." Ua'la'sur mutters, barely loud enough for me to hear, "Just get married already. It would be far less politically messy than the depths-damned dark lord."

As we pass Nakimé in the hallway, Ua'la'sur calls, "I caught you sneaking into my room trying to steal my priceless bow for your practice match. Tough luck, I'm bringing it along so you can't get your sticky-fingered hands on it." She pats the bag over her shoulder. I'd been wondering why she brought such an oversized purse.

Nakimé rolls her eyes. "As if you have any reason to complain after the stunt you pulled with my bedsheets."

"You can't prove that was me."

"Hiding behind legal technicalities, are you, tyrant?"

"Innocent until proven guilty isn't a technicality, thief." Ua'la'sur sniffs. "I'll forgive you if you teach Ho Tan a lesson."

"I don't need you to tell me that. I'll uphold the Dragon Maidens' honor while you're gone." Winking, the redhead saunters off.

I hiss to Ua'la'sur, "Maybe you're the one with wedding bells in your future. Ding-ding-dong."

Face red, she whispers back, "Shut up."

At the fortress gate, Durrian presents me with a carriage decked out in silver and gold. "To make a good impression."

"Thank you." Finally, I'm dealing with someone who understands the importance of appearance in politics. He hands me a scroll. "What's this?"

"A blank document with Lord Kaine's seal."

"It's *what*?"

He laughs at the expression on my face. "Kaine thought you might need it."

With this, I could sell Kaine's kingdom for an aracoin. "This is too much." I try to hand it back.

Durrian raises his palm to block. "Kaine is a very trusting person by nature. Once you're his friend, he'd rip out his own heart and hand you the bleeding organ if you ask. It hasn't killed him yet because he's ridiculously powerful—and because *I* watch his back. If you betray him, we simply won't honor the deal." His tone holds neither threat nor insult. "Keep the seal. You're walking into a nest of blight, and from what the bonehead told me, it's his fault."

I can't argue with that bleak assessment. "Thank you," I say, with extra emphasis. Kaine's trust, foolish though it may be, makes me feel better. It proves he didn't expect me to unconditionally trust him before out of presumptuousness so much as because that's how his brain works.

"A gift in return." I hand Durrian a letter. "I wrote an introduction for Kaine to Urew, leader of the Conollian refugees. If I vouch for his trustworthiness, they'll hear him out." I also included reassurances to my uncle of my safety, since he'll be flipping out about the kidnapping.

"This time I'm sending him with a battalion and his own food." Durrian tucks the letter away. "But thank you, Ysabel."

Traveling in Kaine's carriage lets me slip into the Holy City incognito. At the palace, I inform a guard, "By the will of the Sun God, Holy Maiden Ysabel has been called to attend Queen Bianna's salon."

"You're . . . I thought . . ." The guard gapes. Dammit, the rumors of my supposed abduction have spread outside the court already. My political enemies are probably working to convince the public that the poor, despoiled Holy Maiden needs to be packed off to a nunnery. I brush past, determined to reach the salon before the guards have time to warn anyone.

"It will be fun to see the looks on their faces after they sold you out," Ua'la'sur says, shadows puffing up her dress like a cloud as they whisper dark things. She's clearly in a temper.

"Let the radiance of the Sun God illuminate their shameful behavior," I bluff. My stomach clenches. Without my supposed saintliness, I'm just a jumped-up peasant.

After Yarthor, people told me it was my own fault for writing to a strange man. They brought up how I hit puberty early and looked pretty developed by fourteen, as if that made me less of a child. Worst of all were the bards who called it true love. Apparently since he'd fallen for me after I saved his life, it was cruel of me to refuse him. Please—if everyone I healed took it as a proposal of marriage, I'd need a palace to contain my harem. I suspect Yarthor's attempted rape did more damage to *my* reputation than his.

This time, I have the political savvy to take control of the narrative. I've got one shot at this. My attempt to regain power hangs by a spider's thread.

Teeth bared, I fling open the jeweled door and step inside.

A pair of ladies in green dresses are the first to notice me. They exchange sisterly glances, then shoot in opposite directions to spread the gossip. In minutes the room is silent and staring. Even the servants carrying trays have stopped moving.

A woman—Queen Bianna, based on her crown—sails forward. "Darling Ysabel! We were all so worried about you."

I sidestep her kiss. "Not worried enough to do anything when your husband sold me out to a dark lord."

She freezes, mouth open. "D-did the Sun God strike the dark lord dead?"

"No." After my conversation with Donya, I've decided to stop taking the easy route. The truth I flung at the court last night needed to be said. "The Sun God didn't impose divine judgment on Dark Lord Yarthor either. He's dead because a guard knocked him into my knife. But I wouldn't be worth any less if he'd raped me." An ant's footstep could be heard in the room. My best Holy Maiden smile gleaming, I continue, "Happily, this time I was not driven to violence, as the light of the Sun God shone down on the misunderstanding between myself and dear Kaine."

"'Dear' Kaine?" Bianna asks faintly.

"It's a dreadfully exciting story. I had no idea the man I saved from dying in the gutter was the Dark Lord Kaine." My new plan is to tell the truth, or at least mostly. It would be awkward to admit I saved Kaine knowing who he was. "When he returned to the Holy City, he summoned me in order to offer any boon I desire. Though I attempted to reject his great gift, he pressed this upon me." I wave the blank document with Kaine's seal. Every eye tracks it. *That's right, I'm the one with the power to cut deals with the presumptive winner of the World Games. Better get started on the flattery, bitches.*

Queen Bianna's eyes turn cold. "Yet another dark lord has fallen in love with you? You're quite the seductress for a woman married to God."

My laugh is hollow. "Love blooms slowly like a flowering cactus. This is a business arrangement. I found Kaine an honest soul, unaccustomed to politics. Quoting the wisdom of the Sun God, I've guided him away from violence against the Holy City."

Whispers circle around the room. Bianna crosses her arms. "If you expect me to believe you enthralled a murderous warlord without using your body, then prove you're still blessed by the Sun God. Heal me." She gestures at the rash of powdered pimples on her nose.

I grit my teeth. How much life have I already lost to her menopausal acne? Now I'm no longer clinging to the lie of purity, I don't have to die for her vanity. "My blessing from the Sun God remains, but that proves nothing since gifts have no connection to virginity."

"You can't heal me?" The triumph on Bianna's face is quickly replaced by horror. Without my regular healings, her arthritis would make it hard for her to even walk.

"I'll be attending to my holy duties at my clinic, but I'm afraid my days of healing nonfatal injuries are over. Kaine, sweetheart that he is, felt distressed at the prospect of me losing my life. He can barely accept me healing mortal wounds."

"Then you have sold yourself to him." Anger strips all trace of subtlety from the queen's voice.

I clasp a hand to my bosom. "Such vile lies shame the Sun God, like your lie that Kaine demanded my body in the first place. That was a cheap attempt to damage his good name." I'm going to pin the whole abduction misunderstanding on the royal family because I don't want Kaine to have an undeserved reputation as a rapist. Hey, it's hard to quit lying cold turkey. "My relationship with the man who has an army outside your city is both friendly and influential." I tap her cheek with Kaine's seal.

Then I beat a retreat, leaving her stuttering. Ua'la'sur whispers in my ear, "That was an epic face-slap."

"I've wanted to do that since I was fifteen and she told everyone my jewelry was fake," I whisper back.

Ua'la'sur jerks her head at the wine table. "I need some mental fortification before I apologize to the ambassador's assistant."

"Do you want me to go with you?"

"You have enough to deal with right now. Good luck." Ua'la'sur pats me on the arm.

She's quickly blocked from view by the ladies mobbing me. In such a crowd, it's particularly hard to guess identities. My chest tightens.

"Tell us all about Dark Lord Kaine," one says, then they erupt into questions.

"Is he handsome? The bards say Dark Lord Chingis was handsome as a fallen angel."

"Does he wear a helmet over his face because his eyes glow red?" Nervous titters don't disguise their eagerness.

I sigh. "Kaine is a much better person than the rumors about him claim. He's trying to bring peace and prosperity to his poor, blighted country."

The ladies exchange glances. One whispers, "I think she's using him."

"Mm-hmm. Clever move." An elderly woman gives me an approving nod, and I recognize her by the diamond necklace gifted by her fifth husband.

"You're so unromantic! Ysabel is clearly in love. I've never heard her say such nice things about anyone."

"True. I bet she's doing him."

"A handsome and devoted dark lord? Who could resist?"

Everyone sighs. A teenager casts me a sidelong look. "Are you well, though, Ysabel?" The crowd goes silent, hanging on my next word.

"I'm perfectly safe. Kaine is the type of man who would never harm a woman or disregard her wishes. Please spread that far and wide." I don't want the nobility to look down on Kaine. I'm the only one who can call him a barbarian.

An *oooh* runs through the group. "She does like him."

"Except the Sun God will curse anyone who loves the Holy Maiden, and Kaine is already damned, unless she can redeem him."

"She'll lose her powers if she's tainted by a man."

I cough. "That's a myth. My gift has nothing to do with my private life. I've gone along with that story in the past, but I'm ending it now. We ladies need to stick together against those who would judge us as 'tainted.'"

All eyes fix on me. "So what you're saying is . . . you're in love with Dark Lord Kaine." Squeals fill the air.

This is a lost battlefield. Nothing to do but regroup on new ground. "Let's get down to business, ladies. I have permission to negotiate trade with Conollia."

The room fills with the alertness of panthers on the prowl. "My dear husband is interested in Conollia's diamonds." A lady snaps her fan open. "Only it's sooo dangerous to send caravans into the area." Aha, I have her identity from the way she draws out her *so*; we play cards together.

"Protection would be available," I say. "In exchange, please talk to your husband about lifting the trade embargo on Conollia."

"She's on his side! It's true love!" the lady hisses to her friends. Then she negotiates diamond prices with the vicious bargaining skills of a fishmonger. Next the rest of them have a go at me. When I finally lurch away, I've acquired promises of serious political capital.

A tiny, petty part of me is bothered that I need Kaine to maintain my power. Without his seal, my conversation with Queen Bianna would have gone very differently. But the smarter part of me says to use every tool in my arsenal. A rueful chuckle slips past my lips. I owe him for backing me up, and I'll repay him with the best possible trade deals.

Once outside the circle of my friendly relationships, the first hostile whispers accost me. Someone shouts, "Slut!" before ducking his head out of sight. It's nothing I didn't expect after what people said about me and Yarthor. I cried then, but I'm not fourteen anymore.

A man dressed in a black-and-white-striped doublet steps in front of me. "You're acting like a queen when you've already been dragged off your throne like a common whore."

I can't afford any sign of weakness, and I have no idea who this man is. His injured nose renders his voice nasal and unrecognizable. Fine, I'll act like I'm pretending not to know him. "Have we met? If the Sun God wills our paths to coincide, you may contact my Suzette." I brush past him.

"How dare you!" he screams after me. "You broke my nose!"

Viscount Derall? Phew, good call snubbing him. That guy is small potatoes.

Cardinal Santos enters the room wearing his formal robes: brown with a red and gold sash and a pointy hat. The golden chain around his neck displays the Sun God's symbol of a rose against the rays of the sun. He and Bianna have a mutual loathing worthy of an epic saga, so he would only come here to test me. Santos is a Seer. Eleven years ago, I had to publicly swear to him that Yarthor didn't rape me. My inner Kaine wants to toss a drink in his face then set fire to the room, but I'm a mature adult. Unfortunately.

Weariness and sadness make Cardinal Santos look a decade older. "Ysabel, I'm sorry for your suffering. The Sun God will make the royal court pay for their cruelty. You must accept your fall from grace as His will. The church will support your retreat to any nunnery you choose."

He's dropped the *Holy* from the front of my name. "I remain a Holy Healer. This is ridiculous."

"Can you repeat that for me?" Santos holds out his hand. If I touch his skin, he can tell if I'm being truthful. Any vow made while touching a Seer becomes a life-oath. It's killed more than a few Seers' lovers who blurted out promises during sex. That's their price—to never be able to turn off their power.

I place my palm on top of his. "Kaine did not assault me and never intended to." I'm only playing along so I can clear Kaine's name in a public forum. Warm light dances around our skin.

"True." Santos's brow furrows. "Then have you joined him on his dark path? It's not too late to turn back. You must let Holy Maiden Sarra, who resisted Chingis to her death, be your guide."

"Kaine isn't evil. He's entering the World Games to save his country."

"You believe what you're saying, but that doesn't make it the truth." Santos frowns. "The dark lord is a heretic, and the Conollians were struck by the blight for their sinfulness."

"That's wrong. The blight is a natural disaster." In a lower voice, I add, "Being a Holy Healer doesn't mean my destiny is to sacrifice myself." Santos justified Jiang's plan to kill me with lines from the Holy Book about how healers are an offering from the Sun God. I hold on tightly so he knows I mean what I'm about to say. "You're the one murdering me. God is just your excuse."

He jerks free. "You've been corrupted. I will pray for your sake, but I have no reason to stay in this sinful place any longer."

"Please give it some thought," I call at his retreating back. I don't think he will. I've lost Santos's support. We allied over our mutual dislike of the council's corruption, but Santos thinks the fake me is what a woman ought to be.

My eyes scan the room for other possible alliances. At the pool table, I recognize another cardinal's robes. Orwin has a scantily clad woman on each arm. It does so irritate Bianna when he brings sex workers to her salons. Orwin calls it "doing his part to publicize the disgraceful corruption of the church while making charitable donations to women in need." The ladies love to provoke the queen by acting like dumb sexpots when they're highly educated courtesans. With one nod from Orwin, they make a discreet exit. I gesture toward one of the side rooms.

Orwin takes a seat in a velvet armchair beside the fireplace. "Ysabel! You seem to have come out on top. My favorite position for a woman."

"The Sun God protects innocents and fools. I wouldn't dare speculate about which one I am." I get along with Orwin better than any other cardinal because I can come closer to revealing my real self. Orwin likes his women saucy, so I jest with him like a kitten flashing her fangs, still careful not to reveal too much.

"You're not charming me into moving against the Head Cardinal." Orwin points at me. "*You* have the privilege of tweaking the terrifying bastard because he can't kill you. I don't have the same protection. But I will enjoy the funny faces he'll make next council meeting."

"I'm not expecting you to risk your long, elegant neck." I bat my eyes. "All I want is a teeny-weeny bit of information. Would you care to make a donation to the Holy Maiden Causes Jiang to Make Funny Faces Fund?"

Snickering, he leans back in his seat. "You provide almost as much entertainment as my doves. What are you after?"

"I want the movements of guards on Jiang's payroll, particularly in relation to illegal heretic hunts. I want information on where he keeps important prisoners. Unconnected to Jiang, I'm looking for an enslaved half-elf new to this city."

"You know I don't deal in that business. I have something approaching standards. Those women are flea-bitten and weepy."

"A man, not a woman. He last went by the name Alesh. He's forty-two years old, with red hair and blue eyes. In exchange, I'll provide you with tips on trade investments. Arahasnor is about to experience an influx of diamonds."

He taps the table. "I'll see what my doves know." Orwin's brothels feed him information via pillow talk. "Here's a down payment. When Jiang's previous mistress refused to get an abortion, he had her imprisoned at Saint Lase's Shelter for Fallen Women. All of his charitable donations tend to be fronts, whether for money laundering or doctors who don't mind operating on unwilling women."

I shouldn't be surprised at the depths to which Jiang will sink, but somehow he always manages to sink even lower. This is coming from the man who fought me tooth and nail over the law I sponsored legalizing abortion. "That's very useful. Thank you." I can put Donya's spy to good use obtaining a list of charities funded by Jiang.

"For additional information, I want an exclusive trading grant for one of Conollia's spices."

"Deal."

Orwin laughs, flashing a gold tooth. "If you're agreeing so quickly, I should have asked for diamonds."

"I already promised those to someone else. But I'm a filthy liar." I shift closer. "I'll turn your trading company into the wealthiest in the city if you'll take over as head of the council."

"Dear girl, I'm not interested in challenging Jiang for the last biscuit at breakfast, much less for Head Cardinal." Orwin starts to rise.

A coward who hates responsibility—precisely who I want for a future head of the council. He won't oppose my puppet rule. "I'll handle dethroning Jiang."

"You could never push him off the council, unless . . . are you entering the World Games?" Orwin's eyes widen. "Never mind. I don't want to know. If that's your plan, we can talk after the Games." He more or less flees the room, pausing in the doorway. "For what it's worth, I hope you can break free of Jiang. Good luck, Ysabel."

I consider how much it's worth. He's never once defended me from my grisly fate and probably never will, but still. "Thank you."

That was a promising conversation, except Orwin thinks I'm entering the World Games. Is it such a big difference if I get Kaine's team to beat Jiang's instead of mine? My shoulders slump. It *is* a big difference. Only if I beat Jiang personally will it be recognized as a legitimate transfer of leadership.

I don't know how Alzira could possibly fight without exposing the weakness of her gift. Alzira can bash in heads with her sword alone, but everyone would notice if she didn't use magic. Furthermore, as long as Jiang has Calum hostage, I must pretend to be obedient. I'm shamefully relieved to have an excuse not to fight Jiang openly.

I rejoin the party. The next person I need to find is the old bastard himself.

Sparing me the trouble, a butler informs me that Cardinal Jiang waits for me in a parlor. Time to get this over with.

Cardinal Jiang leans against the wall, fiddling with a wineglass. The firelight dances off the shadows of his face. "I left your knife for a reason, Ysabel. I assumed you'd have the brains to stab Kaine. Did you decide you could obtain more advantages by bending over?"

Behind my back, I pinch myself. It helps the tears well up. "I-it's not like that." I rub my arms as if to ward off an attack. "I tried to kill him. Th-the knife bounced off him."

Jiang's smirk is about as friendly as a shark swimming toward drowning sailors. "Of course it did, you fool. You have to catch him asleep so he doesn't have time to activate his gifts." His pleasure at seeing me broken leaks through his tone. It's infuriating how he speaks to me like a teacher to a student. "Suck it up and pretend to like him, Ysabel. Then he'll drop his guard. It's nothing women haven't suffered since the beginning of time. You don't actually have any purity to protect."

I'd like to slap the smile off his face. But I must convince Jiang that I'm merely pretending to be friendly with Kaine to save face in front of the court. Then it will come as a surprise when I bury a knife in the head cardinal's back. It's embarrassingly easy to sound scared. "Please. I don't want to go back to Kaine. Just let me stay in the city, and I'll do whatever you want."

Setting down his glass, Jiang points his cane at me. "You're stuck with the dark lord until you kill him. You've earned this punishment."

"If you're ordering me to kill Kaine, then I want to see my brother."

"I don't see why I should give you a reward for something you'd do for free." Jiang raises his chin. "If you succeed, I'll let you see your brother."

"I will kill Kaine. I swear," I say, putting all my hatred for Jiang into my voice.

"Good girl," Jiang croons, backing me into the wall. He caresses one of my curls. "It would take a stronger man than that petty warlord Kaine to resist you. You can handle a little boy." *But not me*, his tone implies.

It's not the first time Jiang has acted like a stereotypical villain around a maiden. He hates me, so I assume he does it to mess with me. I'm 110 percent not into men trying to dominate me, but especially not Jiang. He cares for no one in the world except himself, and there's no bigger turnoff than a selfish lover.

Most of the time I ignore him, so he doesn't get the satisfaction of seeing me flinch. Today, he's pissing me off more than usual. I slap away his hand, and when we touch, I feel the sickness inside him. A twisted smirk warps my lips to match his expression. "If you're a big strong man who doesn't need anyone, then why do I suspect you brought me here to heal you?"

His jaw clenches. "It's what you're good for. Get on with it." He grabs my wrist. He always resorts to physical force when feeling threatened.

"Why should I, after you sold me?" I hiss. "I don't know if you've heard yet, but my new master forbade me to heal. You're out of luck."

"Never, ever refuse to heal me." Jiang twists my wrist, making me cry out in pain. He pins my hand over my head to the wall. The firelight makes red sparks dance in his eyes. Teeth pulled back, he's transformed from a civilized cardinal into a beast. "I've allowed you your charity cases, but your gift belongs to me. Cross me, and I will see your Dragon Maidens executed, the refugees massacred, and your brother will take months to die."

Kaine's seal saved me from having to heal the queen, but nothing can save me from Jiang. He has too tight a hold over me. Jiang absolutely could get away with murdering Conollian refugees. When the church first declared the blight a punishment from the Sun God, the subsequent riots killed thousands of Conollians, many of whom had been living in the Holy City for centuries. Those who remain alive are counting on me not to screw up.

Images of Calum flash across my mind, bleeding, starving, and chained. Then his image blurs into my friends and other siblings. I give in. Struggling not to cry for real, I push my power through the place where our skin touches.

This time, it's harder. The magic flows sluggishly. Something is very, very wrong with Jiang. Rot has settled into his organs, covering his liver and lungs. His heart is not even beating. How can his heart not be beating when he's still alive and walking around? I hate him touching me. It makes me feel sick. I can't separate out my revulsion at whatever is wrong with him from my hatred of him as a person. Determined to get him off, I pour out my power. A day of life leaves my skin. But Jiang isn't completely healed.

The power bubbles inside me, but I stop. Sacrificing one day was already painful enough. I refuse to let my worst enemy steal twice my usual price. I pant, too shocked to speak and barely keeping my gift from escaping my skin.

"You should have cooperated from the beginning." Jiang releases me. He pats my cheek. "You will never escape me, Ysabel." He sweeps out of the room like a king.

Alone, I stare into the glowing fireplace. Never before have I needed to use more than one day to completely heal someone. It felt like I was fighting off death itself. Is Jiang working with a necromancer or cursed by a necromancer or both? I'm only certain of one thing: This deadly disease must be why Jiang is so desperate for immortality.

He has a weakness, and I swear I'll find a way to use it against him.

I return to the party. There are a few more people I could seek out for trade deals, but I'm too tired. I find Ua'la'sur at the punch table. "How did it go?"

She shudders. "He drew out the humiliation, the pompous bastard. Next time I'm tempted to let my temper get the better of me, I'll remember what it feels like to have to apologize to someone I despise and hold myself back."

She's come a long way from the bitter, self-centered girl who kicked down my door demanding to become leader of the Dragon Maidens.

I slap her on the back. "For what it's worth, I'm proud to call you a friend."

"From you, Ysabel, it's worth dragging myself out of bed early in the morning to apologize to a jerk." She smiles. "How'd it go—?" She catches the look on my face. "Forget it. Let's ditch this boring party."

As we pass the guard on our way out of the palace, he whispers, "Don't let the posh folks get you down. I'm rooting for your love with Dark Lord Kaine."

The servants' gossip network works faster than any noble's spies. "Blessings of the Sun God to you."

"I love the story of Dark Lord Chingis and Holy Maiden Sarra." He winks.

I fucking hate that story. Chingis was Conollia's king when the blight struck. He conquered half the continent with his necromantic army before the Elven Empire beat his ass. According to the bards, he imprisoned Holy Maiden Sarra after falling in love with her. When his army was defeated, he killed Sarra so the church couldn't take her back, then killed himself. This is what passes for the world's most famous love story. No wonder some people consider Yarthor trying to rape me to be romantic.

At least people gossiping about my forbidden love with Kaine is better than them trying to ship me off to a nunnery. *Ugh. Why do I have to pick between two such terrible fates?* My steps drag as I head toward my healing clinic.

The instant we're out of eyesight of the guards, so perfectly timed they must have been following us for a while, a voice hisses, "Step over here, Holy Healer, or we'll shoot your friend." Five men in black masks lurk in an alley, holding crossbows aimed at Ua'la'sur.

Oh, yay, today's first kidnapping attempt.

CHAPTER FOURTEEN

Shadows explode over Ua'la'sur's body like flowers. When I blink, she's vanished. She reappears behind a thug. Wisps rise off her tan skin to wrap around him. He wails and fires his crossbow behind him into the alley.

The others have their bows pointed at the sky or each other. The leader shouts, "It's not real! Don't shoot!"

"They can't hear you." Ua'la'sur stands on her tiptoes to whisper in his ear. "Let's see what you're most afraid of." Screaming, he curls up in a fetal position pleading with invisible visions. Gradually the wailing stops, replaced by unconsciousness, subdued silence, or thumb-sucking.

The Queen of Nightmares strolls back to me, dumping the cross-bows at my feet like a cat presenting dead vermin. "That was pathetic. I'm insulted."

"Indeed," speaks a new voice. The thugs' swords warp into cuffs on their arms and legs. Alzira leans against the alley wall. "You did an adequate job protecting the princess."

"Were you testing me? Dick move." Ua'la'sur rolls her eyes. "I didn't need your help to handle this lot." Her weakness is that she can't use her power at night, but she's unstoppable under the sun. Furthermore, her bow is a relic capable of completely erasing her presence from both physical and magical detection. She purchased it specifically so she could hide during the hours when her power doesn't work.

"Such a pitiful attempt must have been either a distraction or a minor player attracted by the kingdom-size ransom on my fine ass," I say.

"The latter." Ua'la'sur yanks up the leader to show his face. "Don't you recognize him? Your guards have picked him up several times for petty crimes."

"Oh, right." I've never told Ua'la'sur about my face-blindness. I'm not keeping it a secret from my friends, per se, it's just hard to explain. I've never had any trouble recognizing the only dwarf in the Holy City, so it's never come up.

"What do you want to do with them?" she asks.

"Take them to the guard station, assuming someone hasn't sent for a guard already." I look around the street, which vacated fast. All the residents have closed their windows. "Probably not." People are assholes.

To save time, I ask Ua'la'sur, "When you go to the guard station to report this lot, could you also give them a description of Kaine's brother? Tell the captain I need a list of every half-elf who's entered the city illegally. I know they take bribes, and I'll let it slide if they tell me the truth. If anyone finds him, I'm offering a reward of a thousand aracoins." I'd go higher except that would attract unwanted attention. "Then bring the same description to the safe house for escaped victims of slavery."

"You can count on me." Ua'la'sur pats me on the shoulder before walking away. We leave the would-be kidnappers still twitching on the ground behind us, to be collected later. Alzira, as usual, vanishes as soon as I take my eyes off her.

The streets turn wider as I approach a row of shops and open-air stalls. Cherry trees, tulips, and roses (planted by yours truly) line the road. The sweet scent of flowers intermingles with freshly cooked sausages. A voice calls, "Holy Ysabel! Please hear my plea!"

The man running toward me is dressed too well to be a farmer and not well enough to be a merchant. He must be a shopkeeper, judging from the smell of onions. He bends over, sweat dripping down his baldpate and stubby nose. "Please, Your Holiness. I'm dying."

Oh, my Sun God, this again. A shutter snaps shut around my heart. "If your doctors agree, then they'll add you to my list. I don't heal anyone ahead of their place in line." I never use weasel words like *can't* to justify myself.

"Please!" he shouts. "I won't last long enough for you to get to me. You could save me, right here, right now. Aren't you sent by the Sun God to save us?"

My pace picks up. A woman steps in front of me. "Please, Your Holiness, barrenness isn't fatal, but it would mean more to me than my own life to have a child. It would only cost you a day."

Another shopkeeper hops over his table in his haste to reach me. One person breaking the taboo of approaching the Holy Maiden has unleashed a flood. Soon a dozen people around me are shouting, "Your Holiness!" The desperation in their voices rips at me. An echo in my mind whispers, "It's only a day . . . It's only a day . . ." So many people who want a day from me, like a million mosquitoes nipping into my flesh.

I swallow hard. "Stay back, or the Sun God will strike you down."

The first shopkeeper sneers. "You're just a healer. What can you do?"

"I'll tell you what I'm about to do." I cup my hands to my mouth and bellow, "Alzira, save me!"

"Your Holiness!" Alzira pops up seemingly out of nowhere.

"I'm so scared." I wipe an imaginary tear away from my eye. "Please rescue me, my brave knight!"

Alzira charges forward, swinging her scimitar. "You! To have accosted Her Holiness, I hope you're prepared to pay with your life!" The mob flees. Blue lightning dances on her blade as if in response to her fury. It's the second time I've seen her scimitar spark. Could it be on the verge of becoming a relic? After all, Alzira has strong enough magic power to create one.

"Wait! I didn't do anything! She's lying!" The original culprit gulps, then flees.

Alzira gives chase, crying, "How is it relevant if she's faking it or not? You should be honored to have Her Holiness ask me to beat you, scum."

Suddenly no one on the street wants to come near me. Maybe I went a bit too far. If he's truly fatally ill, I'll feel bad. But most of the people who chase me down do so because they don't qualify for my list. Once a woman tried to stab me over my refusal to heal her, then turned out to have a sexually transmitted illness of the embarrassing but nonfatal nature. There used to be a group of protesters outside my clinic who believed every day I lived wasted a possible life saved, so I should open my clinic doors and heal people until I died.

Alzira returns at a run. "I apologize for letting such trash disgrace your ears, Your Holiness. You could skip healing today and rest."

I'm tempted, but . . . "I can't have Kaine blamed by the people of this city for my failure to show up." The bigger reason is my guilt. People accost me wanting to be healed all the time. It gets to me, having something that other people need so badly. I never asked to hold the power of life or death. I'm not nice enough to heal without rest until I die, but I'm also not cruel enough to turn them all away. I could only chase that mob off without hating myself because I know there's a schedule of people waiting for me to heal them. I'm a coward like that.

At the clinic, the nurse directs me to a room where a woman sniffles. At first, I think she's my patient. Then I see the red-faced, too-small baby in her arms. Children are automatically moved to the top of my list.

When I was ten, my youngest brother was born with his umbilical cord strangling him. My mother wept as her bleeding wouldn't stop. Acting on instinct, I dragged them both back from the grave with a touch. My first healing was truly a miracle. Then a man offered my father a dreadful amount of money in exchange for me, and the rest is history.

For years afterward, I wondered if I would still have saved my baby brother if I knew what it would cost me later. Now it feels like God has placed that choice before me again.

I can only do one thing. Stretching out a hand, I call forth my power. The baby stirs. Limbs tiny from premature birth fill out. Loud, healthy cries fill the room.

The sobbing mother thanks the Sun God. I need redleaf.

Actually, forget the tea—once my healings are done, I go straight for my pipe. The mellow happiness doesn't come. I take a little more, but still, nothing. It must be another bad batch. My hands tremble. I start tapping my cheek to ward off a panic attack. Alzira places an arm behind my back, escorting me out of the city. She's speaking, but I can't hear her voice.

We meet Ua'la'sur at the palace gate. By then, I've calmed down enough to greet her as usual. Alzira tells her, "I'm entrusting you with Her Holiness. Please guard her on my behalf."

"Of course," Ua'la'sur says. Heaving a huge sigh, she mutters, "Now that I've passed your little test, you trust me to walk her back home."

I blink. "Where are you going?" Alzira's guilty look tells me all I need to know. "I told you not to beat up people without asking me first."

"But, princess, they called you such vile things."

"I've been called worse."

"They hand-delivered you to a man who they thought was going to rape you because they owed him a bunch of money, then they called you a slut afterward. I found that *upsetting*."

"I feel the same way, but I'm looking for allies among the nobility."

"I'll put bags over their heads first." Alzira's face tells me I'm not going to be able to stop her.

I groan. "I'll let you scare people a bit. Not the royal family, mind you."

Alzira nods. "Yes, Your Holiness." She mutters, "One of these days, the queen will step into a dark alleyway and I'll be there."

As we climb into the carriage, Ua'la'sur tells me the would-be kidnappers were successfully arrested. More will come to test if I'm still under the church's protection. I could start my own prison block with the people who've tried to kidnap me over the years.

At the gate of the fortress, Kaine bounds over, eager as a dog whose human has returned home. "How has your day been?"

"It went well. I negotiated with nobles interested in Conollia's natural resources"—I notice his eyes glazing over—"and I'll talk to Durrian about the proposed deals."

"Good idea. He loves Mysterious Papers. Whatever he does will be good for the country." Kaine speaks with the absolute faith of a saint or a child. It would be too easy for someone to stab him in his wide open, unprotected back. Touching his seal, I vow to never be that person.

Arm in arm, we walk down the hallway. "I convinced Jiang I'm planning to kill you. Hopefully it will make him less likely to send other assassins after you, but no promises."

"It must be hard for you to resist stabbing his smug face." Kaine scowls. "Just like how you have to strike deals with the people who stole so much life from you."

From behind us, Ua'la'sur calls, "A bunch of snobs called her a slut because of you."

Eyebrows looming, I call back, "Weren't you reporting to Suzette?"

"Yeah, yeah, I'm going."

Stricken, Kaine gazes at me. "I'm sorry."

"Don't let Ua'la'sur give you a hard time." They're overprotective, the whole lot of them. "People call me all kinds of things. Fraud, selfish, seductress . . . This just brought all the muck up to the surface."

"I'm still sorry." He droops visibly. "Why would they call *you* names for what they believe I did to you?"

How to explain this to someone so honest? "The world can be a terrible, cruel, arbitrary place. People want to believe that goodness and justice will triumph in the end. They love the story of a Holy Maiden who struck a dark lord dead with the power of her virtue. But the real world isn't such a kind place. If the dark lord wins instead, people would rather believe she wasn't holy enough. Then they can keep telling themselves such a bad thing could never happen to them, because they say their prayers every evening. If making themselves feel safe means kicking someone else while she's down, that's nothing new."

"I don't get it. Do you want me to punch anyone in the face for you?"

"Alzira is already on that. It doesn't fix anything." I sigh. "But thanks." With that, I let go of what little remains of my anger toward Kaine. He truly didn't realize the damage he'd do to my reputation by kidnapping me. Besides, I decided not to care about the opinions of people like Santos any longer.

"Let me know if you change your mind about the beatings." Kaine's fists clench.

I'd better defuse him. "All I want is to have a nice lunch among friends where I don't have to think about politics."

"I can arrange that." A spring returns to his step.

"Do you have more good wine? My last batch of redleaf was weak. I need something to calm my nerves."

"Didn't you know? Your regeneration ability makes it impossible for you to get drunk or high." He beams like this is a good thing.

No redleaf? "But I *need* it! It's the only thing getting me through my healings!" Having blurted out a little too much, I clamp my mouth shut.

"I've known people who use redleaf without it affecting their lives. I've also seen addicts dying on the streets. The key difference is if they 'want' it or 'need' it." Kaine's gaze bores into me.

"It's just an expression." I don't want to bare my flaws. "Lunch and good company will relax me."

"I'd be honored if you would allow me to provide you with a dress." His tone is questioning. Among Arahasnor nobles, a gift of clothing from a man to a woman signals romantic intentions. *He looked up our traditions? How adorable.*

"Thank you." I smile.

I barely have time to kick off my shoes in my room before a pair of soldiers haul in Kaine's present. I open the box to reveal a fur dress. It's made from a reddish-brown bear pelt with white ruffles on the sleeves and collar. It's a crime against fashion, especially the hat: a tall, round, furry thing with, may the Sun God help me, a pair of ox horns sticking out on either side.

"He probably killed the bear himself. If I don't wear it, I'll hurt his feelings," I moan, picking the hat up by its horns. "Public humiliation or kicking a puppy. Either way, I'm doomed." I take a deep breath, trying to psych myself into this. At least the crocodile skin slippers are cute. The fur on the dress feels like good quality, sleek and shimmering. Ugh, I must really like Kaine to wear something so out of fashion.

After changing, I inspect myself in the mirror. The dress overwhelms my tiny frame, yet it makes me look imposing. Give me a sword, and I could be a warrior queen. Even the stupid hat adds some much-needed height. Best of all, the dress is *comfy*, like wearing a blanket. I'd keep it just for lounging around my room.

Tipping my hat at myself in the mirror, I stride out the door.

Kaine waits to escort me to dinner. The pleased look on his face is completely worth wearing the dress. "Ysabel! You look ferocious as a bear." We're going to have to work on his compliments.

"Thank you for the present," I say, meaning it. Anything he got me would be perfect. "I should have asked earlier: How was your day?"

"I visited the refugee camp again. They wouldn't have let me in without your letter."

"I'm glad I was able to help."

"Do you think you could write me another one? They got mad and threw me out after I beheaded the guy who poisoned me."

"You *what*?"

Kaine blinks. "I told you I was going to kill him, way back when we first met."

He did. I'd forgotten. "Couldn't you have arrested him the normal way?"

"They weren't planning on punishing him at all. They brought him before me and asked me to forgive him." Kaine shakes his head. "I thought I could say 'No, thank you, I'd rather have revenge,' but it turned out to be one of those requests that's actually a demand. For a bunch of pacifists, they turned into an angry mob fast. Urew hustled me out of there before it turned violent. He was muttering about having words with you."

I pinch the bridge of my nose. My headache is coming back. "I don't think anything I can say is getting you back in there."

"Then don't worry about it." Kaine flips a hand. "I wanted to invite them to return to Conollia. That's a favor for them, not me. If they don't follow me, then they're not my people."

"It doesn't work like that. If you're going to become King of Conollia, then you have to look after all Conollians, whether they support you or not." Some of the refugees call me Yarthor's whore, but I'd still protect them from Jiang the same as the ones who admire me. That became my responsibility when I took them into my sect.

Kaine glances at me sideways. "Your sense of duty is why you heal people who mistreat you, isn't it?"

I don't want to return to that argument. "Do you want to be the kind of king who steals from everyone else to prosper a few cronies?"

"Never." Kaine shuffles his feet. "I'll think about it."

Kaine leads me to a private dining room with a feast laid out, enough for everyone who could be gathered on short notice: Ho Tan, Sigma, Ua'la'sur, and Nakimé. The flames of the gas lamps reflect off the yellow wallpaper. Lace dollies and silver candlesticks sit on the walnut table. The silverware is mismatched but very expensive, making me suspect it came from a conquest. The big windows are protected with mesh wiring to block arrows. Two dead animals decorate the walls, this time a crocodile and a deer.

Everything tastes delicious. There are dumplings, steamed vegetables, apple slices, and milk tea. Kaine whispers that he caught and prepared the crispy roast duck himself. Whoever told him men shouldn't cook nearly caused a criminal waste of talent. I have a fascinating debate with Sigma about whether the Moon Devil's portrayal as female is sexist. Personally, I think there are sexist overtones in how my church portrays the Dark Lady as a seductress, but it's still better than pretending all women spout goodness and rainbows from our vaginas and that's why we're too naive to be trusted with any real power. We both agree in the end that assigning genders to deities might be us mortals presuming a lot.

The volume rises from conversations around us. Nakimé and Ho Tan are locked in a friendly debate about who won this morning's practice match. Punching each other in the face a few times allowed the ladies to reach a mutual understanding and respect.

I brush my leg against Kaine's. When he looks up, I mouth, "Thanks." This is exactly the relaxing time among friends I needed to recharge myself after a busy, stressful day. Kaine winks and nudges me back. Emboldened, I kick off my slipper and run my toes down his calf. Soon we're intertwining our feet and enjoying the naughty thrill of no one knowing what we're doing.

When the staff carries in a chocolate cake, I shove my shoe most of the way back on. Three tiers high and dripping fudge, it's a temptation straight from the Moon Devil. A maid kindly refills my wineglass. I take a sip, savoring the well-aged—

There's a funny taste in the back of my throat. My tongue tingles. I try to speak, but nothing comes out. Glass shatters against the table, spilling red wine down my fur dress. I've been poisoned.

"I'm very sorry." The maid grabs my arm. "Let me help you get that off."

Dammit. It's another Dark-Lady-be-damned kidnapping already. My body stands up against my will. She must be using her gift. Shit, she refilled Kaine's glass first! Who sent this woman? Probably not Jiang, since he wants me to kill Kaine for him. It could be a foreign nation plotting to sabotage Arahasnor and obtain my services. Or it could simply be an opportunistic kidnapping. A Holy Healer is worth enough aracoins alive to buy a city. Kaine, people just want dead.

"Aw, I hunted that bear for my own dinner," Kaine says. (I knew it.) "Is the dress ruined?" Unfortunately, he must not be bothering to activate danger detection in the safety of his own fortress.

"We can save the fur as long as we wash it quickly," the maid says. My legs keep moving involuntarily. We're steps from the door.

"Let me help." Kaine brings his cup to his lips as if to chug it. No! I don't even have enough control over my body to cry.

A pro, the maid laughs easily. "This is women's work, Your Darkness. We'll be back in no time."

There's only one thing I can do without control of my body. I heal the assassin. Almost everyone has a tiny bruise or cut somewhere on their bodies. I'm hoping the surprise tingling will make her drop me.

She doesn't so much as twitch. It's over. I taste cold despair.

Kaine sets his wineglass down without taking a drink. "Why did Ysabel's lifespan just decrease?"

Before he even finishes, everyone jumps to their feet and grabs their weapons. The maid puts a dagger to my throat. "It's poisoned with enough Nightwish to kill in one prick."

"I don't like you," Kaine says. His gaze shifts from house-trained dog to feral wolf. The maid's body goes cold and clenches against mine. From the layer of frost covering her skin, his ability killed her instantly.

"Thzzz," I try to say to Kaine. My limbs are back but my tongue isn't completely working. What the hell, I'm going to plant my thanks on his lips. I step forward.

My foot, only half in my shoe because of my games during dinner, slips. In horrible slow motion, I careen into the poisoned knife. It draws a thin line down my arm, forcing a strangled scream from my mute tongue.

Kaine leaps to catch me. "Ysabel!"

People shout around me. It all blends together. This is going to be a very stupid way to die. Sheer anger lets me barely cling to consciousness. I've never found it more unfair that I lack the power to heal myself.

Kaine rips off his sleeve and wraps it around my arm. "Just hold on. You're going to be fine." Holding me tightly to his chest, he runs for the door.

Numbness from the poison has spread up my shoulder. The world dims. The last thing I feel is the warmth of Kaine's arms cradling me close before I pass out.

CHAPTER FIFTEEN

I dream of the first and only time I tried to run away from my dark destiny.

At ten years old, I was enslaved to a crime lord and his gang. They used my healing so frequently, I had to escape or die. One unlocked door later, I slipped out with nothing but the clothing on my back.

I fell in with a pack of street children, all girls. They pushed me around a little and the oldest one stole the ribbon from my hair, but they also showed me how to survive. Then I heard them whispering late at night about my rising bounty.

Mud smeared to hide my face, I begged a ride from a fisher. He guessed my identity partway across the river. When he began to turn his boat back around, I jumped overboard and washed up half-drowned on a bank in the forest.

An old widow found me cramming berries in my mouth as I wept. She carried me back to her cabin, fed me, and made me smile with her age-inappropriate jokes. In gratitude, I cured her arthritis. That night, I woke to her gruff voice telling the men downstairs to "hand over the money."

I jumped out the window. Stumbling through the darkness, I didn't get far before they caught me.

I wept in terror as they shoved me into a tiny cage reeking of piss. Then they let loose the dogs. Clawing through the bars, the starving creatures ripped off a chunk of my hair and savaged my arm. Tears streaming down my face, I curled up in a small ball and begged. *Please. I'm sorry I ran away. I'm sorry. I'll heal anyone you want.* I clung to the one thing people wanted from me like a dehydrated sailor guzzling salt water. My healing power, my gift and my curse, the only reason I lived and the thing killing me, the only worth I had in the eyes of the world. *I'm valuable. I'm not going to be killed because I'm valuable.*

My legs kick a wall. I wake up. Smoke from the candle by my bed makes me cough, and my throat tastes like vomit.

Kaine leaps up from the chair beside my bed. "Water! I have water!" He shoves the cup into my hands.

I take a long gulp, then rasp out, "Are you all right?"

"Am I . . . ?" It takes Kaine a moment to understand. "I didn't touch the poisoned drink. Thank you for warning me." He shifts with nervous energy. "How do you feel?"

"I'm fine." It's mostly true. "You're welcome." I'll accept his gratitude even if it was a happy accident that he noticed my lifespan dropping and interpreted it correctly. "How long have I been out?"

"All day and most of the night. The healer gave you something to get the poison out of your system, then your regeneration took care of the rest." He gestures at my arm, now healed.

"They'd never have used a fatal dosage on me. I'm too valuable." My mouth twists into the smile of a hanged man.

"Can I hug you?" Kaine stretches out his arms like a man sighting water after wandering in a desert. "Please?"

"Come here." I pull him close. He buries his head in my shoulder and clings to me. "Thank you for saving my life."

"It's my fault you were in danger to begin with. I used an ability to uncover the origins of the corpse. She was sent by the nation of Zhaara, likely in retaliation for how I drove them out of Conollia."

"People will be coming after my healing powers regardless. You'll have to fend off a few dozen more kidnapping attempts before it will taper off to a more manageable ten to twelve times a year." As much as it pains me to need a protector, there always has to be someone's army between me and the hordes wanting to use up every last drop of my life.

"Wait, you get attacked every—" Kaine counts on his fingers. "Every *month*?"

"It's not a big deal. I have Alzira. Where is she?"

Kaine points at my bodyguard sleeping on a cot next to mine. "She sat by your bed until she collapsed."

"Let her sleep, then. I'll be here when she wakes up." The pinch of my stomach reminds me I vomited up my last meal. "I'm starving."

"Food! I have food!" Kaine leaps to his feet and tugs over a table overflowing with plates of beef skewers, barbecued pork, and chicken wings.

"Excellent." I dig in. "May I have some fruit to go with it?"

"Fruit!" He looks around like he expects an apple to materialize. "Right away!" He runs off, almost breaking the door, and gallops back with a bowl of grapes. Kneeling down, he presents them to me. "Open wide." His shirt reveals some nice biceps. I could balance a ruler on those straight shoulders.

"You don't have to feed me. I'm feeling much better already."

"I want to. Please?" He's giving me the puppy eyes while kneeling. I have no resistance. Blushing, I open my mouth.

After eating, I wipe my face. I glimpse myself in the mirror. "I look a fright." Someone has washed the powder off my face along with the puke. I always worry about letting a man see me without makeup for the first time.

"Huh? You look the same to me," Kaine says. "You've got a bit of a smell, but I can prepare a bath right away."

A smile tugs at my lips. I wasn't very worried about this particular man.

Kaine's castle has never heard of indoor plumbing, but the bathtub has a bronze shield melted into the bottom—a heating relic. I sink into the water up to my neck and close my eyes.

"PRINCESS!" Alzira bursts into my naked relaxation time. "I've committed an unforgivable sin. I never should have let you out of my sight, not even to beat up fools for insulting you."

"I'm fine," I say, making shooing motions at the door.

"You were attacked! While I wasn't there to protect you!" Tears squeeze out the corners of her eyes.

"Please, could you come back later?" I stretch my arm toward a towel slightly out of reach.

Alzira barely seems to hear me. "While I wasn't there . . . While I wasn't there . . ."

I wave my hand in front of her face. "Alzira, I have a very important task for you."

"Yes, Your Holiness!" She snaps to attention. "Shall I sink the nation of Zhaara into a smoking crater of fire and justice?"

"I need you to feed Evilrina. She's been refusing to eat any mice because she's cranky about moving."

"Understood." She salutes me.

I call after her, "It will soothe Evilrina if you bring her cage back to your room and nap next to her," because it's the only way to trick Alzira into sleeping.

Alzira successfully booted out, I sink back into the water and stay until I'm nice and pruny.

Kaine insists on carrying me back to my bedroom. My legs are maddeningly weak, so it's necessary but also fun. Though I have a long to-do list, Kaine pleads with me to take a break for at least the few hours until morning. He brushes my hair, then arranges it in a lovely fishtail braid. Did he ever braid his own hair? Would it offend him if I ask? My fear of causing harm outweighs my curiosity.

Lying on my bed and nestling my feet in Kaine's lap, I say, "I'm bored."

He massages my feet. "How can I serve you, my lady?"

I was just going to ask for a book, but the way he says that sends heat pooling in my belly. "How about you massage my back?" I roll over.

"I'd love to." He straddles me, the warmth of his thighs blazoning against my hips. As he kneads my shoulders, he infuses my skin with heavenly heat. Mmm, I can feel the tension drifting away. I inch forward to let him access my thighs. "No, don't move. Let me," he whispers, gently repositioning my legs. I'm so relaxed I'd fall asleep if not for the nagging itch of arousal.

I crack an eye open. "You know, I promised you a kiss."

"You did?"

"Inside my head, when I couldn't talk." Leisurely, I sit up and stretch. "You've put me in such a good mood, I might give you a few more treats if you please me."

His breath hitches. I'm not sure which of us moves first. Our lips lock. He tastes like sugar, the glutton, and he eats me alive like one of his pastries. His tongue probes with an inexperienced roughness and a gratifying eagerness. My hands wind in his hair. He sucks a little too hard, so I nip him, then take over the reins, guiding his tongue in a tantalizing dance.

Kaine pants, his eyes glazed over. It only takes a push of my fingertip to knock him onto the bed. I pin his wrists over his head. There's an incredible feeling of power in holding his muscles between my tiny fingers, knowing he could easily throw me off but chooses not to of his own free will. This is true dominance.

"Good boy." I nuzzle his shoulder. His warm body tastes like the sun. "Do you want a treat?"

He whimpers.

"Tell me what you want." I lower my voice to whisper in his ear.

"I want to bite you. I want to leave a mark."

Ooo, hot. "Not where someone might see." I pull down the top of my dress and nudge him toward my collarbone.

It tickles as he licks the skin above my breast. Then he sucks. I moan, long and drawn-out. That will leave a hickey. I'm already hot all over from one touch.

I grab his wrists again, and he buckles underneath me, still careful to keep his wrists exactly where I'm holding them. So good for me. I bury my lips in his neck. A flush creeps up his body, and I realize he's on fire for me. I want to coax more whimpers out of him. As I nibble his earlobe, I map out the broadness of his shoulders with my palms. The hint of a collarbone poking out tantalizes me as my hand hovers over his shirt. "May I?"

"I prefer not to be touched there." He sounds hesitant, so I make a note to be very careful how I ask things. He wouldn't be the first person new to submissiveness to worry about saying no.

"Got it." I keep my voice light. "Do you have another wish?"

"Mark me." His eyes are frenzied. His teeth bare savagely. "Anywhere. I don't care who sees. *I want it to bleed.*"

"Roll over." Straddling him, I tug down his shirt. The strongest man in the world lies pliant beneath me. I take a moment to admire the flat lines of his body and dark skin against white sheets before pressing my teeth against a muscular shoulder, tonguing over lightly sweaty skin and healed scars. Not too high—I don't want it to be visible on his neck in case he only said "anywhere" in the heat of passion. My breathing comes out soft and drugged, even though we've barely done anything. I want to memorize every part of Kaine's body, control the strength in every sinewy muscle, and kiss every last scar. A bitemark no longer seems like enough. I want to engrave myself on his skin so that he won't forget me when I die. Digging my nails into his back just barely hard enough to draw blood, I form a Y.

I'm rewarded with a long moan. "Ysabel," Kaine groans, and the sound of my name hovers in the air. My skin prickles, and I want more, I want to own every part of him. But then Kaine starts to sit up, so I release my prey with a sigh. I shouldn't get too greedy the first time.

"I want to see it." Kaine springs up and runs to the mirror, peering over his shoulder. "It's perfect."

I sit up on the bed. "Look over here." I pull down my emerald lounging gown to expose my breasts. "A peek of the future if you keep being good."

"Good? I'm about to convert to the Order of Saint Nora," says Kaine, the world's most innocent-faced dark lord.

I giggle. All my reasons to take it slow suddenly go out the window. By now I should know myself better. I never resist temptation. "Well, in that case . . ." I pull the dress over my head and toss it to the floor. The silk swishes as it lands. My exposed nipples prickle against the coolness of the room.

Kaine's jaw drops open. I grin. "What a lovely look of worship. As a reward, I think I'll let you touch."

He takes a step forward, then stops. "Are you sure?"

"Yes, I'm sure. But if you don't want to—"

Kaine lunges across the room and burrows his face in between my breasts. "I want every part of you," he breathes. "Ysabel, Ysabel, Ysabel."

True to his word, he licks and sucks every bit. He gives my breasts the same fervent fascination as he does his favorite puff pastries. My back arches as ripples tremble through my body. All semblance of control gone, I grab his hair and push. "Down," I plead.

Kaine attempts to flip me onto my back and slip his mouth between my legs. What actually happens is I bump my head and my heel clips his overly hard skull.

"I'm so sorry!" he babbles. "It seemed romantic at the time."

"I'm fine." Shifting to rest my chin on my hand, I pat him on the head. "I see I'm going to have to instruct you on *exactly* what to do."

His eyes light up. Oh, yes, he likes that. "I'm at your service."

"Kiss the inner part of my thigh. Oh yeah." My breath comes quicker. Heat pools in my belly. "Run your fingers around the edges of the clit, not touching." I guide his hand over. He's a fast learner. A familiar pulse runs up my body. "Now, see that hooded part? Roll it with your fingers, *gently*. A little slower . . . *Just like that, don't you dare stop*."

When Kaine licks a burning stripe, I've lost all coherence. I unwind like a too-tight skein of thread dropped to the floor. My grip on his hair relaxes as I collapse backward with a long moan.

I can feel him smile against me. Then he lies down next to me and snuggles close. I take a moment to breathe.

Turning to face him, I ask, "What can I do to return the favor?"

Kaine shies away. "I . . . really don't like being touched. It's not you. It's my own issue."

I'm a tad disappointed, but I don't let it show. "It's entirely up to you. If I can do anything, just say the word. You've been spoiling me."

"I assure you, I'm getting something out of this, too." He winks. "Are you up for a second breakfast?"

Laughter bubbles up under my chest. Oh, we're going to have such fun together.

Swallowing my last bite of bacon, I set my fork down. "That was delicious. Now I really do need to talk to Durrian about trade deals."

"I'll find him," Kaine says. "First, can I touch your forehead?"

I blink. "That's an unusual kink . . ."

He snorts. "To check how your regeneration ability is settling in."

"Oh, yes, of course." I pull back my hair to let him touch.

Kaine's face breaks out into the broadest grin. "You're gaining back exactly a day of life for every one you live." He yanks me over and wraps me in a hug. His heartbeat feels warm and frantic against my chest.

Mine beats just as excitedly. Even healing three to five times a day, this will gain me at least an extra year. Not as great an impact as I hoped for, but nothing could ever keep pace with the number of injured people in the world.

"I did it!" Kaine crows. "Your full lifespan will grow back! No, even better. Those gifted with regeneration have been known to live as long as elves."

With a sinking sensation, I realize we're doing different math. "Thank you very much. Even a bit of extra time is far more than I ever hoped for."

Kaine's eyes narrow. "You aren't seriously planning to still heal people, are you?"

I sigh. "I was never going to stop, Kaine."

"But why? They started killing you when you were only a powerless child. Now you have friends who would defend you. You have *me*."

"I'm not being forced into this, not anymore. I decided on my own." It brings me a measure of peace to say I'm choosing this sacrifice willingly. Not happily, of course. It's all I can do not to bawl my eyes out. "With just my one life, I can save nearly two thousand people with the time I have left. Anyone would call that a good trade."

"It's not a good trade to me." Kaine growls out each word. His muscles tense. The small room feels like it might break under the pressure radiating off him.

I marshal my arguments. "Suppose you're dying. Wouldn't you want me to heal you?"

"No." Kaine crosses his arms.

"Exactly, and that's how everyone else feels too—wait. Did you say *no*?"

"I said no."

My first instinct is to call it a lie, but Kaine never lies. "You're just saying that because you care about me. If I was a stranger, you'd force me to heal you."

"I wouldn't. I didn't when we first met."

He's got me there. "But you weren't dying then. What if just one day of my life could let us spend the rest of our lives together?"

"Even if I'm dying, I'll never let you heal me." He speaks with simple sincerity.

It's insane, but I believe him. I rub my forehead. "Kaine, I want to heal people."

His nose twitches like a bloodhound tracking a scent. "Don't lie to me. I told you the truth."

Good point. Softly, I say, "People track me down begging to be healed every day. They're desperate. They plead and praise and threaten. I try to harden my heart. But I know my own limits. When a dying child shows up, I tell myself it's one day and I heal them. I can't stop."

Kaine's shoulders slump. "I don't know how to fix that."

"You can't." It melts my heart that he wants to try.

"I'll think about it some more." His lower lip juts out. "I don't let the people I protect die."

"I know. But this time, there's nothing you can do."

"There are many things I could do, but you won't let me. That makes it harder."

"Would you be willing to enjoy what time we have together?" My voice shakes. It's been a sticking point before. My last lover couldn't cope with my grim expiration date, and I can't blame him. Trying to talk Kaine into it would be cruel. I can't guarantee he won't regret loving a dying woman. I wait like an ant for the rock to fall.

"I would love you if you had only minutes left to live. Even if we get only a little time together, I won't regret it. But that doesn't mean I won't fight for you. No matter what you say, I'm not giving up. Not on us and not on finding a way to save you." He brushes a tear off my cheek.

I don't know how to deal with the feelings rushing up inside me. I let out a huge breath. "Look at the bright side: A couple years might be as long as you can put up with me."

He winces.

"Too soon?"

"I'm never going to find that funny."

I enjoy gallows humor, but to each their own.

Kaine leaves to arrange a meeting for me with Durrian. I hate to see him go but love to ogle his backside.

Once he's gone, the shock hits me. I could live. At the rate of one day to replace one day, I could keep on surviving until old age. Why did Kaine have to point out that I might be able to live if I stopped healing? I'd accepted my death until he said that. But I won't give myself false hope, and I certainly won't give false hope to Kaine. I don't know how to stop. Putting my head between my knees, I breathe deeply. I almost want a panic attack so I can stop thinking rationally about this.

Loneliness presses around me on all sides. I need to hear someone else's voice to drown out my own. I open my door. "Alzira?"

As usual, she appears immediately. "Are we going somewhere?"

"No, come inside." I sit down on my bed. "If you were dying, would you let me heal you?"

"I wouldn't allow you to heal any injuries except fatal ones. But if I were dying, I would consider that you still need my services and accept."

"Exactly! That's the normal answer—"

"But I like what Kaine said better."

"Why?" I throw up my hands. "One day of my life is worth far less than all of his."

"Kaine gave the illogical answer—the only answer that allows you to live. He answered out of love." A very tiny smile forms on Alzira's lips. "No man could ever be worthy of you, princess, but it pleases me to think you might find one who passes my minimum standards. He's strong, too. I'd still beat him, of course."

I'm not sure why I talk to Alzira about these kinds of things.

As I put on my makeup and fix my hair, something nags at the back of my mind. What haven't I done yet? I still need to contact Donya! As Bora, I promised to write to her every day. I open our linked book. There's an entire page filled with Donya's increasingly messy writing: *How is Ysabel? Have you and the rest of her staff been able to see her at all? Is she safe? Has Dark Lord Kaine hurt her? Does she need help?* The same questions are repeated over and over.

She hates my guts, and she'd still take on a dark lord for me. This is why I can't dislike Donya no matter how much she dislikes me. On top of my existing exhaustion, I feel a pang of guilt. Donya is the only person who tried to help me when the court sold me out. Yet I've been lying to her and putting her in danger. I haven't even told her that I know her missing maid is safe. She must be stressed out with worry, all for nothing.

Probably Donya heard what I told the royal court by now, but she wouldn't believe it, not after she saw me go into hysterics. The memory makes me cringe. I write, *I'm sorry I forgot to contact you. The Dark Lord Kaine came to repay a favor to Holy Ysabel. He never bore her any ill will.*

Donya writes back so quickly she must have left the book open. *Are you sure that's not just what Ysabel wants her staff to believe? "All a misunderstanding" sounds too good to be true.*

Why does Donya have to be so perceptive? *I'm certain. I've personally spoken to Kaine's soldiers. He has a reputation for being extremely intolerant of any forced attentions, if you get my drift. The best lies have a touch of truth. Also, Kaine gave Ysabel a blank document with his seal. He'd never do that unless he had a heavy debt to repay.*

Huh, that does explain how Ysabel was able to make so many trade agreements. I'm relieved. Now I can go back to detesting Ysabel without guilt.

Heh, she's so cute. I write that while "spying" I overheard Holy Ysabel received some intelligence from Cardinal Orwin, that Jiang uses charities as cover for illegal activities.

Donya promises to order our spy to obtain a list of his donations. Then ink blots the paper as she rests her quill pen down.

Is there anything else I can advise you on? I write.

Do you think it would be morally wrong for me to use Queen Bianna's political influence after what she's done?

Of course not. A politician can't afford such scruples.

She offered to sponsor my bill to remove primogeniture and allow equal inheritance rights to female children. Then she suggested we should hold a hunger strike to draw international attention to the cause while so many foreign dignitaries are in town.

I hastily scribble, *She's lying to you.* Donya's followers have had great success with hunger strikes, though the very notion gives me a stomachache. *You'd have much better visibility protesting at the World Games. Your fasts generally get you thrown in jail. She wants you out of sight by the day of the Games.*

But why? Donya writes.

If your law passes, then King Uctor's much younger sister will become next in line for the throne. Your law has support precisely because everyone is worried about what will happen when Uctor dies, what with the royal family having inbred itself to one withering branch. Bianna wants to hold on to power herself when her husband meets the Sun God. Hence why she got the young princess exiled and even tried to assassinate her a few times. Bianna plans to sabotage you. I hastily add, *Pardon me for speaking my mind, my lady.*

I told you, it's just Donya. That was a very intelligent analysis of the situation.

Oh, it's the natural wisdom of age. Donya is three years older than me, but I'm three thousand years more cynical.

I'd like to continue asking your advice. I enjoy talking to you.

A guilty thrill makes me bite my pen. A bit of feather falls on the pages.

Donya writes, *I'd be happy to buy you a meal at the Dragon's Claw for your troubles if you could meet me there next week.*

I shouldn't. Yeah, I really shouldn't.

Please. Around my friends, I'm forced to always be a leader. It's rare for me to have someone I can confide in like this.

Then I'd be honored. This could go wrong in so many ways. Yet it's such a useful chance to give the dear girl some much-needed political guidance. Everything will be fine as long as she doesn't find out.

After meeting with Durrian to obtain approval for my trade deals, I seek out Suzette. To find Alesh, she's been searching every brothel and sketchy business that deals in trafficked labor. She offered rewards through underworld channels. Her spies stole records from three mob bosses and murdered the city's most notorious trafficker to get her hands on his client list. Yet still, she found not a trace of Alesh. According to her latest report, there isn't a single Dark-Lady-damned half-elf in the entire Holy City. Our lack of luck finding Kaine's brother makes no sense. Half-elves are so uncommon that they should stick out. If the human trafficking scum had one to sell, then they'd brag—carefully, and only to the right people, but they'd brag. The guards haven't seen anyone of mixed elven blood enter the city in a decade. I considered the possibility of someone powerful owning a personal sex slave, so I ordered Alzira to beat up a few nobles who seemed like the type. Although it was fun, it didn't produce any results.

When Suzette looks up from her desk, her lipstick is smeared and her hair untamed, which tells me something serious has happened. "The guards stationed at the skull ritual sites? Their food was poisoned. Ten are dead."

I swallow. "That many?"

"There would have been even more if their dogs hadn't sniffed out the bad food." Suzette holds up a map, tracing a pattern along the skull shape.

I recoil. "The ritual was that close to being completed? What should we do? Fighting crime isn't my area of expertise."

"No need to be modest, you fight politicians all the time." Suzette snorts at her own joke, then turns serious. "I doubled the watch. We're not letting anyone, including the guards themselves, step onto the dangerous ground."

I blow out a breath. "Good, but won't Jiang be suspicious?"

"We got lucky. A guard captain who's widely known for being neutral to politics suggested this could be connected to a ritual." Suzette hesitates. "The watch suspects magical foul play because the bodies of the ten victims have gone missing."

My mouth feels dry. "Who would want to steal a corpse?"

"I have spies around the city investigating precisely that. The door showed no signs of forced entry. It's like the corpses walked out on their own during the night."

I clear my throat. "Uh, remember when my brother gave us the clue 'necromancer'?"

Suzette hisses. "The corpses did walk out on their own! Only a handful of necromancers in history could have done it. Most of them can't raise anything bigger than an ant."

Where could Jiang have met a necromancer? Most Sun God sects prohibit manipulating human corpses as desecrating the dead, a few permit raising dead animals, and half of them persecute necromancers in a disgraceful manner. People don't deserve to be killed for their innate gifts. I refuse to believe I'm better than a necromancer because I was born with healing—in fact, I'd be happy to trade gifts. To avoid the fanatics, necromancers don't live in the Holy City.

But in Jiang's home country of Faan, the corpses of criminals are donated to the court necromancer to use as labor. "Didn't you say a necromancer came with the Faan delegation? Any chance Jiang knows that person?"

"She wouldn't be strong enough to raise multiple corpses." Suzette hesitates. "I'm fairly certain that Jiang isn't from Faan, though. My agents from the area say that he doesn't have the right accent or mannerisms. I've asked people from every region of the Faan Empire."

"His parents could have immigrated here before he was born." Which would be painfully ironic given how he treats the refugees.

"I've had no luck tracing his background, but I'm sure he wasn't born in the Holy City. I would have found him by now."

I frown. "Jiang must have created a fake identity to claim the empty cardinal seat." Sun God worshipers in Faan are a small minority, and the seat went unfilled for decades. "Unfortunately, he has his sect and the cardinals so deeply under his control, I doubt it would make them turn on him even if we could prove it."

"Unfortunately." Suzette sighs.

"Is there any chance the necromancer might be threatening Jiang?"

Suzette looks at me like I've lost my mind. "He's more the type to blackmail other people."

"He's been ill lately. It doesn't feel like a natural illness to me." I don't like to tell anyone how Jiang forces me to heal him.

Suzette taps her chin. "I'll investigate necromantic curses while I'm at it. Honestly, though, many gifts can curse people, and Jiang has plenty of enemies."

We move on to arranging a guard raid on a criminal gang known for trafficking to look for Alesh. Next, I meet with Feiyan to discuss castle security.

Afterward, I eat dinner at my desk while catching up on work. A page delivers a note from Suzette. I read it, then run to find Kaine. He's in the training room, which practically seems to be his second bedroom. Many weapons hang between the stone arches. Targets are set up in the back room for archery. There's a ring in the middle for practice spars. Though the padded floor looks clean, no amount of scrubbing can erase the stench of sweat.

Frowning, he sets down a dumbbell. "Shouldn't you be in bed already? You were poisoned."

I shift from foot to foot. "I've been thinking. What if I heal people until I have exactly one day left, then stop? Then the regeneration will replace one day at the rate of one day and keep me alive. I can maximize the number of lives saved."

Kaine doesn't look as happy about my suggestion as I'd hoped. "Then someone you love will be near death, you'll heal them, and you'll die."

I wince. The people I love do tend to live dangerously. "Uh, I could keep two days?" Surely no one could blame me for not healing if I only have two days left. Except people *would* blame me. They'd bring more dying babies before me, and I'd heal them.

"The only way you're going to live is if you start valuing your life more, or if you lose your gift."

How well he knows me. My shoulders sag. "I'm sorry. I vowed not to give you false hope, but now look what I did."

Kaine steps closer and tips up my chin to look into my eyes. "My hope isn't false. I'm going to make you want to live for me, or I'll do something about your price. I won't give up."

My shoulders heave with a suppressed sob. "Ugh, look at me. I came here to give you good news, something better than my harebrained plan." I push everything else away and smile, remembering the letter in my hand. "Suzette found Bei Ren."

"That's amazing! Thank you!" He sweeps me up in a hug. A very sweaty hug. I surreptitiously wipe my cheek on my sleeve.

"She can see you anytime." My problems wash away in the face of his happiness. "Her gift makes her hair fall out. Every bit, even her eyebrows. Luckily, her hair has grown back enough for her to use her magic again."

"Let's leave now." He towels himself off.

"Do you need to talk to your subordinates first? If you come back looking different and they don't recognize you, it would be a catastrophe."

"I was so eager, I already told Durrian and Ho Tan about my plans." Kaine scratches his head. "Since I used to visit modifiers, my people are used to dealing with my changing appearance. I tried using a tattoo as an identifying mark, but it kept vanishing with the changes, so we have code words. Durrian is a Seer, so he can always verify me. Most people think I have an odd, expensive vanity."

"I take it your closest friends know the full truth?"

"They sussed me out a long time ago." Kaine's eyes become distant. "Except they thought I was a woman crossdressing. Durrian took me aside to tell me that he would back me up as a leader if I decided to come out as a woman. It was kind of awkward since I was trying to come out to him as a man. The more difficult conversation was Ho Tan's well-intentioned attempt to convince me that women could be as strong as men. I kept telling her I already knew that. But they're my friends, so even if it took them a while to understand, they didn't freak out. I know they have my back, no matter what."

I pat the least-sweaty part of his shoulder. "I'm glad you have such good friends. Come on, let's visit the baths."

"Do I have to?" He jiggles with impatience.

I wrinkle my nose. "Yes. Yes, you do."

The carriage drops us off in front of Bei Ren's yellow cottage. The petunias planted along the street are quite lovely, as Kaine kindly points out. He mutters their colors under his breath like he thinks I'm going to test him later, the cutie. Several times, Bei Ren has helped me disguise servants fleeing nobles, so I know it never takes very long. I settle on a park bench under a dogwood to wait.

I'm antsy about so many other concerns that waiting feels difficult. I keep tossing around different theories about the necromantic ritual in my mind. Am I hindering the investigation because I'm bound not to tell anyone the ritual almost certainly ends in my death? Should I be doing more to find Alesh? What more can I do without tipping off powerful players that I'm looking for someone? I wish I'd brought along paperwork to keep myself distracted from these thoughts.

The door to Bei Ren's house opens, and Kaine walks out. With my practice recognizing people, I notice he still has the same confident stride. Most of all, his smile remains pure, as if he loves to be alive from the bottom of his heart.

His new body still has the same black hair and beautiful dark eyes. The squareness of his face has become more pronounced. The shape of his body is straighter now. He's made himself more handsome, of course. Who wouldn't be tempted to give themselves the jaw and cheekbones of a pagan god? His face is longer and his eyebrows thicker. He can barely fit through Bei Ren's door, not only because of his height but also his breadth. His arms are as thick as two soldiers' muscles put together. His thighs could snap a man's neck.

I suppress a tiny bit of disappointment. His original body was closer to my type. I like small, androgynous men who look like they'd bruise if you flicked your finger at them. But it's not my business to tell Kaine what his body should look like. I can understand why, after a lifetime of looking feminine, he wants the manliest bod possible. *They* are *some nice muscles. Look at how they ripple under his shirt.*

Oh dear, the absolute pervert has his hands down his pants, grinning. I'm going to pretend not to know him.

"Ysabel!" Kaine runs toward me, waving. His voice has deepened, which will make life temporarily difficult for me since voices are my primary means of recognizing people. The sun bounces off his teeth. His grin makes it impossible not to smile back.

Giving in, I call, "Looking good!"

He waggles his eyebrows in a way he no doubt believes to be charming. It's a little charming, but I'll never tell him that. "May I kiss you?" He kneels down in front of the bench. Eagerness radiates from his perked-up ears to his tongue darting over his lips. I can practically see his tail wagging. How loveable. I want to kiss him too.

I lean down and place my lips against his. His raw, woodsy taste has grown on me like my first wine. Our bodies press closer together, half-yanking me off the bench. Those hard muscles cushion my fall. I lick his lips, then dive in again. The kiss turns slow and agonizingly gentle as the world fades to nothing but the heat of his body. I'm filled with pure selfish want.

I come up disheveled, my heart racing. Kaine's hair looks satisfyingly rumpled. His tongue is pink against his face.

I want more. So much more. I want to taste every inch of his skin. I want to see him at his absolute limit so I can fill his mind with nothing but me, to burrow so deep under his skin he'll never be rid of it. I want to leave a bruise. What actually comes out of my mouth is "Can I step on you?"

"Why do you think I got on my knees?" He grins. *Naughty boy.*

I slip my foot out of my boot, because it has a high heel and I'm not trying to actually hurt him, not unless he wants me to. The desire in his eyes feels good. Letting my foot trail down his chest, I stop at his most vulnerable point. He whimpers. I laugh and press down. The growl of lust from his throat is the sweetest music I've ever heard. The power and control he's giving me is tantalizing. Without even being touched, I'm getting off on this as much as him.

I should probably stop here. Exhibition isn't one of my kinks, current appearances aside. Regretfully, I pull back. Drawing his head to my chest, I pet his hair until both of our heartbeats calm down. Holding him feels so good. It wasn't just my libido that was lonely before Kaine, it was also my desire for intimacy.

"That was certainly a fun way to try out my new organ," he whispers into my ear.

I laugh. "Time to head back home."

Another day is over. Five years, two months, and three days left, according to Kaine's estimate. By all rights, I should be grateful for the extension. But now that I have someone to live for, I resent every time that count drops one day shorter.

CHAPTER SIXTEEN

Kaine, still trying to be good, has taken to bringing me breakfast in bed every morning. I'm shamelessly encouraging this behavior with little treats. He never takes off his clothes, but I'm not going to press him. I previously assumed that was because of issues with his body, but even after the modification, it hasn't changed. Of course I'm happy with all different types of sex, but I'd like to be able to return the favor to him for once. I get off on giving pleasure, and that's a big part of my sexuality. Plus, I need to touch him if we're ever going to get kinkier. After a few days, I can't resist asking, "How are you adjusting to your new body?"

"It's great. I love it." He says this in the same way people automatically claim to be fine when asked how they are doing.

Hmm. "It's okay if you complain to me about the downsides, too. I'm not going to use that to second-guess your choice. You can tell me anything."

His shoulders slump with relief. "Lately, I've been a little crazy under my skin. I can't stop thinking about sex."

"So it's true what they say about men?" I waggle my eyebrows. "For what it's worth, Suzette said she had something like a second puberty right after the change. It mellowed out with time."

"Good to know. I'm always hungry, too. I've had trouble controlling my new strength." Swiftly, Kaine shakes his head. "It's not that I don't like it! It feels very right. I love my new muscles." He flexes a bicep.

"They're very nice muscles," I assure him.

"I broke two doorknobs and a toilet."

"A toilet? Do I even want to know?"

"With the sheer power of my majestic gluteus maximus."

"Are you complaining or bragging?" I laugh.

"Maybe a little of both." His dimples flash. "Part of the sudden enthusiasm for masturbation is that I like my body now. It's more the real 'me.' I can brawl without worrying that my shirt will rip. I can hug without worrying someone will feel my chest. I'm not having problems disassociating with my body anymore. I'm a lot happier. What I gave up was worth it."

"What did you give up? If you can answer that," I hastily add. Suzette described it as mourning the boy who'd been almost like a separate being from her. She called him her imaginary friend.

"Dresses I can't stand, but jewelry is pretty." Kaine tosses his head as if to shake off his thoughts. "But I've been living as a man for years already, and I've never been one to look back."

"Men can absolutely wear jewelry. Let me buy you some." Leaning closer, I survey him. He'd look sexy with one dangling earring and maybe some rings. "If I can do anything else to help you, just say the word, got it?"

"Will do." A smile spreads across his face. "Despite my complaints, I love it."

"I'm happy for you." I caress him with my gaze. Even though I'm usually into clean-shaven men, his small beard suits him so perfectly I can't imagine him without it. I've gotten used to occasionally swallowing a hair when we kiss. Today he smells of jasmine and sandalwood, a scent I purchased for him. I place my hand on top of his. Sitting on my bed, we lean against each other, enjoying the warmth of shared company. Kaine's indisputably worth waiting for, and I'll take it as slow as he wants.

"Sometimes I feel guilty," Kaine mutters. "About how easily I changed my body when most people don't even know the opportunity exists."

"I could hire bards to spread songs about modification and instruct them to direct the curious to me. We should spread the word in the Elven Empire, where people are more open. What if we started a charitable fund for anyone who can't afford Bei Ren's fees?"

He tousles my hair. "You try to solve everything, don't you? I like that about you."

"I want to make the world better, if I can."

"Myself, I figure if people want something badly enough, they can steal the money for it."

Sometimes I have trouble telling when Kaine is joking. My shoulders are starting to cramp, so I roll them.

"Come to think of it, I get much less back pain now that I don't have breasts." Kaine's grin is mischievous.

I frown. "Are you boasting?"

"No periods, either. Neener, neener."

"It appears you're asking for death, you braggart." Grabbing a pillow, I toss it at his head.

Kaine catches the pillow. "Let me make it up to you." He massages my shoulders.

Ouch—that—ah, that feels good. Lying down, I melt as he kneads my back. "You've earned your right to live," I mumble.

He laughs. "Delighted to hear it, love."

The rest of the week flies by. I seal several lovely trade deals for Conollia and rack up a large number of favors. My brother's fate nags at my mind. Jiang is a slippery fish, so I'm working on a complicated plan to take him down. My evidence of Jiang's corruption won't be enough, unless we win in the World Games. Then his position will weaken enough that his cronies will turn on him. If only I can free Calum, then I can make a serious move to take over the council. Investigating Donya's list of charities has been going slowly. She complained about the obstruction from the authorities at our regular weekly dinner. Even worse, the deadline for Kaine's invasion is fast approaching, and I haven't found Kaine's brother.

Kaine wouldn't truly sack Arahasnor . . . would he? He *is* a dark lord. I'll beg an extension off Kaine even if I have to kiss one out of him. In truth, I wanted to find Alesh most of all for my beloved's sake. But there's not much I can do that I'm not already doing. My spies can't search every building in the city, and even the talented Suzette can't make the information flow any faster. I still believe in my people's abilities, just not that we will finish in time.

After asking a few people, I find Kaine in a basement armory. He moves along a row of cannonballs. Each one glows after he touches it. He looks up, then bounds over to me with a big grin. "Ysabel!"

"What are you doing?" I ask.

"I have the ability to enchant projectiles to always hit their target. Well, in principle. In practice I only improve the odds."

"Huh. You seem like you're preparing for an invasion." I have such a bad feeling.

"That's right. Tomorrow." He smiles even wider. "I can't wait to wage war again."

"About that. Are you even certain Alesh is in the Holy City?"

"Quite certain. I felt a few more pings, and it only happens when I inhale air close to your walls."

I struggle to keep my feelings off my face. "Can you give me another hint about where in the city he might be?"

"Sorry, it's not so precise. Please don't feel guilty about failing to find Alesh. You gave me extra time to prepare my army, so it worked out for the best. Thanks for being a good sport about this." He pats my head. "I know you'll keep our bargain."

From someone else, that would sound like a backhanded threat, but Kaine is sincere. He always keeps his promises, and he expects the same from other people. Suddenly, I can't bring myself to disappoint him. I can't let him invade my city, but at least I'll keep searching for the rest of today before I admit I've failed.

In the city, I harangue Cardinal Orwin for more information, but it's unproductive. As I leave our meeting, I complain to God, "If this really is a task from You, and I'm not necessarily saying it is, I need a hint. I'm stumped."

"What do You mean, right under my nose? Maybe You've gone senile in Your eons of existence?"

"Are You laughing at me? Go shove an angel up Your ass."

In my distraction, I've been walking in the wrong direction. My feet took me toward my shelter for escaped slaves, maybe out of habit. I turn back.

A woman buying bread waves at me as I pass her. Assuming I should recognize her, I wave back.

She smiles. "You should come visit us at the shelter, Holy Ysabel. It would boost morale."

Then she must be one of my volunteers. I'm halfway to the shelter anyway. I could raise the reward on Alesh one more time. First, I decide to stop at my favorite sausage stall, the smell of the bread making me hungry.

The food stall is mysteriously closed, and a single red rose lies on the counter. Today just isn't my day. Groaning, I turn toward the shelter.

I'm in a bad mood now. I fling the shelter door open. The elven ambassador of all people is talking to the receptionist. There's at least one half-elf in the city, but he's no slave. He's the head of the elven delegation, plus he's far too young to be Kaine's *older* brother.

Seeing me, Ambassador Berylseed raises his hand in a friendly way. I glare and think, *Kill, kill, kill* at him until he looks away. I'm still humiliated over the banquet where he read my mind.

If he was less important, I could claim privilege as the owner of this facility to skip the line. Instead, I wait behind him and fume. I have this odd feeling that the Sun God is cursing me out right now. But sometimes I have trouble telling my inner God from my many anxieties.

The old woman says to the ambassador, "I'm sorry for bringing you here for another false alarm, sir."

"Not at all. I want to hear about any lead, no matter how small." His fingers drum on the desk. Tension fills his posture.

"I understand how worried you must be about your brother," the receptionist says in a practiced way nevertheless holding genuine sympathy.

He came here looking for a relative? The irrational anger in my heart melts away. This poor guy lost someone important to him to slave traders, and I was contemplating butting in line. I should be less of a bitch.

"I'm a little confused by the forms you've filled out." The receptionist shuffles her papers. "You're looking for a woman who's a slave or a man who's an escaped slave, but they're the same person?"

"Yes. I'm confident that if he's free, he's passing as a man. If not, he wouldn't have a choice." Ambassador Berylseed hesitates. "Please look for both men and women just in case."

Wait a minute.

"We'll do our best. Kaine is such a common name."

The Dark Lady in an orgy with the Sun God! This isn't possible. There's no way that baby face is past forty . . . Sweet saints, he's a half-elf. Enlightenment knocks me on the upside of the head like the gentle clout of my drunkard father. Half-elves age slower than humans, so Kaine's older brother eventually looks like his younger brother. I'm never going to be able to call Kaine a chicken brain again when mine is a goddamn ant brain.

I tap Ambassador Berylseed on the shoulder. "Excuse me. Is your first name Alesh?"

"Yes, it is."

I jump in the air and scream, "Yes!" Then I kneel down and clasp my hands together. "I'm sincerely sorry, God. You're the best, and I'm dumber than a woodpecker on a steel pipe. I'll be making a ridiculously large charitable contribution here in Your name."

"Are you all right?" Alesh glances at the receptionist. "Is there a doctor on staff?"

Leaping to my feet, I say, "I know your brother Kaine."

"Y-you do? Are you sure?" He grabs me by my shoulders. "Please, this means everything to me."

"We'd better go to a private room. What I'm about to tell you isn't something to spread around." Also, Alesh is probably going to want to sit down once I drop the "dark lord" revelation. I glance at the receptionist. Recognizing me, she hands over a key to a room upstairs.

The entire shelter probably still hears Alesh screaming, "My brother is WHO?"

I send a message ahead of the carriage to tell Kaine the big news. He waits for us at the gate of his fortress. He's wearing the diamond earring and silver rings I gave him, which bring out his big brown eyes wonderfully, if I do say so myself. Upon catching sight of his brother, his face breaks out into the biggest smile. It makes me feel a foot taller.

"Alesh!" he cries. Running up to us, he slides to a stop, his hands twisting together. "How are you? I could barely believe it when Ysabel told me you're an elven ambassador."

"Yes. I've been doing well." Alesh looks around at the fortress bristling with catapults, ballistae, and gargoyles. "I guess we both came up in the world. This place looks very dangerous, uh, I mean nice. Great . . . towers. Very spiky."

"Should I leave you two alone?" I ask.

Two pairs of eyes turn pleadingly on me. "Don't," Kaine says.

"Then I'd be happy to come with you." I understand how they must feel. After two years of separation from my siblings during my enslavement, I felt like I no longer knew them. These two haven't seen each other since they were children.

As Kaine leads us to the sitting room, he asks Alesh, "How did you escape?"

"The slavers who captured me were attacked by elven soldiers a week later. They came because they'd heard someone with elven blood was being held prisoner." Alesh takes a seat on the couch under the buck's head. "They wanted to take me back to the Elven Empire, but I had to find you. Except, by the time I got back to town, I learned you'd been captured too. No one was even certain which war band had grabbed you. I went to the Empire because they have an information network used by escaped slaves to find family."

Kaine runs his fingers through his hair. "I escaped shortly afterward when my gift manifested."

"Mine didn't appear until nearly a year later, while I was living in an elven shelter for escaped slaves. It changed my life. I had colleges offering me scholarships and several noble families wanting to adopt me." Alesh bites his lip and shifts. "I picked the family headed by another mind reader, because he offered to train me. I'm a Berylseed now and a knight."

"That's great. I'm a dark lord."

"I know. Not because I read your mind! I don't invade people's privacy like that. I only use it on the job. I promise I won't read your mind without permission."

I can't blame Alesh for mindreading during the banquet; all ambassadors are informally spies. Dammit, it's going to take a lot of sucking up to repair my hideous first impression. How am I supposed to make Alesh like me when he already knows I'm a liar? Can we please forget all about the awkward fantasies and treat each other as family?

"You can clearly take care of yourself." Kaine nibbles on his knuckles. "I was worried about you. So I'm relieved."

"You look healthy too. Older. And . . . big." Alesh looks Kaine up and down. "How did you grow up so giant?"

Kaine answers the rhetorical question. "I had my body modified to become my real self. It feels great."

"Kaine! Modification is dangerous! Using it too much can kill you!"

"It's okay. I found someone who does permanent, full-body transformations."

"Oh." Alesh sags back on the couch. "I'm glad to hear it. I mean, it's not my place to lecture you anymore."

"It's fine! You were just worried." Kaine nods vigorously. "I know how you feel. I conquered an entire country looking for you."

Alesh's eyes are as wide as whirlpools. "For me?"

"Ha ha. That wasn't the only reason, of course. There were probably other reasons that I can't think of right now. Anyway. It all worked out for the best. You're here now."

The awkwardness in the room is thick enough to drown a rat. I cough. "Kaine, why don't you offer your guest a drink?"

"Great idea!" Kaine leaps to his feet. "I'll get it." He more or less flees from the room.

Sighing, I turn to Alesh. "Sorry, he forgot to ask: What would you like?"

I catch up to Kaine pacing the hall. He clutches his hair. "I don't know what to say! It's Alesh, I know in my bones, but I feel like I'm talking to a stranger."

"It's been twelve years. You *have* become strangers. But you have time to get to know each other again." I stand on my tiptoes to touch his cheek.

"He has noble manners and a new accent, and . . ." Kaine looks at his feet. "I'm not sure he's proud of me being a dark lord."

"Well, it's a lot to take in. He seemed more surprised than upset to me. Remember, he's also seeing the you from twelve years ago. It's probably hard to accept that his kid brother is now the world's strongest warlord." If one of my younger siblings became a tyrant and took over a country while I wasn't looking, I'd probably faint for real for the first time in my life.

"I feel cheated that I didn't get to rescue him. I'd expected we were going to live together once I found him, but he's made a home for himself somewhere else." Kaine shudders. "I'm a h-horrible person. I'm disappointed my own brother was living a happy life instead of being abused as a slave." His voice breaks.

"No, no, you're not horrible at all." I rub his back. "You spent years conquering all of Conollia to save your brother, and now you find out you were looking in the wrong place the whole time. Of course you feel let down. But you freed a lot of other slaves. Your hard work wasn't for nothing."

"Yeah." Kaine shuffles his feet. "I *am* glad Alesh was rescued. This is the best news I could have gotten."

The emphasis sounds a little like he's trying to convince himself. I put a hand on his shoulder. "What's wrong? I won't judge, I promise."

Kaine swallows. "I don't know if Alesh wants me now he's got a whole 'nother family of Rich Nobles who probably don't have any place for a dark lord around the dining table." His hands clench and unclench. Even when he was trapped in a hostile city without his magic, I've never seen him this terrified.

"That's completely wrong." I grab Kaine by his collar and drag him down to force him to look into my eyes. "Do you know where I found Alesh? At a shelter for escaped slaves, looking for you. He wanted to find you just as much as you wanted to find him."

"R-really?"

"Yes, really. If you can charm me, then don't tell me that you can't get along with a bunch of nobles. If they don't like you, that's their problem. You're very lovable." I pat him on the head. "Get in there and have a conversation with your brother. You can't expect to rebuild your bond in one day, so have another conversation with him tomorrow. Show me that dogged determination of yours."

"That's right." Kaine stands up straight. "Alesh is fine, which means everything is all right. Thank you so much for finding him for me."

"Isn't there something else you should thank me for?" I cough. "Didn't a certain sword-happy dark lord have a dumb plan like attacking my beautiful city even though it didn't deserve vengeance after all?"

"I'll make sure to listen to you in the future. Thanks, Ysabel. You're the best." He kisses me on the forehead, then skips back into the sitting room.

Hold up, I had a lot more things to say to lecture him into submission before he admitted he was wrong. Although that's also what I like about Kaine. For a dark lord, he's a sweetheart.

Inside the room, Kaine says, "If it would be all right with you, can I give you a hug?"

Alesh replies, "I'd like that."

I smile and leave to fetch Alesh the apple juice he asked for, walking slowly to give them some time alone.

The Sun God keeps nagging at the back of my mind, telling me we're not done here. "What now?" I mutter. "I found him. Even if I hadn't, they would have met at the World Games, or earlier if Alesh read someone's m—"

I freeze. "He's a *mind reader*! He can tell me where Jiang is keeping my brother!"

The apple juice spills across the floor.

CHAPTER SEVENTEEN

Of course I'll help you find your brother," Alesh says, sitting cross-legged on a wicker chair in Kaine's sitting room. His gaze holds sincere sympathy and warmth. I try not to think about how those eyes can see straight through me if he wants.

I half-jump out of my seat. "Thank you! The next time you meet with Jiang—"

"Jiang refuses to be in the same room as me since the banquet." Alesh sighs. "No one will meet with me now my abilities have leaked. I've been banned from the palace. I can't blame them. If they think I'm spying, they're right."

My shoulders sag. As soon as I find a solution, there's a new problem. I gnaw on my cheek. "How far away can you read minds?"

"My ability works through my eyes, so I have to see the other person." Alesh gestures at his eyes. "I'm planning to do some spying in the Games stadium where people want to see the matches too badly to avoid me. I get juicier information when people know about my powers. Usually, I only pick up on surface-level thoughts. Back at the banquet, Jiang mostly thought about how much he hates Queen Bianna's hats. I had no idea he'd kidnapped the Holy Maiden's brother. But when people know about me, they can't help thinking their darkest secrets when I'm around."

I try very hard not to think about spanking Kaine. *Don't think about that in front of his brother . . . Don't think about that in front of his brother . . . Oh, crap, I thought it.* Since Alesh hasn't run out of the room screaming, then I guess either he was telling the truth about not reading my mind or he has a great poker face.

Trying not to look guilty, I say, "Maybe I could arrange a meeting with Jiang and hide you nearby. But if I get caught, he'll know I was trying to rescue my brother. Calum will die."

"What if Kaine arranges the meeting instead?" Alesh suggests.

"That would be a better idea. Jiang still believes I'm at odds with Kaine." I don't think Jiang will want to meet with a dark lord. What maneuver can I pull so he has no choice? "Does your gift work through binoculars?"

"Sorry, but no. There's a bigger problem." Alesh hesitates. "I have a limited number of times I can read the same person's mind. I've already crept around Jiang a couple times looking for state secrets. We only have two more shots at him."

I appreciate the trust he placed in me by telling me the price of his gift. "Then we'd better make certain the meeting goes off without a hitch."

Unfortunately, the very next day, Cardinal Jiang attempts to disqualify Kaine from the World Games.

One leg crossed, I sit in an armchair facing Durrian's desk, skimming the letter. Cursive has been handwritten on the old-fashioned heavy rolled parchment. My hand crinkles the paper in anger. Until this is settled, no one important will meet with Kaine, including Jiang. They'll be too worried he might kill them if he decides to start a war over this. My plan to save my brother has stalled before it began. Clenching my teeth, I look up. "Ridiculous. No one has ever been banned from playing for having a strong gift. This is blatant rule-breaking." They're claiming precedent on the grounds that the Dragon Emperor has never fought personally—he's too big to even fit on the stage. But that's completely different; he received massive compensation and an automatic place in the top ten.

"They're screwing over Conollia as usual." Durrian shrugs. "Can they get away with it?"

A vote from the Conclave of Kings doesn't have to be fair, merely democratic. Nearly every human kingdom has signed the letter. "Odd, they don't have the Elven Empire." As the winners of the majority of all World Games, the Empire has ample reason to want to disqualify Kaine. "It's true what they say about elven honor." Elves have no love for dark lords, but they respect rules. "But the dwarves signed. Moon

Devil be fucked. I thought they'd refuse out of spite." The dwarves haven't placed well in the last few Games.

"Can they pull off a majority?" Durrian asks.

"Yes, but . . ." I tap my chin with the rolled-up letter. After the elves got fed up with attempts to bias the rules against them, they used their victory in the 201st Games to limit the Conclave's power. "At least two species need to be in agreement to ban a player. If we can persuade the dwarves, we can block this. I'll talk to Ambassador Mo'la'ni." As soon as the words leave my mouth, I remember the risk to Calum if I'm seen helping the Conollians. *Dammit.* Do I have to put my brother at risk to save my brother?

Durrian leans forward, worry leaking into his gray eyes. "To participate in the Games, we agreed on detailed life-oaths to never attack other countries. Fortunately, we were smart enough not to swear magically until the Games actually occur." What he's not saying out loud is, if an agreement can't be reached, it will mean war.

Which means I have no choice but to help, in secret. I'm the one with the political connections. My fingers clench so hard I rip the document slightly. "The dwarves probably don't want to do this. If they allow Kaine's disqualification, the same thing could happen to them another year. The Games only work as a substitute for war because everyone knows a real war would also come down to who has the most powerful Gifted Knights. If the result of the World Games no longer accurately represents who's the strongest, then the system collapses."

"Which is why they're asking us to voluntarily withdraw Kaine." Durrian's lip curls back.

"A lot of players are refusing to fight Kaine for fear of losing their precious gifts." Resting my hand on my chin, my lips form my most charmingly malicious smile. "Could Kaine still win if he agreed not to steal his opponents' abilities?"

"Absolutely." Durrian speaks with total confidence. "By my last count, he has two thousand eight hundred and thirty-one gifts. He's the strongest of the extinction-level gifted."

No, my Alzira is. "If we offer that compromise, most of the nations will withdraw their complaint. Only these won't." I stab the names of the countries located closest to Conollia. "They know Kaine will demand they free their Conollian slaves. But there will no longer be a majority against us."

Durrian strokes his beard. "I can live with that condition."

"Never fear—I'm going to get you some big concessions in exchange for giving up on the chance to steal so many powerful gifts."

"Good. We need Conclave votes more than Kaine needs extra abilities, with how the other nations are aligned against us."

"If you win the World Games, many human kingdoms will start sucking up to you. The Archpatriarch hates Arahasnor's political domination enough to tolerate your part-heathen country." The 549th World Games are going to rewrite global power. My grin becomes even more evil.

"What about your life-oath to Jiang?" Durrian asks.

"On the day of the World Games, I'll blackmail Jiang by threatening to tell everyone about his necromantic ritual. A stadium full of the most powerful people in the world would be the perfect place to shout the news. To keep my mouth shut, I'll force him to wager my life-oath in the Games."

"Kaine will beat him. Your bet will not be in vain."

"I'll repay you by dealing with this absurd attempt to ban Kaine." I strive to sound confident rather than terrified of getting caught. There's no point in complaining to Durrian when he's under enough stress already. The letter I pocket feels like iron instead of paper.

As I head for the door, he calls, "Ysabel?"

I pause, touching the handle. "Yes?"

"Are you sure you don't want Alzira to fight Jiang's team for your life instead? If the victory belonged to you, it would secure your power on the council. We can have her show up at the last minute so Jiang won't realize she's playing until it's too late."

"I'll think about it." Which means no. Alzira's price isn't my secret to share.

"If you're not participating in the World Games to give us an easy victory, you don't need to. We're allies. I would be happy to come to an agreement that no matter which of us wins, we'll hand the Conclave of Kings the same list of demands."

"That means a lot to me." I lower my gaze.

"It makes sense to double our chances of winning and also be able to force more concessions in total if we both place high. If there's a particular reason you've avoided playing in the Games, perhaps we can help."

Did he guess the truth? I whirl around. Durrian regards me calmly.

"I'll think about it," I repeat, my words a sword to draw a line between us. I escape out the door.

Alone in my bedroom, I pace. I reach for my redleaf pipe out of habit before remembering it wouldn't do anything.

Kaine was right. If lack of redleaf bothers me this much, it *was* an addiction. Not a particularly bad addiction, as I was functional . . . I'm making excuses. Just like an addict. How humiliating.

The same panic attacks I thought redleaf helped me treat have calmed down. Ho Tan, a fellow smoker, told me the drug makes some people paranoid. Connections fall into place. How anxious I felt after I came down from the high. The bad trips. Why did no one tell me this before? I'm willing to bet Jiang, who gave me my first dose when I was only fourteen, knew. That bastard never did anything nice for anyone, and yet I'd believed it would help with my panic attacks. So stupid.

My fists hurt from clenching as I pace faster. I'm both tired and too wound-up to rest. If I shut my eyes, I'll remember the first time I tried to enter the World Games . . .

Seven years ago, when I formed the Dragon Maidens, I considered entering my team without Alzira playing. The other ladies alone would have been a shoo-in to at least make it to the top fifteen. None of the other human teams accept women. So if one human team has the best women in the world, while the best men are spread across different teams, then obviously we'll win. Of course the same people who tried to murder Dark Lord Kaine to keep him from competing wouldn't accept being beaten by a bunch of females.

After Alzira first joined my World Games team, fifteen different groups of killers came after her in a week. Half the attackers were cheap thugs either desperate or ignorant about their target. Whoever sent the assassins probably never expected them to succeed but hoped someone might get in a lucky arrow from a distance or catch Alzira asleep. We arranged for me or one of the Dragon Maidens to accompany Alzira everywhere, even to the bathroom. Because I couldn't afford adequate security at my home, Alzira secretly moved to an inn.

A professional assassin tracked her down. The assassin put a dagger in Alzira's side before she woke up. Fortunately Sigma was sleeping in the same room. Sigma drowned the assassin and stabilized Alzira in time for me to reach her and heal her. If the assassin had known Alzira can't use her power except to protect her friends, then he would have killed Sigma first. Then Alzira would have been completely magicless and helpless.

This brought home the nature of Alzira's vulnerability. If the world found out about the price of her gift, she'd be too easy to kill. Catch her alone, and she's just one woman with a sword.

If my Dragon Maidens fought in the Games without Alzira, there would be rampant speculation about why. Even without anyone knowing the truth, Alzira came too close to death. Assassination is a common tactic established countries use against weaker countries with powerful gifted. Even the strongest fighter can be ganged up on or drugged.

I don't have the power to protect my friends. I don't have the power to protect anyone. I never have. And it's all too much responsibility for me to handle. I feel sorry for not letting the other Dragon Maidens fight, but it can't be helped. There's no need to put a permanent target on Alzira's back when Kaine can win on his own, even if we won't be able to get quite as many concessions as if we took both first and second place. Or so I tell myself late at night, staring at the shadows on my wall and remembering Alzira's blood on my hands.

My meeting with Ambassador Mo'la'ni goes exactly as planned. She has no stakes in whether or not Conollia becomes a nation. If anything, the dwarves would be happy to see the powerful human kingdoms weakened. As long as we promise to let the dwarven fighters keep their gifts, and mention how happy Conollia would be to purchase dwarven iron with their Games winnings, she's delighted with the bargain. Next, I persuade Cardinal Orwin to propose my compromise to the human kingdoms, keeping my name out of it. He makes me pay him a great deal of money in exchange for stealing my credit. I seek out Kaine to tell him the good news, only to find him already in conversation with his brother.

Alesh and Kaine are keeping their relationship a secret out of fear of Kaine's enemies taking hostages. It's a legitimate concern. Several people have sent assassins this week alone. Alesh did insist on reporting it to his superiors. He also said his adopted family promised to treat his little brother as their own if he was ever found, though it remains to be seen how well the dark lord revelation will land. In the meantime, diplomatic negotiations give the elven ambassador plenty of excuses to visit.

As soon as I hear them talking on the porch, I take a step back inside, not wanting to intrude. I'm not eavesdropping. Then I hear my name, and from that point on, I *am* eavesdropping.

"I still can't believe you kidnapped Ysabel." Alesh's voice holds a stern note. "I raised you better than that."

"It's not like how the bards make it sound! I was trying to free her from the man planning to murder her. It wasn't a barbaric attempt at romance, it was because I owed her a debt. Although I do like her." I can hear the blush in Kaine's voice.

"I'm just giving you a hard time. Still, you have to admit, a dark lord kidnapping the noble lady he's fallen madly in love with? That's a terrible cliché. If my baby brother must become a dark lord, I expect a higher quality of evil than that."

"Shut up."

"You've become the villain in one of those street shows we used to watch as kids."

"Shut up."

"Who's the hero coming to rescue her? King Uctor is too old, and there's no crown prince. Huh, I think it might be me. We'd have the 'brothers turned enemies' shtick going. I'm the better-looking one, so I'd ultimately win the love triangle."

"Shut up."

I stifle a laugh behind my hand and sink down lower to hide behind the bushes. Whoever designed this miniature garden must be a rare person with both taste and humor. I must meet them for assistance with the rest of the castle. They decorated the dark lord's garden with black flowers. Dark dahlias, hellebores, and calla lilies grow in flower beds on top of and alongside the porch railing. Black roses wind down the support beams. The tulips are a midnight shade of dark purple, and the black-petaled pansies have blue stars inside. The bushes are Zinfandel oxalis, starry lemon-yellow flowers set in night-dark leaves. Alesh and Kaine sit on a swinging seat. The boxes on either side hold bat flowers, which true to their name look like two spreading wings with fang-like whiskers.

"In all seriousness, I got lucky with Ysabel. I keep worrying I'm going to screw it up."

"You have great taste in women," Alesh says (to my profound relief, because I still have trouble looking him in the eye). "How are things going between you two?"

"Wonderfully." Affection fills Kaine's voice. "I'm getting a little antsy to try my new body out, but I can wait for someone like her."

Huh? I've been respecting his wishes and waiting for him to send me a clear signal. Why's he telling this to his brother, not me?

"Have you told her this?" *Good job, Alesh.*

"No, of course not. After the whole accidental kidnapping, I don't dare be forward with her. It's better to wait for her to make the first move."

What the hell! So we're both waiting for the other person like a pair of idiots? If it wouldn't give away my hiding place, I'd be wailing and gnashing my teeth.

Alesh clicks his tongue. "From another perspective, you're forcing her to be the only one who risks rejection. Just ask and be prepared to take no for an answer." My future brother-in-law is getting a large birthday present from me. Actually, I don't even need to marry Kaine, I'll adopt Alesh anyway.

"Do you really think so?" Kaine sounds hopeful.

"It's not like my baby bro, who used to fight a dozen other kids at once, to be a coward. While you're at it, tell her you're crazy about her and want something serious."

Did Alesh glance in my direction? My face heats up. If my hunch is right, I think I'll die of embarrassment.

"You're right! I'm going to find Ysabel." There's a rustle as Kaine rises to his giant height.

Crap. I have to get out of here. I'm almost around the corner when the door opens. Kaine calls, "There you are!" Walking faster, I pretend not to hear. Kaine runs after me like we're playing a chasing game. Right as I shut my bedroom door, he asks, "Ysabel? Are you avoiding me?"

"No, it's not like that!" I open the door so fast I nearly clip him on the nose.

"Why were you outside the garden? Did you overhear what I said?"

"Umm . . ." I should have denied it right away. Now there's nothing for it but to come clean. "Maybe." That was a pathetic attempt at coming clean.

"Great, that makes this easier." He beams. "Want to fuck?"

Want to fuck? *Want to fuck?* I may have indulged in fantasies, but I planned to treat the occasion properly, with rose petals and a bottle of fine wine. Instead, swords-for-brains skips straight to "Want to fuck?" I don't expect poetry from a dark lord, but surely he can do better. I want to beat him, and not in the sexy way. Okay, maybe I also want to beat him in a sexy way. For us sadists, our impulses can get confused. "Not if you're going to ask me like that."

He tilts his head. "How do you want me to ask you?"

"Put a little effort into it. Seduce me. If all you want is to try out your new body, go masturbate."

His pupils dilate. "Can I take that as an order?"

The way he says that gives me the shivers. Hence why I reply, "Sure. It's an order."

"Okay, then." He heads toward my bed.

"Wait, what are you doing?"

"Seducing you." He lies down.

His grand romantic plan is to jerk off on my bed? *Alesh, please explain to me how this fool crawled out of his mother's womb without getting lost.* "Humph, as if such a lame seduction would ever work."

"Is that a challenge?" He lies motionless, waiting for my permission. All that tightly coiled muscle ready to move at my command. It's seriously hot. I swallow.

"Challenge accepted. Do whatever you please, I'm going to ignore you."

He unbuttons his shirt. I sit down and pull out a file of papers. If that's how he wants to play, I'll play to win.

Behind me, Kaine lets out a high, eager whine. My head turns around like a puppet on strings. The light overhead pools in the corner of his collarbone, tauntingly golden like honey. So he likes to play with his nipples . . . angrily, I jerk my vision back straight.

Concentrating proves impossible. In the quiet room, I can hear every exaggerated groan and sigh. The accounting numbers swim in front of me. I shift in my seat, heat pooling in my core. Why hasn't he finished yet? He has some serious stamina. My pen trembles in my hand.

Kaine murmurs, "Ysabel . . ." The sound of my name resonates straight to my bones.

That does it. "Cut that out or I'll take you over my knee and spank you." Huh, that did not come out the way my brain planned it.

His voice drops to a low purr. "Really? Tell me more."

"Listen, I'm a wolf, not a lamb. If you provoke me, don't blame me if I gobble you up." I rise from the chair. If he brought me flowers, I would have been gentle, but now he needs a punishment. A smile tugs my lips upward.

The bedsprings creak as I pounce. Masculine sweat exudes off the body underneath me, and his hardness is visible against his pants. I whisper in his ear, "If you still want to be spanked, turn over."

He complies as fast as if his life depends on it. I drink in the flat planes of skin and well-trained muscle. I bring my hand down once, twice, thrice. We should probably have a clothed discussion before I strike any harder, and right now I've lost my mind. Onto the main course, then. I straddle him and steal a kiss from behind.

Eagerly, he turns to face me. We land on the sheets in a jumble of limbs. His fingers unlace my corset with the skill of someone who's probably worn one, letting it trickle through his fingers to the floor. I rip off his shirt, bursting the seams in my eagerness to taste his bare skin. He shivers as my hands ghost his ribs. I swirl my tongue over the scar there. I'm rewarded with another gorgeous whine. *A little ticklish, how delightful.*

I let my fingers wander downward, barely touching, flaunting my self-control until his own snaps and he buries his face in my breasts. He uses a little too much teeth, as he's prone to when excited. "Let me feel your tongue," I urge, tugging his hair to guide him. He laps delicate circles around my hardening nipples until I whimper, then he *laughs* at me. My blood boiling competitively, I go for the kill. One firm hand pumps him while the other traces around his asshole. He rubs against me, mouth open and gasping. *Oh, I'm going to make him scream by the end.* I'll have the great dark lord himself begging for mercy.

Suddenly I need to touch him everywhere. He seems to have the same idea, and we bump into each other. Kaine catches me when I nearly fall off the mattress, then we're both laughing together helplessly. He kisses me, tenderly at first, then our desire boils over and we go back to thrusting our hips and fucking a tongue down each other's throat. He tastes better than the finest wine. With his sweaty hair, he looks like a cross between a disheveled puppy and a pagan god. His curious eyes are half-lidded as I put a sheath over his length. I need too much to wait any longer.

We push together, misconnecting in our haste. I find the right spot and guide Kaine in. He moves deliciously well, all the power and grace of a warrior translating into an instinct for finding my sweet spots. My nails scratch his back as the sound of our breathing fills the room. The cares of the outside world vanish under the onslaught of pleasure. I've lost track of how many little gasps I've fucked out of him, but I could never get enough.

With that same fantastic howl he makes when he fights, he comes. Barely pausing, he finishes me off by tenderly thumbing my clit at just the right rhythm. He's gotten very good at that, though I enjoyed the days when I used to order him on how fast to go. As I collapse, I feel like all the tension has been pulled out of me. It's the most wonderful feeling in the world. Here, I feel safe and loved. The rhythm of his heartbeat and the musky sex smell relaxes me. Worth waiting for, indeed.

"That was great for round one," Kaine says right as I'm about to nod off.

"Round one?" I ask, grumpy at forcing my eyes open, but not too grumpy, because he's lovely with the sweat glowing on his dark skin like golden rays of sun, and I haven't had enough either. I flip him over and pin his wrists above his head. "There are penalties for disturbing my rest."

"Oh no. Whatever will I do," Kaine deadpans. His magnificent body coils under me.

I laugh before grinding down against him. "I know your weak spot."

"Oh-ho?"

"Right here." I seize his sides and tickle him mercilessly.

He writhes and wails. "Ha! Wait! Ha ha! I wanted! Ha! A more! Ha ha! Sexy punishment!"

"Be careful what you wish for, my dear." I stretch, showing off my gloriously naked body. His eyes ignite as he watches. *Please keep looking at me like that, it inspires my imagination to new games.* I crush my lips into his.

First, I mouth over his hands, tasting the warrior's calluses. I work my lips up his arm and down his chest, playing with his nipples, then his bellybutton, then finally taking him fully in my mouth. He has solid, muscular thighs, a pleasure to tickle and pinch. Then I lick him in the ass too. He never screams even when injured in battle, yet here he screams for me beautifully. That's round two.

For round three he gets on his knees to lick me, loosening me up until a two-headed toy presses in with no resistance. Then he takes the dildo all the way into his mouth and sucks at it where the base goes into me. After a quick conversation, I retrieve a rope from my nightstand and tie it around his cock, looping twice and splitting up his balls to make it harder for him to come. I remind him, "Let me know the instant it starts to feel cold or too tight."

"It's *good*. Now hurry."

"Patience." I flick his dick. The tie has him so sensitive that he howls. His eyes are wide and blown-out. "Look at you, so hard when I've barely gotten started."

Retrieving perfumed oil from my bedside table, I pour it on top of the dildo where my own juices drip down the second end. It's slick enough to slide easily inside him. Facing his back, I thrust. Competitively, he thrusts back. Soon we're both trying to pound each other into the mattress. The headboard slaps against the wall hard enough to rattle my pictures. I should worry about that crashing sound on the other wall, except the stars behind my eyes are too strong. The brutal pace has me nearly sobbing, my body begging for a breather, but I'm too competitive to stop. For his sake, for the man who returned my dreams to me, I'll give him everything he can take. My toes curl, shaking with the force of the orgasm I'm holding back.

Kaine snaps first. "Touch me," he growls, a demand and a plea.

"Not until I've had my satisfaction." I tug the rope. Veins stand out on his neck as I move faster to torment him. Gasps and beautiful pleas echo through the room along with the slap of flesh against flesh. His neck arches, bare and vulnerable. Utterly under my control. I love it.

I'm hot all over with hunger and clinging to my patience with my fingernails. I drop to his ear to whisper, "Now." I bite his beautiful sun-tanned collarbone while undoing the rope. His pleasure rocks my body as my own explodes throughout me, leaving me shaking and breathless.

That was just what I needed. I'm exhausted, I'm overstimulated, and I'm triumphant knowing no one could ever rock Kaine's world as hard as I just did. This victory tastes even sweeter than my political ones.

It's very tempting to collapse and fall asleep with us still locked together. I summon up enough will to drag over a basin and towels. Looking after him is my duty now.

"That was awesome. You're awesome," Kaine slurs.

"So were you. You're absolutely beautiful." I pat his bare ass, then swab a cold cloth across his back. "Turn over." With a nudge, he does so, letting me clean his front. He's very out of it. Good: that means I got him to a natural submissive high. A sudden surge of affection fills me as I gaze at him, sprawled boneless and covered with my marks. Perhaps I've got a bit of dark lord in me, because I have a sudden urge to whisk him away and lock him up where only I can see him.

Sitting on the edge of the bed, I hand him a glass of water. "Do you want anything to eat?"

"I'm not hungry."

Whoa, I got Kaine to a mental state where he's not thinking about food. I'm even more impressed with myself. Still, he should replenish his energy. "How about a treat for a good boy?" I wave a piece of chocolate in front of his nose.

"I have room for that." He opens his mouth so I can feed him.

As I towel myself off, he offers, "I can help," trying to lift himself up.

"There's no need. You're still feeling the subspace, so let me take care of you." I toss the towel to the floor then climb into bed with him, curling up close to his body. I pull the blankets over both of us.

"You're spoiling me."

"Trust me, I get something out of this too." I kiss his neck, his head pillowed against my shoulder. With him next to me, I feel safe, not a feeling I usually get to enjoy. Even if all my enemies busted down the door, my dark lord would destroy them.

I think I drifted off. Kaine definitely did. When I open my eyes, the afternoon sun is just starting to sink, and I'm ready for dinner. If I'm this hungry, Kaine must be . . .

"I'm starving," he says, sitting up. He kisses me on the forehead. Then he kisses me there again, and again. "Since you were so good to me, I'll bring us dinner in bed."

"That sounds lovely," I say. "Do you have a moment to chat first?" I take a chug of water, then hand the glass to him.

He gulps it down. "Sure, what is it?"

"We need to discuss your desires and limits." A conversation I should have had before I jumped straight to orgasm denial.

"Truthfully, I'm not very experienced." Looking away, he runs his fingers through his hair.

I'll have to be slow and careful with him. "That's okay. Start by telling me what you liked about this time. We can talk about your fantasies." Into his ear, I purr seductively, "Then I'll tell you mine."

It's a good talk. I'm pleased to learn he has interests in ropes, forced fantasies, and pain. He showed responsiveness to a combination of orders and praise, giving me plenty to work with. When I mention my kink for sensory deprivation and hot wax, he immediately asks to see my toys, a good sign. He's never heard of aftercare, so we'll have to figure out what he needs together. At a guess, I'd say Kaine draws comfort from food and cuddling.

"You should pick out a safe word."

"Eh, I don't go for fake noes." Kaine flaps a hand in dismissal. "I only say what I mean."

"Then no one has ever pushed you to your limits. You'll know you're ready for a safe word the first time you say no, I stop, and you're disappointed. For now, we can just treat no as no. Safe words are useful and quite versatile. You can use different ones to indicate wanting to slow down or even wanting more."

"I'm tough. I don't see myself needing one."

I crack an eye open to glare at him. "Do *not* get it in your head that there's anything masculine or noble about refusing to say no. It's stupid and hurts both of us." I dumped a man once for refusing to use his safe words, so this is a sensitive topic, making me snap at him.

"I'm sorry!" he says, cowed. "It's not like you could tie me up with anything I couldn't break out of."

"True. But if it comes to that, I've fucked up." I doubt Kaine understands how mentally vulnerable I could make him during subspace. Moderating my tone, I explain, "I need to know where your limits are in order to create fun games. If you have to stop me by force then I'd be a bad domme. I *want* you to tell me when you don't like something instead of making me guess." I swallow. It takes effort to admit the vulnerable truth: "It would devastate me if I actually hurt you. Please don't do that to me."

"Absolutely not! Never!" He waves his hands. "You're adorable, you know that?" He strokes my hair.

"There's, uh, one other thing I wanted to talk about." I wet my lips. This is way harder than talking about types of rope bondage. Overhearing what he said to Alesh has given me courage. "I want to know where you see this relationship going."

"Like where we're going to live?" He motions as if he's sizing up geographical distance. "Durrian will be furious if I don't go back to

Conollia once the Games are over. He's worried about a revolt while I'm gone. Our government is too new."

"We don't need to start that far ahead in the future." I stare at my hands. Asking him about marriage and my dream of exactly two children would be rushing it. I've been fantasizing a lot about a life with Kaine despite all my uncertainties over my future. "Do you want a romantic as well as a physical relationship, of the monogamous nature?"

"The what, now?"

"We don't sleep with other people."

"That goes without saying." He winks. "I'm not the kind of dark lord who kidnaps someone I'm not planning to marry."

"Oh, you." I hit him with the pillow. A smile tugs at my lips. It's nice to have reached a place where we can joke about that.

"Do you want children?" he asks. "Bei Ren said my new equipment is functional in that regard, and I want them."

Screw playing coy. I take a deep breath and decide to be open and honest like Kaine. "I do want children. I'm too busy with work for a large family. Still, my siblings are important to me, so I want that for my own kid. I'd like to have two."

"Yes!" He jumps out of bed and pumps his fist. Still naked—nice view. "Kids with Ysabel would be so cute." His eyes glaze over, lost in the daydream. Luckily types of magic aren't inherited, or I'd be too scared to even think about reproducing.

Oh, right . . . My healing gift, aka the reason why I never thought I'd live long enough to have children. When I'm around Kaine, I forget about my time limit. I'd never have children if I didn't think I'd last long enough to see them grow up. If only I could run away. My life-oath clenches warningly around my heart. For once, I don't mind the pain, because it reminds me I'm alive and fighting.

There might be stronger regeneration abilities for Kaine to steal. I'm not giving up hope quite yet. I want to live.

Sitting up, I take his hands in mine. "I want a future with you. If I can get free of the cardinals, then I'd rather not stay in Arahasnor. This country holds mostly bad memories. We can live in Conollia. I'd go anywhere in the world with you."

He presses his lips to each of my knuckles. "I love you," he murmurs.

My breath catches. I'm not ready—I'm still dying—I need more time. If I say it back, it wouldn't exactly be a lie, but I want to wait until I feel it with all my heart. Instead, I give him my pure truth. "I'm honored. That makes me very happy."

Surging upward, he kisses me deeply and passionately. Fire rises up in my belly, which then unfortunately growls.

Laughing, Kaine says, "I promised you dinner, my lady. I'll fetch us a feast."

"Go, sir knight." I wave. "Wait! Not without clothes!"

He retrieves his shirt and pants from under the bed. The fabric is only a little ripped. Delicious abs ripple below his firm pecs. I run a comb through his hair. He looks good with it neat instead of his usual shaggy look. Would he let me dress him up? I have many wonderful ideas, and it's only fair since I wore the fur dress for him. I gaze at him with my chin resting in my hand. How did I get this lucky? I must be a very virtuous Holy Maiden.

Still blowing kisses at me, Kaine steps out the door. Then he squawks. "Aaah! What are you doing here?"

Alzira says coldly, "This fortress is not yet designated as safe for Her Holiness to be left alone. Nor are you a safe enough person to guard her, although you're getting there."

I sigh. There's another conversation we need to have.

Exhausted, I sleep well that night. Our success has fired up my imagination. All of my previous boyfriends were small, pretty men, often with glasses. But that night, I dream about how much power it would take to hold down Kaine's thick wrists.

I wake up uncomfortably aroused. If my type is changing in order to reflect Kaine, then I've fallen for him hard. *Dark Lady, dammit. I'm in trouble.*

CHAPTER EIGHTEEN

Kaine needs to meet with each World Games team in order to swear not to steal their gifts. It's the perfect chance to sneak Alesh over to read Jiang's mind. We request the meeting in a public park, allegedly for security reasons. In reality, we can hide Alesh in a private gazebo surrounded by high bushes. If he gets caught, we can even claim he passed by coincidentally.

It makes sense for me to stay home—I can't risk being implicated—but that doesn't mean I like it. I pace the narrow confines of my office, waiting for Kaine and Alesh to return.

When someone knocks, my head shoots up.

From Kaine's grim face, I know the bad news before he speaks it. "Jiang noticed Alesh right away. He left in a temper, before I had a chance to ask the right questions to bring the information we need to his mind. Alesh didn't get anything useful at all."

I moan and clutch my hair. "We can try again," I say to convince myself. We have one more shot.

"Does Jiang have a gift? Perhaps related to seeing through objects or detecting living beings?"

"No. Or at least not that I know of."

Kaine's brow furrows. "He noticed there was an extra person in the park even though Alesh didn't make a sound. Also, he refused to shake my hand. People with gifts are often afraid to touch me."

If Kaine's hunch is right, then our plan just got a lot harder. I strain my memory for any clues. Jiang's always been difficult to sneak up on, but I thought he was merely observant. Why would he bother to hide a gift?

A noise comes from my bookshelf. I run for Jiang's book, waving Kaine out of sight before opening it.

Cardinal Jiang's snarling face fills the picture frame. "I thought we were allies, at least when it comes to ending the necro-servant barbarian."

"O-of course we are. Look what he did to me." I hold up my arm, showing where I bruised myself bumping into the wall while going to the bathroom an hour ago. I've already fed Jiang three more stories of my failed attempts to murder Kaine, then cried about my supposed punishments.

Jiang crushes me with one sentence: "Then why didn't you warn me Dark Lord Kaine planned to read my mind?"

"I didn't know!" My heart pounds. He shouldn't have any reason to suspect me. Kaine didn't even have time to ask any suspiciously leading questions related to Calum.

Rage has contorted Jiang's handsome features into something red and monstrous. "Kaine has proven too good at making allies lately. First the dwarves help him sneak back into the Games, now even the elves are doing him favors? That imbecile couldn't charm so many foreign powers without advice. Dark lords have gone downhill in quality since Chingis. I'd believe Kaine's excessive gifts have given him brain damage, except the stories say he's always been a fool."

After so long without Jiang uncovering my negotiations with the dwarves, I thought I was safe. *Cock rot.* I raise my voice. "That doesn't mean I did it!"

"Then who helped Kaine?"

"I don't know!"

"Now that, I don't believe. You're a little sneak. You should have at least warned me about Kaine's new allies." Jiang's spittle hits the image. For him to have gone into a frenzy over the attempted mindreading, he must be hiding graver secrets than my brother. "Did the barbarian's cock charm you into working for him?"

Jiang wants someone to blame. And he doesn't need proof to punish me.

"Please," I whisper. He likes begging. I'll grovel as much as he wants to stop him from taking this out on Calum. I don't look at Kaine, hiding in the corner, but I can feel his trembling fury.

Jiang switches the image.

Two armored men hold Calum up while a third punches him in the stomach. My brother hisses—then laughs. "You call that a punch? You're too weak to pull the socks off a dead man."

"Stop!" I scream. Veins stand out on Kaine's neck from barely suppressed rage.

The man hits Calum again. A mix of blood and bile spews out of his mouth. Aiming his vomit at his tormenters, he hits the tips of their boots. "Rub it on your face. It will improve your smell," Calum slurs, cross-eyed. He's acting brave because he knows I can hear.

"Please, stop. What do you want me to do?"

Jiang doesn't reply. Red-faced, his guard pulls back for another punch. I realize what Jiang wants—for me to suffer. Then fine, I'll give him that.

Placing the book open and face down, I say in a high-pitched look, "Your Darkness, I was only reading. I swear I wasn't trying to communicate with anyone."

Kaine gapes.

I slap my hand against the table, then cry out as if in pain. "No, please!" I've got to make Jiang believe I haven't turned over information on Kaine out of fear, not because we've allied.

Finally picking up on my cue, Kaine growls, "Get back to your room." When he speaks in monosyllables, his acting becomes passable. He chops a chair in two. I cry out again.

The book has gone silent. Jiang believes Kaine knows nothing about our communications. He won't lay off Calum until I give him blood. I grab a letter opener off the desk, but Kaine stops me from cutting my arm. Our eyes lock over the fallen book. Unable to speak, I try to convey to him my desperate need.

He takes the letter opener from me and cuts open the back of his own arm. My cry isn't entirely feigned. Kaine lets the blood trickle down to flow underneath the bent spine of the book. Then we both leave the office, rustling furniture as if struggling.

Once we're safely in the hall, I yank off my headband and wrap it around his forearm. I feel terrible, it should have been me. "I can heal you . . ."

"No," he says definitively.

But healing is all I'm good for. "Please? It makes me feel a bit better about my gift when I get to use it for people I care about."

"I can't stop you from draining your life by healing other people, but I can stop you from using it on me. You have to respect my wishes if I have to respect yours. Fair is fair." Kaine sets his jaw.

With that, I've no chance of moving the rock named Kaine. He's too sweet . . . and too stubborn. Glancing at the bloody bandage, I whisper, "I'm sorry."

"I'm the one who's sorry." Kaine hangs his head. "I didn't carry out our plan successfully. You got into trouble helping me with the dwarves."

"I should have been more careful to not let Jiang find out."

"Let's agree it's Jiang's fault." His eyes crinkle, and he takes me into his arms and holds me until my heart rate calms down. My sense of safety in this castle has vanished, but he brings a bit of it back.

Kaine whispers into my hair, "I bet this makes you wish you could beat Jiang in the Games this year."

"Shows what you know. I'm a coward." I laugh in self-mockery.

Kaine frowns. "Do you want to play?"

"It's always been the dream for the Dragon Maidens. Truthfully, it used to be my dream too. My one shot to change the world. You'll win for me though, right?"

"Sure. But would that satisfy you?" Kaine's gaze makes me squirm.

Forfeiting again certainly won't satisfy my team. They've tolerated it because they know Alzira is our trump card and keeping her price secret overrules all else. I've let them down, especially since Feiyan at least only joined my team for the chance to play. Remembering Calum's pained grunts, I realize hiding behind Kaine isn't what I want either. But if I defy Jiang, he'll hurt my brother again. My mouth flattens. "I'll think about it."

I don't dare risk it. Next time, my plan has to be perfect. There's only one place where Jiang can't avoid Alesh: the World Games. Once the Games start, no one is allowed to leave. Only then can I ensure Jiang can't move my brother even if he figures out my plan. The Games will be my last chance to save Calum.

If I fail again, my brother dies.

Kaine makes it his personal mission to distract me from my worrying and misery over my brother as we wait for the World Games. I can't dwell on it if I want to stay sane, so I let him succeed.

The next couple months blur together in happiness. Kaine drags me along on a hunting trip turned into a picnic. In quid pro quo, I stuff him in a blue doublet and take him to the opera. This spawns a dozen ballads about the great love of Holy Maiden Ysabel and Dark Lord

Kaine. If I hear one more bard call it a kidnapping gone right, then I won't be held responsible for a lute being shoved up an ass. (I'll make Alzira put on a mask before she does it). I personally track down every bard to ask them to remove the rapey elements, only to be told the abduction is (ugh) everyone's favorite part. I could have happily lived the rest of my life without knowing a bunch of complete strangers get titillated at the idea of me being raped.

Kaine writes his own song for me. It's dreadful, but I love it anyway. I move into Kaine's room, although we have sex in every empty room in the fortress. He likes to sit with me in my office while I dig into endless World Games preparations. I'm also teaching him the alphabet. He had absolutely no interest in learning to read until I brought out my checklist of kinks and negotiation contracts, then the adorable blockhead couldn't learn fast enough.

While my nights are spent with Kaine, I spend most of my days with Durrian hammering out our plans. We've constructed a massive strategy to revitalize Conollia's economy, welcome in the freed slaves, and aid the sick and starving. All of our trade deals and funding depend on a World Games victory.

A week before the World Games, and eight days before my scheduled human sacrifice, Kaine shows up at my office, bringing me a bouquet of . . . meat? Each stick of jerky is wrapped with colored paper. "I hunted these myself with the new crossbow you gave me. Except the alligator." He points at the green-wrapped one.

I ordered the crossbow from the Dwarven Caves just for him. "How lovely. You can help me eat it." There's quite a lot. I place the bouquet in a vase. It's pretty, so why not?

I've secured a beautiful tower office with a huge round desk and bookshelves so high I need a ladder to reach the top. Instead of fake gilding, I have real golden candlesticks and a silk carpet. I've hung up a few scent packets from my clinic, and now it smells like home.

"Have you decided if the Dragon Maidens will play in the World Games?"

Oh yeah, I told him I would think about that. Sometimes I lose track of my lies. I fiddle with the bouquet to buy time. "I don't think it's a good idea this year."

Kaine leans against my desk. "Is it because the price of Alzira's gift only lets her fight if you're in danger?"

I stiffen. "Did she tell you that?" If so, I'm going to be annoyed. I trust Kaine absolutely, that's not the issue, but Alzira promised not to tell anyone without talking to me first. My entire team has made a lot of sacrifices to keep Alzira's price a secret.

"I figured it out myself. I've seen her sparring with the other Dragon Maidens, and she never uses her gift. Once I overheard her saying something to Sigma about practicing for when she couldn't use her power. Then I remembered how you jumped off the wall right before she stopped my army outside the Holy City. You're too smart to do something so reckless without a reason. She can only use her power if someone she loves is in danger, right? And she cares about you the most."

"Damn, I'm impressed." There's no point in denying it when he's already completely figured it out. "I hope no one else realized."

"Probably not, I'm good at figuring out how gifts work. Whenever I steal a new one, I have to risk its price. For the more common gifts, everyone already knows how they work, but occasionally people have a different variant."

Because Kaine lets me take the lead in politics, sometimes I forget he's much smarter than me when it comes to battle tactics and combat. I stand on my tiptoes to kiss his cheek. "You've got guts. I prefer them inside your body, so please be careful. You figured us out. Alzira would fight in the World Games with no magic and a sword, but I can't let her reveal her price. She'd be in serious danger if the world knew about her weakness. Perhaps my cowardice is holding the other Dragon Maidens back."

He places his hand on top of mine. "Don't talk down on yourself like that. You have a good reason. Couldn't the rest of the Dragon Maidens play in the Games without Alzira?"

"Someone would guess why. You figured out her price from less evidence."

Kaine considers, chewing on his lip. I wait. Finally, he suggests, "What if Alzira only fights in the match against me? I'll use a couple of my powers to fake it and make it look like she's controlling metal. We can stage the whole thing. A few decades ago, there was a warrior who only fought in one match because he could only use his gift for ten minutes a day. People would guess Alzira's price, but they'd be guessing wrong. No one would question why you'd save Alzira for the match with me. It will be the finals, after all." He beams with total confidence that he'll beat everyone.

"What an intriguing notion." It would even be legal. There's no rule against throwing fights in the Games—people often do so as part of the complicated behind-the-scenes negotiations. A bigger country will offer a smaller country concessions to surrender. I run through every possible outcome in my head, looking for any flaws. If my team doesn't make it to the finals, Kaine could stage a fight on a different occasion. "Then Alzira could go with me to save Calum while everyone else is distracted by the Games." As long as I have her, I don't need anyone else, and as long as I'm by her side, she can fight. "We should be back by the finals."

Kaine winks. "I'll try not to defeat my enemies too quickly in order to give you time."

"If everything goes according to plan, then it will be even harder for anyone to guess Alzira's price. Why, I can strike deals with all the other teams not to use Alzira in their particular match! It will be even more profitable." I rub my hands together.

Kaine chuckles. "I love how you always make my ideas even more diabolical, love."

I throw my arms around his neck and kiss him.

I fling open the door to the Dragon Maidens' practice room. "Ladies, Kaine came up with a plan to let us enter the World Games! He agreed to fake a fight with Alzira. I didn't tell him her price—he figured it out on his own. He's the most wonderful, handsome, and brilliant man ever."

I had more bragging to do, but my voice gets drowned out by the cheers. Feiyan tosses her axe so high it dents the ceiling. Nakimé and Ua'la'sur of all people hug. Sigma has her hands clasped together in prayer, tears glinting in the corners of her eyes.

Feiyan grabs me by the shoulders. "What if someone notices the finals fight is staged?" Her eyes are wild, the expression of someone who does not dare hope until she is certain.

"It's a risk, but so is doing nothing. Kaine figured out Alzira's price from when I jumped off the wall. Others might also have gotten suspicious. If we pull this off, then everyone will think Alzira has a time limit on her gift instead."

"What if we get defeated before our match with Kaine?" Feiyan's eyes water. "If we win, humanity might not continue being foolish about allowing women players. But if we lose, it will be a justification to never let human women fight again."

I take her hand. "I avoided the Games for a long time because I was afraid. Do you want to try?"

Feiyan swallows. "Yes. I want to try." She slumps against the wall.

The other Dragon Maidens surround her. Nakimé shouts, "No time for doubts! We must celebrate! To the pub!"

As the cheering ladies depart, Alzira and I are left standing alone in the room. Alzira hangs her head, looking at the floor.

Her expression breaks my heart. "I'm sorry I couldn't let you fight, too."

"I already accepted that I couldn't." Alzira swallows. "But to throw a fight? I have to lose to Kaine in front of the entire world?"

I wince. In my many calculations, I forgot about Alzira's pride. This is no time to point out that technically she wouldn't be throwing the fight because she'd surely lose to Kaine without her magic. "I'm sorry."

"There's no other way for the others to compete, is there?"

"No. I could ask Kaine to make it look like a very close fight . . ." I'd never ask him to lose. That would be unfair to Kaine with his country's future at stake.

Alzira's lower lip juts out. "Don't. I have no need for pity. For the sake of my friends, I'll set aside my pride. I could never deny them their big chance."

"I need you to rescue my brother. For me, that means more than any Games victory."

Alzira raises her chin. "And to serve you means more to me than any glory." She kisses the back of my hand. "I'll arrange a practice with Kaine. I may be able to use a very tiny bit of magic simply from knowing you would be in danger if my reputation fails." She leaves.

Left alone, the shimmer wears off my joy. I know how badly Alzira wants a fight with Kaine, to determine who is the best. Since Kaine is never going to try to kill me, she'll never get to fight him at full power. A fake fight must feel even more painful for her than none at all. I've considered putting myself in danger so she can fight in the Games, but it doesn't work if she knows it's fake. For me, I'm happier not to put her in danger during the matches. But she doesn't think like that.

I'll never be able to give Alzira her greatest desire.

* * *

By evening, my doubts set in. Every year I get threats to keep my team from the Games. The latest on my desk mentions Feiyan's elderly parents. It would be more concerning if not for her being an orphan. I still need to arrange protection for anyone connected to the Dragon Maidens. If Jiang finds out early, then my brother will suffer for it.

Pacing my bedroom, I call out to the Sun God. "God, do you have a moment? I wanted to ask if I'm making a mistake entering the World Games."

I stop. The Sun God had sent me a conversation with Durrian, a conversation with Kaine, and a conversation with Alzira, all on the same topic. I don't need to bother a busy being for even more obvious hints.

I've made my decision, and this time I have the ability to protect my friends.

Before the Games, I have a few more loose ends to tie up. Donya's spy found Jiang's enchanted books a few days ago. He uses them to give orders to the men holding Calum. If I destroy the relics now, he won't have time before the Games to have new ones made. It ought to save Calum further torment until Alzira and I can get to him. I'll have no choice but to tell Donya the truth so she can get out of town before Jiang traces her spy back to her. Hopefully Donya will be so relieved her missing maid was actually safe all along that she'll forgive me. *Yeah, probably not. I wouldn't forgive me either.*

My hand shakes as I write out the order to the spy to destroy Jiang's book, then make her escape. The page burns away when I'm done, taking my betrayal with it. Then I find the other book linked to Donya and request a meeting at the Dragon's Claw Inn tonight instead of waiting for our usual weekly dinner.

After putting on my Bora disguise, I sneak out of the castle. I ought to take Alzira along, but Donya will hate my deception even more if her hated rival is in on it. Alzira and Donya liked each other the first time they met, at a sword-fighting exhibition. Then Donya asked Alzira, "Why is someone as amazing as you working for an evil witch?" and Alzira shouted, "I'll cut out your tongue for speaking such insolence toward Her Holiness!" and it all went downhill from there.

I enjoy spending time with Donya. I've taught her a dozen drinking songs (although she keeps replacing the curse words with *darn* or *sugar*), shown her how to hide her blushes with makeup, and prevented her from committing political suicide twice. The dear girl needs me. Or so I justify.

The Dragon's Claw is decorated with pictures of dragons, ranging from the armored flyers of Arahasnor mythology to the sinewy long creatures who rule the Faan Empire. The paintings cover the walls in a jumble with little order. Giant dragons wrap around mountains and tiny ones sit on masked ladies' shoulders. A string of lights runs between the pillars, casting a reddish glow on the wooden floor. The main room is dim and perpetually smoky, as if we're inside a dragon's mouth. I've always liked dragons, so I adore it. So many customers fill the room that many are standing, their voices rising into a loud jumble. Several customers brought their dogs. Barrels rest on the ledges above the bar and a narrow staircase leads to the rooms for rent. Though it's tiny and crowded, it has the best food in the city.

Donya's round face broadens into a smile when she spots me. She waves me over to her table. As I sit down, Miss Meaghan places a blue porcelain dish in front of me. I'll always know the innkeeper by her waist-length blond hair. Unbeknownst to herself, Meaghan is Suzette's nemesis: My spymaster takes it as a personal insult that her best agents haven't been able to figure out where the woman came from before she appeared in our city with a sack of gold. Her cooking covers cuisine from around the world, and there's only one item for dinner every day. Today, it's a bowl of beef and eggs over rice.

I blow on my beef bowl as I stall for time. The raw egg coating gives the hot meat a sweet taste. Maybe if I let Donya finish eating, she'll be in a better mood. Or maybe I should tell her the Dragon Maidens will enter the World Games. She'll like that. *Yes, good idea!*

After pretending I obtained my knowledge from spying, I finish with, "Holy Maiden Ysabel has great plans for Arahasnor. After the Games, she'll have the power to ratify your Convention on the Rights of Women. You should work together."

"Then why hasn't she entered the last seven years? An aversion to winning?" Donya's faith in me is sarcastic. "I have no problem working with Ysabel." Her scowl belies this claim. "I just can't see us ever being friends. Every word out of her mouth annoys me."

"A lot of people are different in private compared to public. You should have lunch with her sometime."

Donya snorts. "If I asked Ysabel to meet me for lunch, she'd laugh her makeup off, then mock me for weeks. Snakes go for a bite at the first sign of weakness."

"I bet Ysabel would be delighted if you invited her." I steeple my fingers. "Did you know that although snakes have a reputation for being sly and dangerous, many breeds are actually mild-tempered and cuddly? I have a beautiful python I love very much." My voice trails off at Donya's disinterested look.

I stare glumly at the dregs of my mug. I know Donya's personality. Stubborn. Strong-willed. Loyal to both her likes and her dislikes. This won't end well. I'd better blurt out the whole truth, then run away before she brains me with her bowl.

The air whizzes. A crossbow bolt stops suspended in midair, directly in front of Donya's forehead. *That . . . almost . . . We were just speaking a moment ago, and then a crossbow bolt . . .*

I wish I could help, but instead I hyperventilate.

Donya shoves me under the table. Crouched down, she draws her sword and holds it in front of me. This is all my fault. This must be because Jiang found out about Donya spying on him. I have to do something, but I can't even move.

A twang releases half a dozen more bolts. Somehow they end up in the ceiling. A voice outside cries, "How dare you aim at Her Holiness?"

There's a sudden silence from the open window where the bolts originated.

"Alzira?" Donya exclaims in disbelief. She runs out of the tavern. I quickly follow. Given the assassins only aimed at Donya, she could still be in danger.

Five bodies lie on the ground with their chests bloated in the air and leaking blood. In her fury, Alzira exploded their hearts inside their rib cages.

"What are you doing here? Are you following me again?" Donya demands.

My hooded bodyguard's eyes fall very tellingly on me, then equally tellingly yank away. "Countess Donya. I had no idea you were here." Alas, Alzira is a bad liar.

Donya's eyes dart between us. Her chest heaves. "I did think it was strange. How much you know about court politics. For that matter, how much you know about Ysabel's past." Her eyes plead with me to tell her she's wrong.

One more lie, and we really will cease to be friends. I swallow. "I was trying to break it to you gently." Speaking without an accent, I lift off my wig and wipe my face. Words pour out in a rush: "It's my fault they came after you, I had no idea Jiang would find out so quickly, I just wanted to save my brother."

Donya takes a step backward. "You've been making a fool out of me."

"I never wanted to hurt you. I *liked* talking to you."

"Do you think I'd believe that? I'm not completely stupid." Bitterness dripping from each word, Donya turns on her heel and walks away.

My legs want to run after her, but my brain says I should give her space. Later, I can try to fix this, if Donya will let me. The force of my sigh rocks my tiny frame. "How long did you know, Alzira?"

"I've followed you every time you snuck out of Kaine's fortress." Alzira cocks her head. "Didn't you know? I thought you weren't saying anything because you wanted me to be discreet. I could hardly let you wander at night alone, princess."

If Alzira wasn't my bodyguard, she'd be terrifyingly creepy. "Oh, of course I knew. Yes, please be very discreet about all of this." I run my fingers through my hair, sweaty from the wig. "Donya would be humiliated if anyone found out."

"I'm sorry, Your Holiness." Alzira looks away. "I can't beat up anyone to fix this, can I?"

"No, you can't." I stare down the street where Donya has long vanished.

CHAPTER NINETEEN

Once back home, I write Donya a long letter explaining everything. I give her the location of the maid my brother sacrificed himself to save. That way she can confirm the girl is safe. There's no reply. At least Donya takes my advice to pack up and head to her country house. Alzira escorts her the whole way in secret.

I keep checking my book for a response. By the wee hours of the morning, I give up on falling asleep. I've never been fond of being alone, especially when stressed. Kaine is still sleeping in our bed. Alzira will be at her morning prayers. I head to the common room connected to the Dragon Maidens' training room, hoping to catch a friend.

Suzette sits cross-legged on the couch, munching on a slice of bread while staring at a paper.

"Clearly I've been overworking you." I hold up a deck of cards. "Want to take a break and play Bluffer with me?"

Suzette looks up, a blonde curl falling loose from her ponytail. "First, will you tell me honestly if my idea is dumb?"

"Your ideas are always brilliant." I sit next to her.

Suzette sets down her bread. "Every strong necromancer in the world is accounted for and located somewhere far from Arahasnor. Then there's Jiang's odd illness."

I shuffle the cards. "Which feels necromantic to me."

Suzette nods. "During our failed mindreading attempt, Jiang seemed magically able to notice Alesh. Necromancers can sense bodies and detect if they're living or dead."

"What are you saying?"

"Could Jiang be the necromancer we're looking for?"

My cards fall to the table. I've never considered this idea because Jiang doesn't hesitate to use necromancer-related slurs. What if he's overcompensating? Raising dead humans is forbidden by his Sun God sect, but the rules never stopped Jiang before.

"Wait, what does this have to do with Jiang's illness?"

Suzette strokes her chin. "I think that's the price of his gift. He'd have to be a strong necromancer to raise the dead, which means a higher than usual price."

"It would explain how he came up with a whole new ritual." It would also be the biggest disgrace to the church since the time Dark Lord Chingis declared us to be his national religion. That reminds me: "Cardinal Jiang has always been oddly admiring toward one necromancer. He spouts trash like 'Dark Lord Chingis may have been our enemy, but you have to admire his keen military tactics and how he slaughtered so many pointy-eared tree-humpers.' Crap. You're right. Jiang is our necromancer. Dammit! We wasted so much time looking at the wrong people!"

"At least I have good news about the ritual." The wrinkles fade from Suzette's expression. "Our plan has been working. Three attempts were made to sneak past our guards, and each one was foiled. A mob tried to chase some of Donya's ladies into the ritual ground, but the guards saved them. Not a single death has occurred to complete the skull pattern."

"Good news indeed." I pat her on the shoulder. "We can ask Jiang what his ritual would have done in jail. The important thing is that we've stopped him." Maybe I can even use the scandal to promote church reforms.

"I feel much better now we have the necromancer question settled." Suzette stuffs the last of her toast in her mouth. "I owe you a beating at Bluffer."

"Ha ha, you haven't won yet." I grab my cards and shuffle.

"Do you have room for one more?" Sigma stands in the doorway. "I've been feeling restless. I almost dropped a weight on my toe."

I wave her in. "Come tell us what's wrong."

"Thanks." Sigma sits like a doll perched on the large armchair.

I deal out the deck. Checking my hand, I keep a straight face while groaning internally. As usual, I've ended up with the Fool.

As she sorts her hand, Sigma says, "My dad's health has been failing. I plan to return home after the World Games." She bites her lip. "I'd have to leave the team."

"I'm sorry about your dad. You don't need to hesitate on my account. Either I'll overthrow Jiang soon, or I'll screw up so badly I won't have a sect at all. Either way, I probably won't live much longer to burden you." I laugh. No one else does. "That was a joke."

"Not a funny one." The uncharacteristic sharpness of Sigma's voice slices through the air.

I look away and mumble, "I'm sorry."

"I'm sorry, too." Sigma sighs. "I didn't mean to upset you. It worries me when you spew hate at yourself."

My voice comes back. "I don't hate myself."

Sigma raises an eyebrow. "You call yourself 'stupid' a lot."

"I call everyone stupid."

"Mm, yes, I don't love that either. But you're the hardest on yourself. Stupid, weak, coward—you're none of those things and I wish I could make you believe it." Sigma speaks gently, as if she's handling a glass figurine.

What the frozen hell? I'm right to hate myself for letting people down, exactly like how my stupid, weak, and cowardly dad let me down . . . Oh, shit, Sigma has a point. I need to go and lie down with a cold towel over my head and think about this.

I'm hyperventilating now, and noticing just makes it even harder to breathe. Suzette puts an arm around my shoulder. Sigma hugs me too. Sandwiched between the two of them, I start to calm down. Voice muffled by their embrace, I say, "I'll try to get better about that."

Sigma smiles into my hair. "That's all I can ask."

"Thanks for standing up for me—even against me. I used to think it would be better if no one had to mourn my death. Now I'm glad to have made the best friends anyone could ever ask for and fallen in love." Once I speak it out loud, I realize it's true. I'm in love with Kaine. I need to tell him. "I'm happy to have lived long enough to meet Kaine." A smile tugs at my lips. "I'm even happy to be a woman. I wouldn't have always said that."

I stop, because Suzette gazes at me with tears prickling her eyes. I ask, "Is something wrong?"

"I'm just happy to hear you say that." Suzette dabs her eyes. "Do you remember back when you found out my secret? You said, 'Women are the losing team in life. Why would you possibly want to be one? Do you want to be raped, beaten, and treated as something less than human? If you're a masochist, I could step on you if you beg for it.'"

I wince. "That does sound like me. Did I ever apologize to you? Because I'm really, really sorry."

"Don't. I didn't bring it up because I wanted you to apologize to me for how much life has made you suffer." Resolve fills Suzette's face. "All my life, I'd been told feminine meant weak and worthless. It made it hard for me to accept myself. Then I met you. A woman who was both beautiful and strong. You were my ideal. It broke my heart to learn you weren't glad to be a woman."

I don't know what to say. That might have been the most touching tribute I've ever received in my entire life. "I, uh, I didn't know. But. Um. What you said makes me happy."

"That's all I need." Suzette brushes my cheek with a lily-scented kiss.

"Is someone crying?" Kaine calls from the doorway.

They both release me from the hug. Suzette jumps in with an excuse. "Ysabel is losing at Bluffer so badly we had to comfort her."

Despite Kaine's raised eyebrow, he doesn't press us. He's wearing a lovely embroidered coat I got him precisely because I like my men in tight clothes. The bottomless stomach is munching on cheese-on-a-stick. "She ought to be an expert, seeing how she fast-talks all the Useless Rich Nobles."

"You'd think," I mumble. "I've never won against any of the Dragon Maidens."

"As a human, Ysabel isn't much older than a halfling child, so from that point of view, she's quite good," Sigma says, trying to be helpful and failing.

Suzette laughs. "Ysabel is great at lying to enemies, but she feels guilty about lying to her friends, so she has some obvious tells."

Kaine's eyes widen. "Like what?"

Suzette whispers in his ear.

"Stop that," I say, too late.

"Oh, I noticed that one," Kaine says, nodding.

"What one?" I look between them.

Snickering, Suzette crosses her arms. "We've all agreed as a group. No one will tell you. You already win at every other game."

The joke's on her. I can worm it out of Kaine later. Finally, I will no longer be the one stuck with the Fool.

"I promise not to tell Ysabel either," says Kaine, who never lies. *Dammit.*

Two days before the World Games, I head to the planning room to finalize our wagers. Unlike Kaine's throne room, which is decked out in dead animals, weapons, and drinking-gourd skulls, the nondescript room holds only a round table and wooden chairs. Durrian and Suzette speak together while Kaine plays with a quill pen, yanking off every feather.

I slide into the seat next to Kaine and across from Durrian. We've already established our shared list of demands and are now prioritizing them. Durrian hands a list of wagers to me and I look it over.

The World Games are a proxy war for power and territory. The top team receives tribute from everyone, the second-best team receives a smaller amount of tribute from those below, and so forth. After the 102nd Game, the elves proposed that tribute could also be paid by rewriting the laws of a defeated country. (To make a long story short, they were really sick of humanity's unicorn poaching.)

To paraphrase our demands:

1. Lifting the trade embargo on Conollia
2. Return of all people taken from Conollia as slaves
3. A big pile of money for Conollia
4. Passage of the Conventions of the Rights of All Species (an expanded version of Donya's convention on the Rights of Women)
5. Citizenship for the Conollian refugees around the Holy City should they desire it, with ownership of the unused land in the mountains many are currently squatting on (and used to be part of their country anyway before Arahasnor took it)

I skim the document. "Let's add some money for the refugees as a lower priority. About half don't want to return to Conollia anyway, even with the conflict ended—"

Kaine nods. "They've expressed as much to me, with rotten eggs."

"—so they'll need funds to start over in Arahasnor."

Many refugees have been living in Arahasnor for generations and feel like it's their homeland. As the head of their sect, I've promised to make certain they have options.

I add, "I've also promised the Halfling Confederacy we'll use our power to keep their borders and resources intact. That's all they want in exchange for loaning us Sigma. If we place high, let's lower their export taxes."

"Sounds good." Suzette taps the table. "The trickiest one will be emancipating the Conollian slaves."

"They'll try to cheat us by holding people back," I agree.

"They'll do it or I'll march across the border with an army and free all their slaves," Kaine says, playing with his pen. "We should free all of them anyway. I'll welcome everyone into my country."

"That would simplify the inevitable difficulties figuring out who is from Conollia, who's mixed, and whose owner is trying to pretend they're not from Conollia. Plus, it would be the right thing to do." I nod. "If we can take both first and second place, let's expand our demand to total abolishment of slavery."

Out of the side of his mouth, Durrian says, "If the other nations refuse this demand, I'm not going to be able to stop Kaine from invading no matter what they agree to pay."

Kaine's eyes harden. "I haven't yet found every friend of my friends who's been sold."

"These countries own almost all the slaves." I circle eight small nations near Conollia. Slavery was dying a natural economic death before the blight hit Conollia, creating a helpless populace up for grabs and partly affected neighbors looking for warm bodies to replace their dead farmers. "They're so impoverished you can probably absorb half into Conollia. The rest won't have any choice but to agree to abolition because they don't have the money to pay tribute instead."

Suzette says, "We've been discussing marching Conollian troops in to make sure the decree is enforced."

"Good idea. Conollia isn't necessarily going to be able to feed a giant influx of refugees." *Trust me, I'd know.* "I suggest giving the former slaves some of the land they were working on. They're owed it as unpaid wages. We've got to help them survive on their own or unscrupulous employers will take advantage of them." After Jiang "freed" me from the criminal gang, I had nowhere to go but to him.

"We'd like to claim the land as part of Conollia too," Durrian says, his eyes glinting.

"Fair enough." I write that on the list. "Also, I want to turn the Convention on the Rights of All Species into something enforceable."

"I'd been wondering how much good that would do," Durrian admits. The World Games are good at preventing war because they bind every ruler in the world to obey or die. Social change gets trickier. Even if I force a foreign king to criminalize domestic violence, the common guardsman won't be magically bound to enforce it. I'd rather have a hundred shelters for women than one law no one will obey.

"I want quotas for women in schools and certain jobs. I want an international court. And I want to strike down any law or clause treating people differently by gender, species, race, religion, or social class." I shrug. "I'm not going to get all of that. They'd rather pay me a heap of money. But the countries who can't afford tribute will have to accept some of it. My hope is to turn the Convention into a symbol around the world. Once people see these rights written into law, they'll speak up when they're being violated. If including women in the workforce spurs the economy, then more countries will want the benefits. It's a start."

"Conollia will adopt the Convention voluntarily," Durrian says. "We're short on laws at the moment, and this is worthy of founding a country on."

"Thank you." Donya and I worked damn hard on it during our dinners together. It makes me lonely to think about how much she hates me now. She's ignored three more letters from me, but she hasn't burned our book yet. All I can do is hope and give her time.

"How about the mission to rescue your brother?" Durrian asks.

"Alesh will read Jiang's mind at the start of the Games." In fact, he offered me a brilliant idea for getting Jiang to think Calum's location. "We'll be hiding him in a carriage with curtains over the windows. We have to wait until the Games because that's the only place where Cardinal Jiang won't be able to avoid Alesh. Even better, Jiang won't be able to leave the World Games stadium once the matches start, unless he's accompanying a player." The rule is to prevent betting interference and last-minute assassinations. I don't like waiting, but I only have one shot at this. "This time everything will go according to plan." I say it like I'm convincing myself.

Kaine raises his hand. "As a backup, I'll torture Jiang for information."

I nearly tell him all the reasons that would be a disaster, but with my brother's life at stake, I might get that desperate. "Thank you, dear."

Durrian asks, "Why don't you have your life-oath to Jiang on the li—?"

Laughing nervously, I interrupt, "I have no idea what you're talking about, but I'm sure it's on the longer version of the list." I try to convey with my eyes that Suzette isn't supposed to know. That's why I left it off this list, planning to add it back later after the meeting. Ideally I would like to escape my fate as a human sacrifice without any of the Dragon Maidens ever finding out about the possibility to begin with.

Durrian gets the hint. Unfortunately, so does Suzette. She nudges Kaine. "What was that about Ysabel not having a life-oath to Jiang on the list?"

"What?" He looks around wildly. "Are you still being ridiculous like when you agreed to let him kill you?"

Suzette chokes. I sigh and rub my eyes. *Busted.* "No, dear. I just made a mistake and left it off the list." I don't look at Suzette. "Let's run our terms by our legal experts again to look for loopholes and reconvene later."

"I agree. Ysabel?" Durrian meets my eyes. "You won't be able to get everything you want in one World Game. But keep winning, and more countries will have to accede to your demands. This won't happen overnight."

"But it's a good start," I finish.

"Exactly." He nods. "Kaine, anything else for today?"

Kaine looks up. "Whatever you and Ysabel say is good with me." By now, he's braided every feather from his quill pen.

We make small talk while clearing papers. Suzette doesn't bring up my life-oath. Maybe I can escape back to my room and come up with a plausible story.

As Kaine rolls up a map, I can't help but notice the way his muscles ripple down his back. Detecting my gaze, he leans over and pecks me on the cheek. It leaves a tingle where his lips touched me. He's so damn desirable. Definitely the most handsome man I've ever seen. Funny how I only noticed that over the last week or so.

Dividing up papers with Suzette, I ask, "Is it just me, or is Kaine getting more and more handsome?"

Her voice becomes sing-song. "Isn't it because you're in looove? Weren't you going to tell him that?"

Yeah, yeah, I'm a chicken, bawk-bawk-bawk. I nudge her. "Knock it off."

Her tone turns serious. "Sure, if you'll tell me all about this life-oath."

Just when I thought I was safe. "Sorry, I have places to go. People to meet. Patients to heal. I'm very busy."

Suzette holds up a paper. "Funny, while I was searching, I found this list of demands that doesn't match the one you gave me. Could you please explain to me why you've known for years that Jiang planned to sacrifice you in a necromantic ritual but never told me? I might have figured out much sooner that he's a necromancer."

"Is that really why you're angry?"

"No!" Her gaze burns. "I'm angry because you were planning to die without ever letting me help you."

"We can talk about this later." With a stack of paper under my chin, I make haste for the door.

Hands on her hips, Suzette calls, "Alzira is standing outside the door."

I freeze. Every bit of metal in the room vibrates. A letter opener cracks in two and a gas lamp explodes. "YOUR HOLINESS!" Alzira knocks over my papers and grips me by my shoulders. "How could you? You would have let me fail you without even giving me a chance?" She shakes me. "Where's Jiang? I'm going to *explode his heart*."

"Whoa, stop!" I wrap both my arms around her to restrain her. "You can't! If you murder him, you'll die!"

From the look on her face, she doesn't care. She marches out of the room, dragging me with her. I wail, "Stop! Please! I'm sorry! No kill! Bad Alzira!"

Between the two of them, Suzette and Alzira force the whole story out of me. I might not have been able to stop Alzira's murderous rampage if the World Games weren't so soon.

That evening, Kaine escorts me to the Pre-Games ball. After he sits through an orchestral performance and meets dozens of nobles without punching anyone, I have a reward planned, one we've discussed for weeks. This is for me, too—with all my anxiety over Calum's fate, I want to feel like I have control over something. I've collected information on his health, discussed his kinks (weirdly he hates metal collars in particular, which isn't so weird after I remember his time as a slave), and dug out my rope kit. I'm ready.

* * *

I stand back to admire my handiwork. Kaine is tied naked to a chair with his arms behind his back, a box tie running down his chest and forming a diamond over his dick. To match the blue-dyed ropes, I applied blue eye shadow and painted azure whirls down his arms. His stone face just starting to crack is a blank canvas demanding a painter. I tuck a white lily over his ear, then another under his thigh, then wrap one around his ankle.

"Perfect!" I clap my hands and admire my artwork. The gleaming of the oil I've massaged into his sun-kissed skin. That perfect way the triangles and diamonds accentuate his muscles. The flush creeping up his face, revealing that he's on fire for me. All for my eyes and my eyes alone. Possessiveness surges through me. I brand the image into my memory.

"I cannot believe Useless Rich People waste money on colored ropes." Kaine twists, testing his bonds.

"Someone's asking for a gag." I mean it quite literally. Mouthing off to me is Kaine's favorite way of telling me to turn up the heat. I enjoy Kaine's smart mouth—it always gets my creativity going.

Smiling savagely, I walk forward, Kaine's eyes tracking my every movement. When he gets that look in his eyes, it only makes me want to tease him more. I brought out a special outfit this evening: black fishnet stockings and a leather bikini my breasts mostly fall out of. Silver cuffs gleam on my wrists and ankles. My hair is in a high ponytail.

He opens his mouth for the ring gag. His vulnerability honors me. Although I hate to cover those sexy eyes of his, I slip on the blindfold. Then I stick one last lily into the ring in his mouth. "Gorgeous," I whisper, my voice trembling.

Kaine whines, very quietly. "You're the sexiest thing I've ever laid eyes on," I praise. *See, I can be kind as well as cruel.*

Straddling him, I reach around to squeeze his hands, the signal to ask if he's okay. He squeezes back. I slip a ball into his bound hands. "Dropping this is your safe word," I remind him.

He groans as if to say, "Hurry it up already." This man is sassy even when gagged.

"You're mine to do what I want with. For instance, I could do this." Rising, I press the toe of my leather boots into his dick. He hisses as it begins to harden. "Or I could leave you like this all night and just enjoy the view." I withdraw my foot. Kaine groans and struggles against the ropes. I tied them to hit his pressure points, so this only serves to make him feel good. One knot is tied under his ass. It amuses me to watch him jerk until a sheen covers his skin.

I pull up a chair across from him and rest my feet on his knees. "Aren't you going to beg me?" More nonsense emerges from his lips, opera to my ears.

"Oh dear, you didn't answer me. I'm leaving you here." My two-inch heels click as I walk to the door.

I don't go far, of course, since I have to listen in case he drops his ball. Standing outside the room, I count out five minutes. Anticipation itches under my skin. It's difficult for me to tear my eyes away from my artwork, but he asked for orgasm denial, and his pleasure is my aim.

Flinging open the door, I lunge. Burrowing my mouth into his neck and kissing down his chest, I whisper, "I couldn't stay away. You're irresistible."

He tastes like sun. I leave hickeys, paying careful attention to his nipples and memorizing the curve of his abs and dip of his belly button. The ropes gleam like cerulean brushstrokes across a canvas of night. He's already dripping before I lick a line down his cock. I bring him to the edge—then stop. "See you later," I say, standing up.

He strains and shouts something sounding like, "Evil!"

"Why, thank you." I breathe the words at his crotch, not quite touching. My fingers tease the knot brushing against his asshole. "Do you like that?" His answering sob satisfies me, so I take him into my mouth again. Then, just as I feel his body tense, I stop. He curses some more.

By the end, I make him weep for me, the plea for mercy that he'll never make on the battlefield. I'd howl in triumph if I didn't have a much better use for my mouth. Only *I* can make the dark lord beg. He's all mine. I've sacrificed myself for the world, but this one person would never sacrifice me, and I won't give him up either. Dizziness rushes to my head. In that moment, his pleasure becomes my pleasure, so strongly I imagine I can feel his sensations. The power I have over him becomes indistinguishable from the power he has over me. I take him in deeper, until he almost chokes me, both of our pain indistinguishable from pleasure. Is he moaning or am I? Our gazes lock, and I see my love reflected back in his eyes. That tips him over the edge.

When I taste him, I feel a sudden surge of love. The feeling has been budding inside me for months. Only now, when I'm unencumbered by my responsibilities and completely free, can I acknowledge it. *God, I love this man.*

Kaine's body is deliciously pliant as I carefully untie each knot. I love how he looks with his hair wild, sweat coating his chest, and red marks flowering on his skin. Our bedroom has a giant bathtub with hot water already prepared. Kaine's barely coherent enough to help me clean him off and maneuver him to the bed. I give him a massage to get his blood flowing, then pepper his face with kisses. These little touches afterward bring me almost as much joy as sex. I strip my clothes off before cuddling against him.

Kaine cracks one eye open. "Shouldn't I do something for you?"

"Don't worry about it." I had plans to push the chair over and make him give me oral next, but after he zoned out, I postponed that for another day. I should ask him what he liked or didn't about the scene, but we can do that later. We're both too tired.

Kaine, stubbornly fair, insists, "Next time let's do something all about you."

"All right, you win." I kiss his nose. "Next time you'll be lucky if I let you come at all. Happy?"

"Deliriously so, beautiful." Kaine twists on the bed to face me, propping up his head with his hand. "Can I have another reward when I win the World Games?"

"Confident, are you?" I poke his lovely chest muscles, fully on display. Maybe I should be annoyed that I gave him my sadistic best and he's already asking for more, but I find myself amused instead. "If you defeat *my* Alzira, wouldn't you be asking for a punishment?"

"Either one." He winks.

"I won't sabotage Alzira by giving you more incentive to win. There *is* one bit of encouragement I can give you." I lean closer to whisper in his ear, "I love you." Holding my breath, I wait for his reply.

"Oh, I knew that long before you did. You can be very dense sometimes." He nods. "It's about time you were honest about it."

This bastard is asking for a beating. Good thing we'd both enjoy that. Yanking him over, I crush my lips against his. Like Kaine, the kiss is rough and violent and holds a promise.

By Jiang's count, I have one day left to live. Tomorrow is the full moon, when magical rituals become the strongest, the perfect time to sacrifice me. But I'm not planning to die.

CHAPTER TWENTY

To host the World Games, the Holy City spent two years constructing an arena large enough to seat tens of thousands. Our tax aracoins at work! Since I'm a member of the church not the state, I didn't get to see the royal side of the budget, but I'm very concerned King Uctor went into heavy debt again. We didn't have room inside the city walls, so it was built outside (and I made them pay the refugees who had to move, too). We depart in our carriages early because the stadium is located on the northern side, and Kaine's castle is camped by the southern wall.

The stadium's granite walls rise high toward the misty blue sky. The front row seats have cushions on the stone and canopies to block out rays and rain. There are even servants carrying around trays of vegetables and dip. The back rows are made of only cold stone. Seats spread all the way to boxes high above.

Combatants will be fighting in a giant barren sandy circle walled in by enchanted glass to prevent damage to the audience. It also restricts the power of the Gifted Knights inside to prevent them from bringing down the stadium on all of our heads. To merely touch the glass is to be considered "dead," as is falling unconscious or surrendering. And actually dying, of course.

The night before, I could barely sleep, so this morning I used extra powder to hide the dark bruises under my eyes. For my outfit, I picked a simple white robe tied with a golden belt, sandals, and not a trace of jewelry. This is the moment to capitalize on my image as Holy Maiden. Also, I might need my legs free to run.

The opening ceremony goes on forever—the dancers, the band, and the fireworks. By the historical reenactment of the first World Games, I can tell the audience is getting restless. So am I. Jiang has yet to appear.

In a distant white tent, Captain Feiyan, Ua'la'sur, Nakimé, and Sigma are preparing for battle. They're staying out of view. If only Jiang will show his oversized nose already.

I lurk in a parking area inside the walls. Hidden behind our carriage, Suzette helps Alzira fasten her armor. She wears studded leather, favoring flexibility over strength. My dragon wrapped around a rose is emblazoned on her breastplate. Alzira has tied her favorite blue and green checkered headscarf over her helmet because she's convinced it's lucky. It's too bad they're busy, because I could use a conversation to calm my nerves. My heart clenches. Then all my internal organs do a belly roll as Cardinal Jiang approaches me.

As if speaking to a pet, he barks, "You should have contacted me for orders sooner. My relic books were destroyed by an enemy. Fortunately, it's not too late for you to poison Kaine." He holds out a glowing green bottle. "It took me months to obtain this."

I accept the bottle because it sounds useful. Then my lips turn upward into a cold smile. "I'll consider this my severance pay. Though you'll be the one out of a job, since your team is facing my Dragon Maidens in the first round."

His eyes widen very slightly. But his face is a stone mask. I'm sure there's a rapid recalculation going on due to my double-cross. My palms sweat. I hope my face appears as serene as his. Why can't I ever rattle him as he does to me?

From the circle, the Seer-Referee calls, "Head Cardinal Jiang and Holy Maiden Ysabel, step forward!" I'm pathetically grateful for the interruption.

We both approach the Seer. The gray-robed, green-skinned old woman is an elf. Her dark green braid has streaks of silver. Seer-Referees are drawn from all species and sworn to strict neutrality. They wear masks to cement their interchangeability.

The rage in Jiang's glare steals my breath.

I've spent the last decade waiting for this man to kill me. Even now, I still can't convince myself that he's not about to reveal this is all according to his plan. So I fake it.

Smiling, I extend my hand to touch the Seer-Referee's palm. "Holy Maiden Ysabel, do you swear to abide by the outcome of the Games and fulfill any tribute required of you or forfeit your life?"

The murmurs in the audience rise sharply as magic projects her voice around the arena. This is the first anyone has heard of the Dragon Maidens' participation. Everyone knows about Alzira, one of the six extinction-level gifted. A stampede starts toward the betting tents.

"I swear." I keep smiling through the clench of pain in the left side of my chest as the life-oath takes effect.

"Cardinal Jiang, do you swear to abide by the outcome of the Games and fulfill any tribute required of you or forfeit your life?"

"I swear." Then he drops the Seer's hand so he can wipe off with a handkerchief where the elf touched him.

"Wait," I call in a jovial tone. "I'd like to propose an additional wager. If I win, Jiang will release me from the life-oath I swore to him." The words burn my tongue, and my head spins. Pressure builds under my chest from an oath crumbling. No matter what, I have to force out one more sentence. "If he wins, I'll swear an additional one to never reveal or allow my allies to reveal information incriminating him in a court of law. If you agree, then Alzira won't fight against you in this match." As usual, I'm bargaining with what I never had to begin with. Alzira can't participate. Jiang has always underestimated women in general and my Dragon Maidens in particular. Hopefully he will believe that with Alzira gone, he can win. With the full moon so close, he'll be determined not to miss the chance to sacrifice me. With his illness, he can't afford to be stuck in jail awaiting a trial.

I hand Jiang a paper. It lists my proof of his attempts to assassinate Kaine, of his bribes to the guard, of the people he's murdered on false charges for their money, and most damning of all, of his plans to sacrifice me. I pray it will be enough.

He barely glances at it before saying, "Agreed." I try not to collapse with relief (and a dab of confusion). The heart pain fades away, leaving me dizzy and sweaty. The Seer-Referee has us confirm these additional oaths without comment.

As we step outside the ring, Jiang shifts entirely too close to whisper, "Fool. Your brother will die because you made me do this the hard way."

It has to be a bluff. Doubtless he'll have some trick, but it won't be enough. "I know where you have Calum. My people are already retrieving him from Saint Lase's Shelter for Fallen Women."

He's good. He shows no hint that I've spoken the wrong location. His cane clacks on the stone as he walks away.

Alzira rushes to my side. "Did he agree?"

"Yes."

"Thank the Sun God." She squeezes my hand. "Your brother will be safe now. We'll make sure of it together."

Alesh pulls back the curtains covering the carriage window. "He thought 'Blackweir Orphanage.' I glimpsed an image. They're keeping your brother in a basement." Even if Jiang had known who watched him, the Head Cardinal could not refuse to swear his oaths, so he had to step into mindreading range.

"Got it." Suzette hands me a map with the location circled.

I smile at Alesh. "I owe you." Then I have to lean against the carriage because my legs go out from under me.

Alzira puts an arm around me, but I wave her toward the ring. "Hurry, it's your turn to take a life-oath next." The other Dragon Maidens have already gathered in the ring. With one last hug, I release her.

As Alzira jogs toward the Seer-Referee, the front rows surge forward, eager for a closer look at Humanity's Strongest Monster. From where the monarchs sit on a pair of temporary thrones, Queen Bianna nods at me, which makes her the bravest person present (or the one who hates Jiang the most after me). No one believes I can win against Jiang without Alzira. My hands tighten on my knees. On some level I'm also expecting Jiang to pull off a dramatic, last-minute trick. For so long, he's been my boogeyman.

The carriage pulling up has Donya's crest on the side. Has she completely lost her mind? Shouldn't she be safely out of town? She and the women pouring out are chaining themselves to the torch holders around the arena. I should have known Donya would never miss a chance to protest on the world stage. Since I lost contact with her, I'm no longer in the loop concerning her plans. The Seer-Referees approach angrily as the protesters shout. Someone in the crowd pulls out a tomato.

I tug on Suzette's sleeve. "Please . . ."

"I'll assign agents to protect her," Suzette assures me. "I also have guards standing by to arrest Jiang as soon as his team loses. We'll release all the dirt on him afterward to justify it, but I want to make certain he has no chance to escape. I'll take care of everything."

Behind us, Alesh clears his throat. He holds up a book. "Durrian writes that Kaine has gone missing."

I leap halfway out of my chair. Kaine has always been extremely reliable. Nothing could keep him from the stadium when he knows I'm counting on him. "But he left before me. He got tired of waiting for me to finish my makeup." A nervous energy itches under my skin, demanding I do something even though I can't think of what.

Alesh has bitten one of his nails so hard it's bleeding. "There were signs of a struggle in his tent. Two maids were found dead, and his new bodyguard is missing. Durrian has Gifted Knights tracking the trail of blood."

I force myself to sit back down. "This is Kaine we're talking about. He probably went to rescue his missing man."

"Right into a trap," Alesh mutters.

"If he doesn't arrive before the oath swearing finishes, he'll be disqualified." Doubtless that's what one of his many enemies is aiming for. A glowing illusion in the arena shows a live image of the Elven Empress and the Dharist Spiritual Custodian swearing their oaths. If we've moved on to people not physically present, then Kaine is late.

Suzette touches my arm. "You have to go."

Of course I do. I must leave before the gates close. Calum's life is at stake. Kaine can beat any enemy on his own. I stare at her with wide eyes. My feet refuse to move.

Unfortunately, Kaine will be fighting in the first match. He might have been allowed a bit of leeway if he hadn't been first. The Zhaaran team is in full armor and waiting outside the glass-enclosed ring. Their leader steps away to speak to the Head Seer-Referee.

The Head Seer-Referee's enchanted voice rings across the stadium. "This is the last call for Dark Lord Kaine—"

"Stop being so noisy. I'm here." Kaine's famous black armor is streaked with blood, from the chest to the shoulder spikes, none of it seemingly his. His helmet has a plate covering his face, but his eyes burn through the slit. He climbs onto the stage, cradling a young man with a slit throat in his arms. The crowd around me gasps. I can barely breathe. Alesh says a word in elven that I never thought would leave his prim and proper mouth.

"I'll swear your oath. And one of my own." Kaine holds up the body toward the stunned audience. "His name was Nix. The maids were Delilah and Koroko. I swear to kill whoever ordered this. In the old days, they used to demand an enemy monarch's head after the World Games. I don't care if it's against your supposedly civilized rules. I will have blood for blood." The rage in his voice rocks the stadium. Even I flinch.

Poor Nix. That sweet boy who greeted me when I first came to Kaine's castle died just because someone wanted to slow Kaine down.

The Seer-Referee, too old to fear death, says, "You can't. You're about to swear a life-oath to never attack another member of the Conclave of Kings."

"How convenient. Oaths protect the Conclave, but none of the innocents who get in the way of your conflicts. I will take your life-oath, so I can participate in your Games and win for my people. But I won't let death stop me." Kaine turns to Durrian, who sits near the front surrounded by Conollian soldiers. "I'm sorry. I'm going to kill whoever murdered our people, even if I die. Will you look after Conollia for me?"

Durrian rises to his feet and salutes. "As you command, Your Darkness!" The entire Conollian section breaks out into a cheer that turns into an incoherent roar of Kaine's name.

Kaine turns back to the Seer-Referee. "I'm ready to give my oath." His steady voice cuts through the foot-stomping and clapping. A second Seer-Referee has to step forward to take his life-oath after the first one faints clean away.

I turn my back on him for minutes—half an hour at the most—and he's already trying to start a war! He's set a record by threatening to break his life-oath before even taking it. This time I definitely want to beat him in the unsexy way. I'm not sure if I should laugh or cry. His insanity must be contagious, because I'm starting to find it as endearing as his people clearly do.

Ah, well, after the Games are over, I'll present Kaine with a plan for how to take his revenge without dying. We can use the poison Jiang gave me to assassinate our enemies for maximum irony. In the meantime, he can't do anything crazy as long as he doesn't know the culprit. I must admit, that speech of his will probably cut down on the number of assassins sent after him.

Alesh groans as his head falls forward into his hands. "That does it. I'm not going to worry about him anymore. I'm just going to embrace the insanity."

"That's the spirit." I laugh, welcoming another convert to the Zen of Kaine. "It all becomes so much easier when you stop fretting and enjoy watching him punch people who deserve it."

Alesh ducks back into the carriage and returns with a book. "This is linked to one of mine. I'll write to you about how each match goes."

"Thank you so much." I grip his hands.

"I'm the one who owes you for reuniting me with my brother." Alesh smiles at me.

"That wasn't me, it was the Sun God. No, seriously." My voice trails off as Alesh gets a certain look on his face. When I told him about the series of coincidences leading me to the shelter at the same time as him, he didn't take me seriously. There are some things I can't explain to someone outside my faith.

Time to head to Blackweir Orphanage. Alzira holds open the door for me, and I get back into the carriage.

My carriage barely makes it out before the Seer-Referees close the gates. Since I'm accompanying a player, I'll be allowed to reenter if I get back in time to see the finals. That rule was added after a few too many past competitors tried to delay their opponents from reaching the stadium. The Seer-Referees' job is more to prevent departures, not late arrivals, because of concerns about fleeing assassins and people trying to welch on bets. Hopefully I can watch Jiang get arrested.

I cannot hear Kaine swear his life-oath, but the crowd cheering resounds even outside the stadium, the noise shaking the cobblestones. Loud shouts come not only from the crowd, but also from books transmitting this scene around the globe. The audience knows full well a world war has been prevented. This is the first time a new nation has been accepted into the Conclave in two hundred years. It's a pity to see Kaine's great power forever restrained to the laws of the Conclave, but if we can change those laws without war, then that's worth it.

I have my own battle right now. I have to trust that Kaine can handle his. Yet I find myself remembering him picking out his Dharist grave tree in preparation for the worst.

* * *

The scenery turns from countryside to forest as the world blurs by outside my carriage. The carriage is a relic enchanted to move far faster than any horse could. Alzira looks over my shoulder to read as Alesh writes: *Kaine won his first match. Not surprising. The Zhaaran team wouldn't have tried to sabotage him if they thought they could beat him fairly.*

Alzira whoops and punches the air. I write back, *You think it was Zhaara?*

I was referring to their last assassination attempt. I have no idea who is behind the latest one, but they're high on the suspects list. Kaine swung by to see me. He's uninjured. He wants you to know he won with only three of his two thousand eight hundred and thirty-one abilities. Is he bragging?

I told him to avoid revealing too many powers early in the matches, but yes, he's bragging. I smile before I remember the Dragon Maidens are up next. They're facing Jiang's team. *Can you tell me everything that happens in the Dragon Maiden's match, play by play?*

Alesh promises. I stare anxiously at the book before eventually his words start forming.

They're lining up. The match started. Jiang's team dropped some bottles full of yellow gas on the ground.

I moan. This is it. Jiang's big plan. He's poisoned my friends. I'm not near enough to heal them. Panic sends shivers up my limbs. What if they die?

Sigma controlled the water in the air to push the gas away. Nakimé tied them all up in vines. The Dragon Maidens won. Jiang's team surrendered.

Wait, what? That's it? Maybe I should have let them fight years ago.

My chest tingles, and I clutch the front of my dress. My life-oath is gone. The invisible chain around my heart has left. I'm free.

Why am I not happy? I'm no longer bound to become a human sacrifice. I should be delirious with joy. Instead, I just feel . . . empty. Is it because I'm too tired? Or because I don't fully believe this is real?

I want to be proud of my Dragon Maidens' victory. I *am* proud. Since no other cardinal would compete against Jiang, I've taken over the church with this victory. But it was too easy. As much as I respect my friends, that fight should have taken longer than a few minutes. Why was there no secret weapon or surprise trick? I can't see Jiang letting his precious immortality ticket escape without more of a fight than this.

Alzira cheers and hugs me. "You're free! How do you feel?"

"My life-oath is definitely gone." I look at the book, rereading the message and trying to understand. "Are we sure we stopped Jiang's necromantic ritual?"

"Positive." Alzira squeezes my hand. "Cardinal Jiang never had a real chance in the Games after Kaine wiped out his original, first-string team during the failed assassination. His confidence was probably a bluff."

"I bet he's the one who lured Kaine away," I mutter, hands clenched. I want that to be true. Then we would have already thwarted Jiang's secret plan. Because he always has a secret plan.

Alzira regards me with concerned eyes. "Jiang isn't invincible, princess."

"You're right." I straighten. In front of my friend, who fought so hard for me, I force myself to smile. I don't want to ruin her celebration with my doubts. She's right—I've built Jiang up too much in my head when he's just another corrupt cardinal. "I'm tired of being afraid of him. Now I no longer need to be. I'm free."

I watch the book carefully for news. King Uctor's team surrenders to Kaine without a fight. Boring. This will look quite bad to the court. I'm going to dominate Arahasnor this year.

Kaine beats the dwarven team. Serves them right for booting out Ua'la'sur. His matches all seem to end in the first five minutes. The only player strong enough to last half an hour is the Lavamaster, another extinction-level gifted. After Kaine punches out a volcano, his enemy collapses.

The Dragon Maidens have been progressing steadily as well. They've defeated half a dozen human kingdoms. Nakimé can use her toxic flowers to knock out any teams without resistance to poison, and Ua'la'sur can trap the rest in nightmares.

"It's to our advantage that we entered late," Alzira says, reading over my shoulder. "A lot of teams didn't have time to prepare for us. Not that it would have made a difference."

I envy her easy confidence in our friends. "What if someone gets injured?" Fatalities are rare in the World Games, but there always seems to be one every couple of years. *No one died last year! Does that mean we're overdue?* I should be there in case I need to heal my friends, except I have to stay close to Alzira in order for her to use her magic, and I'll certainly need to heal my brother. That thought gets me fretting about him too. Who knows what condition he might be in?

Alzira puts a hand on my shoulder. "The best doctors in the world are on standby at the healing tent."

I nibble on my hair. "Sigma took a cut on her arm in the last match. Alesh said it was shallow. You don't think he'd lie to me, would he?"

"He wouldn't dare, princess."

"We're here," Alzira calls. This jolts me from staring at the book. I close it. I need to have faith in my team.

We leave the carriage at a distance and walk on foot. Crouched down behind a bush, we share a pair of binoculars. The Blackweir Orphanage resembles the prison it actually is: a square, obsidian building lacking a single window, clearly past its prime. "Are there any children present?"

She closes her eyes and concentrates. This close, she can detect the blood in people's veins and even their rough sizes. "No children. There are two dozen grown men though. I feel a few heartbeats on the upper floors, but most are guarding the trapdoor to the basement. I count one prisoner underground, wearing iron manacles. It's just as Alesh told us."

Unless the prisoner isn't Calum. What if this is a trick from Jiang to let me think that I won? I bite my cheek, using the jolt of pain to stave off intrusive doubts.

"Good, we can go with the original plan." Standing up, I cup my hands to my mouth and shout, "Hey! Over here!"

The watchman on the top floor whirls, his crossbow pointing at me.

As soon as I'm in danger, Alzira's powers activate. The second story of the building hits the first story, which hits the dirt. Dust saturates the air. Our enemies are squashed in an instant. Burying the basement should forestall any attempt to take Calum hostage.

A spark of electricity dances down Alzira's sword, another sign that it's becoming a relic. Because of her unparalleled power, that could be happening early. When magical power is channeled through an object, it starts to linger, with unpredictable effects. I'd rather not deal with unpredictable right now.

A Gifted Knight explodes from the rubble, his skin silvery and metallic. He swells up to twice his height. Alzira clenches her fist, and he falls, his heart crushed within his chest. I've seen death often enough not to flinch.

Something isn't adding up. Why did Jiang leave someone strong enough to survive a fallen building here, instead of entering him into the World Games? Had Jiang already given up on competing because of Kaine?

I glance down at Alesh's book. The Dragon Maidens are fighting the Dharist church. I want to read on, but Alzira has formed a tunnel through the rubble. She offers me her arm. "I don't detect anyone left alive except the prisoner, but stay close to me just in case."

The ground is uneven, and the air smells stale. I hold a glowing relic shaped like a wand for light. Our tunnel stops at a trapdoor. Alzira pushes me behind her, then opens it.

A man hangs on the wall. I know from the scar on his face that it's Calum. I put a fist to my mouth to restrain a cry. Rushing past Alzira, I reach for Calum. Both his legs are bent at funny angles, and his eyes are bruised shut. But he's here. He's safe. I want to weep. Once I'm done, I will. Touching his cheek, I heal him.

Calum's legs straighten. Skin grows over his many cuts, leaving a crust of old blood. He opens his hazel eyes identical to mine. "You shouldn't have, Ysabel."

"For you, as much of my life as it takes," I say and mean every word.

"I have so much to tell you. Jiang—" He sags in his chains. His eyes slide shut. This is normal—people with serious injuries often feel drained of energy after I heal them. My power does not erase the need for sleep.

Alzira points at the chains and grunts. Nothing happens. She sighs. "Now that you're out of danger, I can't break them."

"We should have left one enemy alive," I joke. Using her ability, Alzira detects the key from the rubble. We unchain him. Then Alzira carries Calum out to the carriage.

As our carriage flies away, Calum tosses and groans. I touch his forehead. He feels feverish. My pulse quickens. I've never before encountered any ailment that my gift couldn't heal with one touch—except whatever is wrong with Jiang.

The strangeness brings back all my fears. Anxiety itches under my skin like an animal trying to claw its way out. Taking a deep breath, I tell myself I can do this. My power, as much as I hate it at times, has always been effective.

Brushing back Calum's sweaty bangs, I heal him again. The color returns to his face. That's good.

Groaning, Calum sags. His head rests in my lap. He mumbles, "Jiang . . . You have to stop Jiang . . ."

"It's okay." I brush his hair. "We're going to arrest Jiang soon. You're safe." Calum's skin feels hot again. Panic chokes my throat. To my gift, it feels like there's a hard, rotten lump under Calum's chest. The ickiness is exactly like Jiang's ailment.

"Why isn't your healing working?" Alzira asks.

"It can only be magic." I frown. "Did Jiang somehow transmit his illness to my brother?" I reach for Calum again.

Alzira pushes away my hand. "Your Holiness, each time costs a day of your life. You shouldn't use your power for nothing. Jiang has been ill for many years, and you've never been able to completely heal him. At least Calum is stable thanks to you. Let us get him back to safety. Maybe a doctor will know what to do."

That's a good point. Kaine—Kaine will be able to save my brother. He must have some gift in his thousands that can help. I want to return to the stadium anyway, to watch over the battles of those I love. I glance at the empty coachman's seat. "Let's go as fast as we can."

We can't make the magic move any faster, but still Alzira says, "Of course, princess."

When our carriage arrives at the stadium, I hand over the paperwork to the Seer-Referees, allowing us back into the Games. Calum moans in the carriage, but Alzira clamps a hand over his mouth before anyone can question why we're bringing in a sick man.

Calum's entire face has turned red. His sweat has soaked the rags he's wearing. Every time he breathes, he makes a pained rattle. Jiang never got sick again this fast after I healed him. *What the hell did that monster do to my brother?* Healing has long been my curse, but at least it meant I could save anyone I loved. How can it fail me now?

As we enter, a referee booms, "Conollia's team has defeated the Elven Empire." Massive cheering comes from the audience. This crowd wouldn't normally cheer for Kaine, but the locals are pleased to see a human beat the elves for the first time in several decades.

Using a complex and secretive system, the Seer-Referees arrange the matches to have the strongest teams face each other last. The Elven

Empire has dominated the World Games since their creation. Our technology and magic pales before theirs, and they have two of the six extinction-level gifted. I would have liked to have seen Kaine's match, or at least read about it in the book. Right now I'm too wired to even celebrate.

I step up to a Seer-Referee at the bottom of the stairs. "Has Dark Lord Kaine returned to his tent? Can you direct me to him?" My voice shakes. My mind has scattered in a thousand pieces.

"That's classified information." He grinds his pike into the dirt.

I attempt a smile. "I'm Holy Maiden Ysabel, an ally of Kaine's. The Sun God has called me to speak with him on an urgent matter."

"You can't. You're his opponent in the next match." Barely visible behind his mask, his eyes narrow. He points at Alzira, with Calum on her back. "Hurry up and take your player to the stage. It's about time you got here."

"I need to see Kaine first." I swallow.

The expressionless mask turns on me. "You have no business with your opponent right before the match starts unless you mean sabotage or collusion."

My throat seizes up. Yes, we plan to rig the fight, but he can't possibly know that. "Such baseless accusations insult the Sun God. My brother is sick—"

The Seer-Referee scowls at Calum. "Ah, so you're planning to infect Lord Kaine with an illness."

Several more Seer-Referees surround us. "Contestant Alzira, you're late." Four words convey an ocean's worth of disapproval.

It's getting harder to keep a smile on my face. "As you can see, my bodyguard is currently carrying my ailing brother. The Sun God has called Kaine to heal him."

A ring of skeptical eyes fixes on me. "Are you not the Holy Healer, capable of curing any illness?"

"I haven't been able to heal this one. It's a magical curse." What an insanely fishy excuse for me to need access to my opponent right before the finals of the World Games. Even I wouldn't believe my own story.

"With all due respect, Holy Maiden Ysabel, if you bring a strange magical curse anywhere near Dark Lord Kaine right before the finals, then I will disqualify you. If Alzira is not on the stage in the next couple minutes, I will also disqualify you."

"Your Holiness?" Alzira taps the air with her sword, requesting my signal to attack.

If I start a fight with the Seer-Referees, then I know Kaine will join in to help me. Then we'll both be disqualified. The lives of millions rest on this final match. I have a duty to uphold. In truth, I don't even know if Kaine can help. I look at the bright red face of my brother, radiating heat so strong I can feel it on my skin, a small gurgle lodged in his throat. My heart cracks a bit more with each pained sound he makes.

I tuck a lock of hair behind my ear, the signal for Alzira to stand down. In a soft, defeated voice, I ask, "Could one of you please take my brother to the healing tent?"

The closest Seer-Referee nods curtly. Reluctantly, Alzira hands over her charge. She salutes me. "I'll do my best to bring you glory in this match, princess." I detect the wistfulness in her voice, that she will be acting out a play instead of fighting for my victory. Then the Seer-Referees surround her and take her away.

Running ahead of the man carrying Calum, I tell myself that I did the right thing. Surely the best doctors in the world will know what is wrong with my brother.

The doctor's tent is pure white and nearly as large as a hospital. It's marked by a blue star on the canopy. From the outside, it's completely silent. This fabric is enchanted to be soundproof, so that patients feel like they can freely tell doctors the price of their gifts if need be. The stench of blood and herbs fills the air.

Two Seer-Referees guard the outside. "Only World Games fighters and their immediate relatives are allowed into the tent," one of them barks.

I'm pissed, but I get it. Assassins must be a huge problem. "Where's the medical tent for audience members?" At the Games, people often pass out from heat or fall down the stairs. I distinctly remember arranging for a second medical tent.

The Seer-Referee points. The man carrying Calum is already headed in that direction. I sprint past him and lift the flap.

A portly middle-aged elven woman stands behind a desk. "Another one who fainted?"

"It's more serious. He's sick." I'm not sure if that's the right word. Should I say cursed or poisoned? On the Seer-Referee's back, Calum twitches. His hand dangles ashen and still.

The doctor nods professionally. "Follow me." She guides us down a row with many beds separated with thin cloth walls. The doctor pushes back a curtain. Inside, there's a single cot. "Lay him down here."

The Seer-Referee places Calum down carefully, then leaves.

Touching Calum's forehead, the doctor frowns. "I'll get him powdered unicorn horn for the pain before I diagnose him."

Calum groans again. I kneel down to touch his clammy hand. He mutters something incoherent. It sounds like Jiang's name.

Since Alzira isn't here to stop me, I heal my brother again. If I've always been destined to die, I at least want to spend my life on the people I love. A bit of color returns to his face, but that rotten core still lurks under his chest, wrapped around his heart. The beats have become weak now.

The doctor returns with a glass bottle containing glittery powder. She carefully measures out a very tiny pinch in a spoon, then sprinkles it over Calum's head.

As soon as the first sparkle falls on him, Calum screams and thrashes. The powder turns dull and jet-black.

"What did you do to him?" I shout, whirling on the doctor even though I know unicorn horn is entirely benign.

"He's under a necromantic curse. Only one type of magic reacts like that to unicorn horn. Necromancy comes from death, and unicorns are natural bringers of life."

My breakfast threatens to come up. I should have known that bastard of a cardinal would never let me save my brother even if I could find him. He left a contingency plan to ensure that Calum would die either way.

On the bed, Calum whimpers. I turn my attention to him. "Can more unicorn horn heal him?"

"Weren't you listening to me, young lady? Unicorn horn can't do anything for a necromancer." Contempt fills her eyes as she spits out that last word.

I'm so surprised it takes me a moment to find words. "My brother isn't a necromancer! He has a disguise gift. I think he was cursed by a necromancer."

"Oh, I'm sorry to hear that." Her lined face becomes drawn. "We know very little about necromancy. It's too rare. I will consult with my colleagues."

"Can I take my brother outside?" I ask.

She looks at me as if I've gone insane. "I daresay it won't make his condition any better or worse."

The doctors don't have any idea how to help me. Only Kaine can help me. In his thousands of gifts, surely he has at least one to break curses. If not, I'll force him to take my regeneration and give it to Calum instead. I should never have let the Seer-Referees keep me away from Kaine.

Heaving my brother onto my shoulders, I stagger out of the tent. It's slow going. My back aches by the time I push open the flap to the brilliant sunlight. I collapse to the grass, barely lowering Calum down before I drop him. His head flops onto my lap. We're not going any farther, I fear. I'm too tired.

Besides, I'm also too late. In the ring, Alzira and Kaine face each other. The healing tents are in the back of the stadium, giving me a clear view. Kaine has taken off his metal armor. His hair is barely long enough to be pulled back into a ponytail, and he flashes his familiar cocky grin.

Now their fight has begun, no one can stop it. The World Games are sacred. I look down at Calum. "Just hold on a little longer. Then Kaine will help you."

His head feels like a hot coal in my lap. The fever is already back in full force. He does not so much as twitch. I recite a prayer.

The Referee brings his arm down. Thousands echo his shout. The finals begin.

Alzira draws her scimitar as Kaine pulls a stone hammer from his back. They run at each other. Around the stadium, a shout arises: "Win, Alzira! Humanity's Strongest!" It completely drowns out Kaine's handful of soldiers. I have a strong suspicion this cheering is less pro-Dragon Maidens and more anti-Kaine.

Sword and hammer lock together. They clash, withdraw, and clash again. Vines, rocks, and wind buffet Alzira. Floating metal shields around her deflect the objects. Given that Kaine is secretly the one manipulating both the magical attacks and defenses, his control must be amazing. As they planned, Alzira dances around a miniature tornado, each step in this fight choreographed.

The ground shakes, and metal balls rise up from the dirt. Kaine is using a telekinesis power. It must have taken him an incredible amount of finesse to only grab metal.

The balls pelt Kaine. Alzira backs up nearly to the wall. If Alzira was actually the one controlling the metal, it would make sense for her to attack him at a distance so he can't steal her gift. It would also make sense for her to call down her meteors, but Kaine can't do that.

A violet-white shield forms over Kaine's head, deflecting the balls. One slips through and hits him on the cheek. The crowd cheers. I know he did that on purpose, but I still wince.

Kaine swings his hammer at Alzira's waist and grabs for her wrist. In their practice fights, they planned for him to miss. Sure enough, she dodges around him and traps his hammer on the ground with her foot. Kaine tosses her into the air. She backflips and lands behind him. Her scimitar arcs forward . . . Aaah! That almost hit his neck! I know they practiced carefully, but did they have to script so many close calls? Why does everyone I love have a limited sense of self-preservation? My hands clench.

Calum groans, and I stroke his sweaty hair. I just want this fight over with.

Kaine blocks the blade with his grayed stone arm. A pit forms under Alzira, sending her running—straight into a blow from his hammer. She blocks. Metal screams against stone. With a flick of his wrist, Kaine sends Alzira flying. She barely gets her feet under her before she hits the glass wall.

Missiles form in the air around Kaine, from tiny knives to glowing sigils. They fly forward. He pretends to let the metal balls deflect them.

A shadow falls over the sand. The crowd gasps. It's fake. Kaine used a power to generate a shadow, because it would look strange if Alzira never tried to use her meteors. Now he'll run forward and pretend to steal her gift.

Alzira braces her feet. Her brow furrows with concentration. She's trying desperately to summon even a little magic. Perhaps she wants to make the show look good, or perhaps my proud Alzira refuses to surrender without a fight. A tiny spark flickers on her blade, only to die out.

Calum convulses in my lap, then coughs up liquid. I mop his face with my handkerchief. At first I think it's blood. Then I smell the decay coming off the black gunk.

I don't have time to wait for Kaine. I grab my brother's hand and heal again.

One day of my life slips away, a chill under my skin. I keep on pushing, pouring my life out through my hands. A week slips away. Then a month. A year is eaten by the endless, howling void. I've destroyed some of the darkness, but it's not enough. Maybe even my entire life won't be enough. I should stop now. Tears fall down my face.

I remember the first time I healed, my hands on the baby's soft face. Calum had snuck into my bed the night after with an apple tart to comfort me. I'd cried because the hollow feeling of my life leaving had terrified me. I remember the look on Calum's face as Jiang's guards dragged him away from me at the clinic. I let go of him back then, but I won't let go of his hand this time.

I guess I always knew it would end like this. Of course I would die healing. That's the reason why I was born into this world. At least I'm going to die saving someone I love.

Everything pours out of my hands as I heal Calum again and again, all my hopes and dreams for a future with Kaine. I burn out the rot. There's still one more bit I'm chasing, the core of pulsing darkness. *Please, Sun God, let my last bit of life be enough. I can't die for nothing.* I weep, my hands shaking with energy.

Calum's eyes snap open. His face is rosy and healthy, but he flinches upon seeing me. "Stop, Yzzy! You're going to die!"

It's already too late. I've made my choice. I want to speak some touching last words, but my lips won't move. My body is freezing up. Even as my hands grow cold, I burn away the last bit of darkness.

Calum rips his hand from mine and shoves me away with all his meager strength.

When our skin loses contact, the healing ends. No strength left, I topple sideways. I land with my cheek prickling the grass. The world starts to dim. It would feel nice to slip away into the darkness. But first, I have to check on Calum. My body feels like a heavy lump disconnected from my mind. Though I try to rise, nothing happens. My eyes slip shut.

Through the darkness, I hear a scream: "PRINCESS!"

I open one eye. Alzira stares directly at me through the glass. Her face contorts with horror. Kaine stops, seeing that his opponent isn't trying to block his attack. He turns around and sees me as well.

Lightning erupts from Alzira's sword and crackles down her body. Her hair stands on end. A shadow falls again, but this time it isn't fake. A meteor the size of the stage is hurtling toward us.

The sun flashes in and out. The air roars. Sulphur overwhelms the stadium. The glass surrounding the stage shatters. Bits of the priceless relic fly everywhere. The magic-repellant was created by the very first Elven Emperor for the first World Games. The audience screams. No one ever believed the glass could break. It has held against extinction-level gifted for centuries, but there's always someone with stronger magic.

Right now, that someone screams as a swirling storm of metallic dust floats around her. Iron rips up from the earth and deposits itself in a twisted heap at Alzira's feet like an offering before a goddess.

I've never been so close to dying, and as a result Alzira has never been stronger.

With the glass broken, Alzira's magic runs wild. The air wails as a thousand meteors blot out the sky. The crowd is screaming and trying to flee. Gifted Knights line the aisles, using wind magic to force people apart and prevent a stampede. Another Gifted Knight raises a glowing shield over the stadium. The first meteor breaks straight through to shatter into the stairs. People scream louder.

"Stop," I croak.

Alzira sways on her feet, her eyes dazed. "Your . . . Holiness?" The smaller meteors snap together into the larger one, making it even more massive, enough to crush the entire stage. A dark shadow falls over me. The giant rock starts to rise away from us. Before I can be relieved, it slips down again. More metal bubbles up from the ground, all around the ring. There's too much magic, more than her frail mortal body has ever contained. Alzira's power exists for the sake of protecting. With me dying but nothing she can do to stop it, there's nowhere for her magic to go.

Oh, sweet Sun God, I don't think Alzira *can* stop.

I have to make Alzira believe that I'm all right. That's the only way to calm the raging missile threatening to break the sky. With all my remaining strength, I lift myself up onto one elbow. I fake a smile, like I've been faking it my entire life. Stretching out one hand toward her, I beg, "Please, I'm fine. See? I'm okay, Alzira. So please . . . don't destroy everything . . ."

The Gifted Knights turn and ready their weapons, pointed at Alzira. She can no longer hear my voice.

But Kaine can. He fastens his hand on the back of Alzira's head. The metal whirling around them cuts into his chest. Then the rock falls.

CHAPTER TWENTY-ONE

When the dust clears, Kaine and Alzira are both lying face up, the giant rock hovering just barely above them. A splash of red drips from Kaine's chest, and his arm is bent funny.

Then the billowing dusty wind obscures them from view again, and I collapse, face-first, into the grass.

When I wake up, a booming voice rings out over the stadium. The Head Seer-Referee sounds in shock. "It's a draw. The first draw in World Games history. I must consult with the Conclave." *I don't give a damn! What happened to Kaine and Alzira? By the Sun God and all the saints, if they're unconscious, what's keeping that massive meteor hovering above their fragile, squishable heads?* All I can see, over and over again, is Kaine bleeding. If my Alzira has killed my Kaine, then . . . I . . .

I pray like I've never prayed before that I make it before Kaine dies. Terror gives strength to my legs. Tottering like a newborn fawn, I stand.

I shove Calum into the healing tent, where the doctors will obey their life-oaths to look after the sick or they'll answer to me. Then I stagger toward the stage.

Gifted Knights surge forward. I find myself pressed between multiple bodies, all stronger than me. I'm carried forward by the crowd, then knocked away.

I land on my bottom. The impact stings. I stare up at the blue sky, blinking watery eyes. My fears for Kaine and Alzira war with my guilt for abandoning Calum. If my brother is awake, then who knows what panicked thoughts must be going through his mind?

I grab a Gifted Knight by his shin and use his armor to lift myself up. "Let me through! I'm Holy Maiden Ysabel." Shamelessly, I add,

"Touch me and be stricken dead by the Sun God!" That and a few kicked shins clear me a path.

My heart stops at the sight of the meteor lying on top of cracked glass. I grab the nearest woman by her collar. "Tell me someone with half a fucking brain rescued them before the fucking rock fucking fell!"

Stammering, she nods at the medical tent.

I kick my way to the front of the tent. Two Seer-Referees carrying pikes stand guard. "Let me in."

"Only immediate family of the injured are allowed into the tent." The masked man speaks in a voice stripped of emotion.

"I'm the Holy Healer. I can help."

"Only immediate family to the injured are allowed into the tent," the second man repeats. The Seer-Referees' adherence to rules is legendary.

"Give me a moment." I turn and hunch my shoulders. Drawing the blank parchment with Dark Lord Kaine's seal from my bag, I write rapidly. Then I whirl around, face flushed and triumphant. "See! I'm Dark Lord Kaine's fiancée."

A Seer-Referee takes the document from my hand. It's not much of a marriage contract, but with my signature and Kaine's seal, it's legally binding.

"Please step this way." The Seer-Referee gestures me into the tent.

Behind me, whispers erupt. "The Holy Maiden is marrying the Dark Lord."

This will get complicated later. I'm too terrified to give a damn. I stumble into the tent.

My heart only starts pumping blood again at the sight of Kaine and Alzira on their beds, being attended to by doctors. Alzira only has light bandages on her hands, thank the Sun God. Kaine lies flat on his back while the doctor presses ice against his arm in a sling. Another doctor stitches the cut on his chest. He holds up a cloth to stem the blood from his nose. Bruises dot his face.

He waves at me. "Ysabel, did you see me fight?" His gleeful grin fades away at the look on my face. "I'm fine. I only broke one arm . . . in three places."

Screw the rumors. I throw myself at his prone body and kiss him.

His tongue is just starting to get frisky when the doctor taps me on the shoulder. "Excuse me, I'm still attending to the player's wounds."

Sheepishly, I stand aside. The doctor tries to stitch Kaine up, but his regeneration power forces the thread out. He's healing, but large injuries like his arm will take longer.

"Are you in a lot of pain?" I inspect Kaine closely. My gaze snaps to Alzira next. "How are you doing? I'm sorry! I should never have let you see me like that." This wouldn't have happened if I'd healed Calum inside the tent.

Alzira drops to her knees before me. "I apologize, Your Holiness. I've failed you. I endangered you with the power meant to protect you."

"It was just as much my fault." I yank her to her feet. "Neither of us knew your gift would react like that." I've never been nearly dead before. We've learned a valuable lesson that too much power for Alzira can be as deadly as too little.

"It most certainly was not your fault," Alzira insists. "And I would not feel better if you'd tried to die somewhere I couldn't see."

Kaine mutters, "Maybe you shouldn't have nearly died at all instead of trying to do it out of sight."

"I swear this will be the first and last time I lose," Alzira declares.

Kaine shakes his head. "If anyone lost, it was me. If you hadn't controlled the meteor to slow its fall, I would have been crushed to death before I had a chance to steal your power."

"We both would have been crushed to death," Alzira points out.

I cough. "So it's a draw?"

"It's my loss," Alzira says, her face mulish.

"No, I'm the one who lost," Kaine says, like it's a point of pride. I'm never going to understand sword-brains.

"Does it matter?" I ask.

They both stare at me. "Of course it does!" Alzira says. "If we don't settle who's the strongest, then we'll have to fight again."

"You will not," I growl. My heart can't take it. "You were both knocked out in the end. It's a draw."

Alzira considers, then nods. "A draw." She turns away, talking under her breath about needing to train even harder.

At least I'm confident Alzira won't be fighting in the next World Games. She'll be banned after nearly murdering the audience. That gives me a good excuse to keep her out of the matches without revealing the price of her gift. Also, Kaine won't be fighting next year because he'll be spending all future World Games safely tied to my bed.

. . . Fine, not happening, but I can fantasize.

Kaine gestures with his good arm. "Alzira, touch me. I'll give you back your power."

"Sit still," both the doctor and I order. Kaine returns Alzira's gift while still being stitched up, the stoic idiot.

"I came here to heal you, but—"

Kaine's eyes pierce into me. "You're not allowed to heal me. You promised."

"If you'd been dying—"

"You're not allowed to heal me even if I'm dying." Kaine glares in a way that reminds me why most people are terrified of him.

I wave my hands. "I was going to say it's lucky you don't have any fatal wounds because I'm rather tired at the moment."

I'd expected this to appease him, but instead Kaine's eyes narrow. "*You* are too tired for healing? What exactly happened?"

"My brother was under a necromantic curse, according to the doctors. I healed him, but it was . . . tricky." I try to keep my tone casual, but from their identical looks of disapproval, I'm not fooling either of them.

"How much life did it take from you?" Kaine demands.

Alzira says, "More than usual. I could feel her dying."

I wince. "Look, I had no choice. Calum was coughing up pure darkness. I didn't need to study medicine for years to know he was about to die. But I healed him! I'm almost completely sure of it."

Kaine's voice drops. "I don't have any right to criticize you when I would have done the same if it had been my brother. But I hate what your gift does to you. Please let me check how much life you have left."

My cheeks flush. I'm scared to know, but I nod.

Kaine's eyes glow. All color drains from his face. "Ysabel, you have *one day* left."

"That's not possible," I say stupidly, even though I know full well I nearly killed myself breaking the curse on my brother.

"One day?" Alzira glares at Kaine as if this is all his fault. Then the full seriousness of my situation hits her. "Oh no. Oh no. What are we going to do?"

Kaine's mouth flattens into a hard line. He locks eyes with me. "You're going to stop healing."

My head spins. "What if someone I care about gets hurt?"

"They'll have to see a doctor, because your life is worth as much as anyone else's."

He makes it sound so easy. Plenty of people don't view my life as worth very much at all. Without my healing, what value do I have to anyone? "I . . . I . . ." I look away, unable to meet his eyes.

"I'll explain to everyone that you have no days left to spare. If anyone asks you to heal, then they'll answer to me." Iron lurks behind Kaine's mild tone. "Then your regeneration ability will replenish one day for each that you live, and you can finally have a long life."

I'm starting to come around to this idea. I've never been able to tell anyone that one day of my life is worth more than all of theirs. But now I have the perfect excuse. It will kill me to heal even once more. One life is the equivalent of one life.

"I'll kill anyone who requests healing before Kaine can do it," Alzira adds.

"There's no need for that." I choke out a weak laugh. "I'll stop healing. I promise."

When Kaine opens his mouth, I fear he's going to scold me for letting myself get down to one day or doubt my promise. Instead, he says, "I'm glad you saved your brother."

"I love you, you know that?" I kiss Kaine. "And I love you, too." I kiss Alzira on the cheek. "I hate to abandon you two, but I have to check up on Calum. He's in the separate healing tent for the audience."

"We'll be fine without you." Kaine blows a kiss at me, before the doctor slaps his hand down, then goes back to tending to his injuries.

I wrap bandages over my head in a cheap disguise. As I leave, I spot a massive crowd swarming the betting tent.

In a voice magically projected around the coliseum, Durrian speaks: "Luckily, we were allies with the Dragon Maidens in the World Games. We've already prepared a mutual list of requests. For the future, it would be a good idea to come up with a rule for draws."

No wonder everyone who placed bets is going into hysterics. I wonder if anyone bet on a draw. This year I didn't bet, since I would have needed to testify before a Seer about not having any inside information.

In the second healing tent, I find Suzette already standing next to Calum's bed. "I ran as fast as I could through the crowd. The other tent wouldn't let me in, so I came to look after your brother."

I sprint to the bed. Calum is still asleep, but when I touch his forehead, it feels cool. There's no tug to use the meager remains of my gift. The rot is gone.

Pressing a kiss on his forehead, I whisper, "Thank you for staying alive and saving me, big brother." Because of his information, I'm free of Jiang now.

"I took Jiang into custody," Suzette says. "I've called the other Dragon Maidens over to guard Calum."

"Thank you." I hug her. The events of the day and my near brush with death catch up to me, and I start sobbing.

Suzette rocks me back and forth and rubs my hair until the tears subside. I straighten and brush leaves off my dress. "I need to talk to Durrian." As the joint winners of the World Games, we have a lot to discuss.

"Go." Suzette waves her hand. "I'll take care of everything here."

As I fight my way back through the crowd, my disguise is knocked off. Someone points and shouts, "The Holy Maiden!"

The crowd mobs me. "Holy Ysabel, are you engaged to Dark Lord Kaine?"

"Was it a task from the Sun God to redeem him? Has he converted to the True Faith?"

"No, she had to marry him in order to stop his dread conquest of the world."

"He had to marry her in order to take responsibility for their wild night of passion after she saved his life!"

Less than fifteen minutes since I created the fake marriage contract, and the situation has already spun out of control. At least this is distracting everyone from the destruction caused by Alzira. I can't afford to pay for the broken glass. I look for an escape route, but I'm trapped on all sides.

Guards in the livery of the Council of Cardinals push their way through. Rakir with his identifying and ornate turban calls, "Holy Ysabel, I must speak with you at once."

I bet he wants me to pick him as the next head of the council, since a woman isn't allowed to hold the role. *Sorry, I've selected Cardinal Orwin, but you're all welcome to send bribes my way if you want.*

Cardinal Rakir lowers his voice. "We must make arrangements for an affair of importance. The full moon is tomorrow."

This horrible twat still expects me to become a human sacrifice. The sheer appalling nerve is almost as bad as the part where he's trying to murder me. "I have no idea what you're talking about," I say. He's trying to shush me with his hands, but I ignore him. "Any life-oaths I swore to Jiang were voided as a result of our match." The horror on his face amuses me.

"Your position on the council is already in jeopardy because of your loose affairs."

Just days ago, I would have panicked and denied any relations with Kaine. Now I don't want to stay on the council. I never enjoyed a single one of those damn meetings. As long as I have the love of Kaine and my friends, what do I care? It's a very refreshing feeling. I raise my head high. "I've done nothing to be ashamed of—unlike *you*."

Rakir gestures to his guards, and they advance on me. I open my mouth to scream if they try to drag me off.

"Ysabel!" Kaine runs forward, lifting people out of the way with his magic and depositing them off to the side. "This way!" He sweeps me into a princess carry with one arm and runs for the Conollian tent. Furious cries follow after us. This will only spur on the rumor mill.

Inside, Durrian leans over a table covered in maps. He raises a hand to greet me. "Please tell Kaine that he can't demand the heads of all enemy nations who might have been behind the murder of our staff, no matter how satisfying it would be."

Ah, right, Kaine's dramatic declaration of war. "You can demand, but you're not going to get it." I slip out of Kaine's arms. "Even if we can prove the culprit's identity, the rules allow them to pay you off with monetary compensation."

"People's lives can't be purchased with money." Kaine has a stubborn glint in his eye. "I'll handle this *my* way."

I cup his cheek. "Monarchs can get away with murder. It's not fair. But starting a war would hurt even more innocent people. To say nothing of you dying, which would break my heart. Didn't you ask me not to heal any longer? Then you turn around and charge to your death?"

Kaine's shoulders slump. "Fair point."

"Send your own assassins. Give me some time to investigate the true culprit and make arrangements. The other nations might even respect you for using such a civilized method." Probably not, but I'll be sure to point out the ironic justice to them.

The wrinkles relax off Kaine's face. He turns to Durrian. "Never mind, we don't need to go to war after all."

"Goody," Durrian says. There's a dead look in his eyes. I should hint to Kaine that his second-in-command needs a vacation.

Durrian hands me requests from a few hundred countries for in-person meetings and counteroffers on our Games demands. We get out a map and start drawing the border lines for Conollia's new territory, but unless we want a border shaped like jagged teeth, someone's town always gets chopped down the middle.

This will take longer than I thought. We agree to reconvene tomorrow. I need to reassure Calum that Jiang is under guard and no longer a threat. Then I need a new outfit because I'm not showing up for the World Games closing ceremony with dirt on my white clothes. My makeup is a fright, too.

After Durrian leaves, I turn to Kaine. "Thank you for saving me from the crowd. It's always intense for the winning team after the World Games."

"What's this about us getting married?" Kaine steps closer.

I swallow. "It was the only way the Seer-Referees would allow me into the tent. I'm sorry for misusing your seal." I hand him the parchment. "I won't hold you to it, of course."

"Who says I'm not going to hold *you* to it?" There's a glint in his eye. I grab for the paper. He holds it high over my head.

"That's not legally binding," I lie. "Give it back."

"Don't you want to marry me?" He switches from mischievous to pouting.

"Well, uh, it's not that I hadn't thought about it, it's only, you can't pick a future queen without carefully negotiating—"

"This agreement looks fine to me." Kaine would be more convincing if he held the paper right-side up. "I've been pondering what you told me about the duty of a king. You're right: The people of Conollia deserve a monarch who will care for every last one of them, whether they like him or not. That person can't be me. It goes against my nature. But it could be you. If you become Queen of Conollia, you can protect everyone. Then I'll protect *you*."

I press a hand to my mouth. Kaine's faith touches me. "I'm not as perfect as you think I am."

"You *are* perfect, and I'm going to spend the rest of our lives showing it to you. I want to marry you because I love you with all my heart and soul. Let's have two children, a boy and a girl."

"You can't control their genders."

"Then you agree to have my babies?"

"That's not what I said."

Kaine kneels down. "Please marry me, Ysabel." Light glints off his white teeth and chiseled jaw. Seeing him in this position arouses a primal hunger in me. I'd let him have whatever he wants as long as he lets me have him. My lips are moving. Sound presumably comes out.

Kaine leaps to his feet. "Yes!"

Blinking, I snap out of my daze. Why am I such an absolute sucker for a man on his knees? I can't let him find out my weakness or I'll be in real trouble. Bluffing, I say, "We're going to have a long engagement."

"Sure." He picks me up and spins me around. "Just as long as you're mine, and everyone knows it."

My heart softens. I also want the world to know that Kaine belongs to me. "Dearest, we have a deal."

A new voice says, "Let me know when you have a wedding date so I can arrange my visit." Alesh stands by the tent flap, smiling.

Kaine bounds over. "Did you see me out there? I tied for first place in the World Games!"

"You were amazing." Alesh ruffles his brother's hair.

Kaine grabs Alesh and ruffles his long red locks back. "I'm bigger than you now."

"You'll always be my little brother." Alesh hugs him. "I'm proud of you."

"Do you *have* to return to the Elven Empire?" Kaine clings tighter. "You should come back to Conollia with me. Tell the Elven Empress I'm willing to fight her for you. Single combat, to first blood, no magic, she picks the weapons."

"I'm not going to say that to a venerable millennium-old elder." Alesh holds his brother off with both hands. "I can arrange to be made ambassador to Conollia though. I've developed a reputation as one of the few people who can deal with a certain dark lord."

"Yay!" Kaine claps Alesh on the back hard enough to send him reeling. "Ysabel, did you hear that?"

His happiness is infectious. I grin. "I heard."

"I can't wait to show you the new Conollia. I bet you'd love the gardens in my capital. Well, you'll love them when Ysabel has finished them. Her designs look amazing. I'd like an outdoor wedding. Ysabel gets flowers, and I get to hold a tournament." Kaine extends his arms broadly enough to encompass all of his big plans. I can already predict my future—me, who likes to be in charge, will be thoroughly led around by the nose by him. Strangely, it makes me smile.

When I move to Conollia, I won't have to worry about the council booting me off. I'll be out of range of the sneers of the royal court. I can finally live for myself.

After Alesh leaves, I whisper to Kaine, "As soon as you're recovered, let's plan something special for my conquering champion."

"A broken arm is no obstacle to being tied up." Kaine winks. "We could play 'priestess and captured heretic.'"

I hesitate. He raises an eyebrow. "Not to your taste?"

"I don't find it sexy to be reminded of work during play." Plus, every man wants me to dress up in the white Holy Maiden robes. It gets old. "But I'd be willing to do it for you."

"Hey, we don't have to do it at all. You know what else I love? Barbarian princesses. Wear the fur dress."

I laugh. "You have yourself a deal." Since he's so understanding, I'll indulge his other suggestion on some special occasion, like his birthday. Maybe we could confiscate Jiang's desk and defile it. Suddenly, I'm very much into this idea.

I wet my lips. "Kaine. There's something I want to tell you." I swallow down a lump. "I'm glad you saved my life even when I'd given up. Because of you, I have everything I've ever wanted. Thank you."

"It's my pleasure," he says, tracing a finger down my jaw. Did I think he was the most handsome man before? Funny, he's gotten even better-looking since then. "You've saved me several times, too. I never dreamed I'd be able to find someone like you. Thank *you*."

I don't know how I got this lucky, but I thank the Sun God with all my heart.

After that, it seems like a great idea to push him into a chair, straddle his hips, and kiss him. Then Alzira bursts into the tent.

"I've failed you!" she wails. She takes two tries before speaking. "Jiang escaped."

"Please knock first," I say, sliding off Kaine. "Wait, what?"

"The guards were found dead. People saw him leave escorted by dozens of what appeared to be zombies. The cowards feared the undead too much to stop him."

I grind my teeth. "This isn't your fault. I knew Jiang would have another twist up his sleeve. I knew it!" To think I'd convinced myself I was just being paranoid. Where in the name of the Sun God did he get the corpses from? He can't have summoned zombies all the way from the city—he's not Dark Lord Chingis. Only one necromancer in history was that powerful, and if Jiang had that strength, then someone as power-hungry as him would have tried to take over the world.

I turn to Kaine. "I have to go." The royal court and the Council of Cardinals will have returned to the city in preparation for the Post-Games parade. I need to borrow relics to look for Jiang and send the guard on a manhunt. "Jiang isn't as much of a threat now I've stolen his position, but it would really anger me if he escapes justice."

Alzira trembles. "That's not all." There are tiny tears in the corners of her eyes. It takes her a few tries to speak. "Your brother is gone from the healing tent. There were signs of a struggle."

No, no, no! This isn't fair! I saved Calum! He can't be gone already! Then my brain catches up. "Who was guarding him?" Which of my friends is also in danger?

"I'm not sure," Alzira whispers. "There were no dead bodies left behind."

Given we're dealing with a necromancer, that's not as comforting as it would normally be. I tell myself that Jiang would prefer my friends as hostages. If he went after my brother, then he still wants me for his evil ritual.

Oh, Sun God, just when I believed myself to be free, now I'm back to bargaining with my life again. I take deep breaths to keep myself from breaking down.

"How can I help?" Kaine asks.

"Please send your soldiers to guard the roads." I'm already heading out of the tent. There's not a minute to waste. Kaine's army is located on the opposite side of the stadium, and his soldiers won't be allowed inside the city. I don't have time to gather an army. The gate guards won't let Kaine enter the city without royal permission either. "I need you to guard the Southern Gate while we enter from the north." Kaine can loop around to the other side of the city in case Jiang tries to leave that way. I can't risk Jiang escaping the country with my brother and any other hostages.

As long as I'm with Alzira, we'll be okay. She's stronger than any army—dead or undead. She can manipulate the blood in the undead as easily as the living. With her ability to puppeteer people, she's the perfect person to have during a hostage situation.

With long strides, Alzira easily catches up to me. "We'll get everyone back. I vow it."

I want to say, *It should have been over.* Instead, I say, "I have faith in you."

There aren't any guards at the Holy City's drawbridge. That's not just odd. It's utterly terrifying. "Alzira . . ." I hiss.

Her face hardens. "I'll protect you."

I exhale. With Alzira by my side, I don't need to be afraid. We're going to rescue everyone, then go home together.

The streets are deserted. But there's no sign of violence. Maybe people are hiding inside their houses. No matter how loudly we shout, there's no reply.

The air smells of decaying meat. I hesitate, looking at Alzira.

"Dead bodies. Recent ones," she says.

I bite my lip. I'm a healer, skilled even without the use of my magic. Someone might need me. Part of me is screaming to get out, but that's my cowardice talking. "Let's investigate."

"Stay behind me, Your Holiness." Alzira takes the lead.

The coppery stench gets stronger as we head down the deserted street. Alzira throws up her arm. "Don't look!"

Of course, I look anyway. The bodies hang suspended by metal wire around their necks, though the injuries that killed them range from stab wounds to crushed skulls. Bile rises up my throat. I know these people. The crowns make it easy to identify King Uctor and Queen Bianna. Then eight men in cardinal's robes. One is missing, though I can't tell who. I recognize Orwin by his favorite diamond ring. His entrails hang out of his stomach. I take a step backward, then another, my stomach heaving. Dozens of nobles are strung up, continuing down the street, not in a straight line but slightly curved. These houses here are deserted, with yards overgrown and windows shuttered. I remember why we evacuated this location.

This place fills in the top of Jiang's skull. With these murders, his ritual is complete.

I no longer care about being a coward. "Go! Run!" Following my own advice, I turn around.

Jiang stands behind me. He's flanked by the guards who should be protecting this spot. A rotting stench comes off them, and their nails are pitch black. The one with his head half falling off makes it the most obvious that they are zombies.

Close to a hundred undead shuffle aside to reveal Feiyan, Sigma, Nakimé, and Ua'la'sur, all bound and gagged, held by the Gifted Knights who made up Jiang's personal guard. Except I should call them former guards because they're all dead. Very sharp swords point at my Dragon Maidens' throats.

The Sun God has not smiled down on me today. Jiang has *all* my friends. I thought I had him cornered. I thought everyone would be safe. Instead, he was planning this all along. No wonder he didn't care about the World Games. No wonder he let me destroy the fake orphanage. His men are more dangerous dead than alive.

Slowly, I lift my eyes to Jiang's smirking face. He draws a blade from his silver-headed cane as another zombie tosses Calum at him. My gagged brother struggles briefly before the sword settles at his throat.

Scimitar drawn, Alzira demands, "How did a necromancer swear the oaths against dark magic required to join the Council of Cardinals?"

"*A* necromancer?" Jiang's lips pull back into a snarl. "Don't talk about me like I'm some street magician who decided to try his hands at raising a dead cat to dance for coins. I have existed before the Sun God sects formed a council, and I will exist long after its destruction. I'm *the* Necromancer. I am Dark Lord Chingis."

"Impossible," Alzira snaps.

My first reaction matches hers. Maybe Jiang has lost his mind. Maybe *I've* lost my mind and have been hallucinating everything since I collapsed at the stadium.

Except it's not impossible. I know that immortality exists, since I nearly died for Jiang to obtain it. Jiang—Chingis—must have been granted longevity from the first healer he murdered, Holy Maiden Sarra. I can't understand why he seems to hate his own homeland Conollia, but then he's always been the type to despise the weak for their weakness. If he's truly Dark Lord Chingis, then perhaps he could survive breaking a life-oath and take over the Holy City. The greatest dark lord had many powers. How can we possibly defeat a figure out of legend? "What do you want?" My voice comes out high-pitched. I'm skirting the edge of panic. If I start spiraling, then I might faint for real.

"I want you to fulfill your bargain with me. Or your brother and your subordinates all die." He strokes his sword down Calum's cheek, drawing a line of blood. Calum hisses.

"Stop! Please don't hurt him! Alzira, lower your weapon."

Alzira gives me an odd look. "Princess, allow me to act."

My heart restarts as I realize why Alzira seems undisturbed. She could shatter every blade here before they have time to break skin. "Rescue them," I order.

Nothing happens.

Jiang lifts his hand and points. The zombies lumber forward. One slaps Alzira across the face, knocking her to the ground. She touches the blood trickling from her nose as if it's the twisted opposite of a miracle. "My gift isn't working!" Color drains from her face. "I'm sorry, princess!" The zombies surround her.

Even without her gift, she fights. Her sword cleaves off a zombie's head, then she kicks it into another. Whirling around, she plants her sword in another zombie's chest. But that fails to stop the undead monstrosity from swinging its sword at her. She barely pulls her weapon free in time to block. Alzira wises up and takes off its head with her next swing, but another zombie grabs her from behind. Growling, she drops low and skewers it. That gives the others time to pile on her. They have no care for stabbing through their own fellows to get at her. Sheer weight bears her down. They kick and punch her as she lies on the ground.

"Alzira!" I try to run forward, but the blank-eyed undead block me. She falls horribly silent.

Jiang snickers. "I'm tempted to give you one free pass because that was funny. But I did tell you what would happen if you defied me. Promise made"—he slices his sword across Calum's throat—"promise kept."

CHAPTER TWENTY-TWO

Calum hits the cobblestones at my feet. He makes a horrible sound between a whimper and a whistle of wind. Blood splatters my sandals and seeps into the white hem of my robe. I crash to my knees and slap my hands down on the spurting injury as I call forth my power.

How right Kaine was, that day back in the training room, to tell me that I would never stop with one day left. I knew he was right, but I didn't know it would happen this soon. I'm sorry for breaking my promise to him, but I'm going to heal my brother anyway.

Nothing happens. I try again. Nothing happens. Nothing happens. Nothing happens!

"How futile," Jiang says. "My ritual has disabled every gift but mine in this city. My power feeds off and absorbs all other magic, like I feed off lives. I've spent centuries crafting rituals to enhance my magic. I had plenty of bodies to experiment with."

The words ring in my ears like a funeral bell. Calum gargles and coughs up blood. He's trying to talk but he can't. His eyes lock with mine. I can't move. I can't breathe. My shoulders tense as if a monster's claws grip my neck. My insides flip. I might be about to vomit. I have a mad desire to run, but tingles consume my hands and feet so I freeze instead.

It's all my fault. It's all my fault. It's all my fault. It's all my fault.

I have to hold it together. Calum needs me. He's counting on me to save him. Fighting through the haze around my mind, I lift my arm. Each shaky movement feels like I'm forcing my way through gelatin. Shakily, I touch Calum's cheek with my blood-soaked hands. I summon my power. I know this is the last healing I will ever perform. But he can have every single last bit of my life, if that's what it takes. I pour in everything.

Still, nothing happens.

"He's dead. Extremely dead," Jiang says. "I would know. Shall I make him stand up and dance a jig? I can do that to the *deceased*."

Because of me . . . He killed Calum because of me. My big brother. My hero. He'd suffered. He'd drowned in his own blood while I sat useless. The one time in my life I needed my cursed power the most, it failed me. Calum looked straight at me, and I couldn't save him.

I topple backward to the ground.

"Don't pass out yet. I'm not done with you." Jiang frowns. "If you dare ignore me, I'll kill another of your people. Shall I beat your obnoxious bodyguard to death next?"

I have to stop him. Except I can't move. It's as if I'm watching this scene play out from a distance. The sky. It's very blue. Something is . . . is wrong . . . I can't . . . Alzira is going to die because I'm stupid and worthless.

Spitting out a chunk of her gag, Sigma strangles out, "She'sh hava panic attack. She can'sh help it."

"Yes, she can. Watch," Jiang says. "Stab Alzira's shoulder." A zombie brings down its sword with an awful squelch. "Ysabel, I'll keep doing this until you stop acting like a baby."

"W-wait. I'll do anything." My panic attack still courses through me. It's all I can do to talk. I can't think rationally enough to figure out what I have to offer Jiang. All I can do is beg. "Please. Please."

"Yshabel," Sigma whispers. The other Dragon Maidens plead with their eyes.

I can't let anyone else die. A certain calm settles over me. It washes away all my thoughts and stills my shaking hands. I've always known I'd end up this way: killed for my healing powers. There's no need for my friends to go down with me. And Kaine . . . What I had with Kaine was a brief mirage. My fate has come.

In a state of pure, overwhelming emptiness, I tell Jiang, "I'll come with you if you let them go."

"How very much like you—trying to bargain until the bitter end." He laughs. "You have no cards left to play, little girl. I have a city full of hostages. My ritual puts everyone to sleep. All I have to do is turn up the intensity, and they'll fall into permanent slumber. Then they become useful to me." He caresses the cheek of a dead guard. "Every last person in the Holy City is at my mercy. I have an excess of hostages. Why shouldn't I kill one of your friends? Or all of them?"

My mind goes white. "Please. Don't." I find a stronger voice. "You need to sacrifice me in your damn ritual to gain immortality. I'll cooperate if you let everyone go."

"You'll take a life-oath first." He fiddles with his cane-sword. "I'll bind myself to release them at the same time."

"The entire city."

"The entire city," he agrees. This is the best I can hope for.

"I'sh too easy," Sigma whispers. Feiyan and Ua'la'sur nod frantically. Jiang taps his blade at Sigma's throat to silence her. Helplessly, I watch with all-consuming horror.

They're right, but what choice do I have? Nothing matters more to Jiang than extending his ancient life. If I can save everyone by dying, then that's something I resigned myself to a long time ago.

"Lead the way," I say, raising my chin with the dignity of a Holy Maiden.

Jiang marches us to the royal castle, his undead carrying the unconscious Alzira. The bastard wouldn't even let me bandage her up. Her blood has stopped dripping but her entire face is swollen.

Up close, the scent of decay drifts off Jiang even through his perfume. Raising so many zombies must have taken a high price and rotted his body. In other words, he wouldn't have been able to use magic if I hadn't been healing him all this time. I hate myself even more. Jiang used me to the very last drop he could drain from me. He will kill me with exactly one day left. I'll die to save the man who murdered my brother. A brief, mad impulse seizes me to throw myself at him and strangle him. No life-oaths would stop my heart, since Conclave signatories are allowed and encouraged to kill dark lords. But the zombies surrounding me would definitely stop me.

A creepy sight greets me at the palace entrance. All the guards are slumped sideways in sleep. Servants lie fallen over in the hallway. Jiang's zombies force my Dragon Maidens down the stairs to the dungeons. At least they won't have to watch Jiang kill me.

The stench of Calum's blood contaminates my nostrils. If only I'd never tried to escape Jiang. It's all my fault. No more fighting back. I only made everything worse.

In silence, I follow Jiang to the throne room. His zombies form a line along the carpet. A man in cardinal's robes stands held up by two undead. That moustache and pointy hat—Santos. Jiang must have left the Seer alive to bind me to a new life-oath. Murmuring prayers under his breath, Santos doesn't look at me. An ugly part of me wants to ask if he's rethought his conviction that all misfortune is the will of the Sun God, but I'm not that cruel.

A mirror perches on Queen Bianna's former seat, the royal relic for peering over long distances. The mahogany frame shows zombies patrolling the palace walls. This must be how Jiang gives them orders. His army numbers at least a thousand.

Jiang settles on King Uctor's throne. "Repeat after me: 'I swear to allow myself to be sacrificed at the next full moon tomorrow. I will not take any action to escape the castle. I will do nothing to harm Cardinal Jiang directly or indirectly. I will not leave the eyesight of himself or his minions.'"

I wish the full moon would come right now. Even one day is too long to suffer. "You go first."

"Very well." He sighs. Since he has hostages, I suppose he doesn't fear me trying to back out.

Nervously, I say, "Wait, magic doesn't work here."

"It works when I allow it," Jiang says. "Only the spells I specifically will, so don't get any funny ideas."

Jiang's zombies drag Cardinal Santos forward by his armpits. His prayers become louder. Jiang slaps him across the face, then grabs his chin. "I swear that I will safely release everyone in this city once Holy Maiden Ysabel dies in ritual sacrifice next evening. Afterward, I will make no further attempt to harm them." A blaze of light completes his vow and proves to me that the magic took.

Thank the Sun God. A little tension eases from my shoulders. I can accept my death now. Tears prickle my eyes, as much from joy as grief. Taking Santos's wrinkled, clammy hand in mine, I repeat the oath Jiang asked of me. It's almost comforting to feel the tightness settling over my heart. All I have to do to save everyone else is die. I'm good at dying. I've been doing it all my life.

"Satisfactory," Jiang pronounces. He smiles at me. Very tentatively, I smile back.

Then Jiang draws the blade from his cane and rams it into Santos's heart. I leap backward and scream as more blood sprays my dress. Pulling his cane-sword free, he recites, "With this, let my life-oath be taken to the grave." Light flashes down the blade.

Jiang's cane is a relic allowing him to break life-oaths. Of course! How else could he attack the Holy City? How else could he have sworn the oaths against necromancy to join the Council? For that matter, this explains a few of Dark Lord Chingis's historical betrayals. I had all the clues, yet I stupidly let him trick me.

I drop to my knees. "Please." I don't even know what to beg. *Please don't kill my friends. Please don't destroy my city.* I have nothing left to bargain with. I've already given him everything he wants. All I can do is cry, muffling the sound with the back of my hand.

I have one hostage left.

Myself.

I slide backward, not taking my eyes off Jiang. "If you don't keep your promise to me, I'll kill myself by breaking my life-oath." The chains begin to tighten around my heart. I force the last syllable out through the pain.

Santos rises off the ground, a dead-eyed zombie. His still-warm arms wrap around me as I try not to scream. Blood seeps into my clothing, reaching my skin. Leaning down, Jiang strokes a lock of my hair. I retch. He yanks, sending my forehead smacking into the floor. "You wouldn't dare, you spoiled child. I could make you pick between a fast death for your friends or a slow one, and still have hostages to spare."

I don't try to get up. Past beatings tell me not to provoke him. I use an arm to protect my face. "I'm sorry." Begging is all I have left. "Please sacrifice me." I hate pleading for that. "I was always fated to die for the greater good. I was wrong to fight it. Only please let my friends live."

"Apologize for the trouble you've caused."

"I'm so, so sorry. I never should have defied you." I grovel on the floor. "Please don't kill anyone else. I'll do whatever you want." I try to think of something to offer him. My political expertise? My foreign allies? My healing power? All will be gone once he sacrifices me. "Please." I lift my eyes off the floor to his maniac grin of triumph.

"You're the only one who needs to die for the ritual. My immortality was incomplete the first time because I shared it with Holy Maiden Sarra, and even killing her later didn't rectify that mistake." He kicks me in the stomach. "I ought to slaughter them all to punish you. Luckily for you, I do have something I want. Do it and your friends live."

Live! Yes, they have to live. I grasp onto that thin thread of hope with all my might. I need him to be telling the truth. Daring to raise my eyes, I scan his face.

I'm confident he's not lying because I know him too well. We've fought, lied to, and tricked each other many times. I know his tells. This is his truth. "I'll do anything," I whisper.

Jiang tips my chin up with his foot. "That upstart dark lord who stole my throne has come knocking on my door. Be a good girl and get rid of your pit bull."

Alone, I step across the drawbridge. I'm sweltering in a coat covering my bloodstained clothes. Jiang waits in a carriage pulled by zombie horses. Several hundred of his undead monsters hide against the walls, waiting to attack. In an instant, Jiang can order the zombies back at the palace to murder my friends. I have to make this good. I have to send Kaine away.

My foolishly courageous love stands alone before the city wall. As far as he knows, nothing can harm him. He's a walking army of one. Except once he steps through the gate, he'll become as helpless as Alzira. Jiang would enjoy murdering the man who's caused him so much trouble. I must keep Kaine out of the city, safe and alive, no matter what I have to say or do.

Kaine waves at me. "Ysabel, everyone in the stadium fell asleep, including my brother and friends." On this rare occasion I see true concern on his face—not for himself, but for the people he cares about. "Luckily I have an insomnia power I never thought would come in handy." His eyes narrow. "Where's Alzira?"

He's suspicious already. No matter what excuse I come up with, he knows it would make no logical sense for me to send away Alzira, when she needs to be close to me to use her power. My throat dries up. I can't speak.

Kaine examines my face. "The sleeping spell hit a good part of my army, but the outskirts are still awake. Who are we fighting?"

I can't let Kaine bring his army into the Holy City, or his life-oath will kill him as an "invader." I refuse to let him die for me. *Refuse.*

I clench my fists, summoning my resolve. Then I step forward, my Holy Maiden mask on my face. "There's nothing wrong. I've taken over the Holy City."

"How? Why didn't you say anything to me?" A tiny trace of hurt shows under the worry knotting his brows.

"Obviously because you aren't useful to me any longer." I throw back my head and laugh. "It was a triple-cross, you fool. I've been working with Jiang all along. Did you really think I cared about the brother who betrayed me and sold me into slavery? I faked a sob story so you'd be my useful meat shield in the Games. Thank the Sun God that's over with."

"Bullshit. You love your brother," Kaine says.

His instincts have always been good. All I can do is hurt him so badly he'll stop caring about me. It takes every scrap of my experience as a liar to hold my voice steady. "I never loved you. I could never love someone like you, a brain-dead barbarian with no class or style. I'm not sure where you got the delusion that you were adequate for me, a Holy Maiden. Know your place."

His eyes widen and his shoulders hunch over. "Why are you saying this? I don't understand." He looks as pitiful as a puppy tied up in a sack and tossed in the river. My heart clenches. I can't . . . but I must. A vision of Calum dying slowly on the pavement fills my spine with steel. If I don't send Kaine away, he'll die too. The instant Kaine steps past the gate, he'll be struck down by the zombies without even knowing why.

To make him give up on me, I have to take this all the way to the bitter end. Loving someone means knowing exactly how to hurt them the most. And I know what words will trigger Kaine's deepest fear and override his reason: *You truly thought I would marry you? I only like men. Not a sad little girl pretending to be one.*

Except no words come out of my mouth. I try, once again, to speak. A low "ung" emerges. Blood drips down my throat. I've bitten my tongue too hard.

It's better to hurt Kaine than see him die. I fail out of simple selfishness. I can't bring myself to destroy Kaine's love for me. Not when I needed and craved to be loved like that for so long. To the very end, I'm a coward.

My mind gropes for Kaine's second sorest spot. It will have to do. "Frankly, it was disgusting to have a former slave touch me. Never show your face in my city, or I'll have you beaten and tossed out like a beggar." A drop of blood trickles from my mouth. I turn my back to hide it . . . and so I won't have to see Kaine's face. With this, it's over. He'll never forgive me. Hopefully that will make it hurt less when I die.

"Do you think I'm an idiot?"

I whirl around. Kaine stands puffed up with his fists clenched and his face red. "Well, I am an idiot! But I know why you always lose at Bluffer!" His lower lip juts out. "It's because you know exactly how to trick your friends—but you can't bring yourself to do it. You can't hurt the people you love even when it's a game. If you want me to leave you, you know what you have to say. So go on. Say it."

God. Do I have to hurt him even more? Do I have to cross the line to make him leave? My lips twist into an ugly sneer. "I have nothing else to say to you, you"—*sham of a man*—"dark lord." Again, I failed.

Softly, Kaine says, "You've got blood on your shoes."

Bad, bad, bad. Kaine knows. But I have one card left with which to save his life. "I don't want you to help me. I'm telling you to leave me alone. What are you going to do, kidnap me for my own good again?" I snarl, knowing he won't, not when he promised me to never do that again.

"N-no." He draws his shaking body up. "This time I won't do anything against your will. I'm not clever enough to figure out how to help you unless you tell me. But I'm going to wait for you. I'll wait as long as it takes. All you have to do is ask me to save you." Too-perceptive eyes burn into me. "I won't regret it even if I die."

Goddammit, I love him. I've never been more overflowing with love than watching him stand there, proud and tall. I love him too much to watch him die for me. If I tell Kaine the truth, he'll bring what remains of his army to the Holy City to save me, even knowing it will stop his heart. Without another word, I turn and walk away.

As I climb back into the carriage, Jiang says, "He hasn't left yet. I'd better not have any trouble from him."

"Don't worry. Kaine always keeps his word. Since he promised me, he won't move a muscle until it's all over."

The zombie horses start forward and the carriage rattles down the street. I sit with my hands clenched on my lap, tears falling onto them.

CHAPTER TWENTY-THREE

Jiang imprisons me in a tower bedroom for diplomatic guests. I beg him to let me stay with my friends, or at least see them, but he refuses. For all I know, he's already killed them. I tell the nagging voice to shut up. I've done everything he wanted. I just have to keep obeying him, and he won't kill anyone else.

The pale blue room is stuffy. The curtained bed hasn't been made up with sheets, the fireplace lacks wood, and the desk's inkwells lie empty. The ebony dresser and mirror are dusty. The window isn't even locked, because my life-oath prevents me from trying to escape. I pace the bearskin carpet, nibbling on my hair. Three zombies stand around the room, still wearing the armor of the King's Guard. Their horrible pits for eyes and rotting stench nearly drive me to vomit. In a twisted way, I long for the full moon to come faster so Jiang will kill me sooner instead of leaving me alone with my fear for my friends, my guilt at hurting Kaine, and my grief for Calum.

When the doorknob turns, I suddenly decide I don't want to die after all, and plaster myself against the wall. My arm brushes one of the corpse-guards, and I whimper.

A brown-haired woman rushes into the room. She takes off a zombie's head with one sword blow, then whirls on the second one, gutting it. The intestines dripping down don't bother the motionless creature, so she kicks it to its knees and chops off its head too. Then she lunges for the last one.

"Wait, whoever you are!" I jump between them. As soon as it no longer sees the sword, the zombie stops moving.

"You're pretending not to recognize me? Are you a child?" *Ah, got the voice now.* It's Donya.

People don't tend to understand face-blindness, so instead I say, "Sorry, I'm in shock."

Donya's expression melts into sympathy. *Damn, she's easy to trick.* Thank the Sun God she's not dead. What in the heavenly choir is she doing here?

"If you kill all of them, I'll die. See, it's not even attacking you. It's only under orders to watch me." I point at the motionless corpse.

"You'll die?" Donya asks, uncomprehending. Sweat sticks a curl to her forehead. She wears trousers under her dress and has a breastplate tied around her torso using rope. It looks ridiculous, yet the barely contained aura of murderous energy about her has *me* flinching away.

"I took a life-oath to Jiang not to escape or leave his zombies' eyesight," I explain.

"What did you do a goshdarn stupid thing like that for?" She waves her bloody sword.

"To stop him from killing everyone!"

"Brilliant job, then. Your friends broke out of the dungeon with me minutes after he left."

"I didn't know that!"

"Did you make him give you a guarantee his hostages were alive?" Donya glares. "You always give up too easily!"

"Like how you gave up on our friendship?"

"You lied to me! Used me! Let me pay for all our dinners!"

"You volunteered!"

"Because I thought I was richer than you!"

"Sorry! I'll pay you back!" Realizing I'm screaming, I stop.

Our lungs spent, we stare at each other, panting. Donya sighs and lowers her sword. "I would have helped you save your brother if you'd told me the truth. Do you believe me?"

I think of Donya, who risked her life to save a harassed maid, who stood up for me against the court when she had every reason to hate me, and who's here to rescue me after I stabbed her in the back. "I believe you. I'm sorry."

"I'm sorry I said so many mean things about you when I didn't know it was you." Her face turns bright red.

"Donya, you say worse things to my face all the time." What's she so embarrassed about? It's no secret she hates me.

"Don't remind me." She covers her eyes.

"Look, I really am sorry about everything. How did you end up here?" I lower my voice as I should have done from the beginning. In my defense, I've had a rough day. "I thought you'd still be chained outside the World Games stadium."

"The royal guard arrested me. Not because of the protest—Queen Bianna flipped out because I was the only person to bet on a draw in the finals so I won all her money." Donya pauses. "I think I won everyone's money. We can open a lot of schools together, assuming we get out of this situation alive."

"I didn't even know it was possible to bet on a draw."

"I was angry at you, so I bet that both your bodyguard and your boyfriend would lose to each other."

How Donya-like. "If you were with the queen when Jiang came to kill her, how did you survive?"

"Jiang wanted to interrogate me about why I'd spied on him. I should thank you since I avoided being sacrificed." It's hard to tell if she's joking. "I'd already chipped away at the lock on my cell when your team got thrown in with me. We're hiding—"

I raise my hand to stop her. "What I don't know, I can't reveal." Already I can guess too well. Nakimé's told me about a few secret passages around the palace she used during her thieving days.

Donya pauses. "Let's focus on escaping." She turns around to show me Ua'la'sur's silver bow decorated with ebony roses strapped to her back. "Relics still work inside Jiang's spell, so we all agreed to send one person with the Bow of Concealment to rescue you. I drew the long straw."

I shake my head. "Why would you come to save me?"

"No one's gifts work, so I'm as useful as any of your Dragon Maidens."

"I meant why would you care?"

"I care." Donya swallows. "We need to talk, but now's not the time. Let's tie up the zombie and take it with us so it can keep its 'eyes' on you."

"That won't work." I clench my eyes shut. "I swore not to escape."

"Did I mention how stupid that was? It's worth repeating."

"You all have to flee the city without me."

"Who said anything about fleeing?" Donya's eyes blaze. "As soon as you're safe, we're coming to kill Jiang."

"Are you crazy? You have no magic! He has a zombie army!"

"We found a Bookmaker's relic and sent a call for help to the refugee camp. They can fight Jiang without breaking any oaths, since they aren't acknowledged as a country." Donya nods like this is a clever plan, not utter madness.

I grab her by the shoulders and shake her. "Have you lost your mind? They're pacifists!"

"Saint Nora's vows don't prevent them from putting down what's already dead. Urew is on his way with several hundred people. More are gathering weapons."

"That's impossible." I dig my fingers into my hair, twisting and hurting. "They'd never come for Kaine or Arahasnor."

Donya says quietly, "They're coming for you."

It takes me a moment to understand. "They . . . they actually . . ."

"The refugees will take down the corpses and bless the ground to break Jiang's spell. The Dragon Maidens plan to bust into the palace and kill Jiang. If he dies, the zombies go back to rotting peacefully."

My legs go out from under me. I sit down on the bed. "Don't. You can't fight Jiang—no—*Chingis*. He's too strong! He'll kill you all!"

"If his ritual succeeds, it will cause another blight." Donya speaks with cold determination. "We found his battle plans. That's what happens when he sacrifices someone to extend his life."

I shake my head. "That's not possible." Except it makes sense. The blight occurred shortly after Dark Lord Chingis kidnapped Holy Maiden Sarra.

"The blight starts the moment you die. He's counting on the chaos for his world-domination plans. Tomorrow, he'll lure Kaine into the city to kill him while he's powerless."

"But he promised me . . ." My words sound horribly weak.

"Did you have any reason to believe the creepy old necromancer's promise?"

"N-no." It's too much. I cover my face with trembling hands. "He has a sword in his cane, a relic allowing him to renounce a life-oath whenever he kills someone with it. No promise can bind him."

"He'll turn everyone in the Holy City into an undead army. They'll murder their way across Arahasnor to swell their numbers. He's heading for the refugees first. They *have* to fight."

I'm such a fool. I should have known Jiang would never keep his promise to spare Kaine, who defeated and humiliated him. I hurt Kaine for nothing. He'll die anyway.

Millions will die because of me. The desert of Conollia flashes across my mind. The tornadoes. The children who arrived at the camp with skeletal limbs and swollen stomachs. The next blight will be my fault. The world spins.

"Are you all right?" Donya sheaths her sword and steps closer. "Look, we're going to stop the blight and rescue you. I'll tell the others about the cane-sword so we can free you from your oath."

"You can't fight him!" I whirl on her. "He has a thousand zombies."

"I can't abandon millions of people to die." Very lightly and very awkwardly, Donya pats me on the shoulder. "We have to try."

"You'll all be killed! Don't! Please!" It's better to just run away. Calum would be alive if I'd run away.

"I used to think you stayed passive because you didn't care enough, but I've realized it's because you care too much. You're afraid for so many people who you care about. I'm afraid too, but I'm not going to give up." Donya shakes her head. "Sorry, I'm not trying to accuse you. But we're going to fight. We're going to save you and everyone else we can." She turns for the door.

I grab her sleeve. "You should kill me. Kill me before he has the chance. Then he won't be able to sacrifice me, he'll lose his immortality, and he won't be able to cause a blight."

"With every passing moment, he's slaughtering more people in the Holy City and adding them to his zombie army. We'd still have to fight him." Donya pries off my fingers.

I don't have an argument for that. "At least fewer people would be at risk if I was dead!"

"Ysabel, you could kill yourself at any time if you want to avoid the sacrifice. Just act against one of your life-oaths. But please wait. Please trust us. Please let us try and save you." She lays Ua'la'sur's bow down on the bed. "Maybe this can protect you. I won't leave you without any weapon. Just hold on a little longer. If I return here to find you dead, I'll never forgive you!"

"Are you insane?" I glare at her, disheveled and wild-eyed. "Are you really naive enough to throw away your life and risk a blight just to save your enemy?" My one life isn't worth anything when weighted against many other people. That truth has been ingrained into my soul.

She stops at the door. "No, I'm not naive enough to risk the fate of the world for an enemy—but I'm naive enough to do it for a friend." The door shuts behind her.

"Stop!" I leap to my feet, but they've gone numb. I trip, crashing into the carpet. When I stagger over to the door, Donya is already gone. The zombie blocks me from leaving. I'm too late to stop her.

Donya is going to die. Alzira is going to die. Feiyan, Ua'la'sur, Nakimé, and Sigma are going to die. Everyone in this city is going to die. Uncle Urew and all the refugees will die. *Kaine will die.*

It feels like I've been sucker punched by an orc. My mouth tongue sticks to the roof of my mouth. All I want is to run, but I can't flee from this. My heart beats under my chest like a caged bird. *No, not now.* If I have a panic attack now, I'll become useless!

It's not like there's anything I can do. I screwed everything up. By giving into Jiang's threats, now I'm a hostage and a tool to cause a genocide. Donya was right: I always give up too easily. I've been giving up since childhood. At my core, I'm a coward.

"God, if you have a moment, I . . ." My throat clenches. Even though I've always felt the Sun God at my worst moments, now there's nothing. I'm such a disappointment even God has abandoned me.

The panic attack roars over me like a wave, and I drown in it. Rolling on the floor, I shout, "Help me! Help me!" I scream until my throat is hoarse. Tears stream down my cheeks faster than I can wipe them away. "I don't want to cause a blight! I don't want to be sacrificed! I don't want my friends to die! Please, help me!"

"Of course. What do you need me to do?" Kaine's distant voice pierces my mental fog.

I sit up. Staggering to the window, I look down. Kaine jumps off the palace wall. Landing on the lawn, he waves.

It can't be. But it is. Despite not knowing anything, despite having every reason not to forgive me, he's still come for me.

The tremors coursing through me silence my tongue. My brain feels foggy.

Kaine begins to look nervous. "Are you angry I came?" he shouts. "Who do I have to punch to make you feel better?"

The zombies! They're approaching from his right! I squawk and wave my hands. Nothing coherent comes out. Even now, I keep failing.

Emerging from the ornamental trees, Alzira clamps a hand over Kaine's mouth and drags him behind a bush. "Shhh! They have awful eyesight, but they're sensitive to sound."

"What are?" he asks, not quietly at all.

"Jiang's undead monsters."

"Undead? Here I thought I just punched that one guy a little too hard and his head fell off." Kaine rubs his neck sheepishly. "So basically all our problems will be solved if I kill Jiang?"

"Of course. The vile fiend entrapped Ysabel with a life-oath."

"Is that why she's not talking to me? I thought she might be angry because I broke her city walls to get in. She's dreadfully touchy about those walls."

"Her Holiness is *here*?" Alzira shoots to her feet. "Ysabel! I'm coming to save you!"

Dozens of zombies stagger toward them, drawn by the noise. They flee. Distantly, Feiyan shouts something about murdering both of them for destroying her ambush. Then comes the sounds of battle. Zombies fill the courtyard, over a hundred strong now. My friends won't be able to reach me. They may die regardless.

The panic drains out of me, leaving in its place total exhaustion. Growling, I slap my cheeks. This is no time to collapse. It turns out I always had people who value my life, people who will help me if I ask, people who love me. My walls were just so high that I couldn't see. There has to be something I can do to help my loved ones. Except I'm stuck in this room and if I try to harm Jiang, I die. My current resources suck. *Think, Ysabel, think.*

Something is off about Jiang's actions. Why let my friends live? Why even temporarily spare his mortal enemy, Kaine? Jiang went to great lengths to keep me from learning about his world domination plans and convince me I could save everyone. Why all this song and dance? Why didn't he just drug me unconscious, then strap me to an altar until the full moon?

My thoughts slip away from me like the slimy frogs I used to catch in the river as a child. I'm missing something. All of Jiang's lies have been aimed at manipulating my mental state. Why? What makes *me* so important?

Jiang wants immortality. He wants it more than anything. But his previous sacrifices failed, leaving him desperate and at the end of his lifespan. I don't think all of the story he told me was a lie, because I trust my ability to read him. First: Holy Maiden Sarra. The ritual worked, but it didn't make him fully immortal because he split the power between the two of them.

I'm confident that Jiang killed Holy Youth Noretho. Why else did he join the church except to obtain access to healers? But there was no second blight. If he'd obtained his immortality then, he wouldn't be so frantic about sacrificing me now. One spell succeeded and one failed. Jiang must have needed Holy Maiden Sarra's cooperation, or he never would have shared his precious immortality with her.

I've got it! The Holy Healer has to be sacrificed *willingly*! Hence why he wants me to go to the altar begging him to kill me because I believe it will save my friends.

"I have to be able to use that against him somehow. What do you think, God?"

He's back. The warm voice in my heart was always there. I'd just been too frantic to hear it. New strength lets me sit up and rub away my tears. "I'm not scared anymore. I'm tough enough to do whatever it takes."

"Huh, You think that would work? It would be an asshole move. I like it!"

"Yeah, yeah, I'll be careful. I don't plan to die. I'm not going to make You worry about me anymore. Love You too. And . . . thank You for everything."

Jumping to my feet, I shout, "Jiang, I'm leaving this room so you'd better control your minion to follow me!" My voice echoes around the dead castle. I throw open the door.

Stepping outside, I glance over my shoulder. The zombie is moving toward me. Actually, it's running after me. *Crap.*

I flee down the hallway. Cold dead hands grab my shoulders and lift me into the air. My struggles are no use. It's taking me to Jiang. *Err, yeah, exactly as planned.*

At the throne room, the smelly zombie tosses me face-first to the carpet. I drag myself to my feet and face the snooty bastard sitting on the throne, fiddling with the head of his cane.

The mirror shows a ragtag army of Conollian refugees. Armed with pitchforks, butcher's knives, and pots, they battle a mass of zombies. They've taken the city walls so they can hurl stones and hot oil.

The image shifts to the palace hallway. Kaine and Alzira with Ua'la'sur and Nakimé fight back-to-back. Kaine wields his hammer with only his left arm while his other hangs in a sling. Alzira's neck and one shoulder are heavily bandaged, and she's bruised everywhere. To replace her bow, Ua'la'sur has stolen a sword off one of the former guards. It's chipped and has a finger hanging off the tip. Feiyan bleeds profusely from three injuries, while Sigma frantically bandages her. Donya guards them, holding off five zombies at once. Fear dries out my throat, but I swallow it down.

In a voice ringing all the way to the high ceiling, I cry out, "I know you need me to sacrifice myself willingly."

The look on his face is pure beauty. I want to have a portrait painter capture it and put it in a locket for me to wear around my neck forever.

I smirk. "If you knew you couldn't use an unwilling victim, how did you screw up so badly with Holy Youth Noretho?"

"All I did was kill one commoner maid, and after that nothing I threatened him with mattered. He hated everyone else for stealing his life." Jiang clucks his tongue. "If I'd known virginity made no difference to healing ability, I wouldn't have cared about him getting his dick wet. I lost my only good hostage."

That's why he's yet to kill my friends. "If I die, I take your immortality with me. What are the odds another healer will be born before your life runs out? All I have to do is say, 'I renounce my life-oath not to harm Ji—'" I stop, bent over with pain, my point made.

He rises from his throne. "I can bring your friends here and torture them to death in front of you one by one until you beg me to let you sacrifice yourself."

I clench my teeth. *Sun God, give me courage.* "You don't have them yet. You'd better not kill a single one of them, or I'll kill myself. I'm counting every single one of the refugees, too. They're my *family*."

"You're bluffing."

"Am I? You know me. I'm a drug addict with suicidal impulses. A coward at heart who takes the easy way out." As I know Jiang well enough to see through him, like it or not he's become equally familiar with me. "Just hurting one of my friends might drive me to despair. I'm such a fragile flower." I bare my teeth.

In the mirror, Nakimé screams, "Ua'la'sur! No!" My dwarven friend's stolen sword has broken. Blood drips from her forehead. Nakimé jumps between Ua'la'sur and the zombie guard's blow, bringing her own weapon up to block—too slowly.

I scream, "I renounce my—"

The zombie's sword stops inches from Nakimé's chest. He moves to club her unconscious instead, but she already has her whip wrapped around his hand, jerking it clean off.

His voice as cold as the top of a winter mountain, Jiang says, "Do not imagine you've done them a favor by forcing me to take them alive. There are worse fates than death."

His obsession with immortality gives me power over him. "You'll have to catch them first." Whirling around, I draw Ua'la'sur's bow. An arrow of pure darkness pierces the mirror.

Glass shatters, breaking the connection allowing Jiang to view his zombie army outside. The zombies pile on me and wrench the bow from my hand. My chin hits the floor. With the taste of blood coating my tongue, I grin. "Can't control them now, can you?" I've given my friends all the advantages I can.

Just minutes ago, I'd have used my one shot to kill Jiang, even knowing it would mean my death, too. But I've decided to believe in my friends. Call it selfishness or love. I won't give up any longer.

Also, I probably couldn't have hit a target as small as Jiang's blackened raisin heart.

I expect it when Jiang backhands me across the face. Closing my eyes, I make no sound. He kicks me on top of my bruises. I smile.

It infuriates him. "Don't play the martyr with me. You've always rejected your natural role as the Sun God's sacrifice."

"How dare you?" Indignation cracks my calm. "Are you trying to tell me you're a believer? After everything you've done?"

"The Sun God granted me my throne by divine right. Only the foolish subjects of Conollia failed me. All my actions must be approved by Him, or I wouldn't be winning."

Oh, he's that *type.* I snort, losing interest.

He shouts as he beats me. "You're a fake! Just like *her*, like all healers, I know you must hate and curse the Sun God for your fated death."

"I have *never* lost my faith," I say, and something about the burning intensity in my voice makes him recoil.

Shouts and the clash of blades reach our ears. Jiang jerks me up by my hair. I go limp out of spite as he drags me up the curved interior stairway leading to the commoners' balcony overlooking the throne room. With a grunt, he throws me against the wall and draws Ua'la'sur's bow.

My friends tumble through the door, bloody and bruised. Kaine leads the charge, beheading a zombie in one blow. Jiang aims the shadow arrow at him.

I jump in front of him, arms outstretched. He curses and jerks the bow downward. While he's surprised, I grab the bow. My life-oath won't let me toss the relic to Ua'la'sur, so I throw it behind the throne. Then I shout, "Up here—"

Jiang's sucker punch cuts off my shout. I double over, gagging. Bile drips down my chin and mingles with the blood in my mouth.

"Get your hands off her!" Alzira screams, barely blocking an undead guard's sword as she turns to glare. Kaine shoots Jiang a look of raw, murderous promise.

"Ignore me! That's an order!" I shout. "He won't kill me."

Jiang kicks me to my hands and knees. "If it looked like you were about to be rescued, I'd definitely kill you. If Sarra couldn't live, you're sure as hell not going to."

His next blow breaks my nose. Through the throbbing mess of pain, I refuse to cry out. At the very least, I don't want to be a distraction.

Jiang drags me upright. His cane-sword slices open the front of my dress, drawing a line of blood from my collarbone to my bellybutton and revealing the many bruises on my stomach. He holds the blade at my throat. "Whether you win or lose, she'll die."

Alzira shakes, her teeth grinding as loud as a sword against a whetstone. The buckles of her armor are rattling. Her power smashed the antimagic barrier around the stadium. Perhaps she can do it again. The closer the cold metal presses to my jugular vein, the stronger Alzira gets. "Alzira, *destroy everything*."

Jiang laughs. "Have you gone mad with fear? You might as well pray for a miracle."

Alzira closes her eyes and bows her head, her sword pointed at the sky. Jiang gapes. "Are you actually praying?"

"I'm praying for forgiveness." Alzira opens her eyes. They blaze like the darkest night. "Because after what you've done to Her Holiness, I'm going to enjoy killing you."

A distant rumble sounds above. Alzira's scimitar has nearly become a relic, one capable of operating even under Jiang's curse, one which does . . . what, exactly?

A hundred lightning bolts rip through the ceiling. They catch on the tip of Alzira's blade, wreathing her face in dancing shadows. She swings. The bolts sear dead flesh right and left. She's not done yet.

After the lightning comes the meteors. They rip giant chunks from the ceiling and crush the zombie reinforcements pouring in the door. One head-sized meteorite lands entirely too close to me, knocking a chunk off the stairs and making my ears ring.

Through the hole in the roof, the sky overhead has darkened. The moon blocks out part of the sun. Alzira is *causing an eclipse.* I scream. "Whoa, stop, please! I'm begging you, calm down! I only meant for you to destroy Jiang, not the entire world! It was a metaphor!"

Jiang shouts, "One more rock and I'll—" But his hand has frozen, the blade refusing to cut into me. Alzira's magic is definitely back. He cries out as a lightning bolt strikes him. I shout too, from surprise not fear. The electricity dances away from my body. He goes limp, his hands falling off me.

I push him away and stumble—straight into very familiar arms.

Kaine, like an absolute madman, has climbed straight up the wall with one broken arm via dedicated footwork. He takes off his coat and tosses it over my shoulders. Then he deflects Jiang's blade coming at us. In Kaine's haste drawing his weapon, his grip is wrong. The hammer slips from his hands and falls over the railing.

Jiang has risen off the floor. I bite back a gasp. His skull peeks out of his burned flesh. Glowing patterns dance underneath his skin. Eternal "life" might not be the right word for his immortality.

Kaine punches Jiang in the face. The monster of a former cardinal rocks backward. "How can you possibly be here?" Jiang snarls. "You took a life-oath!"

"My life-oath said I couldn't attack this city with my army or my magic. But it said nothing about attacking with just myself." Kaine beams like he found a clever loophole instead of absolute insanity.

"I stripped you of your legendary gift, yet you still dared come?"

"You've disabled our magic? I guess that explains why no one else is using their powers either." Kaine shrugs. "Wait, what about Alzira?" My bodyguard totters on her feet, her magical strength depleted yet still trying to fight her way past the rubble to reach me. The others use their gifts to lift aside rocks. My regeneration scabs over the cut on my throat and tingles as my nose straightens. The refugee team must have finally succeeded in purifying the skull ritual and unlocking our magic.

My city is saved.

Kaine says, "Eh, they're using their gifts now."

Jiang glances at me. "Someone like you fell in love with someone this stupid?"

I make a rude gesture at him. Only I'm allowed to call Kaine stupid.

"I don't worry about the details. You hurt Ysabel, so I'm going to kill you."

Go get him, darling. I'll just be cowering in this corner.

Kaine swings his fist again. This time he misses. The force of his blow knocks part of the railing down.

"You came all this way without even knowing the reason she cruelly tossed you aside?" Jiang's eyes widen in disbelief. "Why are you doing all this for a woman who's scheming and treacherous, who's excessively proud despite being utterly shameless, and who bows down before no man unless it's to get low enough to headbutt him in the crotch?"

Kaine scowls. "Huh? Why are you calling my fiancée absolutely adorable? Are you in love with her too?"

"Not a chance in hell!" Jiang and I shout at the same time. Dammit, he's the last person I want to be in sync with.

Not looking convinced, Kaine asks, "Is this all because if you can't have her, no one can? Too bad for you. We're madly in love."

Growling, Jiang thrusts his sword again. Kaine deflects with his fist.

"You're an idiot! A barbarian! A drooling moron!" Jiang shouts.

"But I can beat you." Kaine's punch rips the flesh from Jiang's face and sends him flying into the railing. My friends' magic has mostly cleared the rubble from the stairs. Soon, everyone will arrive to finish Jiang off. Alzira is already climbing up the broken staircase.

A skull's grin warps Jiang's hideous face. "I won't let you have the satisfaction of killing me. And I'll take her down with me. Ysabel, I'm dying because of you!" Jiang flings himself over the railing.

I double over, gasping, the pain in my chest overwhelming all of my cuts and bruises. My actions are leading to Jiang's death, which means I am breaking my oath, sealing my own fate. I'll die next. The fist tightens around my heart. I know what my last words have to be.

If I had time, I'd apologize too, but what's most important to say is: "Kaine, I love—"

Kaine jumps over the edge after Jiang.

With the energy of desperate fear, I run to the railing. Burning pain and tears blur my eyes. Alzira's arms fasten around me from behind, although I wasn't planning to jump off—I think. As they fall, Kaine snatches the cane-sword from Jiang and rams it into his heart, shouting, "With this, I free Ysabel from her life-oath."

The pain crushing my heart vanishes. The physical one, at least, but the smack as they hit the ground damages my soul. Kaine lies a broken twisted figure on the stone floor. He screams and sobs. I've never before heard him cry out in pain during battle.

"Ysabel, I'm so sorry," Alzira whispers.

I don't want to hear her pity or its implied meaning. This is beyond what regeneration can heal, and I would know. I run for the stairs and leap over the broken part. My tired legs can't make it. I nearly fall, before Alzira's power lifts me up and pushes me over the gap. Then she collapses to her hands and knees, her energy completely spent.

My nose aches, my legs tingle, and the cut on my chest throbs with each step. None of it matters next to the terror gripping my heart. Little pleas to the Sun God slip from my mouth, even though I know better than to pray for miracles.

The others reach Kaine's side first. Sigma is doing her best to clot his blood while Donya rips down curtains and Feiyan turns them into bandages. It won't be enough. Three of Kaine's limbs are twisted and broken. His hair is drenched with blood. Internal injuries blossom under his shirt like red flowers. His skin tries to knit together, but not fast enough. The injuries are fatal.

Beside him, Jiang lies dead. The relic killed him where likely no natural weapon would have. My brother has been avenged.

Dropping to my knees, I place a hand on Kaine's chest. Tears mingle with the blood running from my nose. No, this can't be happening to me again. I refuse to watch yet another person I love die. "It's going to be all right. I'll heal you."

He cracks a blood-crusted eye open. "No."

"No?" One word is all I can get out through my disbelief. No one ever turns me down on the point of death. Then I remember. I have only one healing left, and Kaine knows it.

Deep down, I never believed anyone would value my life over their own. I expected that if he was truly dying, he would change his mind. But he glares at me with the same determination as the day we first met. It fills me with both happiness and sorrow, because this does not change my decision. I refuse to watch yet another person I love die while I'm unable to heal him. I can practically feel Calum's blood soaking my hands. "I'm sorry." Even if Kaine doesn't forgive me, I'm going to heal him. I would have done anything to save Calum. There's no way I can stand by and let Kaine die. I slip my hand under his shirt and begin to heal.

"I will never let you," Kaine growls, his words choked by the blood dribbling down his chin. His back arches, writhing in pain.

An odd tingly sensation runs through my body. Something is being pulled out from under my skin. The intruder claws at my insides. Kaine is stealing my power.

It never once occurred to me that Kaine could take away my gift by force. It probably occurred to him from the first time he asked me to stop healing people. Instead, he respected my wishes. But according to Kaine's rigid sense of fairness, if I use my power on him against his will, then he can do it back. It would be easy to let him remove my gift, then live a long life without guilt or responsibility for healing anyone. But I don't want to live at the cost of Kaine's life.

"No!" Seizing my power, I yank. It's like trying to hold onto quicksand. I should be able to stop him from taking my gift, as long as I have a strong enough will. I've never wanted anything in my life more than I want to heal Kaine. Still the magic slips away from me. The sound of my panting mingles with drops of sweat hitting Kaine's chest. "I won't let you!"

"I won't let *you* die," he croaks out. His will slams down against mine even harder.

No! I can't allow Kaine to die in my place! I love him!

Two equivalent needs lock together. Two people trying to save the one they love. The world spins and doubles. Through blurry eyes, I see Kaine's injuries start to knit themselves together. I feel strange. It's as if energy is rushing into me, instead of leaving me.

We both fall over sideways in a tangle of limbs and blood. The last thing I'm aware of is his warm arms wrapping protectively around me before the darkness consumes me.

EPILOGUE

"Close your eyes, and I'll make it better." I place my hand on the toddler's forehead. As my power surges through him, his crying stops. The sores on his arms and legs melt away.

His mouth hanging open, he feels his body. A grin spreads across his chubby face. "Thank you, Holy Ishabel!"

"You're welcome." I pat him on the cheek. Children are still my favorite to heal.

The boy's mother accepts him back from my arms. "Thank you, Holy Maiden Ysabel." Her brow creases. "If there's any way you could accept a day of life from me instead of him . . ."

"I'm sorry. My new power can only take from the patient." I smile. "With such a loving mother to look after him, this child will surely grow up happy."

Giving her thanks again, she steps aside to let the line move forward. It's a much longer line because now I'll heal anyone who wants to be healed for free. After all, it costs a day of their life, not mine.

My clash of wills with Kaine had an unexpected result. I ended up with a bit of his power, allowing me to drain life from people whenever I heal them. Though I can still use my own life if I want to, I'm not telling anyone that. An astonishing number of people whine about sacrificing one day of their lives in exchange for miraculous healing when no one ever had a problem with *me* doing it. Luckily the Queen of Conollia doesn't have to put up with anyone's crap.

The former Dark Lord and current King of Conollia is in excellent health—and always will be, thanks to the ability to instantaneously heal his own body, which he stole off me. He paid a price from our power swap: Kaine can no longer steal gifts. He can still give away gifts, but he'll never again obtain a new one. I felt terrible about it, until Durrian pointed out Kaine still has two thousand eight hundred and thirty-two gifts and thus will not cease to be indestructible.

Then Durrian had words with me about how Jiang's threats were no excuse for hurting Kaine's feelings. The mere memory makes me break out into a cold sweat. Kaine himself teased me for weeks about being "dumb" enough to believe Jiang's lies. But that's the only way he's ever brought it up. I'm a damn lucky woman, and I'm never letting him go. As my lifespan recovers each day, I'm looking forward to a long life together. A smile tugs at my lips.

The doctors carry forward a burn wound victim on a stretcher. They can barely fit in the cramped space between my desk and my medicine cabinet. I step over a box to heal him. My green skirt swirls around my ankles. Since I left Arahasnor, I haven't once worn white. Though I don't hate the color, I'm tired of it.

I built this clinic first thing after I married Kaine and moved to his homeland. The hasty construction shows in the slapped-on white paint and lack of decoration. At least I have a vase of lilacs on my overstuffed desk, courtesy of my husband. A cabinet tilts slightly, the shelves only held up by stacks of books. The boxes piled high in the corner have yet to be unpacked. A sign on the door reminds people to thank their healer, the first thing Kaine wrote after learning to form sentences, and I swear I didn't put him up to it. There's less need, now my cause for bitterness has vanished. I left the window open, bringing in a breeze to chase out the dusty scent. Sunlight falls across half a dozen beds with white sheets. We don't have any waiting room chairs, and the line circles all the way around the building twice.

Plans for a better clinic have been drafted, with plumbing and room for a dozen surgeons. I've just been so busy. I helped the refugees who decided to return to Conollia settle in while also establishing the new city for those who stayed in Arahasnor. After how they saved the Holy City, they were the recipient of aid and favorable trade agreements.

With the council and much of Arahasnor's nobility wiped out, it left a dangerous power vacuum. This also proved an opportunity for reform. Donya stepped up to form a temporary government and draft a new legal code. I made certain the new cardinals were all sincere believers and good people, even if it meant having to promote from the lowest ranks. I'm optimistic about the future of Arahasnor.

There's just one hitch. Arahasnor still doesn't have a new monarch. The king's much younger sister should be next in line for the throne. However, she'd been exiled to the neighboring country of Sherda and has yet to return despite dozens of increasingly undiplomatic letters. With our princess still a child, we can't even tell if she doesn't want to return or is being prevented. Nakimé says we don't need a monarch at all, but Arahasnor might not be ready for that much change that fast. If the nobles start squabbling for power, the country could fragment.

Sigma returned home to the Halfling Confederacy. Feiyan, Nakimé, and Ua'la'sur stayed in Arahasnor because competent personnel were desperately needed to keep order. Tomorrow, they're coming to visit me. They haven't decided where they want to settle down for good, but they're leaning toward Conollia. Obviously, it's in my best interests to show them the finest hospitality.

Happily, I persuaded Suzette to stay with me via a hefty raise and a lot of begging. I paid her expenses to relocate her entire polycule, and it was worth it. Without her help, who knows how I would have organized the burgeoning royal court or survived two assassinations and five kidnapping attempts. We've been hard at work creating a system to distribute Conollia's reparation money as payments for every citizen. It's been a massive endeavor to stop anyone from slipping through the cracks. At least now I can take credit for my accomplishments instead of having to pretend the cardinals did all the work. Tomorrow's visit will be the first vacation in months for both of us.

Alzira, of course, stayed by my side as my bodyguard, as she will until the day one of us dies. After I finish my healings, she helps me close up the clinic and escorts me to Kaine's wheeled castle, anchored next to a lake. Baby willow trees sprout around the water. The lovely petunias lining the road? Mine. I also added the garlands around the gargoyle's necks, made from dried flowers so they don't need to be changed as often. Our evil fortress must look fashionable.

Since Jiang died, the blight has started to fade away. It's as if he was draining the lives of many to sustain his own in a twisted reversal of my gift. Conollia has high hopes of plentiful crops this summer. A ridiculous number of people claim the renewal of the land happened because King Kaine brought back a Holy Maiden as a bride.

I've become open about my belief that healing is a regular gift not a sign of religious favor, though the people who praise my modesty seem to be missing my point. Although I'll always bear the title of Holy Maiden, I'm much happier since quitting the Council of Cardinals and all other religious duties. Now that it's no longer killing me, I get satisfaction from healing people. My faith has become stronger than ever.

As Kaine desired, we held a massive tournament for our wedding, but the ceremony itself was only for close friends and family. I wore an evil-queen style black lacy dress with a wicked scalloped collar. Even with my fashion experiments, I wouldn't have dared wear it for a large audience. Kaine loved it so much he left it in tatters the night after.

We've started trying for children. I'll let Kaine pick the name if we have a girl, because I want to name a boy Calum. Because of my shame and guilt over his death, I haven't even been able to tell my younger siblings what happened, despite Bora's increasingly pointed questions. Sometimes I sit up at night thinking of all the ways I could have saved him and concluding if I'd just rolled over and let Jiang kill me, then my brother would still be alive. I know it's irrational, but I can't stop. During these nights, when my sobbing wakes Kaine up, he wraps his arms around me and holds me. It helps. The bad nights have become less frequent.

The soldiers at the gate greet me, pointing at their name tags. Kaine's guards insisted after he told them about my face blindness. It's unnecessary but incredibly sweet of them. I greet both of them by name (yay!). After exchanging pleasantries and asking about their families, I head inside. We have a very cheerful castle for a battle-scarred, unstable kingdom. My theory: Kaine's kindness is contagious.

In the entranceway, Suzette waits to ambush me. "I know it's late, but this letter has the seal of the Conclave of Kings."

I open it on the spot. "Oh, good news for a change of pace. The Conclave of Kings has decided to hear our protest about Sherda holding onto our future queen. In other words, at the rate the Conclave moves, it will happen in a few months. Still, the Conclave hates disorder and rulerless countries. We're guaranteed to win. Sherda's probably been stalling to get concessions out of us, but the Conclave will slap them down. All will be well in Arahasnor."

Suzette arches an eyebrow. "That sounds like famous last words."

Alzira barks, "Her Holiness never has famous last words."

I sigh. "No, she's right. I was tempting fate."

Alzira squares her shoulders. "In that case, I'm sure Her Holiness's famous last words will turn into an absolutely legendary international incident."

"Stop jinxing me," I groan.

Suzette says, "It's late in the evening. We'll analyze the political situation tomorrow. You should be with your husband."

"And you should be with your lovers." I shoo her away. The Queen of Conollia's problems never end, but I'll face the challenges as they arise.

Working late, I've missed eating dinner with Kaine. I slip to the kitchen to pick up dessert for us to share. The massive black-and-white tiled palace kitchen could fit several rooms inside. So far, I've added the window flower boxes and the golden decorations around the cabinets. It's empty except for the night crew doing dishes. The gas lamp on the windowsill makes their shadows long and illuminates the white bone of the counters. Frying pans in a row hang off hooks on the top shelf like big bats. Lemon scent rises off the splashing water, each clank from the dishes echoing off the high ceiling.

Crouched low behind the counter, I sneak across the porcelain tiles on my tiptoes. At my side, Alzira does a better job of being quiet. It makes me feel like a little girl again to pilfer two napkin-wrapped blueberry tarts from the icebox into my pocket.

At the sound of my name, I freeze, briefly wondering if I've been caught.

"Holy Maiden Ysabel and Dark Lord Kaine." The kitchen maid sighs, placing a plate on the drying rack with a rattle. "It's hard to believe they'd suit."

"Now, now, opposites attract." The second voice is older and saucier. "The appeal of a barbarian to a noble lady is 'that.'"

"That?"

"I mean 'that.'" The older woman lowers her voice. "A man like Kaine must be a beast in bed."

The first maid squeals. "I believe it. Have you seen how tired Queen Ysabel looks in the morning? Yet King Kaine is always completely refreshed."

Hey, I'm not a morning person, and thanks to the power he stole off me he barely needs sleep. And yes, he does have monstrous stamina in bed.

The younger woman continues, "I passed him in the hallway carrying some strange things. I only got a glimpse inside the box, but they looked *terrifying*."

"I'm telling you, she loves it," the older woman says. "It's natural for a woman to want a man to conquer her."

Snorting, I head for the door. In the hallway, I can finally straighten my back and stretch my arms.

Alzira scowls. "Would you like me to set the story straight?"

The notion of Alzira explaining my sex life to a couple of kitchen maids fills me with horror. "Please don't. People will think what they want to think." And I've come to accept that. I never could completely squash the rumors of the dark lord carrying me off by force. Let people believe what they want to believe. I'm living my life as my honest self now.

"Are you happy, princess?" Alzira asks.

I grin. "Deliriously so."

"That's all that matters." She kisses my forehead before taking up guard duty outside the royal bedroom.

Our large quarters have a sitting room with a bedroom and bathroom attached. I find Kaine pouring out his box of sex toys on the breakfast table and stomp over. "Could you be more discreet with those? You scandalized a maid." Titillated might be more the right word.

His face lights up. He always makes me feel like he's delighted to see me every time I walk into a room. It's one of the many things I love about him. "Sorry. I was just too eager."

My heart softens at the sight of him. Tall, broad, and dreamily muscled, his shaggy black hair falls over his brilliant big eyes. His jade wedding ring matches the forest-green coat I picked out for him. Tight gray pants cover his perfect legs. This gorgeous specimen is all mine. I smile. "I'm sorry for being late. The evening is all for us. I brought dessert." I set the pastries down on the table. He swallows his down in one gulp while I savor mine more slowly.

"I got us presents too." His mouth stuffed, he holds up a strap-on and a cock cage.

"So I see," I say with a raised eyebrow. After last night, he's already hungry for more. No wonder the maids noticed I look exhausted, though they have the wrong idea about why. It's actually far more work to be a top than a bottom! My arm is about to fall off, and he's the one who comes out relaxed. At least Kaine appreciates my efforts.

"Can we use this one tonight? Please?" He holds up a whip with barbs on it.

"I don't know. That looks like it might draw blood. I'm not really into blood . . ."

"I heal right away. See, I brought some wax, you know you love that." He bats his eyes at me. "Come on, it doesn't hurt enough when you use your hand."

I roll my eyes at this old argument. Kaine keeps telling me to hit him harder because he's not delicate, when I'm already hitting with all my strength. It's not my fault his butt is solid muscle. "Maybe another night. I want to be fully rested before our guests arrive."

"I'll bring you breakfast in bed so you can sleep in." Kaine drops to his knees in front of me. "Please, Ysabel."

The jutting pout. The big puppy eyes. The magnificent power of his body coiled to my will. He'd look absolutely lovely bent over my knee. I wipe the drool off my chin. "I guess . . . a little . . ."

"Thank you, light of my life," he says, a smug glint in his eyes. It can't be—it is! He's figured out my kneeling kink! *Moon Lady, take me to hell now. I'm in serious trouble.* He's going to use this to get whatever he wants from me whenever he wants it.

"Go easy on me," I say, an acknowledgement of my total surrender.

"You won't regret it," he purrs. "Let me earn a reward." His nimble fingers unbuckle my skirt's belt, then let it trickle through his fingers to the ground. My body already starts to clench deep inside. These days, his most featherlight touch can immediately excite me. When doms fall in love, they're the ones who become enslaved. I'm doomed.

"I love you," he whispers, nuzzling my inner thigh.

"Love you too," I breathe, inhaling the musky scent of his hair.

I, Holy Maiden Ysabel, am completely wrapped around Dark Lord Kaine's finger. And I wouldn't have it any other way.

ACKNOWLEDGMENTS

No book is ever written in a vacuum. Thank you to my parents for reading my childish attempts at writing and telling me they were good. Without them, I never would have stuck at it long enough to write something publishable. Extra thanks to my sister for brainstorming ideas with me. This book has been through many rounds of edits with many critique partners, and I am profoundly grateful to all of them. A special shoutout to the people who read it more than once: Kelly Barina, Becky Bosshart, and the Lexington Prose Group.

Thank you to my wonderful agent Stevie Finegan for her enthusiasm, support, and editing skills. Everyone at Podium Publishing did a fabulous job whipping this book into shape. Thank you in particular to Cass Dolan, Stephanie Beard, Taylor Bryon, Erin McClary, and Marinda Valenti. And of course, thank you to the readers so dedicated that they even read the acknowledgments.

ABOUT THE AUTHOR

Katy Nyquist is an economist in Washington, DC, who writes humorous fantasy novels to take a break from the constant math jargon. She has had short fiction published in *Abyss & Apex Magazine, The Arcanist, Every Day Fiction*, *Strange Changes*, and *Magic, Mayhem, and Monsters.*